PRAISE FOR *DRIFTLESS*

"After what had to have been years of effort beyond the usual struggle of trying to make a good novel, we get [Rhodes's] fourth, and, I have to shout it out, finest book yet. *Driftless* is the best work of fiction to come out of the Midwest in many years."

—*Chicago Tribune*

"A profound and enduring paean to rural America. Radiant in its prose and deep in its quiet understanding of human needs."

—*Milwaukee Journal Sentinel*

"*Driftless* is a fast-moving story about small town life with characters that seem to have walked off the pages of Edgar Lee Masters's *Spoon River Anthology*."

—*Wall Street Journal*

"Comprised of a large number of short chapters, the novel opens with a prologue reminiscent of Steinbeck's beautiful tribute to the Salinas Valley in the opening of *East of Eden*, with a little touch of Michener's prologue to his novel, *Hawaii*. The book moves at a stately pace as it offers deep philosophy and meditative asides about life in Words, Wisconsin, in the Driftless zone—which is to say, about life on earth."

—NPR, "All Things Considered"

"Few books have the power to transport the way *Driftless* does, and it's Rhodes's eye for detail that we have to thank for it."

—*Time Out Chicago*

"A wry, generous book. *Driftless* shares a rhythm with the farming community it documents, and its reflective pace is well-suited to characters who are far more comfortable with hard work than words."

—*Christian Science Monitor*, Best Novels of 2008

"A symphonic paean to the stillness that can be found in certain areas of the Midwest. The writing in *Driftless* is beautiful and surprising throughout, [and] it's this poetic pointillism that originally made Rhodes famous."

—*Minneapolis Star Tribune*

"*Driftless* presents a series of portraits that resemble Edgar Lee Masters's *Spoon River Anthology* in their vividness and in the cumulative picture they create of village life. Each of these stories glimmers."

—*New Yorker*

"Rhodes consciously avoids drama to deliver a portrait of a real rural America as singular, beautiful and foreign as anywhere else."

— *Philadelphia City Paper*

DRIFTLESS

ALSO BY DAVID RHODES

DRIFTLESS

David Rhodes

MILKWEED EDITIONS

All rights reserved. Except for brief quotations in critical articles or reviews, no part of this book may be reproduced in any manner without prior written permission from the publisher:
Milkweed Editions,
1011 Washington Avenue South, Suite 300,
Minneapolis, Minnesota 55415.
(800) 520-6455
www.milkweed.org

Published 2009 by Milkweed Editions
Printed in Canada
Cover design by Christian Fuenfhausen
Cover photo by Corbis
Author photo by Lewis Koch
Interior design by Wendy Holdman
The text of this book is set in Dante.
09 10 11 12 13 5 4 3 2 1
First Paperback Edition

Please turn to the back of this book for a list of the sustaining funders of Milkweed Editions.

The Library of Congress has catalogued the hardcover edition as follows:

Library of Congress
Cataloging-in-Publication Data

Rhodes, David, 1946–
    Driftless / David Rhodes.—1st ed.
       p.   cm.
    ISBN 978-1-57131-059-0 (alk. paper)
    1. Wisconsin—Fiction.   2. City and
town life—Fiction.   I. Title.
    PS3568.H55D75 2008
    813'.54—dc22
                              2008020881

This book is printed on acid-free paper.

To Edna

ACKNOWLEDGMENTS

T HE *DRIFTLESS* STORY TOOK OVER TEN YEARS TO COMPLETE AND IT'S not like I wasn't trying. One reason may be the characters who wanted to be written about. They were for the most part not the kind of characters who usually find their way into print—very private, never satisfied with their assigned roles, always wanting their voices to be more accurately rendered and their feelings better dramatized. Some were more comfortable with my wife, Edna, than with me, and for over a decade she tirelessly advocated on their behalf. Her assistance was instrumental throughout the entire process.

The work would never have been finished without the additional help of many generous people. The life and times of my friend Mike Cannell provided vital inspiration. Others helped with sage advice, editing, critical insights, living facts, and invaluable intuitions. These include: Mike Austin, Pam Austin, Steve Barza, Barry Clark, Jenny Clark, William Davis, Peter Egan, Jim Goodman, Francis Goodman, Rebecca Goodman, Darrel Hanold, Linda Kiemele, John Kinsman, Charlie Knower, Patti Knower, Lewis Koch, Jim Kolkmeier, Leslie Kolkmeier, Jerry McConoughey, Judy McConoughey, Kathleen Nett, Jim Noland, Bronwyn Schaefer Pope, Luther Rhodes, Stephen Rhodes, Paul Schaefer, Ed Schultz, Alexandra Stanton, Blaine Taylor, Judy Taylor, and Peter Whiteman. I'm grateful to my agent Lois Wallace, and I especially want to acknowledge Milkweed editor Ben Barnhart for his creative discernment and priceless suggestions on structure and tone. Thanks to all.

CONTENTS

DRIFTLESS

PROLOGUE

IN SOUTHWESTERN WISCONSIN THERE IS AN AREA ROUGHLY ONE hundred and sixty miles long and seventy miles wide with unique features. Its rugged terrain differs from the rest of the state. The last of the Pleistocene glaciers did not trample through this area, and the glacial deposits of rock, clay, sand, and silt—called drift—are missing. Hence its name, the Driftless Region. Singularly unrefined, it endured in its hilly, primitive form, untouched by the shaping hands of those cold giants.

As the glacial herd inched around the Driftless Region, it became an island surrounded by a sea of receding ice. There, plant spores and pollen, frozen for tens of thousands of years, regained their ability to grow. Moss fastened to the back of rocks. Birds and other creatures carried in seeds, which sprouted, rooted, and prospered. Hardwoods and evergreens rose into the sky, with warmth-loving tree tribes settling on southern hillsides and cold-loving tribes on northern slopes.

Rivers and streams—draining fields for the glaciers and migratory paths for animals—poured into the Mississippi River valley. The waters rushed thick with salmon, red trout, and pike, which in turn attracted osprey, heron, otter, mink, and others who lived by fishing. In time, larger animals moved in, including bear, woolly mammoth, giant sloth, saber-toothed tiger, mountain lion, and a two-hundred-pound species of beaver. (The name *Wisconsin* is believed by some to be a derivation of the word *Wishkonsing, place of the beaver.*)

With the wildlife came humans, and for thousands of years people about whom there can now be only speculation conducted civilization from those ancient woods. The summer camp of the Singing People was once located in the Driftless.

The first Europeans to arrive were trappers, hunters, and berry pickers—men who lived much as the people who were already there, often mating and living with them. In time, trading posts sprung up along the larger rivers, attracting more trappers and hunters. Rafts piled high with furs floated downstream, until the supply of cash animals was nearly exhausted.

Then a larger wave of immigrants came, displacing the frequently moving trappers, hunters, and foragers. Trading posts gave way to forts, farms, and villages.

The new arrivals, almost without exception, came in search of homesteads. Families as numerous as church mice rode in wagons on wheels with wooden spokes pulled by oxen and mules, dreaming of Property. When they arrived, they climbed out of their wagons, sharpened their axes, and moved into the Driftless to harvest a ripe and waiting crop: timber. Logging roads and lumber mills invaded the hills, and within a single generation the Driftless forests—like the rest of Wisconsin's virgin oak, pine, and maple—were cut, floated downstream, and made into railroad ties and charcoal.

After the settlers cut down the trees and dug up all the lead and gold they could find, many abandoned the Driftless in search of flatter, richer farming. Those who remained were generally the more stubborn agriculturists, eking a living from small farms perched on the sides of eroded hills. Like the Badger State totem that burrows in the ground for both residence and defense, they refused to leave. For better or worse, their roots ran deep.

Small villages blossomed with schools, post offices, and implement dealers; dairy and grain cooperatives; hardware, fabric, and grocery stores; filling stations, banks, libraries, and taverns. And the Driftless farmers moved into these villages after their bodies wore out. Old men and women sat on porches in work clothes faded by the sun and softened by innumerable washings to resemble pajamas. They talked in whispers, shelling hazelnuts into wooden bowls, telling stories, endless stories, about long ago.

The young people listened but were skeptical. It didn't seem possible for men and women to do the things described in those stories: people didn't act like that.

"They don't *now*," the old people complained.

It was impossible to explain how in those days, in earlier times, in the past, there really were giants—people who did things, good things, odd things, that others would never do. Those giants were at the heart of everything. Nothing could have been the way it was without them, but how could anyone explain them after they were gone?

Over the years, most of the Driftless villages grew into towns and cities. Other villages, however, grew up like most other living things, reached a certain size and just stayed there. Still others, like Words, Wisconsin—a cluster of buildings and homes in a heavily wooded valley—noticeably shrank in size, and entered the twenty-first century smaller than years before.

To get to Words you must first find where Highway 47 and County Trunk Q intersect, at a high, lonely place surrounded by alfalfa, corn, and soybean fields. The four-way stop suggests a hub of some importance, yet there are no other indications of where you are. This lack of posted information can be partly explained by the constraining budget of the Thistlewaite County Highway Commission and partly by the assumption of its rural members: people already know where they are. No provisions are made for those living without a plan.

Still, there is some mystery why a four-way stop should be placed here, impeding the flow of mostly nonexistent traffic. Grange, for instance, with a population of five thousand by far the largest town in the area, has a justifiable need for four-way stops and even several stoplights; but Grange is fifteen miles to the east on 47.

Red Plain, to the west, has grocery, feed, and dime stores, a gas station, a grain elevator, four taverns, and one stop sign on a highway that connects after sixty miles to the interstate.

Heading south on Q does not take you directly anywhere, but for those knowing the roads this is eventually the shortest route to Luster.

Eight miles north of the intersection, the unincorporated village of Words has no traffic signs at all. County Trunk Q is the only way into the tiny town, which sits at the dead end of a steep valley. Few people go there. State maps no longer include Words, and though Q is often pictured, the curving black line simply ends like a snipped-off black thread in a spot of empty white space. Even in Grange, most people don't know where Words is.

NO REASON

THE MORNING RIPENED SLOWLY. TEN O'CLOCK FELT LIKE NOON.
July Montgomery cut open a sack of ground feed and poured it
into the cement trough. He looked out of the barn window into his
hay field, where a low-lying fog stole silently out of the ground, filling
space with milky distance. Beyond the fence, the tops of maple, oak,
and hickory formed a lumpy, embroidered edge against infinity.

July had lived here for more than twenty years, but because of
the dreamy quality of the morning, the landscape now appeared almost unfamiliar. The row of round bales of hay—which he'd placed
near the road only weeks before—seemed foreign and completely
removed from any history that included him. The road itself looked
different, and when a hawk stepped off a utility pole, opened its wings,
and sailed up the blacktop road toward the nearby village of Words, it
disappeared into the looming fog as though entering another world.
July marveled at how easily the characters of even the massive, stationary things of reality could be changed by a little moisture in the
atmosphere.

On the other side of the barn he could hear his small dairy herd
hurrying back from the pasture. He had let them out just an hour before, and it seemed odd that they would be coming back. Normally,
they preferred to graze all day, knee-deep in grass, even in the most
inclement weather.

Several cows anxiously butted their heads against the wooden
sides of the building and he opened the doors, allowing them back
into the barn. Agitated, they bellowed and crowded against each
other, milling nervously from one area to the next, swarming in slow
motion.

Something had frightened them, and July stood in the opening
and searched for an explanation—a pack of dogs, perhaps. But he

7

could see nothing, and indeed it wasn't always possible to identify the reason for a herd's agitation. Like the fear that often seizes human society, it sometimes had no tangible cause. Given the social nature of animals, an errant yet terrifying idea could flare up in a single limbic system and spread into the surrounding neighborhood, communicated with the speed of a startled flock of birds. Before long, a climate of fear was established, perpetuated through the psyche's network of instinctual rumor.

A movement caught his eye. Several hundred yards away, at the very edge of where the fog swallowed objects wholesale, a large black animal jumped the fence into his hay field, turned around in an almost ritual manner, and looked directly at him.

Now there's something, July thought, staring back. It appeared to be a very big cat, a panther, also known as a cougar, puma, or mountain lion. He'd seen them out west and up north, but never here. Though they had once been native to the area, there had been no reports of them, as far as he knew, for generations. It wasn't even necessary to actually see one, of course; a stray scent of the beast—inhaled by a single cow—and the whole herd would vibrate with primordial anxiety.

Moving slowly, the panther paced with elastic ease along the old fence, carefully measuring its distance from the barn, keeping partially hidden in the fog, like a ghost not willing to assume corporeal form. As it moved, it continued to stare at July, and July continued to look back.

He wondered why a panther would reenter an area its ancestors had long ago abandoned. The larger reasons, of course, included the encroachment of human civilization and depletion of natural habitat; but July wondered what the urge itself must have felt like—from the inside—to compel it to leave its familiar haunts. If it was a male, the pursuit of a female might lure it into the unknown; a female, on the other hand, might venture out in search of food or the protective seclusion needed to raise its young. July also imagined that both male and female might, like some people, simply enter an unknown area for the sake of discovering how it compared with what they already knew.

As he watched the panther striding slowly, elegantly on the edge of the woods, July also saw no reason to deny to the creature the possibility of acting without a compelling motivation. Perhaps it ended up in his hay field without knowing why it had come.

July remembered his own journey to the Driftless Region, more than twenty years ago.

He recalled first that nothing had hurt. He'd woken up in a surprisingly comfortable ditch along an unrecognizable road in the middle of the night, near the end of September, somewhere in Wyoming. The stars seemed especially thick and chaotic above him, brilliant but mixed up, as though they had been stirred with a silver oar. He had no memory of how he'd come to be here—wherever *here* was—and he felt to see if some parts of his body were perhaps broken, bleeding, or missing. But nothing seemed out of place, and nothing hurt.

After more checking, he discovered that his wallet was missing. And his duffel bag, lying next to him in the long grass and weeds, had been ransacked. Most of his personal belongings—rope, stove, cooking utensils, hatchet, knife, compass, lantern, bourbon, dried food, candy bars, matches, soap, maps, and a couple books—were gone. All that remained were a couple items of clothing, his sleeping bag, and his water bottle.

But nothing hurt and that seemed like a good omen. Things could be much worse. Whoever had left him here had not found the flat canvas money belt tied snuggly around his abdomen. He then fell back to sleep and woke up an hour later at the sound of an approaching vehicle.

A pickup moved east along the highway. It was closely followed by a noisy single-axle trailer, pulled by a bumper hitch. As though extending a carpet of light before its path—a carpet it never actually rode on—the truck came to a rattling stop at the nearby intersection. The driver climbed out and walked back to check on the trailer. Cramped from sitting and arthritic with age, he moved stiffly.

July dusted off his clothes, walked out of the ditch, and joined the old man at the trailer.

"Everything all right?" he asked.

The old man seemed startled at not being alone and warily inspected July and the duffel bag extending from his left arm.

"So far, so good," he said, and resumed shining his flashlight through the open slats in the side of the trailer. The dense circle of yellow light moved over a massive Angus bull. The animal's warm smell had a sweet yet acrid quality and when it shifted its weight from one set of legs to another, the trailer groaned respectfully.

July walked to the other side of the road and urinated on the gravel shoulder.

It was a clear, summerlike night, and the sky glowed with unusual green luminance.

The spilling sound reminded the old man of his own full bladder and he also peed on the edge of the road. Far in the distance a dog barked.

"You need a ride, young man?"

Inside the truck, the driver adjusted his billed hat and lit a cigarette. July shoved the duffel bag under the seat and sat beside him. "Where you going?" he asked.

"Wisconsin. Ever been there?"

"Nope," said July.

As they rode through Wyoming, the old man explained that he and his brother kept a herd of Herefords in southwestern Wisconsin. They wanted to breed up some black baldy calves, and the old man had driven out to the stockyards in Cheyenne, looking for a long yearling with eye appeal. At a late auction, he'd bought one.

July liked the way the old man talked—his accent and choice of phrases. On this basis he decided to continue with him.

"How long you been in Wyoming?" the old man asked.

"Eight or nine months, working on a ranch."

"You from around here?"

"Nope."

"Where you from?"

"Everywhere," said July. "Never been to Wisconsin, though."

"Where were you before you were in Wyoming?" asked the old man, openly exhibiting the interest of someone who currently lived in the same house he had grown up in.

"Unloading ships on the docks in California."

"And before that?"

"Hauling wheat in Canada," July said. His window was open and the warm night air blew against the side of his face. "I spent almost a year in the prairie provinces, driving truck. While I was there I met a man, a logger with a plastic leg who could run faster than anyone I'd ever seen. And at night he'd take off his leg and count the money hidden inside it. Other people were always betting him he couldn't outrun them."

"How'd he lose his leg?"

"Cut it off by mistake with a chain saw, above the knee."

It was the kind of talk people make in bus stations and other places when they do not expect to see the person they're talking to again—stories about other people, maybe true and maybe not. It was good-natured talk, well suited to the thin, fleeting comfort shared by strangers. Ghost talk.

They traded driving in South Dakota and continued all the way into Wisconsin, where the old man began to anticipate returning to his brother and their farm more eagerly.

"It's not that far now," he said. "Only about twenty miles past the next town. My brother should be waiting up for us. The coffeepot will be on and we can have a real meal."

The trailer rattled loudly after running over a large pothole in the pavement, and the old man stopped at the deserted intersection and went back to check on his young bull. It was dark, and after looking at the tires, he inspected the interior of the trailer with his flashlight.

July got out and stretched.

When the old man climbed back behind the wheel, July stood in the road and drew the large canvas duffel bag from under the seat. He pulled the strap over his shoulder.

"Thanks again for the ride."

"My place is just a little ways ahead. Look, my offer for a place to sleep is good."

"Thanks, but, well, no thanks."

"At least let me drive you into Grange. I don't feel right leaving you here in the middle of the night."

The young man looked away. He was uncomfortable with not

complying with the older man's wishes yet remained determined to be on his own. "Where does that road go?" he asked, nodding north.

"To Words—nothing up there but a handful of houses. Look, my brother will be waiting for me. Our place is only a little ways from here. You can spend the night, and in the morning—"

"I wonder why they put so many stop signs here?" asked the young man, neither expecting nor waiting for an answer. "I really appreciate the ride."

Smiling, he closed the door.

"Wait," said the old man. "The sandwiches—there are a couple left. You paid for them." And he handed a greasy, lumpy paper sack through the open window.

July tucked it under his arm. "Well, thanks again, and goodnight."

He stood in the middle of the road and watched the glowing taillights move beyond his sight. The clanking and banging sounds of the trailer faded and disappeared. A grinning yellow moon dissolved all the stars around it and threw a greenish-blue glow over the countryside.

July set his pack down and took out a denim jacket, replacing it with the paper sack.

"Okay," he said, "which way now?" He hadn't thought further ahead than this unknown intersection.

He stood in the middle of the road wondering which way to go, waiting for some inspiration—a beckoning or sign. After receiving none, he decided a town called Words was good enough.

His boots made clumping sounds against the road's hard surface, which continued north in a meandering manner up and down hills. Moonlit fields of standing corn, hay, and soybeans merged with evergreen and hardwood, marshland and streams. Crickets, frogs, owls, and other nocturnal creatures called out to him as he passed. Of particular notice were the unidentifiable cries—the raw sounds of nature that refused to be firmly associated with mammal, fowl, or insect.

Set off from the road, an occasional yard light burned near a barn. The houses themselves remained dark, their occupants sleeping.

It had been some time since he'd been in the Midwest, and July attempted to picture himself in the central part of the United States once again. He'd been born just southwest of Wisconsin, in Iowa, so this seemed like a homecoming of sorts, or as much of one as his habitual homelessness could imagine.

In the distance a firefly of light appeared, disappeared, and reappeared at a different location. Once it was out of the hills, it advanced more earnestly, then disappeared for a longer time, only to float up into view a mile away. The single light rounded a corner and divided into two parts, accompanied by a harsh, rushing sound. Then the headlights grew brighter, bigger, and louder, like an instinct merging into consciousness.

July stepped off the road, behind a stand of honeysuckle. He'd become accustomed to his own company again and did not wish to share it with anyone or explain where he was going when he didn't know himself.

After he had been walking for another half-hour, the faint yellow glow of a town in the near distance cautioned him to wait for morning before going further. He began looking for a place to pass the night.

Beyond the Words Cemetery a collection of old-growth trees ran downhill away from the road. He walked between several dozen gravestones, climbed the woven wire fence, picked his way through mulberry and hazelnut bushes, and found a small hollow of land covered with long grass, sheltered by an overhanging maple. In places, the moonlight fell through the branches and spotted the ground. The thick underbrush he hoped would announce the movement of any large intruders, and the rising slope of the cemetery blocked the view from the road. A short distance further down the hill, the rhythmic burbles of a stream could be heard.

July unrolled his sleeping bag. He folded his denim jacket for use as a pillow and ate one of the sandwiches from the paper sack. Then he drank from the water bottle, took off his boots, put his socks inside them, lay down, and zipped himself inside. He loosened the money belt that contained his savings from the past five or six years. Somewhere in the distance a barred owl loosed its mocking cry,

"Who-cooks-for-you, who-cooks-for-you-aaaaalllll." The light from an occasional star found its way through the tree above him, blinking on and off with the shuttered movement of leaves in the wind.

Closing his eyes, he tried to place the experiences of the past several days in a reasonable perspective: the drive from Wyoming, the wandering conversation with the old man, the walk down the mostly deserted road. The dark foliage above him seemed to draw nearer and a spirit of fatigue invaded his senses, disrupting his review of recent events. Blocking it out, he focused his attention and struggled for several long minutes to keep the images in his mind from sliding through the cellar door of nonsensical stories, and fell asleep.

Hours later, he woke up with sudden, blunt finality. He knew why four stop signs had been placed on a remote intersection: there had been an accident. Some time ago, people had died at the crossing and two extra stop signs had been put there. They were erected as memorials.

And so it was: the dead forever change the living. Even those unknown to the dead are required to stop.

The sky was still mostly dark, but morning stirred beneath the horizon and birds rustled about in their lofts in the trees and bushes, conversing through murmured chirping.

Climbing from the sleeping bag, he put on his socks and boots, unfolded his jacket, and siphoned his arms through the sleeves.

Why had he come here, he wondered, and walked down the hill. At the stream, he sat on the bank and stared into the dark water.

The air—warm and thick—filled with noises, and mingled with burbling water, rustling birds, and the dry ruckus of squirrels came the distant sounds of humans. Doors slammed, vehicles started, and an occasional, indecipherable, barking voice could be heard. A heavy truck moved along the road beyond the cemetery.

Why had he come here?

Not everything has a reason, he told himself. His arrival amounted to a whim of circumstance, a living accident. In the same random manner he had arrived in Chicago, Sioux Falls, Cheyenne, San Francisco, Moose Jaw, and many other places. There was no reason.

At least this is what he'd been telling himself for years, but he could no longer quite believe it. He now suspected that somewhere between his actions and what he knew about them—in that vast chasm of burgeoning silence—grew a nameless need, pushing him from one place to the next.

Something shiny near the water's edge caught his attention and he investigated.

A rusty flashlight, half covered in dead grass and dried mud. Most of the chrome had been chipped or worn off, the cylinder dented in several places.

He wondered to whom it belonged. Had it been intentionally discarded or simply lost? But the artifact refused to divulge any information about its owner. Yet *someone* had obviously occupied the same space that July currently inhabited, and this coincidence begged for explanation.

He absently rubbed the dirt from the glass lens with his thumb and pushed the corroded switch forward. To his astonishment, a beam of light leaped out.

It seemed impossible, or at least highly improbable, and he experienced an unexpectedly good feeling over having a valuable object in his hands. The dead had come alive. A personal connection grew up between the previous owner and himself: *I have something of yours, something worth having.*

But as soon as this cheerful happenstance had been announced, the light dimmed to faint orange. It flickered as though trying to communicate, glowed feebly, and went out.

He shook the flashlight and worked the switch forward and back several more times. Nothing.

He tossed it on the bank beside him, then picked it up and tried again. Nope.

Loneliness soon visited him, and though he had learned to cherish his own private loneliness, this particular feeling had a more universal character. The previous owner of the useless flashlight somehow participated in it. *I have something of yours, and it is worthless.*

July looked back at the dark water and understood that he had gone as far as he could. His life had grown too thin, and he was nearing the end of himself. He was living but didn't feel alive. He knew no one in the sense of understanding them from the inside—feeling the center of their life—and no one knew him.

He had come here, he knew then, as a last stand—to either become in some way connected to other people or to die. He could no longer live as a hungry ghost.

He retrieved his duffel bag, climbed the woven wire fence, crossed through the cemetery, and began walking into Words. Whatever people he found there would occupy him in one way or another for the rest of his life. For better or worse, this place would become his home.

All of these memories visited July as he watched the panther pacing along the fence in the fog. To show the animal that he too knew how to play the game, he stepped out of the barn and walked toward it.

The animal stopped pacing, leaped effortlessly over the fence, and disappeared.

A NATION OF FAMILIES

V IOLET BRASSO HAD A PROBLEM THAT GREW BIGGER EACH TIME she visited it, and she visited it often. The familiar pains in her chest and back were coalescing into a single, clarified anguish: What was she going to do about Olivia? What would happen when she could no longer take care of her younger sister?

It was hard for Violet to imagine two people more different than she and Olivia. If archaeologists dug up the Words Cemetery thousands of years in the future, after all the tombstones had washed away, they would assume she and Olivia were from different subspecies. It would never occur to them that such variation issued from the same family.

Everything about Violet was large, not fat, but big. Though she was feminine to the core, her bones were twice the size of Olivia's, her shoulders wide. Her brown eyes nestled deep beneath a sloping brow, lending her facial expressions the proclamation *plain*. Her hair, which she usually gathered into a bun, grew out straight and thin. Her hands were bigger than her father's had been; she was tall and moved slowly. People had always thought of her as old, partly because she stooped to look shorter.

Olivia, in every way, was tiny and preternaturally cute. She looked twenty-five, if that, though she was actually thirty-eight. Her face resembled a child's, with darting, bright blue eyes; her hands were so incessantly busy they seemed to have separate agendas. Those who met her for the first time, especially in the company of her sister, often found themselves later in the day reminiscing about collector dolls—the kind that are too expensive to actually play with. Her hair sprang out of her head in curls so thick and tumultuous that, after being cut and falling to the floor, they bounced.

Most members of the Words Friends of Jesus Church assumed

Olivia's youthful appearance had something to do with having been cared for all her life. Born into a tightly knit, protective family, the cherished invalid had been passed from one relative to another. The stress of adulthood had never caught up to her, so she had naturally remained young in appearance.

In a moment of weakness, Violet had once told this to Olivia—why she looked so young—and regretted it immediately afterwards. Olivia's reaction was so vehement and sustained that it seemed they would never get over it. She refused to eat and stopped talking altogether. For weeks, Violet found small pieces of colored paper, neatly folded and placed in the kitchen and bathroom drawers, under cushions, in the refrigerator, with carefully written quotations from Scripture, in ink.

"He looked round about on them with anger, being grieved for the hardness of their hearts" Mark 3:5.

"Judge not that ye be not judged" Matt. 7:1.

The pains in Violet's chest returned, and she was reminded that at the first opportunity she and Olivia needed to have a talk. She needed to explain that it was time to begin thinking about other arrangements. She needed to guide Olivia firmly through a realistic assessment of her own situation, to remind her that many years separated them; her older sister's health was now failing and some changes were in order.

But the opportunity seemed never to arrive, partly, Violet suspected, because she dreaded the encounter. Talking to Olivia, about anything, usually brought out one of Violet's shortcomings: she could rarely say what she meant, or at least what she said was often not *heard* in the right way. Things perfectly understood in her mind came out jumbled. Olivia, on the other hand, had the gift of speaking clearly and authoritatively on practically any subject, and could run right over most people with her talking. Her uncompromising spirit flowed seamlessly into language. Despite the diminutive size of her vocal organs, her voice resonated in an astonishingly deep, full, and commanding register, imparting to her words a gravity-based sense of importance, even when they weren't important at all.

So Violet tried to avoid thinking about her problem. But now the subject of death and its inevitability was in the air. A funeral had been scheduled for Thursday afternoon—one day away—and the basement in the Words Friends of Jesus Church was in shambles. Late summer rains and a clogged eave spout had conspired to bring three inches of water running down the foundation wall, and even after the sump pump from the Words Repair Shop had removed the muddy liquid, the church smelled of mold. Cardboard boxes filled with quilting supplies and Sunday school materials rested on dark, sagging bottoms, gaping open in places like the mouths of dead fish. To make matters worse, following the first cleanup effort someone left the back door open. Dogs came down during the night, rifled through the pantry, and left a mess that pet lovers could never adequately describe.

Yet the need for everything to look its best had never been greater. The deceased had been a long-standing member of the community, with a large family. Many people, some of them new to the church, were likely to attend. As the senior member of the Food Committee, she had made the necessary calls to coordinate main dishes, salads, and desserts, but there was still much to do.

"Nothing is more important mostly than a funeral," Violet said as they ate a noon lunch of soup and sandwiches. "The whole point of a person's life—or the lack of a point if it's more or less rounded—can't help popping out at a funeral." She wedged the last triangular bite of wheat bread, cucumber, mayonnaise, and lettuce into her mouth and chewed deliberately.

Olivia helped herself to another puddle of tomato soup. The ladle wobbled dangerously in her small hands, and tipping the liquid into her bowl summoned a wincing blink into her face. She eased back into the wheelchair and rested before picking up her spoon and beginning her comments.

"When the end comes—for whomever it comes—it is the duty of the church to hold them up and present them to God."

Violet picked at the bread crumbs along the edge of her plate. "Funerals remind us that nothing ever for very long has ever lasted for very long ever and always things change."

But Olivia would have the last word. For decades, she had accepted

the burden of spiritual insight, devoted herself to assiduously reading Scripture, study, and prayer, eventually gaining the respect of and
measured control over her immediate family. Deciding she had eaten
enough after all, she abandoned her spoon and pushed away from
the table several centimeters.

"Ecclesiastes twelve-fourteen," she said. "'For God shall bring every
work into judgment, with every secret thing, whether it be good, or
whether it be evil.'" Then she added, "A funeral, Vio, is our last chance
to contribute to people's lives before they step into the past."

But as the sisters well knew, stepping into the past did not mean
Gone, and the Brasso home offered as many walkways into that
frozen zone as there were stars in the southern sky. Their white clap-
board house provided a veritable launching pad into the past. Every
book, chair, teapot, beveled windowpane, spring-wound clock, and
door frame covered in darkening layers of varnish offered direct passage into a time somehow more established, meaningful, and real
than the present moment.

At the end of one long, dusky hallway was a room; in the room
was a small table near a window; on the table stood a framed photograph. The picture beneath the glass had yellowed until there was
no visible image, only an oblong space of cloudy mustard colors. Yet
Violet and Olivia would often stare fondly into it, contemplating the
likeness it had once contained.

Happenings, friends, neighbors, relatives, and others who had long
ceased filling their lungs with air had left indelible clues to finding their
current hiding places, and anyone able to decipher them could at once
begin solving the mystery of their seeming, habitual absence. The sisters were constantly surrounded by the presence of things not there.

This was equally true of the village of Words. Like the Brasso sisters
themselves, Words attached more firmly to the past than to the present, and only tentatively engaged the future. Named for the surveyor
who had first donated land for the village, Elias Words, the community
had little to contribute to the modern world, having already forfeited
all of its inhabitants who entertained a keen interest in actually *being*
somewhere. Indeed, the only residual relevance of Words remained

more a subjective secret than an objective fact—a secret collectively shared with other small towns throughout the world.

As three generations of rural people had migrated to cities like woodland creatures fleeing fire, the current denizens of Words remained stubbornly rooted in an outdated idea. Like people who refuse to update their wardrobes, they simply ignored all evidence that their manner of living had expired. Their fierce loyalties were often provoked but never progressed, and they clung to the particular, the vernacular, in the face of ever-encroaching generalities. Consequently, they were losing their habitat, and empty buildings accumulated—somber, withered monuments lacking inscriptions—memorializing a once-functioning cheese factory, school, post office, dry goods store, lumberyard, mill, grocery, furniture store, dressmaker, garage, wagon factory, implement dealer, and gas station.

The town stood in its own shadow of better times, when families depended on agriculture for their livelihood, on work for exercise, on common sense for intelligence, on each other for entertainment, and on faith for health. Seasonal rhythms of nature had permeated every aspect of living and everyone, in one way or another, had danced to the same fiddler. Shared ethical standards fought crime, and inexorable obligations linked individuals together in a single, unbroken human chain.

Violet helped settle her sister onto the living room sofa, tucking a quilt around her. She cleared the dishes from the table and packed away the leftover food. Placing water, pills, remote control, and telephone on the end table, she told Olivia she would be home before dark. In case there was more talk of the mountain lion that people kept hearing at night, she brought in the police scanner. On the chance that their young neighbor might be outdoors doing something interesting—like last week when she jumped up and down on her lawn mower—she pulled back the curtains on the south-facing window.

More groceries were needed for the lunch following the burial service, as well as additional cleaning supplies. Mildred Fletcher, Rachel Wood, and four others were meeting Violet in the church basement at two o'clock. Their pastor might also come, but this was uncertain. Her movements had been unpredictable lately. The young woman was highly sensitive and overly intelligent—not stable traits in a pastor. Her heart was too full to be completely trusted with the customs of the church, and for some unknown reason she had asked the pastor of the Methodist church in Grange to conduct the funeral. She had done this with the permission of the family, of course, but it had been her suggestion, and no one knew why.

Violet's Buick started without hesitation and she drove slowly through town toward the highway.

The golden years of Words, she speculated, must have begun sometime after the territory joined the Union in 1848 and then extended somewhere into the post-European War period. They did not, however, reach as far as the resignation of President Richard Milhous Nixon on August 8, 1974, which coincided with the death of Margaret Brasso, the mother of Violet and Olivia and wife of James Brasso, pastor for twenty-five years of Words Friends of Jesus Church. During those blessed times the nation had defined itself in terms common to Words—farmers, shopkeepers, and reliable traditions. People had mattered then, and provincial citizens had waxed confident in the knowledge that they represented—in every movement and thought—the soul of the nation.

But times changed. First the railroads came, or rather didn't come to Words, then electricity and telephones, cars and interstate highways, all promising more community, commerce, and culture. But one by one, those promises were broken to Words. The economy restructured, large families divided, and Words filled with abandoned homes, rusted automobiles without wheels on streets named for families no longer there.

Driving slowly over Thistlewaite Creek Bridge, Violet remembered the exodus years, when people she had known all her life, even whole family trees, simply vanished into the wider civilization. And even when some had tried to return, something prevented it. They had forgotten how to be themselves; the old ways of thinking could no longer conceive. The human chain had broken inside them.

The new, dominant culture moved on, forgot about Words and

thousands of similar rural communities as though they had never existed.

But of course they did exist, and of the people presently living in and around Words, about half could remember the village as a vital business and community center, though this group was rapidly aging. A smaller portion of the local residents were the offspring of this shrinking majority, who refused for whatever reasons to follow their brothers, sisters, cousins, and children into distant cities. A third group, smaller but growing in relative size, were people now escaping those same cities, moving into the area from Chicago, Milwaukee, Sheboygan, Minneapolis, St. Louis, and Des Moines. Generally better off, this group usually built new homes and, to Violet, seemed like tourists on permanent vacation. And finally, there were the Amish, coming in with their black buggies, blue bonnets, and strange Anabaptist customs. About them, no one knew what to think.

But in real numbers, the population of Thistlewaite County had been shrinking for decades. Sometimes the only reflection of earlier homesteads was patches of daylilies and iris growing in ditches, perennial reminders of bygone housewives sowing blue and orange along driveways.

The only businesses in Words today were the Words Repair Shop and the church. And though some would argue that a church was not a business, it was, as Olivia was fond of pointing out, "God's business."

In the Grange grocery store, twenty-three miles away, Violet accepted a free cup of coffee at the bakery counter and spoke with Florence Fitch about the funeral. Florence was bringing her Crock-Pot chicken and dumplings, and her cousin Margie was making her usual macaroni and four-cheese casserole, with ham. She wondered if Violet had arranged for anyone to bring a bean or rice dish.

They discussed the deceased briefly. Both already knew the pertinent details of the death and the family, and they soon exhausted all there was to share on the subject. Then they drifted into a more fertile conversation about the national decline. Things had changed for the worse.

The whole country, it seemed to Florence and Violet, suffered from a moral ailment whose symptoms could be readily identified: high divorce and crime rates; profanity; drug and alcohol use; pornography in movies, on television, and inside popular magazines; promiscuity; homosexuality; personal and corporate greed; political corruption; and misbehaving children. The symptoms were stark and clear—but not the cause. Today, Florence thought the blame could be unequivocally assigned to taking prayer out of public schools. But for her part, Violet feared the problem might be more complicated.

Violet had thought a lot about the national erosion of morals and the difficulty of assessing it. First, she could admit that she and others often regretted getting old. Mourning the passing of their youth made them jealous of young people and resentful of all the things young people do. Consequently, she and other old people inclined to remember themselves in childhood not as children but as miniature adults and their parents as patron saints of irreproachable stature. They did not recollect ever stepping outside the margins and viewed willfulness in modern children as a sign of emerging pathology.

Even when the tendency to edit memories was taken into consideration, however there still remained firm differences between the present and past. And from a moral point of view those differences could only be seen as skydiving from grace. The family, for instance, had been nearly torn apart, and as the nation was nothing but a large number of families, the nation had itself fractured. Despite rising incomes and larger homes, old people were routinely discarded into nursing homes to die from institutional cleanliness. Professionalism had replaced real compassion, and nothing made Violet angrier than families that did not act like families. Selfishness was something she could not abide.

At sixty-six, Violet was well acquainted with duty. She had outlived two husbands, caring for both through their last gasping minutes. Later, because of the nursing skills she had acquired, it seemed appropriate for her grandmother, and then her mother, to move in with her. Still later, at the request of her father, she had moved back to Words to care for Olivia.

That was eleven years ago, and during those years she had had plenty of opportunity to witness the nation's calamitous decline.

Since she had no children of her own, other people's children remained the focus of Violet's historical assessment. Children were the meter of change, and an indication of cultural decline could be found in the prodigious resources and effort now required to raise them. It was apparently impossible that families had ever lived in drafty houses filled to the rafters with unplanned offspring. Now, radio and television programs routinely featured experts guiding parents through the minefields of having children. Books, brochures, and videos apprised grandparents of their august responsibilities. Elementary and secondary schools, which in Violet's youth were rickety wooden buildings in vacant fields, had mushroomed into hospital-sized compounds with squadrons of specialists skilled in interacting with another squadron of state and federal departments, lawyers, accountants, psychologists, medical consultants, testing agencies, welfare workers, and law enforcement officers. Clearly, mere living had become so complicated that these intervening bureaus were actually needed to prepare children for getting older. And to argue, as some did, that as a result of this deathless regimentation young people were now better prepared, well, it simply wasn't true. The size of the current prison population was one of many facts militating against this wishful notion.

The wrong people were winning. Those who were completely without morals were now in control. Decent homes were under siege and every ounce of vigilance was required to protect them.

SCHEDULED VIOLENCE

G RAHM SHOTWELL WAS MAKING A BOMB IN THE SHED BESIDE THE barn while his wife and two children slept in the farmhouse. His dog, Gladys—curled up yet wide awake—lay on the floor next to the kerosene heater, and Boxer the family cat sat on the sill staring out of the smudged window into a barnyard lit by the blue-green light from a gibbous moon. An old tube radio crackled and spit in the corner, occasionally emitting music from *The Gospel Hour*. A single hooded bulb cast a cone of yellow light onto the workbench.

Grahm set a foot-long section of pipe into the vise, locked it in place, and selected a three-inch die from the collection his father had bought at a neighbor's auction a generation ago. Inserting the die into the ratchet handle, he made threads in both pipe ends, applying a fresh supply of cutting oil after each several turns. Slow work, but the metal yielded to the strength in his arms in a satisfying way. When he was finished he wiped the metal shavings and oil from the threads and with a loose-jawed wrench screwed an iron cap on one end until he could turn it no more. He drilled a small hole in the middle of a second iron cap. Seated at the table, he poured used bolts, screws, and nuts into the pipe until it was approximately one-third full. These would act as shrapnel, which he separated from the rest of the interior with a small, clean rag.

From a green tin Grahm poured black and gray powder into a paper funnel, the shiny, slick particles sliding over each other and cascading into the pipe's open throat until it was filled within an inch of the top. The mounded surface shimmered like live hair. With wire cutters, Grahm snipped off several feet of orange dynamite fuse from a spool hanging on the wall and clamped the pipe into an upright position in the vise. After screwing on the second iron cap, he inserted one end of the stiff, coiled wire through the drilled hole until he was sure it nestled safely within the black heart of the powder. To keep the fuse from moving, he applied a generous glob of epoxy, forming a collar where the fuse entered the pipe. With a single turn of the vise, the Promise of Just Vengeance was freed, and Grahm held it before him for several minutes in the yellow light, contemplating the scheduled violence contained in the heavy, mute, smooth, compact form. He then put it in the corner of the shed under a rumpled tarp, extinguished the kerosene heater, silenced the radio, turned off the light, and opened the shed door. The dog scrambled to her feet and bolted through the narrow opening, nearly toppling Grahm in her race to be first outdoors.

A fine mist had developed in the air, drifting through the moonlight, settling like breath on the grass. Grahm walked to the barn, through the milk house, and into the darkened interior.

Not wanting to turn on the light, he carefully made his way along the north wall as his Holsteins slept, chewed, groaned, and switched their ropy tails. Lulled by the nocturnal peace of the animals, he sat for several minutes on a bale of straw near the freshening cow he had come to check on. Because she was not breathing heavily, the flesh around her pin bone was still soft, and she was standing calmly, he thought her calf would not try to come out until sometime tomorrow. He listened to animal sounds in the darkness and thought about crawling under the covers with his wife, her body warm, smooth, and pliant from sleep. He tried to imagine her welcoming him, eager for touch, but his imagination failed.

MOTTLED SUNLIGHT

T HE TELEPHONE RANG AS GAIL SHOTWELL WAS RINSING SHAM-
poo from her short, curly blond hair. "Drat," she sputtered,
invoking a childhood curse she had never managed to purge from
her adult vocabulary. She had no intention of leaving the steaming
shower, but the ringing nagged at her warm, watery comfort.

Rinsed, she stepped from the stall and pulled a blue towel from
the wooden rack. Several jars of cream, liquid soap, and perfume fell
from the overcrowded ledge and clattered horribly into the porcelain sink.

"Drat."

Dried and seeing better, she opened a hole in the foggy mirror,
fluffed out her hair, returned the jars to their earlier congestion on
the shelf, and brushed her teeth.

On the way downstairs, she inspected her home disapprovingly.
So far, she was turning out to be a mediocre home owner. Her parents, well, her father, to be more accurate, had given her the little
house on the edge of Words two years ago as a way of saying that
Grahm and Cora were getting the farm—all of it—so obviously her
subconscious harbored some unresolved feelings about keeping
it clean. Still, she was glad to have it, even in its unkempt and un-
repaired state. Most of the people she worked with at the plastic
factory rented, even couples who both worked.

How nice it would be, she thought, to have someone steal into
your house in the middle of the night and straighten everything up,
the Snow White Silent Night Maid Service. Perhaps this was the origin of many fairy tales—storytellers wanting their houses cleaned
up by unobtrusive, unpaid workers.

From the refrigerator she took a diet soda and the last, slender wedge of caramel fudge cheesecake, so narrow it leaned and

threatened to collapse. She transported breakfast into the living room. The telephone rang again and she returned to the kitchen.

Buzz Scranton, her band's drummer and booking agent, was irritated, his voice shooting over the wire in menacing chirps. Mike's Supper Club had canceled Thursday night due to scheduling problems with a wedding party. The Straight Flush wouldn't play until next Saturday, six days from now, at the county fair. They would have to leave early to set up the equipment. Jim had the van. She could meet him in the trailer park.

This brief conversation had the effect of chasing away her mostly good mood. To be more accurate, she became aware that she must have been in a good mood earlier when she noticed a desperately sinking feeling inside her after hanging up the telephone. She returned to the living room and discovered her cat gulping her way through the cheesecake.

"Oh, you shameless thing!"

Gail reclaimed her soda and carried it onto the back porch along with her electric bass.

Late-morning sun dove through leafy hickory and sumac branches and arrived bright and mottled inside the screened-in enclosure. Looking into her back yard, she felt welcomed by the quiet assurance of domestic privacy, the blessing of home ownership, insulated from the rest of Words by a thick tangle of fortifying vegetation.

Tossing the towel over the vacuum cleaner handle, she eased onto the broken glider and stretched out her legs, playing soft, deep tones that boomed from the twin fifteen-inch woofers inside the house. Shafts of sunlight struck the painted front of the guitar in a clear, spangled display.

Since early childhood, Gail had disliked wearing clothes. They never fit right, never looked right, never *seemed* right. A cloying, dolorous sensation always accompanied dressing. She suffered under clothing like violets under blankets. It was far, far worse, of course, in winter—living inside mattresses—but clothes were never good. In summer, and occasionally at other times, she let her skin recklessly inhale open air. And why not? It was her house, her porch, her back yard, her day away from the plastic factory, and her life.

Some people might be most comfortable immersed in their jobs, others while navigating a narrow channel into open water; Gail was inordinately at home in her body. It felt right, natural in the naked sense of lacking pretension and the classical sense of having ap-propriate proportions. She liked herself, and her surrounding self liked her. When others in moments of uncertainty and fear might close their eyes to locate a safe center, Gail found courage in her own manifestation, the sight of her knees or feet, her hands, the pressure of her fingers gripping her arms—the way she was expressed.

She plucked the coiled steel bass strings and resumed gazing into her back yard.

Soon, however, the sense of sunny peace drained away as she struggled to play the bass line to a song by the Barbara Jean Band. Gail had both of Barbara Jean's recordings and had been trying to learn the songs on them, but they were very difficult and something always remained out of reach.

She returned to the living room and pushed the CD Play but-ton. The room filled with the recorded singer's darkly searching voice. Gail tried to remain neutral, unmoved, critically appraising the haunting melody, but, as always, Barbara Jean's music evoked in her feelings of undying sadness, longing, joy, reverence, and quaking awe—all at once. There never seemed enough of her to experience the song fully, and each time she heard it a new dimension tunneled open, unexplored. She leaned against the sofa and clasped her hands together as the first verse lilted toward the refrain and into a place beyond the uncanny skill of the musicians, beyond words, beyond notes, beyond music itself—a place where the sublime simply ex-ploded inside her heart.

Gail hurried back to the porch and tried to play along with the recording, but she sounded awful. Her fingers couldn't move fast enough. Some of the chords were elusive, unknown. Her tone lacked clarity, and it was not just a failure of technique. She, as a person, lacked depth, imagination. The musicians on the recording were not only more practiced, they were different in kind, better.

This was the reason she played in a second-rate country band, where her audition had not involved any bass playing at all, only, "Turn around once, slowly."

She put her bass down and just listened, staring into the back yard. Though she could not play as she wished, at least she knew what was good. Barbara Jean's voice floated through the doorway and merged with the mottled patterns of sunlight. After several minutes Gail looked down at her hands, watched them fold into her arms, and smiled.

GRIEF

THE CRYING BEGAN WITH RISING, SONOROUS HOWLS. THEN A shrill, hysterical whine joined a succession of rapid yelping barks. Primeval moans intoned the interminable sorrow of abandonment, mocked by a wild, warbling laugh. Taken all together, they sounded to Jacob Helm like demons at a drunken feast.

But of course there were no such things as demons, and in the next instant he wondered if eight or ten people had decided for some reason to come to his remote home on the edge of the woods in the middle of the night to scream at the top of their lungs. He moved quickly away from the kitchen table, where, unable to sleep, he had been rebuilding an old carburetor, and stood beside the open window. But the frightful sound was not quite like people screaming, either, at least not normal-sized people. Little people perhaps. Very small people might be capable of . . . and then he knew what they were: coyotes.

He'd never heard them this close before.

Their voices continued. Coyotes—he was sure of it now. He'd read about them after moving into the area five years ago. *Canis latrans,* creatures of the forest and fields, often heard but rarely seen, also called prairie wolves though not as large as wolves. Nocturnal predators, they ate mostly mice and insects, supplemented by road-kill. They were not generally aggressive but were opportunistic. They lived in groups for mutual protection, mating and raising pups, though they mostly hunted individually or in pairs. Membership was for life. Packs rarely accepted new members.

"I hear you," he said through the screened window. "Go away."

When the howling finally stopped, Jacob glanced at the clock. He returned to the table, wrapped the carburetor in newsprint, closed his eyes, and attempted to think about sleeping. He needed at least a couple hours of unconsciousness. His body ached with the frustrated desire for rest, but his mind's thirst for wakefulness remained unquenched.

Then he heard them again, further away—on the ridge above him—this time even more shrill and desperate.

And out of the center of these sounds came something much wilder. A new cry cut through the night air in a single shaft of terror. And if the earlier sounds could be said to resemble the screaming of little people, this more primitive voice could only be compared to the screaming of people who were big. Something was out there, and it did not primarily eat mice. Its voice not only invoked spirits from a nether world, it provoked them. Jacob had never heard anything like it. He found his flashlight and went outside.

Assisted by light from a clear sky, he climbed up the wooded hillside, through the underbrush. The distant yapping, snarling, and shrieking of coyotes diminished to a solitary barking voice. He did not hear the other voice again.

The air seemed unusually warm, laden with the humid leftover smells of late summer. By the time he reached the open field there were no sounds at all: utter silence ruled save for the vegetative rustle of wind in tall grass. Panning his flashlight from side to side, he waded in. His pant legs rubbing against the headed-out tops of grasses made irregular loud swishing sounds. After some time he walked down into a narrow swale, and next to a pool of water lay the half-eaten carcass of a white-tailed deer and the mud prints of a cougar or some other large cat. Nearby were four dead coyotes. Mottled reddish-gray, the furry, bloody bodies seemed roughly the size of spaniels. Scattered in several directions were three more, ten or fifteen feet away, torn to pieces. One was still breathing. It raised its head and without blinking stared into the flashlight.

Jacob continued searching and then returned to sit next to the dying animal, not near enough to alarm it, but close enough to make a connection. He turned off the flashlight and listened to the creature's labored breathing.

Later, following a rustling movement, a half-grown coyote emerged from the long grass and entered the swale, its eyes reflecting greenish light from the sky and its body shaking visibly. It regarded Jacob with little interest, perhaps having already taken his measure, approached the dying animal, and sat next to it. Five or ten minutes later the labored breathing stopped. The young coyote stood up, sniffed the lifeless form, looked at Jacob, and gazed briefly into the western sky, as though unsure what to do next. Then it climbed out of the swale and disappeared into the grass.

Jacob remained sitting on the ground. Why had he been called to witness this if he could do nothing to prevent it? On some fundamental level it made no sense. What purpose had been served? No doubt the coyotes had come upon the cougar eating the deer carcass and, unfamiliar with the strange beast, were overly confident in their numbers. Even so, how could one kill seven? Wouldn't their mistake have been obvious in the first moment? Why didn't they simply run in all directions after discovering the evil they had unlocked? Wouldn't their individual survival instincts outweigh pack allegiance? What perversion of nature had unfolded here? How was it possible for one to kill so many? What future awaited the lone pup, and would he live only to wish he hadn't?

Jacob lay on his back. The stars looked back at him from ten million years ago, their light just now arriving. He wondered if there were other places in the universe where the rules of the living did not require feeding on each other—where wonder could be discovered without horror and learning the truth did not entail losing one's faith.

Unwilling to go back home and face the ordeal of trying to sleep, Jacob continued in the direction the young coyote had taken, west.

He often walked at night and was familiar with the woods, streams, and valleys for miles around, including the heavily forested area inside the reserve. He knew which families owned dogs, where coon hunters hunted, the narrow ravine with a corn mash still boiling in late summer, and where the local militia—forty or fifty armed men—held meetings at night.

At the end of the field he followed a narrow path along the chain-link fence surrounding the Heartland Federal Reserve, stopped at the rope bridge he had strung across the river, listened to the moving water, and eventually reached the gravel road.

Morning light grew in the sky.

On either side of the road were the DO NOT SPRAY signs he had put up two years ago. He had won that particular battle, but after he convinced the township to stop spraying herbicides they bought a radial arm shredder. The chewing device ripped through plants with ear-splitting efficiency, leaving saplings and bushes severed between two and four feet above ground, their decimated tops splayed out like beaten stakes. It was a war of factions. The road crew wanted safe, wide roads and managed ditches; Jacob was making more signs.

Some distance later he came to his driveway—two parallel tire-wide tracks trailing off through the grass and weeds and into the trees. He looked in his empty mailbox and straightened the bent flag. Geese flew overhead.

He followed the driveway half a mile to his ramshackle log home. It was the last remaining building in a former logging camp, and he had added onto it one room, porch, door, garage, loft, and solarium at a time. It now stood as a tribute to afterthought. Solar panels were mounted on the south-facing roof, and, beneath them, were storage tanks for rainwater. A composting outhouse sat partially hidden in honeysuckle and snow pine with a satellite receiver on top, providing access to the Internet. A dozen small round windows salvaged from boats were set into the front of the cabin, giving it a hivelike appearance.

Inside, Jacob showered and shaved and dressed in coveralls for work. He moved the carburetor and newspapers to the far side of the table, ate two tomatoes, and drank a glass of orange juice for breakfast.

Before leaving the house, he glanced at the framed picture of his wife taken two years before her death. She looked lovely, though because of too much sunlight the photograph was beginning to fade.

PAINTED BODIES AND ORANGE FIRES

I NTIMACY HAD NOT ALWAYS BEEN DIFFICULT TO ACHIEVE FOR Grahm Shotwell and his wife, Cora. Not at all—until about a year ago, when finding a way to close the door on the rest of the world became harder. Problems that couldn't be solved kept stealing into their mutual space, making it impossible to experience each other with the spontaneous delighting freedom that they both desired. It was maddening to them both because it always seemed as though they should have the mental strength, the courage, to close the door and keep all the unwanted concerns outside. And they should be able to have the integrity to not blame each other for what neither of them could control. But they couldn't. Banished from each other, they endured in their lonely spaces, and the grief was all the more unbearable because of their well-remembered history of comforting sensuality.

In fact, their relationship had been forged, as it were, in the furnace of physical inspiration, when Cora, a young woman working for her father's insurance company in Milwaukee, attended a concert by the Barbara Jean Band with a couple friends. Dressed in a flaming red dress and heels, her black hair gathered on top of her head with long, waving strands falling along the sides of her face, she stood next to a folding table covered with Styrofoam cups, cold cider, and hot coffee. She surveyed the crowd and wondered what she was doing in a place that resembled a page out of a ten-year-old JCPenney catalog.

Her roaming eyes fell on a young man on the far side of the room, beyond the musicians, wearing a suit too large for him. He seemed almost comical as he attempted to negotiate his medium-sized frame through the room, armed with only rustic formality and a broad smile that flashed like fireworks from inside his neatly trimmed beard. Many people apparently knew him and reached out to shake his hand, whisper, joke, and touch him as he tried to move around them, causing him to blush again and again in shy retreat.

His slow progress appeared as though it had been filmed earlier and was now being replayed at reduced speed, and it took him nearly five minutes to wend his way through the mostly-seated crowd. Unaware that such mannerisms evolved naturally from the habit of walking among large, excitable animals, she could not take her eyes off him, even after it became clear that his destination was the very table she was standing in front of. His slow movements seemed overly practiced. His oversized suit, she became convinced, was neither borrowed nor stolen, but a deliberate choice to cover up more of him—extra folds of material to hide within. It seemed his ambition, frequently obstructed by people who clearly enjoyed his company, might be to remain unnoticed.

He continued moving until he almost reached her and then stood on the edge of her personal space, looking at the floor. They continued standing this way until Cora realized he had come all the way across the room for a cup of coffee or cider and was now too shy to look directly at her, say what he wanted, or come close enough to reach for it. The realization that she was effectively blockading an entire field of refreshments with her own slender presence gave her— as soon as she recognized it—a surprisingly pleasant sense of power.

"Oh," she said, moving to her left, "excuse me."

Grahm stepped forward and captured a Styrofoam cup of coffee with his rough-looking left hand. They stood together without speaking for several minutes, sipping from their drinks. Grahm noticed the perfume evaporating from Cora's neck, and Cora discovered an interesting pattern of swirling thread in his jacket sleeve, next to the button.

Left alone, they could discover no conversation. But out of the crowd, fate provided two young boys chasing a third. The pursued— running pell-mell in the direction of the exit door—was more concerned with his pursuers than with what lay directly in his path and was busily engaged in knocking chairs to either side of him and scrambling around them.

It seemed inevitable that all three would rapidly collide with Cora, who put out her one free hand in a pallid imitation of stopping traffic and grimaced in anticipation of being driven onto the field of drinks in an undignified collision of overwhelmingly social significance. Instinctively, she closed her eyes and held her drink away from her dress, and in that selfsame instant felt herself grasped about the waist, lifted into the air, and set down again. When she opened her eyes, she was on the other side of the bearded young man, while he absorbed the combined force of the rushing boys, gathering them into his arms and ushering them off again in another direction with the reproof, "Don't run indoors, boys."

Though her drink had not spilled, something was decidedly overflowing. Her first sensation issued from just above her hips, where she retained the impression of two gripping hands rearranging her place in the world. The next came from the realization that the man had taken time to set his own drink down, and now he drew it back to his mouth, his eyes twinkling in amusement.

"I can't breathe," she said, unsure if this was either a legitimate concern or an appropriate topic of conversation.

He smiled, unable to find anything to say.

"I'm Cora," she said.

"I'm Grahm Shotwell," he said, and his voice expanded like summer.

"Pleased to know you," said Cora. She offered her hand. Grahm took it, entangling them in a mutually inquisitive texture of fingers and palms. The most primitive parts of themselves immediately began speaking to each other, without permission. Their imaginations entered caves deep in unexplored forests, and joined painted bodies dancing around orange fires. The thin membrane keeping the watery world of dreams from diluting the hard substance of reality stretched to breaking. Through a quick organization of bodily fluids, Grahm's face turned bright red, and Cora tried to pull her hand away but found she couldn't move it.

"Oh, no," she said.

"Let's find a place to sit down," said Grahm.

So began an acquaintance that in many ways proved too strong

for them both. And though they fought bravely against falling fool-
ishly, pointlessly in love, they remained hapless victims. Even their
most venomous arguments, accusations, declarations, and final
good-byes resulted only in bringing them closer together, clinging
to each other in exhausted defeat. Episodes of soaring exhilaration
were succeeded by evenings of heroic despair—depressions so dank,
clammy, and dark it seemed they would live the rest of their lives
underground.

The one hundred miles of expressway and sixty-eight miles of
back roads separating them became so familiar that it sometimes felt
as though they lived in vehicles. During one emotionally momen-
tous month Grahm drove to Milwaukee twenty-one times.

There was always something left unsaid. Telephone bills arrived
in envelopes with extra postage. Their need for each other grew
at a pace impossible to appease, like disease feeding on its own
symptoms. They tried to save themselves by making rules: times to
call and topics never to discuss because they contained labyrinths
of meaning. They bought candles and vowed to let the burning of
them determine the boundaries of their lovemaking, hoping in this
way to leave room for all the other things they weren't getting done.
But they always forgot to light them, or ignored them when they
burned out.

Cora hoped to be able to transplant Grahm from his rural surroundings into her clean, comfortable, and convenient urban apartment. But Grahm could not be separated for very long, it seemed,
from his 246 acres of rocky, hilly ground and forty black and white
spotted cows. It was as though he had been born with two umbili-
cal cords—one attached to his mother, successfully severed, and the
other to his great-grandfather's farm.

Farming provided Grahm with a mission as urgent as it was
unquestioned. The duty to save the family business infused him
with an unwavering sense of his own importance, and he never
struggled with problems of identity or other social anxieties. He was
indispensable to his own quest. It was as if his ancestors gathered on
an hourly basis to communicate from the Other Side: *We're counting
on you, Grahm.* Even the land seemed to conspire with the dead to

gain his unconditional loyalty, and as a result he simply revered the forty-acre stand of old-growth maple trees at the back of his farm and walked through it as if it were an ancient cathedral.

"It isn't fair," she complained. "My work, friends, family, everything that is me is here. Why should your life be more important than mine?"

"It isn't," he said. "But I have cows. You can't just put out food for them as if they were cats."

"When will I see you again?"

"I'll call tomorrow."

"Don't leave now."

"I have to."

"Wait, I don't want you to drive alone."

It seemed the only way to end the madness was for Cora to move out of Milwaukee and into the farmhouse, which she did. She gave up her job with the insurance company, gave up her apartment and the friends she had made over the years but never saw since attending the performance by the Barbara Jean Band. She even gave up her family name, not wanting to be bothered with a hyphenated future, yet had every intention of going back to work after settling into her new home.

But settling took longer than she had anticipated. All of a sudden there were two children two years apart and enough responsibilities to fill two lifetimes. A natural process that began with vague, alluring images on the back wall of her mind ended in the numbing details of daily living, the currency of dreams spent on cooking meals, doing laundry, and making ends meet. Whatever remained of her youth evaporated in the worried heat rising from unending physical movements.

GATHERING EVIDENCE

C ORA TOOK OVER THE FINANCIAL AFFAIRS OF THE FARM AND AT once became alarmed when she examined the records, which Grahm kept in shoeboxes in the bedroom closet.

"We're going broke!" she exclaimed.

"Farming isn't easy," said Grahm, trying to coax her back to the bed and away from the ocean of papers spreading over the bare wooden floor like great sheets of sea foam.

"Grahm, stop. We aren't being paid for our work. For crying out loud, who sets the price of our milk?"

"It's complicated," said Grahm.

Over the next several months Cora decided to find out how complicated it was, and she began pouring over receipts and canceled checks and consulting with the Wisconsin Department of Agriculture, Trade and Consumer Protection and the local chapter of the National Farmers Union. The answers seemed clear enough: a century of government policies directed at favoring industry at the expense of the rural economy was still achieving its goal, reducing farmers from 70 percent of the population to 2 percent. And what the government did not accomplish through laws and regulatory boards was completed by giant agribusiness.

She confronted Grahm in the barn as he went from cow to cow attaching the milking machine to the animals' soft, leathery udders.

"It's all wrong," she said, balancing her daughter—an uneasy child—between her right arm and hip. "Our milk prices are set by the people buying it, with government help."

"It's always been like that," he said.

"It's unfair," said Cora. "Every year the price of milk in the stores goes up while the farm price doesn't change. The people selling to us and buying from us are making money. We aren't."

Grahm looked at his hands. He tried to keep his life manageable by limiting his attention to things he could control. Open discussions of government agricultural policies caused him great discomfort. His otherwise reasonable and beloved grandfather had been so sure that the big chemical and seed companies were single-mindedly undermining his livelihood and his health that he occasionally exploded in apoplectic fits of red-faced fist waving at the dinner table. In his declining years his grandfather imagined corporations taping his telephone conversations, filming his trips into town, and discussing his farming methods behind mahogany desks in St. Louis.

Cora returned to the house to make supper. The next day she began looking for work, and babysitters. The following week she took a part-time job as a waitress. Two weeks later she found full-time employment at the American Milk Cooperative, a nationwide farmer-owned organization that marketed milk from more than 40,000 dairy farms, including theirs. Within the first year, she was awarded two pay increases at the branch office in Grange and the following year became an assistant bookkeeper.

Their situation improved. Though much of the money Cora earned went toward the farm operation, they now had a fairly reliable automobile, a roof that did not leak, and a refrigerator with a self-defrosting freezer compartment.

At the same time, their lives became more hectic, a frantic race from one workstation to another. The children were alone, they feared, too much. Cora often found reason to believe that Seth and Grace had grown bigger—grown up—during the space of a single day away from her.

In an effort to lower debt, Grahm added five more cows to his herd. He began leaving the house at 4:30 a.m. and did not return until after 8:00 p.m. They no longer kept a garden and had little time on the weekends for anything other than chores they neglected during the week. And for Grahm, weekends merged seamlessly with weekdays, as indistinguishable as links in a chain. Like most of their neighbors, they came to accept a state of perpetuating fatigue.

In April, Cora returned from work and found Grahm in the

machine shed kneeling beside a grain drill. He set down the grease gun, with grease scrolling out of the nozzle's end like a red transparent worm, and went to her.

"What's the matter?"

"Grahm, they have a second set of books. There was a discrepancy in the shipping sheets. When I reported it to my supervisor, I was told I could find the correction in the main building in Madison. I drove there this afternoon. There's a second set of records in back of the main office. Maybe I wasn't supposed to see them. I don't know—I'm just an assistant bookkeeper—but there's a whole wall of file cabinets."

Grahm stared mutely forward.

"I told my supervisor, but he told me not to worry about it. He said it only concerned upper management and they had a different accounting system."

"What does this mean?" Grahm asked, feeling much like he had when he'd learned Cora was pregnant, both times. There seemed to be nothing for him to do. Something was happening that greatly concerned him but he had no way to assure that everything would turn out all right, and this somehow seemed like a personal failing.

"Maybe there's another explanation. Maybe it's just a mistake."

"It's no mistake, Grahm. With one hand they steal from us farmers and with the other they lie to the government. They're breaking the law and it's not right."

Cora decided to gather enough information to prove her suspicions. The next evening she brought home two Xeroxed spreadsheets, folded and tucked into her purse. And she continued collecting evidence.

She also began having difficulty sleeping, migraines, and finally a doctor prescribed pills. But even then she often could not sleep.

Grahm and Cora's intimacy dried up like attic furniture.

Grahm felt increasingly frustrated. Voices in his mind told him to *do something,* but he had no ideas. Like most of his neighbors he had devoted his life to farming. He liked farming. All he wanted to do was farm. Farmers had a long, proud history of avoiding social,

economic, and political issues. They enjoyed nature, work, and solitude, and they eschewed everything that might be considered grist
for the nightly news.

But after a lifetime of successfully defending his private life from
the baneful affairs of the world, his wife had rolled a pestilential
army of scandalous problems through the front gate. And now they
were in his house, in a cardboard box beneath their bed.

One afternoon he drove his pickup to July Montgomery's small
farm, several miles away. Grahm didn't remember exactly when
Montgomery had moved into the area. He'd arrived unnoticed and
blended in so well with his surroundings that it seemed he'd always
lived in the old brick house, taking over a farm that had been for
sale for a long time. Tim Pikes, the drunkard and former owner,
had lost the battle against bank payments when Grahm was a small
child. Most of the land had been sold off, and the remainder with
the buildings—only a hundred acres—didn't seem like enough for a
viable farm, but apparently it was for July.

His place was easy to identify, with MONTGOMERY JERSEY FARM
painted in large white letters across the upper front of the red barn.
Each word sat on its own board, and the third board had recently
come loose on the "m" end and now hung perpendicular to the
ground.

Grahm pulled into the driveway just as the middle-aged man in
a checkered shirt came around the side of the barn with a double-
hung aluminum ladder. He planted the metal feet and pulled on the
rope, hoisting the upper half of the ladder into its uppermost position. When the ladder was fully extended, the highest rung came
within a couple feet of the hanging board, twenty feet in the air.

Grahm got out of his pickup and walked to the barn. "Hello, July,"
he said. "Can I help?"

"Do you have a hammer?"

"Sorry, no."

"Then I guess you can't help," said July and headed up the ladder.

"I can hold the ladder."

"Good, you do that," he said.

Watching him climb, Grahm wondered about July. He seemed

odd somehow, and because he didn't look especially out of the ordinary or deformed in any way, Grahm imagined the reason for this impression must come from something July had experienced beyond the normal range of what most people experience. His history, in other words, contained a deformity. And for some unknown reason this made him easier to talk to. He never seemed to be passing judgment.

Standing on the next-to-highest rung, July reached the errant board and worked it underneath the ladder. When it reached the horizontal level of MONTGOMERY and JERSEY, he took a nail from his shirt pocket and drove it into the wood. Then he dropped the hammer into the denim belt loop and climbed to the ground.

"Thanks," he said.

They collapsed the ladder.

"You got a minute?" asked Grahm.

"Sure. You want some coffee?"

"No thanks, coffee makes me too nervous." They carried the ladder over to July's machine shed and hung it on an inside wall. July leaned against the back tire of his Minneapolis-Moline while Grahm paced back and forth over the dirt floor.

"I didn't know who to talk to. I think we're getting into trouble, my wife and I. I mean I think we really are."

"We're all in trouble," said July. "We're farmers."

"Cora and I ship to American Milk, and Cora works in the office."

"I ship to them too. Not many independent plants left. American Milk bought up most of them."

"Cora says they keep two sets of books, and there are other things. One big farm is shipping watered milk; several others routinely test positive for antibiotics and listeria but are accepted anyway. Cora's making copies of shipping and accounting sheets—stacks of them. She says they will prove everything, and she won't stop."

July took off his hat, rubbed a hand through his short brown hair, put his hat back on, and said, "Look, Grahm, this is serious. AM is a Fortune 500 company. The people who run it are wealthy and powerful, and it's better to just leave them alone."

"They're not above the law."

"Maybe not, but they're not as far beneath it as we are." In some ways he looked more worried than Grahm.

"My grandfather and some others started American Milk during the Depression. He was a charter member and it wasn't a crooked outfit back then."

"No, maybe not," said July.

Grahm continued pacing.

July once again took off his hat and rubbed his hand through his hair.

"I don't know what to tell you," he said. "Make more copies of the copies your wife brings home. Put them somewhere safe. Everything depends on them. If those papers get out of your hands, you're done. Show them to people you trust. Do you have a lawyer?"

"We don't need a lawyer."

"I think you need a lawyer."

"We can't afford one."

"Then maybe you can't afford to be involved with this."

"We shouldn't need a lawyer. We haven't done anything wrong. This is the United States of America."

"No country is immune to human nature."

Grahm reached the end of his desire to talk. He regretted coming. Talking to people was difficult enough, even in the best circumstances. Now he felt angry, and he drove away.

THINK LESS, DO MORE

JACOB HELM CLIMBED INTO THE JEEP, BACKED OUT OF THE GARAGE attached to the side of his log home, and drove the eight miles into Words. He had bought the Words Repair Shop building soon after moving into the area, converting it from what had once been a creamery. At the time he'd known little about running a business, but he needed a new beginning. After Angela's death, he'd quit his job of eleven years (he'd been an engineer for an electrical component company), sold their suburban property, and left Sheboygan. He ended up here, determined to immerse himself in anything that bore no resemblance to his past.

The old creamery was bigger than he'd needed for a repair shop—even a shop where he worked on everything from tractors to watches. He added a craft room, managed by Clarice Quick, who opened and closed the building when he wasn't there. She knew the local people, ran the cash register, and did the billing.

The smells from the two parts of the building competed for dominance. Oil, grease, gasoline, hot metal, fermenting leather, burned-out electrical components, tobacco, mildew, mud, and workbench solvents did battle with the thinner but better defined odors of scented candles, dried flowers, paraffin oil, fabrics treated with fabric softeners, lemon furniture polish, air fresheners, Clarice's lavender body wash and her hair spray. The combined fragrance one encountered in the doorway adjoining the two rooms, if truth be told, resembled nothing else on earth.

"Good morning, Mister Helm," Clarice said when Jacob came in. He suspected she would refrain from using the formal title if she ever thought about it, but when her mind was consumed with other things—in its normal state—she relied on the expression her upbringing had prescribed to her for addressing teachers, shopkeepers, and employers. "We have an order for eight quilts, Mister Helm."

"Someone must be reselling them."

"They said they would make good Christmas presents."

"I forget who makes them."

"Olivia Brasso—the cute one in the wheelchair. Her sister Violet, the bigger one, usually brings in her things. They work as a team, you might say. Always have for almost as long as I can remember, though if you ask me it would be no picnic taking care of Olivia. Despite her small size and her infirmity, there's something quite frightening about her. I don't know if others have noticed it, but, oh, yes, and Mr. Shrinkle left a wheel from his farm wagon. I guess it needs a tube or spokes or something."

Jacob stopped listening and resumed welding a hay rake that he had begun working on the day before.

Mid-afternoon, five men dressed in olive fatigues came inside. Jacob had seen them before but did not know them by name. For several minutes they walked from place to place, not speaking. The largest man closed the door into the craft shop. Another turned off the radio beside the air compressor.

"You the owner?" asked the oldest of the five, a muscular man with small eyes set inside a wide, square face.

Jacob nodded.

"Know anything about guns?"

"Not much."

"Know anything about machine guns? Ever work on them before?"

"Some. I was a mechanic in the Guards."

"We have several we want you to check over."

"If they're Chinese nine millimeter, forget it. They're junk."

"These are American and Israeli, thirty and fifty caliber."

A tractor stopped in the road and backed an empty manure spreader toward the open double doors into the shop.

"We'll bring them over to your house," said the man. "We know where you live." And they left.

July Montgomery climbed off the tractor and came inside.

"What did those men want?" he asked, watching them climb into an SUV with tinted windows.

"Nothing," said Jacob. Three years ago July had pulled Jacob's jeep out of a ditch after he'd had too much to drink, and after that awkward meeting they got along well. July even occasionally showed up at Jacob's house with beer and cigars. They played chess and cribbage next to the woodstove. Though July was ten or fifteen years older, he was the only person Jacob ever talked to, in the sense of really talking to someone.

"That was Moe Ridge, and those men are in his militia," said July.

"I know who they are."

July turned toward his spreader. "Chain broke," he said. "Bearings are making noise and she needs new grease cups."

"Might take a while, I'm busy."

"You look tired, Jacob. You should get more sleep. Where's the soda machine that used to be here?"

"Company took it back. Said they'd replace it, but I haven't seen them for two weeks."

"Too bad. I was going to buy you a soda. Say, there's a lawn mower on the edge of town that won't start."

"Bring it over sometime next week."

"The woman who owns it doesn't have a way to get it here," said July. "It's a big one and she doesn't know anything about motors."

"You can show her," said Jacob, opening the door to the craft shop and returning with a can of soda from the refrigerator on the other side of the cinder block wall. He handed it to July and turned on the radio.

"Thanks," said July, "but I want *you* to show her."

"Don't have time."

"Poor thing's lawn is getting away from her."

"Don't have time."

"Jacob, this is a good idea. She needs your help."

"How old is she?"

"I don't know how old she is. Ask her. She's at the end of the first road after the bridge, right over there," and he pointed behind him. "Her name's on the mailbox: Gail. Tell her I sent you. If she isn't home, go back. Her schedule is hard to predict. Gail Shotwell, don't forget."

"Clarice can call her."

"Don't do that—she'll say she doesn't need any help."

"I don't think so. I don't like talking to women I don't know. I just don't think—"

"That's your whole problem, Jacob. Think less, do more, that's my motto."

PROTECTING PAPERS

G AIL SHOTWELL WORKED THE NIGHT SHIFT AT THE PLASTIC FAC-
tory in Grange and drove home in gray light. She made a piece
of toast with peanut butter, ate half of it, partly undressed, slept
three hours on the sofa in the living room, woke up, and ate the rest
of the toast. She played a CD and felt pretty good then in a sleepy
kind of way. She thought about eating another piece of toast, but
before she could get a slice of bread into the toaster a loud knocking
arrived on the front door.

Gail had so few visitors that at first she did not recognize the ex-
plosive sound. Then she had no idea who it could be. There were
only thirty or forty people living in Words at any one time, and she
was on speaking terms with only a few of them. Lacking stores
of general interest, the little village afforded few opportunities for
strangers to get acquainted without going right up to each other,
which no one would ever do. There was the Words Repair Shop,
of course, with its heaps of old metal and claustrophobic room of
crafts in back, but the owner was not someone she especially wanted
to meet. Her nearest neighbors in the Victorian beyond the hedge,
old Violet Brasso and her sister, Olivia, were fanatically religious by
all reports, and Gail assumed they disapproved of her. They rarely
left home for anything other than church.

She opened the front door and on the other side of it stood her
brother, Grahm. Behind him his wife, Cora, had her arms wrapped
around a cardboard box as big as an orange crate. Because of the
direction of the sun, both looked carved in granite.

"We came last night," said Grahm, "but you weren't home."

"We waited until after eleven," said Cora.

"I worked last night. What's in the box?" asked Gail.

"These are copies of something *very important*," said Cora in her

usual manner of assuming everything in her life was very important. "We need you to keep them." And she marched into the house,
walked down the hall, and put the box on the kitchen table.

"Grahm thinks you're our best hope," she said, appraising the
kitchen with a scowl. A mound of Styrofoam take-out containers,
mismatched ceramic and paper plates, cups, glasses, and plastic wrappers rose out of the sink and spilled onto both sides of the counter.

"You guys want some coffee?" asked Gail as Grahm and Cora
seated themselves at the table.

"Look these papers over when you have time," said Grahm. "Keep
them in a safe place."

"They probably won't mean anything to you and it's not necessary they do," added Cora. "We just need you to have them."

Gail started coffee and set three cups on the table. "Either you tell
me what this is all about—right now—or take your old box home."

"You tell her," said Grahm.

"These are shipping records and report forms that prove American
Milk is stealing from farmers, defrauding the government, and selling tainted product."

"Holy shit," said Gail. "Where did you get them?"

"I took them."

Cora talked for quite a while longer and Gail realized somewhere
near the end of the narrative that she hadn't been listening. The picture in her mind of her sister-in-law making off with papers from
work had crowded out everything else. The coffeemaker groaned
twice, grueling sounds of concentrated mechanical anguish ending
in a gasp of caffeinated steam. As though in response, the CD player
in the living room turned off.

"Coffee?"

"Sure," said Cora.

"No thanks," said Grahm. He was currently feeling guilty about
bringing his sister into the same awful business that had been de-
stroying his relationship with Cora for the past six months. Gail gave
him some anyway, and he drank it after pouring in enough milk to
bring the liquid up to the rim of the cup.

"You should get milk from us," said Grahm. "This stuff from the
store has been boiled to death."

"Yes, but they take all the fat out and I perform for people on a stage."

"Doesn't seem to interfere with your drummer's eating."

"Men don't have to look good, especially behind a set of drums. Everyone notices women."

"Tell me about it," said Cora, pouring herself a cup of coffee. "Our society is shot through with double standards."

Gail frowned at her but didn't say anything. As far as she was concerned Cora had directly benefited from those double standards. She lived on a farm inherited in the final act of a long drama of double standards, mostly written, directed, and acted out by Gail's mother, who expressed her preference for boys in general and Grahm in particular with every embittered fiber of her being. The leather strap she kept hanging beside the stove might as well have had "Gail" embossed on it, so seldom was it used on anyone else.

"What am I supposed to do with these papers?"

"You won't understand what they mean," said Cora, burning her tongue and spilling several teaspoons of coffee on her sweatshirt. "Just keep them in a safe place."

"People get in trouble over these kinds of things," said Gail. "You hear about it all the time."

"Oh, calm down and stop being so dramatic," said Cora, who privately admired her sister-in-law's talent for walking around un-surrendered in her underwear. She had a figure, for sure, but who didn't before having two children? And she probably exercised, what with all the free time she had. Still, there was something intrinsically unwholesome about just wearing underwear, even clean underwear. "As long as we have these papers we have nothing to worry about," she said. "There are laws that protect us from lawbreakers."

"By the way," said Grahm in his getting-ready-to-leave voice, "what's the matter with your lawn mower? It's sitting out by the road."

"It won't start."

"I'll look at it on the way out."

After they left, Gail put the cardboard box in the closet and found her bass. She was feeling lucky and ready to try to learn the Barbara Jean song again.

KEEPING A RESPECTFUL DISTANCE

W INIFRED SMITH HAD BEEN IN FULL-TIME PASTORAL MINISTRY for six years. At thirty-three, she remained confident that God had a plan for her, a purpose, but she did not yet know what it entailed. And though she eagerly anticipated the joy that would accompany embarking on her life's mission, she avoided imagining in any detail what her future might hold—for fear vain predilections might block the Way in which unseen forces were guiding her. Allowing things to develop all by themselves would open doors of experience.

In just this manner she had been led to the Words Friends of Jesus Church and into her current circumstances. The opportunity had come unexpectedly, while she was waiting for a barber to trim her hair in a tiny three-chair shop in Cincinnati.

As the steady snipping of long-handled stainless steel scissors performed thin, rapid, rhythmic, metallic insect music, she turned the pages of limp glossy outdoors magazines. Oily smells from colored bottles on the shelf along the mirror combined with the odor of men in vinyl chairs and pictures of trophy animal heads to create a not exactly pleasant atmosphere, and her discomfort—not with the room itself so much as her condemnation of it—was reflected in her face shrinking around her eyes.

"So you attend the Bible college," said the barber nearest to her, resuming a conversation he had attempted to start earlier. Of the three men cutting hair, this one seemed the most dedicated to establishing personal connections, and Winnie thought he might be the owner. His arms, hands, and wrists moved with an effortless, rubbery fluidity. As the youngest person in the room and the only female, she assumed she was fair game for conversation. One of the social obligations of being younger, and female, entailed letting people talk to you.

"Yes, I'll graduate soon."

"Congratulations to you, Ma'am," the barber said, gesturing with his rubbery limbs. "We need good preachers and I understand there's a shortage of them in all denominations."

"Whether I will be good remains an open question," said Winnie. "I will try to be." She put down the magazine and smiled in what she hoped was a professional manner.

"As far as I'm concerned," spoke a man sitting next to her, waiting to have his hair and beard trimmed, "women make just as good pastors as men. The Man Upstairs made both men and women and I doubt there's a whisker's worth of difference between them in church work." He smiled at her in a kind manner, though his mouth seemed somewhat crooked.

Winnie attempted to ignore the problems caused for women in the church when even those men in favor of gender equality thought in terms of men upstairs and measured the lack of difference between men and women in whiskers. She reminded herself to listen for the intention of what people say and ignore the words. And the intention seemed reasonably cheerful.

Besides, this was one of those rare opportunities for her to be available, open to others—when divine matters had been spoken of in public. As she knew, most people thought very little about God. Their busy lives consisted of eating, drinking, social climbing, fornicating, and all the attendant thoughts needed to secure perpetuity for those activities. They marched in an ultimately joyless parade of orifice functions finding expression in a complex society. Only on rare occasions did the human spirit break free from these fugacious concerns and seek a greater joy. And Winnie's primary responsibility, as she understood it, was to nurture those moments while not intruding into other people's privacy.

"I don't imagine genitalia matter much," she said, trying to look both amiable and sincere.

"You both are missing something," said a middle-aged man with sideburns seated on the middle stool, staring at himself in the mirror. He spoke with authority, as though he was accustomed to having people listen to him. "The reason there aren't enough preachers is that fewer and fewer people believe such rank superstition. Religion is irrelevant to the modern world."

Winnie gathered her long skirt carefully around her hiking boots, tilted her head back, and shook it. She then remained suspended in a moment of hesitation, as though standing at the end of a high diving board from which she felt the compulsion to jump.

"Actually," she said, leaping forward, "there has been an increase in church attendance in the past twenty years. People flock to churches because modern life leaves them longing for something more. Especially the fundamentalist and Pentecostal faiths have experienced a sustained resurgence in membership. But I'm truly interested to know what you see as superstitious."

The man with sideburns spoke again. "Fewer and fewer people attend church on Sunday. Television evangelists have completely soured the well of religion and people now see it as just another pocketbook scam."

Winnie laughed. "I love that phrase, 'soured the well.' Thank you for using it. I wonder where it comes from. The images it brings to mind are so vivid. I'm afraid, however, we must be very careful to not take our personal experiences as representative of society as a whole. If you know fewer and fewer people attending church on Sunday, it is probably due to your associating more and more with like-minded fellows. Reliable statistical data confirm that more and more people are attending. As for television evangelism, which you are right to criticize for its sometimes shameless tactics in fund-raising, it is just one more example of how people thirst for the Word in these modern times. Even the most flawed messenger can find acceptance."

"Look around you," the man said, gesturing with his open hands. What do you see? Over here, a leader of a church stands behind a pulpit and condemns sexual immorality and the next day is found in bed with animals. Over here, Christians maim, torture, and kill Muslims, and Muslims maim, torture, and kill Christians because of their religion. And just yesterday, out in some backwater town not far from here, a man murdered his wife and children—shot them in the head—because God told him to get them to heaven as quickly as possible. Turn over any rock and you'll find a politician pressing his hands together in public prayer while he's accepting bribes, cheating on his wife, and sending his neighbors' jobs overseas. If there's one critical imbalance in the world, it's too much religion."

Winnie continued to smile. "But all the examples you've given are of men violating religious principles, not acting in sympathy with them. You've cited exceptions to the general case, which is why they are put into headlines. The religions of the world offer hope in times of darkness and assurance that moral integrity is rewarded. The majority of people find courage in knowing that charity is divinely supported and goodness will eventually prevail. It helps them to be better people."

"Then how do you explain the lack of preachers and priests?" He was now inspecting Winnie's reflection in the mirror.

"The economy presently allows people to better provide for their families outside the ministry."

"You mean they can make more money if they are not professional followers of Christ?"

"I suppose that would be fair to say, though your choice of words is a little harsh."

"Then despite the growing number of people in churches, few of them let religion interfere with their material ambitions. I guess that would make them hypocrites—isn't that the word for people who profess one thing but do another?" He smiled straight into the reflection of Winnie's eyes in the mirror, as though to drive the final nail into her argument.

"Oh, no," said Winnie, rising to her feet and smoothing her skirt over her narrow hips until the finely woven material fell without a fold or wrinkle to within an inch of the floor. "Serving God is not limited to working inside the church. People serve wherever they are. In whatever line of work they choose, many people are doing their part. It's simply that fewer are choosing full-time ministry. You yourself may choose to serve God while having your hair cut. You may—"

"I see," the man interrupted. "Then perhaps everyone at every moment is serving God. Perhaps even thieves, rapists, terrorists, murderers, and other criminals are serving God as they go about their crimes."

The haircut concluded, and the barber unclipped the neck cloth
and tipped the chair into its upright position. The man took several
bills from his wallet and accepted no change. He abruptly crossed
the room, opened the door, and walked outside.

Winnie went after him.

"No one can serve God while hurting others and no one can serve
God unconsciously," she said, walking briskly beside him. "That's impossible. Service is a form of worship, and worship requires more
conscious attention than anything else."

"Being conscious of a lie and insisting everyone must believe it
doesn't strike reasonable people as reasonable," he said.

Winnie's long legs matched his, stride for stride. She continued:
"I'm afraid you've committed another error in your thinking, which
is common among people just beginning their spiritual journey and
you should not feel badly about that. Dogmatism plays the part you
are attempting to cast for belief. In truth, the same vital intuition
that informs reason even further informs belief. Believers are more
ardently concerned with removing the Great Lie than nonbelievers."

Followed halfway around the block, the man stopped and turned.
"Leave me alone. My parents used to talk just like you. I've had many
very bad experiences with cruel, greedy, and ignorant people who
call themselves religious. They beat you until their fists are bloody
and then read from the Bible. My childhood was a nightmare of perverted religion."

"Oh," said Winnie, touching her face with her hands. "Oh, I'm
sorry. Really, I didn't know. What you talk about is a real problem,
for sure. I'm sorry. Believe me, I'm very well acquainted with night-
marish childhoods. My own was—"

"You're a hopeless fool," he said. "I doubt if you'll ever amount
to anything or if anyone will ever care anything about you."

The man stepped from the curb and moved quickly through traffic to the other side of the street.

Winnie walked back. *You did it again,* she whispered to herself.
*You did it again. Why can't you pay attention! It's not right to intrude too
far into other people's lives. Let them say whatever they want. You must*

learn to respect that. You keep forgetting. How many times do you need to be whacked on the head by something you already know?

Back inside the barbershop, the older gentleman who earlier had been sitting beside her had taken the place of the man with sideburns on the elevated chair. Winnie sat down, folded her skirt carefully around her boot tops, and blushed.

The barber grinned from ear to ear. "There are some people born to preach and I believe you are one, young lady. You'll do a bang-up job. And I know for a fact there are many churches looking for pastors. My sister, for example, attends a little church in Words, Wisconsin, which is an area so rural that God left His shoes there. They haven't had a full-time pastor for over a year."

"What an astonishingly odd name," said Winnie.

In the library that evening she looked up Words, Wisconsin. Then she found an old Wisconsin map with Words on it and immediately experienced several short bursts of panic, beginning in her stomach and radiating into her extremities. The area in southwestern Wisconsin where God had left His shoes and apparently intended to send her was not far from the town that her father and mother had grown up in, as well as the place they had lived together, married, and eventually separated when she was a child. But she trusted that her guardian savior would not allow her father to hurt her again, even if he found her.

To be further satisfied that no harm would come to her, she found a telephone book for Thistlewaite County and searched for all the listings under Smith. There were of course a number of them, but none with the first name of Carl, and she assured herself that the others had no relation to her.

HUMPED FLOORS

RUSSELL (RUSTY) SMITH NEEDED SOME WORK DONE ON HIS house. The paint had peeled, especially around the upper windows, and the roof leaked in two places. But the retired farmer had long ago stopped climbing ladders. After sixty years of milking cows, carrying sacks of feed, and jumping off tractors and wagons, his knees had given out. He also had problems inside, where the hardwood floor in the guest bedroom buckled into hills and valleys. To make matters worse, his wife's sister had called, announcing her intention to visit at the end of next month, and after hanging up the phone his wife, Maxine, had instantly reordered her collection of things to worry about, placing house repair at the very highest peak of concern.

Rusty called all the lumberyards—even in Kendall, more than fifty miles away—and was told there were no construction crews available. He called all the listed carpenters and contractors.

"This is always the worst season," said Rodney Whisk at Whisk Lumber. "Everyone puts off construction until frozen ground is just around the corner. There's more building now than you can shake a stick at."

"I need someone," said Rusty, flipping his spent cigarette to the asphalt and grinding it beneath the pointed toe of his cowboy boot. He tried to keep from reaching again into the pocket of his insulated vest, failed, found another cigarette, and lit it from a disposable lighter.

"Everybody works for the big boys now," said Rodney. "Pete Hardin was in last week looking for someone to finish the addition on his house. He finally hired some Amish."

"Don't want Amish," said Rusty. "Don't want to encourage them to keep moving in."

"Appears they don't need any encouragement," said the lumberyard owner as a tractor-trailer load of Canadian plywood backed toward them from the street.

"The wife doesn't like to drive at night," said Rusty. "Afraid of hitting 'em."

"They finally put electric lights on their buggies."

"Didn't do it until they forced 'em."

"They're hard workers," said Rodney. "Give them that."

"Never said they weren't. Never said they weren't. Just think they make poor neighbors."

Rusty paused to remind himself why he had a right to complain about religious groups and anything else. He had grown up in an always-hungry family that never took charity. His father never held a steady job for more than three months, never owned his own home, and didn't live past the age of forty. Rusty had dropped out of school in the eighth grade to work as a farm laborer, as did his younger brother.

From one rented room to another, Rusty had worked seven days a week, fourteen hours a day, year in and out. He had worn other men's clothes, slept on cement floors, and hidden rice in soiled pockets of his overalls. He'd plowed with horses, shoveled manure, butchered animals, and cleared timber. He had worked for some of the most miserly farmers in the area—well known for their cruelty to family, animals, and themselves.

When he was old enough to be legally employed, he had worked nights as a grinder in the foundry. At thirty-eight he finally made a down payment on his own farm and a year later married a school-teacher. Then for the next thirty-five years he farmed with a moral ferocity that more resembled mortal combat than work, until he had paid, in full, for every blade of grass and splinter of wood on his property. Meanwhile, his wife had raised their two daughters, who eventually attended the state university, married young men from the suburbs, and provided his two grandchildren with lives of nurtured indolence.

Rusty Smith had the right to talk about other people. In a culture that valued work, he was a living testament to that virtue, a gnarled emblem of relentless toil.

He continued, "The Amish don't pay gasoline taxes but use the roads and leave horse manure all over them. Their steel wheels cut deep into the cement. They don't use electricity, so the rest of us have to pay higher rates. They don't follow the same school laws. They get special privileges when it comes to having outhouses. Hell, for ten years my neighbor tried to build a hunting shack, but they wouldn't let him unless he put in a complete sewer system. They say crapping outdoors is part of their religion."

Rusty rarely talked about anything, but this was one of the few issues he had well rehearsed. "Amish don't believe in owning cars, but they sure like to ride around in them. They don't believe in owning phones, but they sure like to use them. They don't believe in medical insurance, but they run to the hospitals in every emergency. They don't believe in owning power tools, but they sure like to borrow them."

"Do they borrow your tools often, Rusty?"

"Not mine."

"You're a hard man," said Rodney, "and I'd like to talk to you more, but I've got to check over this plywood before they unload it."

"Suit yourself."

Rusty returned to his dual-wheeled pickup and began the drive back to his farm. Well, it really wasn't a farm anymore, he reminded himself. Two years ago he had sold the land to Charlie Drickle & Sons. All his equipment had been auctioned. Now he just owned the house, the barn, and four acres. Drickle had wanted the barn, too, but Rusty refused, even though it stood a long ways from the house. "I'll build you a big garage," Drickle said.

"Not the same thing," said Rusty.

At home, Rusty went directly into the basement. He always changed clothes down there to keep the smell of the farm out of the rest of the house. There was a shower next to the washer and dryer. After stepping out of his city clothes, he put on a pair of forest-green coveralls that zipped up the front and exchanged his leather cowboy boots for insulated rubber.

It was the only place in the house where he smoked, and he squatted onto his old milking stool and lit a cigarette. His knees hurt.

From above him came the sounds of Maxine and the vacuum cleaner. The humming and bumping gradually moved north. Running out of electric cord, she turned off the cleaner and returned south to retrieve the plug from the socket.

The telephone in the kitchen rang and her footsteps reversed, then stopped directly above him. Though he could not understand individual words, the fleeting sounds of occasional laughter led him to suspect the caller to be one of the girls, Maxine's mother in Milwaukee or her sister in Chicago. About 90 percent, or more, of their calls could be traced to these sources. Rusty lit another cigarette as he listened to her pull a chair out from under the table and sit on it. Her voice lowered as she settled into the conversation, and the silences grew periodically longer as superficial greetings ended and more vital communication began to flow.

Rusty didn't like talking on telephones. His circumstances had frequently made it unavoidable, yet he could not remember a time when he had ever *agreeably* dialed a number. And as he had so often demonstrated, it always proved easier to drive twenty miles to see if a store carried a desired item—or if it was open—than call. Holding a telephone against his ear had the same effect on him as entering a room filled with tourists in flowered shirts. He was not gregarious in that way. To be honest, he was not gregarious at all. His entire social capital had been invested, wisely and exhaustively, in Maxine. He hadn't talked to his own brother or sisters in over fifty-five years. He so rarely thought about them that they seemed little more than characters in a mostly forgotten book.

Finishing his cigarette, Rusty groaned to his feet and climbed the cement stairs into the yard. He let the white bull terrier crossbreed out of her pen. The enormous dog limped through the wire gate, reminding him of her untreatable arthritis. Together they completed the long walk to the barn, which sat on the edge of a woodlot.

The building's interior looked more like a museum than a barn. After selling the farm, Rusty had turned his attention to all the things he had promised to do whenever he found time. He oiled, repaired, and arranged all his tools. Then he made a pegboard to hang them from. Though he had resisted buying certain tools during his farming life—not wanting to spend money on things he would use only infrequently—he now purchased them to complete his collection. He built a new workbench, with oak drawers to sort the nuts, bolts, screws, washers, nails, clips, pins, wire and wire fasteners, insulators, brads, tacks, rivets, and other things he had accumulated over the years, labeled and arranged according to size. He painted his vise. He painted his gasoline and oil cans and set them along the wall. He painted two metal storage barrels and put them at the end of the bench. He painted a wooden sign and hung it on the pegboard: TOOLS. He painted the doors and window frames. By the time he had finished, the inside of the barn looked like a Walt Disney production.

He backed the Oldsmobile out, drove it up to the house, parked it next to the water spigot, and began hosing off the dust and road dirt. On Wednesday nights Maxine volunteered in the library, and she often took Leslie Weedle, the librarian, home afterwards.

Keeping vehicles clean seemed important. Cars and trucks were extensions of the home and reflected their owner's character. Like ragged clothes, a dirty car said a number of things Rusty did not wish to be associated with. Though he didn't give a nickel what any particular individual thought about him and even held most of his neighbors in near-contempt, the mass of all of them together—the community—had considerable weight.

He began to go over the Oldsmobile with a chamois cloth to eliminate water stains. Maxine came out of the house and stood beside him. "The library's closed tonight," she said. "Someone is waxing the main floors."

"Won't hurt to have the car clean," said Rusty.

"No it won't, Russell. Anyway, Margie called and it looks like Mother might be able to come with her. She talked with the doctor and called the airlines. She can take her walker on the plane."

Rusty wrung out the chamois and wiped off the trunk.

"We'll have to put Mother in the girls' room," she said, turned, and spoke again. "It's been almost ten years since they were both here—clear back before the girls were out of high school."

Rusty finished with the trunk and continued until all the water streaks had been removed. Then he rewound the hose and drove the Oldsmobile back into the barn. He stood beside the workbench and lit a cigarette. He didn't know what to do. He had to find someone to work on the house. Maxine was beginning to panic. At this point she could contain herself, but she wouldn't last long. He should have found someone to do the repairs early in the summer, but he'd put it off. The bitter fact that he couldn't do the work himself had made everything else easier to ignore.

He checked the oil in his lawn-mowing tractor, took a deep breath, and climbed stiffly onto the seat. With a turn of the key, he was out of the barn and moving along the fruit trees like an insect perched on a noisy green leaf, the giant old dog ambling alongside as well as she could.

While he had been farming, their yard could be mowed in fifteen minutes with a push mower. After he retired, the mowing area gradually expanded until it now took three hours. The mower deck beneath him chewed into the thick damp grass and sprayed cuttings onto the blacktop road halfway to the centerline. The roaring and churning sound was punctuated at odd intervals by an occasional *ping* from a piece of gravel coming into contact with the whirling blades.

He made two passes along the orchard, and a white pickup stopped on the shoulder of the road, maybe twenty yards away. A man climbed out. From this distance, without his glasses, Rusty couldn't be sure he knew him, but with both of them moving toward each other he soon recognized July Montgomery, a Jersey farmer near Words. Jerseys, Rusty smiled, were for people who were afraid to milk Holsteins and too ashamed to milk goats. He shut off the engine and lit a cigarette as a way of saying hello.

"Rusty," said July, smiling with a sincerity that Rusty interpreted as feigned. "I've been meaning for a long time to stop. How are you?"

"I'm okay."

"How are those knees holding up?"

"I'll let you know. What do you want?"

"Dog won't bite, will it? Looks mean."

"Take your chances like everyone else," said Rusty.

"Remember that grain drill I bought from you?"

"No refunds."

"How did you set the boxes for barley?"

"Set the outside box on about the sixth notch, the inside ones on the tenth."

"Sixth notch outside, tenth notch inside."

"Worked for me."

"A little wet to be mowing, isn't it?"

"Not really. Want a job doing carpenter work?"

"No. What kind of carpenter work?"

"The house needs a new roof, among other things."

"I found a good carpenter last summer. Eli Yoder and his boys Isaac and Abraham. They built my new shed."

"Don't want Amish," said Rusty.

"I thought the same thing," said July, taking his cap off. "But I hired them anyway, and it was the drop-dead best thing I ever did. They work like mules but you only have to pay them like horses." He laughed. "No, seriously, they did a good job. Eli lives—"

"I know where he lives."

"Say, have you seen any signs of that cougar?"

"Nope."

"Me neither. But they say it's around. Many people have heard it and some people have seen it. I saw it myself."

"First time I see it will be the last," said Rusty.

"Big cats used to be all through this part of Wisconsin," said July.

"Maybe so, but people back then had the sense to kill the buggers off."

A ROOM WITHOUT FURNITURE

WHEN CORA HAD GATHERED ALL THE EVIDENCE SHE NEEDED to prove that the American Milk Cooperative was shipping adulterated milk, shortchanging its patrons, and manipulating government reports, she told her supervisor she didn't feel well and took the afternoon off. On the drive home she kept her hands from shaking by gripping the steering wheel until her knuckles turned white.

The farmhouse seemed cold, and she turned up the thermostat. As her husband moved back and forth through the north windows pulling a chopper and wagon into a field of July hay, Cora poured a cup of hot coffee and drank it, thinking it might calm her down. Then she telephoned the number written on the back of a pink memo card. With the box of photocopied documents sitting on the floor in front of her, she listened to three distant rings before the Wisconsin Department of Agriculture, Trade and Consumer Protection answered.

"May I please speak with the compliance officer in charge of dairy," said Cora.

"Who's calling?" asked the secretary.

"A concerned citizen," said Cora, bracing herself for the questions that would follow.

"I see," said the voice on the other end. "I'm afraid Mr. Wolfinger is not available."

"I have something important to speak with him about," said Cora. "Very important."

"I'm sorry, but Mr. Wolfinger is not in his office at the present time. Perhaps you can call back later."

"I must talk to him."

"I'm sorry, but Mr. Wolfinger is not in his office at the present time. If you wish, you may leave your name, telephone number, and the nature of the business you wish to discuss, and Mr. Wolfinger or a member of his staff will contact you as soon as his schedule allows."

Reluctantly, Cora gave her name and, in a very general way, said something about the information she had to report. Neither elicited a response.

Outside, the thick sound of the chopper's whirring vegetative violence ceased. Her husband drove out of the hay field, out of view. A short time later the auger could be heard running beside the bunker feeder.

Three cups of coffee later, Cora called back.

This time, a different voice answered.

"Hello, this is Cora Shotwell. Mr. Wolfinger is expecting my call."

"One moment, please."

"This is Mr. Wolfinger," said a pleasant alto voice.

"I have something you will be extremely interested in," said Cora.

"Excuse me?"

"I have something you will be interested in," repeated Cora.

"To whom am I speaking?"

"This is Cora," she said. "I have really important information to turn over to you." She steadied her breathing and spoke again. "You will want to send someone immediately. It's all here."

"Could you tell me what this is about?"

"It concerns highly illegal actions taken by a very large milk-processing cooperative over a period of roughly six and one-half months. I have proof—all of it. I have it right here. For instance, on this May billing sheet the testing line for the ratio of butterfat and the dates are . . . "

"Excuse me, where are you calling from?"

"The farm."

"What farm?"

"We live in Thistlewaite County."

"How did you come to have this information?"

"My husband and I ship to American Milk. I also work for them as an assistant bookkeeper—at their plant in Grange—and became aware of extremely illegal actions at the main office. I have records that prove everything. When will you be sending someone out?"

"Can you spell your name—last name first."

"S-h-o-t-w-e-l-l, C-o-r-a."

"One r?"

"Yes."

"Your telephone number?"

She gave it.

"And address?"

After giving her address she anticipated that directions would be needed and began explaining how to reach the farm from Madison. Before even getting off the interstate, she was interrupted.

"Pardon me, but I have enough information for right now. Next week you will be notified about a time to come into the department. Thank you for contacting us."

Cora put down the phone and tossed the papers she was holding into the box on the floor.

She felt undone, unfinished, like a room with a fresh coat of paint but no furniture. How could someone register so little interest in what she assumed would be the lifeblood of his agency?

Not wanting to remain in her tomb of arrested expectations, she drove into town to pick up her children and save them a long bus ride.

FAITH KEEPS NO TREASURE

W INIFRED SMITH OFTEN FELT SHE LIVED TOO MUCH INSIDE her own head. She thought about things longer than she should and this presented quite a problem, especially in the ministry. It made her appear out of place.

Sharing reality with others had always proved difficult for Winnie, a problem made much worse after the death of her mother. Child Services had placed her with a foster family whom she suspected would without a second thought jam her into the coal-burning furnace in their basement if her roasting would result in an additional payment from the state. She later understood this probably wasn't true, but at the age of twelve her imagination fashioned whole garments out of the soiled cloth of her despair. Her inconsolableness over the loss of her mother gave her the demeanor of belligerence, loneliness made her seem aloof, and the perpetual fear she lived in caused others to think she might be mentally challenged.

Lying awake at night in her first foster home, she knew she had nothing. She was nobody. No future waited for her and she had no answer for the tiny yearning voice inside her that asked over and over: *Am I going to be all right?*

After months of listening to this, one night Winnie noticed another, deeper voice. At first she couldn't make it out—only that it was not asking the same fearful question. This new voice was making a statement and the feeling attached to it gave her comfort, and the more comfort she felt the more clearly she could hear the voice. It was telling her something about herself. She could be somebody after all: a Christian.

But what did this mean? Other children called themselves Christian and they seemed to get this blessed identity from their parents, like being Norwegian. But Winnie's mother and father had belonged to nothing. They had no religion.

What did it mean to *have* a religion, she wondered, and thought about this incessantly. Inordinately shy, she had no skills in talking to strangers, and everyone now was a stranger. There was no one to ask, and she had to figure everything out for herself.

One by one, things were revealed, and her young mind built from them a safe fortress to grow up in. Christian membership, she decided, was unlike other ways of belonging. It was a community of faith, and so long as you had faith, you belonged—a home of shared convictions. In the family of Christians, togetherness was maintained not by similar physical characteristics or spatial proximity, or even knowing each other, but through the fellowship of sharing beliefs. In the privacy of your own mind, when you thought about these special beliefs you could find safety in knowing that others shared them. Your thoughts were theirs. They conversed agreeably in exchanges of encouragement and goodwill. Sharing in these beliefs was like talking with a friend under a warm blanket, or knowing something in your heart, something good, that someone else also knew. And not just any beliefs would do—only the right ones. The wrong beliefs left you outside, alone, with no firm identity.

As she was transferred from one foster home to another, she continued to work out these beliefs that qualified her to be a true Christian. She read the Bible from beginning to end, and then started over. Slowly she began to understand what was required, and as her understanding grew her confidence in herself as an authentic person strengthened.

At fourteen, she was placed with a Christian family and experienced a cautious elation at finally arriving in her mind's outward community; but the elation quickly faded when she attended church for the first time and was placed in a class for religious instruction. She had lived too long, it seemed, in her own fortress, and the walls had become thick.

She tried to talk to the other Sunday school students about the beliefs they shared with her, only to discover that they didn't share them. Not only did they not share them, they had never heard of them and had no interest in learning about them. Even her teacher seemed unfamiliar with many, and those he seemed familiar with he had obviously spent too little time thinking about.

After six months Winnie asked to be excused from the confirmation ceremony following the completion of her religious instruction class. Her teacher was "cut to the quick," he said, because she was, he said, his best student. But she did not think any legitimate sanctification could be granted solely on the basis of affirming belief, because, she said, a person could be filled with the Holy Spirit and still not believe, in the same way that someone could be electrocuted but not believe in electricity. Professed belief was an insufficient agency between God and woman.

She of course wanted to accept the things her teacher insisted she must, but as long as there remained the slightest *wanting* on her part, surely it couldn't be faith. True faith kept no treasure in wanting. True faith wanted nothing to make it whole; it simply was, and grace could only be called "sufficient" when the Grace of grace was present, and no one, she told her teacher, could say that grace was always present because that would make living outside of Grace impossible. And if one never lived outside Grace, one could never know the experience of living under its benevolent rule. After all, Grace was not just a word for which a meaning could always be assigned and a definition found. Grace was something real that made all the difference, something that could be experienced, and because of this it had to be admitted that it could also *not* be experienced, and if it was *not experienced* it could not be sufficient.

And as far as the Holy Trinity was concerned—this was of course a wonderful idea so long as you did not worry about the need for All to be One rather than All to be Three, but what Scripture, exactly, was it based upon?

Her teacher placed his head in his hands, looked at her through the spaces between his fingers, and called her a "bad girl."

After leaving church, her foster parents took her home and whipped her until she bled, but this was expected, because suffering at the hand of others, she had come to believe because of many resounding examples in the Bible, was a sign of having true beliefs. Within the month, she was taken to another foster home.

That was a long time ago, she reflected on her way back to the parsonage behind the Words Friends of Jesus Church. Now she was no longer a child and did not expect other people to share her thoughts or beliefs. It wasn't necessary. The Holy Bible Theological Seminary had taught her that. There were hundreds of Christian denominations and all of them had different practices and different shades of belief. They talked about believing the same things, but when it came right down to it, they didn't. Whatever unity there was came from a shared agreement to not be very specific about what those beliefs entailed. And only odd ducks, like herself, bothered to look very deeply into them.

The congregation she currently served belonged to the Society of Friends. She had known little about this denomination but studied up before coming for the interview.

Their mid-seventeenth-century founder, George Fox, had experienced the living spirit of Jesus Christ, in England. Convinced that such personal encounters constituted essential Christianity, Fox attracted a number of equally convinced followers, and they openly criticized established religious and governmental practices. They called themselves Friends and suffered appalling persecution from other Christians for their iconoclastic beliefs.

Friends came to the New World as many others, seeking religious freedom. Their numbers in Pennsylvania once comprised a majority and their views on pacifism, plain dress, alcohol abstinence, and the shunning of music and dancing were well known. William Penn had been a prominent member of the group. They worshipped in "meeting houses," in silence, seeking direct communion with God, the males on one side of unadorned rooms, females on the other. There were no paid pastors or priests among them, as they rejected the idea of spiritual intermediaries. Each individual believer, they thought, enjoyed the same direct connection to the Deity. Their nickname, Quaker, currently used to advertise breakfast cereal, mocked the way some members' untrained voices quavered when they delivered inspired messages to the rest of the meeting. They advocated for better treatment of mental patients and criminals, and the Society of Friends included many women who were instrumental in spreading the early faith. In later years, Friends contributed to the abolitionist movement. The Underground Railroad was believed by some to have been engineered by them.

In the late nineteenth century, the Great Awakening, also known as the holiness movement, swept across the United States in a wave of evangelical tent meetings led by charismatic, European-trained ministers. The movement owed much of its emphasis to John Wesley and profoundly influenced Quakerism. Soon, an acrimonious dispute over practice and doctrine divided the Society. Afterwards, there were many Friends congregations that to an untrained eye resembled Wesleyans, except for omitting water baptism and other rituals relating to the sacraments, which were rejected in favor of less demonstrative forms of devotion. Gone were the plain clothes and peculiar speech—replaced with collection plates, organs, pianos, and singing. In time, evangelical Friends came to depend upon the services of paid pastors and even called their local meetings "churches." The Words Friends of Jesus Church was one of these.

Winifred Smith lived in the little parsonage behind the white church. The roof leaked and the toilet flushed with the kind of diminished enthusiasm that often precedes serious septic difficulties. She had a forced-air oil furnace with no air-conditioning, the majority of windows were painted shut, and the floors were covered with linoleum and flowered carpets. The downstairs served as office space for a copy machine, Sunday school library, donation center, and church answering machine. Even the refrigerator was best regarded as communal property, with pictures, calendars, notices, and articles held to its front and sides with magnets glued to pieces of painted, colored clay, made in Vacation Bible School. The upstairs, where Winnie actually pictured herself living, like a swallow in an attic, consisted of two small bedrooms with partial ceilings.

The majority of her congregation, gray-headed and stoop-shouldered, lived under the continuing influence of Depression-era memories. They could easily recall events—and spoke of them in earnest detail—that occurred before electricity, telephones, and interstate highways. Many had spent their entire lives (excepting, in some cases, military service) in the same geographical area, and every hill, valley, road, and building held familial volumes of association.

These frail, dignified ladies and gentlemen formed the core of her church, supporting it with near-sacrificial fervor. Though many were living on Social Security or the dwindling income from the sale of their farms, their generous giving provided the lion's share of her salary. Their attendance at church functions bordered on fanatical, and their views on how the church should operate were tantamount to ancestral codes. As one member said during a heated business meeting, "I care more about this church than about anyone in it." And while he possibly would have eventually conceded that the church *was* the people in it, he nevertheless had hit upon a significant truth.

People, Winnie discovered, related to organizations, and those institutional relationships were often more meaningful than the fleshly kind because they could be sustained over longer periods. People came and went, but the local church and its unchanging programs remained, and her duty was to uphold them.

Winnie Smith cherished her new position as guardian of traditions that were not her own, even though she feared that her acceptance was tentative, a little like the welcome extended to a poor relative. She suspected she might present something of an enigma to people whose lives rooted in family, where the first question asked in getting to know someone was not "What do you do?" but rather "Who are you related to?"

Still, she did not intend to fail.

Winnie conducted two Sunday services, one in the morning— with the largest attendance—and a less formal one in the evening. Both included announcements, a sermon, prayers, and hymn singing accompanied by Betty Orangles, an octogenarian pianist with snow-white hair, a soft pedal foot, and a narrowly construed sense of rhythm. Sunday school preceded morning worship, where Winnie taught grades two through six (three children). On Tuesday afternoons she met with the Women's Missionary Union in the church basement, participated in a noon potluck, and helped make blankets for people needing a "touch of sympathy." On Wednesday night she led Bible study. Thursday nights were devoted to her youth group— two teenagers, if everyone showed up. Twice a month she visited area nursing homes, calling on residents who had once sat in the pews at the Words church and holding Protestant services for those who could be coaxed out of their beds. There were also regular committee and business meetings, visiting the sick and shut-in, holding dedication services for newborns, officiating at weddings, and attending local ministers' association meetings. So far, she had been able to arrange for other pastors in the area to hold the only funerals that were required, for which she was thankful. In addition to these responsibilities were the numerous and sundry little things that consumed most of the rest of her waking hours: correspondence, individual and marital counseling, building and grounds oversight, and activities too diverse to mention.

BROKEN THINGS

W HEN JULY MONTGOMERY PICKED UP HIS MANURE SPREADER
at the Words Repair Shop, he reminded Jacob Helm to work
on the stalled rider on the edge of town. "Send me the bill," he said.

In the craft room, Clarice Quick called Gail Shotwell about her
lawn mower, but there was no answer. "I've tried three times," she
told Jacob.

"I'll stop on the way home," he said. Several hours later he walked
out of the shop, padlocking the double garage doors behind him.

The sun had faded from its yellow brilliancy to resemble a golden
bowl filled with late afternoon. The air felt warm, humid, and sleepy-
still.

The painted black mailbox read GAIL, in white stick-on block letters. He parked his jeep near an orange-red mower surrounded by
tall grass, mired like a rowboat abandoned in seaweed.

Providing mechanical remedies appealed to Jacob in much the
same way that healing appealed to physicians. Broken things *wanted*
to function properly and were tragically prevented from doing so.
When they were fixed, they returned to their normal state and
resumed their activities, happily cutting off the tops of grasses or
whatever else they had been created for. Ending their uselessness
constituted a noble calling: liberation mechanics.

A short time later he located the problem: a faulty switch designed to allow the engine to start only when the mower blades
were disengaged. The best solution required a new switch, but in the
meantime he could bypass the safety precaution with a small length
of spliced electrical wire. The appearance of the lawn suggested that
the owner would probably want to mow as soon as possible.

After returning his toolbox to the jeep, he walked along the

assorted collection of wooden planks thrown down for a sidewalk
to the house and knocked.

No answer, yet inside the house he could hear a low, unsteady
noise.

Jacob knocked again, louder. Again no answer. The staggered,
muffled noises inside the house grew louder and more rhythmic.
Someone, it seemed, must be inside.

He decided to try the back door and walked around the yard,
climbing with some effort through blackberry brambles and hickory
saplings.

The sounds could be heard more clearly here, rambling yet melodic, each tone flowing away from the previous one in a mocking,
playful humor, as though the ground itself were making up earthy
songs about the foibles of nature. Then he recognized something
familiar in the melody, and while he was pondering this familiarity
he walked around the corner of the house and discovered inside the
screened-in porch a young, completely naked blond woman, seated
on a broken glider, her head tilted to one side, playing a bright red
guitar. Her eyes were closed, her mouth partly opened, an expression of concentrated effort on her face.

A wide, sequined guitar strap fell over her right shoulder, and the
additional weight of the instrument rested in the cleavage between
twin pale thighs. The slender fingers of her right hand plucked vigorously at the four coiled strings as her left hand darted up and down
the neck as quick as a weaver's, searching for some combination of
movements to free the notes she hoped to coax from the instrument.
The motion of her hands was relayed by a thick black cord issuing
from the front of the guitar onto the porch floor, around her naked
right foot, and through the back door, leaving the impression that
the house itself amplified the muted stirrings into heavy, spacious,
romping tones. Because of the angle of the guitar, her left breast
remained partially obscured, hidden. The other stared amply ahead,
apparently aimed through its ripe focused nipple at the bridge of
his nose.

She opened her eyes, raised her head, and looked directly at him.
The music stopped at the same moment that her uncommon beauty

announced itself inside Jacob's mind, like the bright pain following
with brief delay after an openhanded slap.

Jacob felt accosted. A barrier had been breached and he was immediately surrounded by a number of aggressive and uncomfortable
revelations. He was thirty-eight years old, and his feet were stuck
in a pivotal spot in history in which six million years of instinctual
male responses to naked females of childbearing age meeting the
highest standards of pulchritude needed to change. Indeed, it had
fallen solely on Jacob, the responsibility of crafting a Better Way of
reacting to young, unclothed women, based on unassuming con-
tractual and egalitarian considerations, shared ideals, and mutual
respect. His obligation, it seemed, required him to ignore the synaptic and endocrinic associations that men were assumed to hold in
regard to such women: leafless bouquets, genetic rewards, orgasmic
flutes and funnels, slippery wine skins, squeeze toys programmed
by Nature's Cunning Twin to reduce even the most sober, mechanically oriented minds to mush. He reminded himself that beauty was
subjective, interpretive. The viewed object-in-itself did not possess a
wild nympholeptic spirit able to reach inside him and command his
allegiance. The only reaching going on within his present circumstances lay within his own jurisdiction. Everything happened inside
him. His memories and loneliness were directly contributing in some
unknown but potentially understandable way to the perception that
Diana herself had come to be seated inside the porch—Diana or
some other mythopoeic creature of such alarming loveliness that
ordinary human relations became temporarily suspended. He was
projecting these alluring symmetries onto her and he needed to
take responsibility for doing so, now. A woman on a porch, nothing
more. Everything else about the situation he was simply making
up. Someone dying of thirst and stumbling upon a cavern filled with
dark, wooden casks of chilled wine will not be the most reliable
judge of viniculture.

In addition, a hateful thought soon informed Jacob that the
young woman before him so far surpassed his late wife in physical
beauty that they could not be compared. In other words, there was
a comparison but no one who loved his wife or at the very least the

memory of her would propose it. This woman communicated an exuberant compact burgeoning that had years ago departed from Angela, whose bodily form had been consumed in a losing battle against disease. But even in her best days, Jacob feared, before illness had begun to exact its limping toll, Angela had never possessed this creature's combination of raw visual appeal and unrehearsed grace. She glowed with health. Her neck, stretching out of the extraordinary suppleness of her shoulders, mimicked in every detail the curving stem of a lily rising to its flower. And the problems posed for him by the rondure of her hips were addressed in his imagination, one after another, before they blossomed into conscious questions, only to be posed anew.

Jacob felt ashamed of these thoughts. Protective of Angela's memory, he attempted to lay them aside. It could only mean that fate had endowed one at the expense of the other. Angela had not escaped the harsh levies that fall on all who would be honorable and true, while the beauty of the young woman before him obviously issued from outrageous good fortune, undeserved luck, and perhaps even outright theft.

As though to confirm this thought and wound him further, Gail shifted slightly, and in this nearly imperceptible twitch of positioning her beauty became even more pronounced—a trick of proportioning magic. She had instantly crafted an enhanced visage through which to be seen, arriving in it with an effortless flinch. A wicked shiver moved through Jacob.

Gail looked up and discovered someone behind her screened-in porch, someone in stained clothes with greasy hands.

Her first conscious thought was terror. Her imagination dutifully informed her of impending doom, illustrated in lavish detail from its arsenal of anticipated horrors, but this soon subsided. Even strangers can know things about each other, and the stance of her unannounced visitor seemed too upright, his gaze too worried, his hands, though thick, unwilling to play the roles her imagination scripted for them. Indeed, all those brutish qualities he shared with other men were supervened by a determined refusal to face up to the fact that he had them. This guy thought too much, lived too much in his head, and, whoever he might be, he was no threat. Something about him was broken.

Her next worry concerned her privacy. A sense of violated propriety—her house, her yard, her porch, her *her*—found expression in contemptuous anger mingled with mild curiosity and surprising embarrassment at being discovered naked. Without looking away from him, she rose to her full height, slowly untangled herself from the sequined strap, set the guitar on the glider, turned around, walked in hieratic, ceremonial steps inside the house, and closed the door.

A minute later, she emerged in denim cutoffs, yellow top, and yellow running shoes.

Both pretended the earlier moment had not occurred. Something completely unrelated to it caused them to be unable to make eye contact.

"July Montgomery said I should come over and check your lawn mower. I'm Jacob Helm."

"Hello," she said, without offering her name.

"I called earlier, there was no answer . . . I knocked on the front door, but, I'm sorry . . ."

"July should have said something to me. I hate him. Nobody minds their own business anymore."

"No, I don't suppose."

She stepped off the porch and into the back yard. Jacob looked away from her mouth to the ground, but soon had his attention drawn to a yellow shoelace, untied, falling loosely over her instep and quickly gathering significance—a drama threatening to invoke the scene of her ankle—and he looked up again.

"Did you look at it?" she asked.

"No," he said.

"It has gasoline but it won't start."

"What?"

"The lawn mower."

"I mean yes, I did look at it. A switch needs replacing. You can use it, though, while I order a new one, but you have to remember not to start it with the blades engaged. It's hard on the motor and solenoid."

"You're the owner of the repair shop," said Gail, as though making a general announcement.

"Yes, and I'll be leaving now. Remember not to start the engine with the blades engaged."

"What do I owe you?"

"Nothing. I was on my way home anyway . . . and that was a Barbara Jean song you were playing. I recognized it: 'Cradle of Your Smile.'"

Gail tried to keep her face still, but a pleased-with-herself smile that she couldn't swallow crept into her mouth.

"Really?"

"Really. It's unmistakable."

HOT MILK

THE MORNING FOLLOWING CORA'S CALL TO THE DEPARTMENT of Agriculture, Trade and Consumer Protection, early, her husband, Grahm, walked to the barn. The air seemed unusually fresh, and the sky drew the dew away from the ground in long curls of smoking water—hundreds of tiny, silent geysers erupting.

Unlike on other mornings, the dog did not greet him. Once Grahm was inside the barn, he discovered the north door, which he routinely closed each night after milking—a door that could only be fastened from inside because of a broken latch spring—wide open. But this seemed of no consequence.

The dog appeared in the afternoon, with dried blood in her fur and a lump above her left ear, but Grahm thought no more about it until the following day when the driver of the milk truck handed him a bill for $5,314—the cost of a tanker-load of milk.

"What's this?" he asked.

"Sorry, Grahm," said Hubert Shorn. "Your antibiotics contaminated the whole load."

"Can't be," said Grahm.

"Sorry. There it is—black and white. I don't do the testing, just haul milk and bring in samples."

"There's some mistake."

"Talk to the lab about that, or management. The whole lot was hot. Had to be dumped. Your sample, when tested, turned as green as food coloring."

"It says penicillin."

"That's what they mostly test for."

"We haven't used penicillin since summer before last. We applied for organic certification and they won't allow it. Don't use antibiotics."

"Like I said, I just haul milk."

"Five thousand dollars!"

"Talk to management. Hell, I'm on your side."

Grahm drove to the branch office in Grange, met with the plant manager, and talked to the head of the testing lab. He insisted they run a second test on a sample he had brought with him. The test showed no antibiotic residue and Grahm asked how his milk could be contaminated one day and clean the next.

The technician rearranged utensils on the counter. "Milk from treated cows was not put in the bulk tank today," he said.

"But the amount of milk was the same. If I'd withheld milk it would show up in volume. If I'd added water, the butterfat would be off."

"Perhaps treatments were discontinued, or milk was brought in from another farm. Ninety-five percent of hot milk clears up the second day."

"Are you calling me a liar?"

"Of course not," said the branch manager, stepping between the technician and Grahm. "Mistakes are always possible. If you want to contest the assessment you can file a complaint with DATCP. They set the standards and make the rules."

By the time Grahm returned home, his thoughts were swimming in mud. He needed help. He needed Cora.

But when Cora came home, Grahm could tell from clear across the barnyard that something was wrong.

"What's the matter?" he asked when he reached her.

"The second set of files in the Madison office—the filing cabinets—are gone. They just disappeared. I asked about them and everyone ignored me. That woman, Harriet, who has worked there for twenty years said she couldn't remember any file cabinets."

An hour later a solid blue Chevrolet pulled into the drive. A deputy sheriff walked disdainfully around the tractor ruts and through the yard. Cora met him on the porch and he placed a legal summons in her hand. It ordered her to appear before an administrative judge at the Wisconsin Department of Agriculture, Trade and Consumer Protection.

Monday morning, Grahm and Cora dressed in their best clothes and drove into Madison, the cardboard box of photocopied documents in the back of the station wagon.

Inside the slate gray building they were directed to the fourth floor. They waited in an empty waiting room for almost an hour, sitting in sculptured plastic chairs.

"Cora Shotwell," said a woman with short reddish-orange hair, carrying a yellow notepad. "Come with me, please."

Grahm rose to follow but was told to remain. Cora walked behind the woman down a long hallway and into a room with men seated at tables. She was told to sit down, and she did.

The five men seated at the tables appeared to be reading from papers in ringed binders. Because of the position of her chair she could not face them all at once. They continued reading and paging through the thick volumes without speaking.

"We understand you have a grievance with your milk plant," said one of the two men seated at the furthest table from her.

"It's not a grievance," said Cora, turning her chair to address her comments in his direction. She thought he might be a judge, but wasn't sure. "I have proof American Milk has been robbing farmers, keeping a second set of records, and selling illegal milk."

"How long have you been working for the cooperative?"

"Five years."

"What position do you currently have there?"

"Assistant bookkeeper."

"How long ago did you begin to think irregularities were taking place?"

"Seven months ago, and they're not irregularities."

"Why didn't you report this immediately?"

"I had no proof."

"Did you report your suspicions to your supervisor?"

"Yes, and it become clear that if I continued to ask questions I would lose my job. He said the main office had a different accounting system."

"What did you do then?"

"I made copies of the reports and billing sheets. I have them outside in the car."

"Did you have authorization to make these copies?"

"What do you mean?" asked Cora.

"Were you given permission by the American Milk Cooperative to make copies of their internal records and reports?"

"No."

"Are you aware that making unauthorized copies of proprietary information and other data can constitute a felony?"

"No, but I have the documents outside in our car."

"Let's not get ahead of ourselves here," said a man seated at the table directly behind her. "This agency is not in a position to accept any documents before a review panel can be convened."

"Nothing was said about this when I called last week."

"We are bound by law," said the man seated closest to her, without looking up.

"I talked with Mr. Wolfinger. I told him—"

"I *am* Mr. Wolfinger and I never told you we could accept your papers before a department review had been convened."

"Then why am I here?"

"We have begun a preliminary investigation and American Milk has offered to cooperate in providing us with all the information we require."

"I can't believe this. I have the documents in my car. They prove everything."

"During this phase of the investigation it would be improper for us to accept them."

"I can't believe this!" shouted Cora, rising to her feet. "Shame on you."

"Sit back down, Mrs. Shotwell."

"I will not."

"Let me assure you, Mrs. Shotwell," began a very large man seated near her, his silhouette resembling an enormous pile of unfolded laundry. "Let me assure you, Mrs. Shotwell, that we are making a thorough and diligent effort."

"I don't believe it," said Cora. "I don't believe it."

"This is only a preliminary hearing," said the man she thought was a judge. "As we move forward, our own independently verified real documents will be forthcoming under department rules of discovery in compliance with the judicial administrative code. Until that time, I must ask you not to discuss this matter or other issues related to this with anyone."

"Why not?"

"It may interfere with our investigation."

When Cora reached Grahm in the waiting room, her face glowed bright red and she was shaking. "Let's get out of here," she said. "This is an unholy place."

"What happened?"

"They insulted me."

On the way home, Grahm said, "Maybe they didn't mean to."

And Cora said, "I guess if that were true you wouldn't need to do anything about it."

HIRING HELP

JULY MONTGOMERY AND HIS TWENTY-EIGHT-YEAR-OLD NEIGHBOR
Wade Armbuster sat at a round metal table on the front deck
of July's house. They were drinking coffee and eating the last of a
peach pie. Despite the cool morning air, a cloudless sky permitted
an uncommonly brilliant sun to heat up everything it could reach
into, and their clothes and the brick front of the farmhouse were
saturated with warm comfort.

Wade wanted to borrow July's block and tackle to pull the engine
out of a car he was fixing up.

July wanted help with his third crop of hay.

The negotiations were complicated. Wade worked at the cheese
plant, and his schedule was inflexible yet erratic. He had the strength
of two ordinary men and would be good help, but July wasn't sure
he would bring the hoist back.

July forked another piece of pie into his mouth, contemplated the
texture with his tongue, and gazed into the shrubs growing along
the edge of the house.

"How long you need the hoist?"

"Long enough to trick out the motor—pistons, rings, stroker
crank, roller cam, and three-way valves."

"Sounds expensive."

"Power costs money," said Wade.

"Young people get hurt in cars like that."

"People get hurt doing lots of things," said Wade, his face thin
and intense. The sunlight reflected from the jewelry in his ear and
nose. "How much hay you got?"

"Two full days, maybe four. Can't pay you much."

"If I can use your shop—here—I'll work for nothing. You've got
good tools."

"Here?"

"That way the folks won't be nagging me."

"You still on probation?"

"I guess so."

"Sounded like a bad deal to me—what I heard," said July. "Wasn't entirely your fault. Someone backed you into a corner and you came out of it."

Wade looked away, following a sound on the road. He admired July but didn't care for him to know it. The older man lived alone and made his own rules. No one told him what to do and something in his eyes said two things at once: I like you but I don't compromise on anything important.

Over the eastern horizon, Rusty Smith's dual-wheeled pickup came toward them, eventually turning like a bloated silver fish into the narrow tributary of the driveway. He stopped at the edge of the yard, then drove another thirty yards to the open machine shed, where he climbed from the cab and stood waiting for July to speak with him in private.

"Here's the deal," said July. "You can use my shop, but I don't want any of my tools disappearing and I've got to talk to your parents first. I know you're old enough to do whatever you want, but that's just the way it is. I don't want any trouble with your folks. And I don't mind if you occasionally drink around here, but I can't tolerate drunks."

Wade left.

July swallowed the bottom half of his coffee and joined Rusty in the machine shed. They discussed the weather for several minutes, milk prices and road construction.

"Those Amish," muttered Rusty. "When you hire them, how do they get back and forth from work—in buggies?"

"That's right," said July. "If you want them quicker, pick them up."

"I've got a lot of work to get done. How do you call them?"

"You don't call them, Rusty. They don't have phones. You go over. It's the old way of doing business."

"I'm not saying I'm going to."

"Going to what?"

"Hire them." Rusty spit on the ground in an almost friendly manner, climbed back in his pickup, and drove away.

Fifteen minutes later, he turned into Eli Yoder's barnyard. A
dozen or more chickens, geese, and guinea hens performed a clam-
orous and feathery retreat. A black and white dog barked anxiously
from a safe distance away. Stepping from the truck, Rusty looked for
signs of human life among the shabby collection of wood-framed
buildings, sheep pen, cement silo, and an overturned cart. Chestnut
draft horses grazed beyond the barn and a curl of smoke rose from
the tiny, unpainted house.

Hoping to find someone outdoors, Rusty walked to the barn. Road-
hoppers flew out of his path, their papered wings rasping. A barefoot
child—perhaps four or five years old—darted from a nearby shed
carrying a pail. She glanced fearfully at him from beneath her white
head scarf and continued running along a dirt path to the house,
where she closed the door behind her.

Finding no one in the barn, Rusty followed the dirt path to the
house and knocked on a windowless door. It opened and a large
woman stood directly inside, holding a broom, her head covered
with a coarse dark-blue bonnet with strands of gray hair poking out
around the edges. A full-length dress of matching blue provided a
shapeless background for the untied apron falling from her neck.
Her bare feet seemed surprisingly large, imposing and immanently
functional, as though two normal-sized feet were protectively hidden inside them. She did not speak but continued staring at the floor,
gripping the broom with red-knuckled hands. Three children under
school age stared wide-eyed from a darkened corner of the room.
Rusty shifted his weight inside his cowboy boots and pulled his right
ear lobe with his left hand. "I'm looking for Eli."

No response.

"He here?"

"Nope," said the woman without looking up or offering another
explanation.

It seemed an unusually masculine reply, putting Rusty partly at
ease, and he continued, "You know where I can find him?" He took a
cigarette from his jacket pocket and inserted it into his mouth.

"Fillin' silo over to Bontrager's."

The three children cautiously moved out of the darkened corner and were now about halfway across the little room, keeping the woman between them and the door. The boy—the youngest of the three—continued to stare at Rusty with extreme anxiety, as though Rusty were someone he had been specifically warned about. The only light in the room came through a single window, partly obscured by curtains, and the smell of kerosene lay heavy on the air. The smell nudged something loose inside Rusty—a memory he held for a moment then let fall.

"Where's that?" he asked.

"Three places over," she said, jerking the broom handle to indicate north. "Pumpkin patch by the road."

Rusty lit his cigarette and blew out smoke. "I'll be going over there, then."

Rusty found the farm. Six buggies parked in front of the house—some with horses still in harness. Amish men were filling silo next to the barn. Several stood on a wagon piled with bundled cornstalks, feeding them into a gasoline-powered chopper. Other horse-drawn wagons could be seen in a nearby field, where more Amish loaded more cornstalks. All wore straw hats, blue coats, and black boots. The older men had beards without mustaches; the youngest were clean-shaven.

As Rusty approached, the operator of the chopper walked out to meet him. "I am Levi Bontrager," he said in slightly broken English over the roaring sound of the chopper. "Can I be of help to you?"

"Looking for Eli Yoder," said Rusty. He reached for a cigarette and then decided against it. Levi Bontrager turned and shouted in German to the workers unloading the wagon. A tall, thin man with a narrow black beard jumped to the ground and came forward. Bontrager returned to his position beside the chopper.

"July Montgomery said you do carpenter work. I need work on my house."

"Jha," replied Eli, looking out from under his hat like a badger looking out of its burrow. "What kind of work?" It was impossible for Rusty to judge his age, not only because his clothes, hair, and facial grooming did not communicate the usual signals, but also because of his general comportment. He might be a young man unusually mature, or an older man unusually immature. His teeth, for instance, were in deplorable condition, but his posture was markedly erect; while it seemed inconceivable for a young man to have such rotten teeth, it seemed equally inconceivable for an older man to stand so straight. His eyes were proud, even vain, but not arrogant. The teeth again captured Rusty's attention. You just didn't see bad teeth anymore, not like you used to. Rusty's father had bad teeth—real bad—and he quickly forced the memory away from him.

"Roof work, windows and trim, and humps in the bedroom floor," said Rusty. "Shouldn't take longer than a week or two."

"When you need this done?" Eli asked, absently brushing curls of dried corn leaves from his sleeves.

"Need it done right now."

"You say you know July Montgomery?"

"Yup. I'm Russell Smith, and my farm's not too far from here."

"People call you Rusty?"

"Some do," Rusty replied, disturbed at being identified by someone he knew nothing about.

"I should take a look at what you have."

"When can you come?"

"Right now."

"All right. I've got my truck here, I mean I suppose it's okay for you folks to ride in a truck, I mean if it isn't . . ."

"It's okay," said Eli. He walked straight to the truck, climbed in, and closed the door.

Rusty hadn't anticipated this. He was unaccustomed to sharing the interior of his truck with anyone and could count on one hand the number of times a passenger other than his wife had sat beside him. He lit a cigarette before settling behind the wheel and noticed a strong smell of human sweat mixed with corn silage.

On the road, he could think of nothing to say. Every topic seemed likely to violate some religious sensibility or unnecessarily accentuate the many obvious differences between them. But while the silence gnawed at Rusty as if it were a rat imprisoned in a wooden box, Eli Yoder appeared unperturbed. He gazed at the passing landscape from beneath his hat, occupying his place on the seat with an indifferent ease.

"Hope the smoke doesn't bother you," said Rusty, nearing the end of his cigarette.

"It don't."

Rusty lit another and they continued until they reached the state highway.

"If you don't mind, I'd like to stop at the convenience store," said Eli. "If you have the time."

Rusty parked on the lower side of Kwik Trip, where posters announced cheap cigarettes, beer, lottery tickets, bananas, and frozen pizza. Eli went in. Rusty remained in the truck, wondering what business an Amish could have here. Even Rusty disliked going inside, where teenagers abounded, middle-aged women talked in shrill voices, and everyone seemed to move in a fluorescent world of forced humor and snacks wrapped in plastic. Beneath advertisements for a video featuring a blond girl screaming beneath a man with a knife in his teeth and a sale on toilet paper, Rusty could see the top of Eli's hat. Five minutes later he came out and climbed in the truck carrying a plastic mug of coffee and a pastry filled with raspberry jam.

"Thanks," he said, sipping from the mug. "I needed to make a telephone call and they had free doughnuts with a cup of coffee. I didn't get any breakfast."

Rusty backed out of the lot. "Didn't think you people used phones," he said.

"Try not to," said Eli. "But you got to make a living."

They went the rest of the way in silence.

At Rusty's home, Eli looked up at the roof and learned that twenty-five years had passed since the asphalt shingles had been replaced.

"Fifteen years is usually the end of shingles," said Eli. "But that steep slope I suppose added to their life. You got good surface underneath?"

"Got the old shingles underneath," said Rusty.

"Should tear them out, put in new plywood."

"Plywood's blamed expensive," said Rusty. "No sense in fixing something isn't broke. Another set of shingles will outlast me no matter what's under 'em."

They walked all the way around the house, looking at the siding and paint.

"Rotten boards here," said Eli and poked a finger into a hole beneath a window frame. "But the boards could be replaced, I suppose, without replacing it all."

"It's a matter of time," explained Rusty. "This has to be done—all of it—in a month. Wife's mother and sister are coming. Has to be done."

Eli nodded. He understood the need as well as the deadline.

They went inside to inspect the floor in the downstairs bedroom, where Rusty explained that some minor flattening was in order. Eli began tugging his beard at the sight of the hump along the outside wall. "Don't like this," he said.

His fears were confirmed in the basement. "Your joists rotted off as the house settled," he announced. "Water running down the side of the house rotted away the plate, and over here you can see all the way through to outside."

"What we talking here in the way of time?" asked Rusty.

"Can't tell until we get in there—new plate, break out all this old cement, hard to tell."

Rusty felt a coiled cinch tighten around his neck. "Can you still be finished by the end of the month?"

"I should think so," replied Eli.

"Does that mean yes or no?"

"God willing." And he smiled a smile from which his beard seemed to be expressing more than his actual face—the kind of smile, Rusty feared, that could also be employed when everything was not finished on time.

"When can you start?"

"End of the week or beginning of next, I suspect."

"Sooner the better. Do you have tools?"

"We have hand tools. The work would go faster with electric, but it makes no difference to us. My sons and I are familiar with either."

"I have power tools," said Rusty. "You can use them. How much do you and your boys charge?"

"Fifteen for myself, seven for my youngest and eight for the oldest."

They were both distracted by the sound of footsteps on the basement stairs. "Russell? Russell, are you down here? Is everything all right?"

"Everything is fine. Go back upstairs."

"What are you doing down here?"

"We're almost through. Go back upstairs, Maxine."

"Is there some problem down here?"

"No. Go back upstairs."

"Hello, I'm Maxine, Russell's wife," she announced after discovering Eli standing beside her husband.

Eli looked at the cement floor in greeting. He was unaccustomed to talking with women, at least English women.

"What's your name?" she asked.

"Yoder."

"Are you here about the repair work?"

"Jha."

"Where do you live?"

Eli turned partly around so as not to be facing her directly, but not so far as to actually turn his back to her. "Over Bundy Hollow."

"Close to the Williams' farm?"

"Three places south."

"Oh, I know where you live. You have all those ducks and chickens that come out to the road. It's a nice spot. How long have you lived there?"

"Three years in November."

"Where did you come from before that?"

"Pennsylvania."

"Do you have a family? That's a small house."

"It's large enough for us."

"How many do you have in your family?"

"My wife and I have seven children, and my mother-in-law lives with us."

"Didn't a barn burn down near you?"

"The Millers'—lost half their cows last year."

"I heard you put the roof on the new building."

"Along with my boys."

"I thought that was you. Eva Miller comes into the library regular. She said you did excellent work. How old are your children?"

"Isaac is seventeen and Abraham is sixteen. The younger ones are younger."

"Do you have any daughters?"

"Three."

"Russell and I have two married daughters. Only two grandchildren, though—a newborn girl and a toddler. His name is Brian. Do you have any grandchildren?"

"No."

"Is it true that your children don't go to school past the eighth grade?"

"It's our way."

"Russell doesn't even have a seventh grade education, but that was more usual in his day. It kind of limits a person's opportunities—I mean in the modern world. You don't have any problem with your knees, do you?"

"No."

"That's good. Russell can hardly walk, I'm afraid. Can I get you something to eat or drink?"

"No."

"Well, I'll leave you two men alone to do your work. It's been nice meeting you, Mr. Yoder. I suppose Russell explained that the old wood shingles will have to be taken off the roof and new plywood put down. My sister says that's absolutely essential, and she's in real estate. And we need roof vents."

Maxine labored with thick steps up the creaking staircase.

Rusty and Eli did not look at each other and continued discussing the rotted joists.

On the way back to Eli's house, Rusty was surprised when his passenger asked—without the slightest embarrassment—if there was time to stop at the feed mill for a bag of ground corn, a roll of fencing, and a pair of sheep shears. The sheep shears had apparently been left by another Amish living on the other side of the county and waited to be picked up. Yes, there was time, Rusty said, *my time.*

When they arrived at Eli's little house, the frowning older woman appeared again in the doorway—still barefoot and still clutching her broom—and three little children bolted past her, rushing into the yard in wild anticipation. Ignoring Rusty as if he did not exist, they seemed delighted with the arrival of the items from the feed mill. Only the little boy shot him a quick, fearful glance. Eli lifted the chicken feed and wire out of the back and placed them in the children's eager arms, and they staggered off happily toward the rickety outbuildings. Rusty did not get out of the cab.

On the way home, he stopped at the lumberyard to order the needed materials.

"I hear you're hiring Amish," said the lumberyard owner.

"Who told you that?"

"July Montgomery was in here a while ago and said you were going to hire Eli Yoder."

"Something wrong with that?"

"Not a thing."

"Make sure these materials are delivered before Thursday," said Rusty. "And put a tarp over them when you drop them off. I don't want them rained on."

PERPETUAL PERISHING

G RAHM SHOTWELL WAS RUNNING LATE. WHEN THE LOADING-dock worker threw the last sack of ground feed onto his pickup and the box sank another coil spring groan lower, three o'clock had become a pillar of the past. His children, Seth and Grace, were out of school, pressing papers and books against their jacketed bodies, looking for him. He was seven miles from home and ten miles from the school. "Put this on account," he told the mill hand.

"Can't do that," said the young man, climbing back onto the loading dock and taking off his dusty hat in a gesture of apology. "Talk to them in the office. I don't make the rules."

Grahm hurried around to the front of the building and into the office. The owner and the owner's cousin, Mildred, sat behind a long counter layered with papers. Both looked up, Justin from the telephone cradled beneath his jaw and Mildred from an adding machine with a scroll of white tape arching up and onto the floor like a paper fountain. "I guess I need to talk about my bill," said Grahm.

Mildred lowered her head to signal that talking about bills did not fall under her department. Still, her eyes darted up from time to time from beneath her reading glasses. Justin rustled among the papers before him and in a darting movement seized a small pink sheet as though it was attempting to escape. "You're getting a little behind, Grahm," he said, pointing at the bottom line on the paper. "You haven't made a payment in a couple months."

"I've always paid."

"I guess you have, Grahm, but I don't remember you ever being this far behind."

The two men looked at each other. Grahm broke the silence: "I haven't got the checkbook with me. I'll stop in tomorrow morning and settle up half. Pay it all after corn's in."

"See you in the morning," said Justin, lowering his head and re-suming his telephone conversation. Mildred punched a number into the adding machine and the paper fountain jumped a notch.

Grahm glanced at the clock on the wall as he went out.

Inside the pickup he was confronted by the edge of his checkbook sticking out from the sun visor. He didn't remember putting it up there, pulled it out, and turned toward the office. Then he stopped, consulted his watch, took off his hat, adjusted the sizing band, and climbed back into the pickup.

On the highway, Grahm pushed the accelerator to the floor. The pickup gained speed, noisily, until the speedometer hovered between fifteen and twenty miles per hour above the posted limit, a full thirty miles per hour faster than he usually drove with a load of feed.

He considered the likelihood that driving this fast was reckless. The ton of additional weight seriously lengthened the distance he needed to stop. If anyone pulled in front of him, turning quickly to either side would be impossible without rolling over. But he was late, and if nothing bad happened it would mean something good.

Late had recently become a habitual companion in a more gen-eral condition of dread. He felt unable to remain completely sane. He drove himself so hard it seemed he was being driven by outside forces. His inner life felt like a theatrical production in which the major players did not even bother to show up and the minor players attempted to continue without them. Everything he touched stole from his center, until nothing remained except an exhausted empti-ness, a perpetual perishing. The nightmare that waits for young people to grow old before visiting them with visions of permanent inadequacy visited Grahm on an hourly basis. He had contracted the penultimate social disease—falling behind—and had joined the infamous ranks of people predetermined to fail.

Grahm remembered several reprobates from his childhood, men who could not keep body and soul together and for whom disorder and distress seemed a way of life, and he shuddered to think he could now be seen standing among them. Tim Pikes, for instance, had lost his farm outside Words. "A poor manager, but a good drinker," the neighbors had said before Pikes moved his threadbare family to somewhere else, leaving a broken-down farm and two acres of trash. Septic with failure, the old Pikes place had remained for sale a long time before July Montgomery finally bought it after the bank had auctioned off most of the land. Everyone else feared owning it.

As a small child Grahm had attended the Pikes's auction with his father, and he remembered walking through the farmyard where the things to be sold were sprawled out in ragged, rusting rows. It seemed like a battlefield after the dead had been removed. All that remained were the last things the soldiers had touched before they died—weapons and helmets that failed to protect them. There were tractors, household appliances, tools, furniture, dishes and silverware, farm machinery of all descriptions, miscellaneous boxes of junk, wagons, vehicles, children's toys, light fixtures, motors, welding equipment, and items too numerous and varied to recall. His father had taken his hand and moved carefully along the rows as if picking his way through a warehouse of leaking chemical drums. They left without bidding, and it seemed to Grahm that his father had been afraid of bringing anything infected with the inefficiency disease home with them.

Grahm continued at full speed. In his farmyard, he bailed out of the still-moving truck, ran into the house, shed clothes through three rooms, and climbed into the shower. Five minutes later, he was in the station wagon, back on the road.

Just before the school, Grahm slowed down to keep the tires from squealing around the corner. He saw his children at the edge of the deserted schoolyard, Seth standing on the curb and Grace sitting in the grass, both wearing masks of fatigue over worried eyes. His love for them swelled up in his throat. They were so vulnerable, their future so unformed, their purchase on life so uncertain that it seemed they could easily cease to exist—evaporate like mist—without fundamentally disrupting the laws of nature. They were too fragile, too good, to be living in such a corrupt world.

At the same time he understood the resiliency of children, a survive-at-any-cost capacity that had allowed the human species to slosh through eons of muck, drought, starvation, plague, and war. Children and beasts had more in common than anyone usually cared to acknowledge, and it was only during the first few years of life that they required enormous amounts of nurturing. After that, they were able to ascertain and secure the elemental necessities, endure unspeakable hardships, and face the cruelest realties. In fact, if parents abandoned their offspring as soon as they could adequately balance on their feet, the human race would not cease to exist; in overwhelming numbers, survivors would plod inexorably into the future. Gone, however, would be anything resembling civilization— so it was not species survival that engendered the nagging worries about his children, but the preservation of a world worth surviving in. The compulsion to protect children from physical and psychological damage provided the cornerstone upon which all civilization had been built, one guilt-ridden decision at a time.

Seth and Grace clambered into the car beside their father, their expressions somewhat improved due to the novelty of sitting in the front seat. (Their usual driver—their mother—always relegated them to the back seat, where according to official safety reports they were more likely to survive an accident.)

"Guess what!" said Grahm.

They couldn't guess what. They were entirely unfamiliar with their father picking them up at school and felt speculation to be pointless.

"It's your mother's birthday! We've got to get over there before she leaves for home. We'll surprise her and go out for dinner. Won't that be fun?"

Seth and Grace regarded him silently, knowing about their mother's birthday but confused about why he intended to play a part in it. Grahm looked back at them and knew himself to be far out of character, no longer the deaf, dark shape that lumbered through the house without speaking. He wanted to plead for understanding: this was how desperate people acted just before things got better.

EPIPHANY

WINIFRED SMITH GOT UP BEFORE THE SUN—A HABIT FORMED early in life after her mother had found work cleaning motel rooms. She settled onto her prayer mat, lit a candle and placed it on the floor beneath the east-facing bedroom window, arranged her shawl around her thin shoulders, closed her eyes, and centered her mind. In a rhythm created by her heart and lungs she silently repeated: Now I am breathing in God's good and wholesome spirit; now I am breathing out God's good and wholesome spirit. When other thoughts intruded, she nudged them aside, shooing them away from her consciousness as if they were downy chicks in the path of bare feet. With equal care she crept past her most obstinate enemy— the possibility that lifeless subatomic particles moving in monotonous paths of least resistance explained everything—arriving safely in the space of mystical freedom beyond.

Satisfied with her progress so far, Winnie prayed for individuals, holding their names and images before her, hoping Grace and Light would enter their lives. If they suffered from a known infirmity or some other circumstance that needed correcting, she held these problems before her mind. By doing this she did not hope to actually heal or improve another life per se; neither did she presume to direct the attention of an absent-minded Being. She prayed in order to participate in the Activity of God, much like a daughter who dutifully cans vegetables—not because she likes vegetables or contributes significantly to the canning process, but because she wants her mother's company. She then prayed that her father be forgiven for his vast cruelty, deserting Winnie's mother when she became sick and forcing Winnie into foster homes. In considering him, which sometimes attracted so many hateful emotions that they ended her devotions altogether, she thankfully experienced a bit more ease and softness of heart.

Finished with her prayers for others, she then prayed for herself. She repeated *Jesus Christ, Son of God, have Mercy on me* until these words also dissolved, without residue, into her breathing, and entered a state of consciousness that both dreamed and did not dream.

After she had been sitting for about forty-five minutes, distant stars began to disappear beyond the bedroom window, obliterated by light growing beneath the horizon. Morning was arriving. She then prayed that someday, somehow, if it was God's Will, she might have children, or at least have one child of her own. As soon as the plea escaped—as soon as she thought it—she tried to take it back, but of course she couldn't. Her selfishness had, once again, shown itself. Her greedy nature wanted things that maybe she was not meant to have, maybe she didn't deserve. She blew out the candle and went down the narrow staircase.

While she was making tea and toast in the narrow parsonage kitchen, she recalled her dreams from the night before. In one, she had woken up in her earliest home, where she lived before her parents divorced. The house seemed much bigger than she remembered, with many large, interconnected rooms so elaborately furnished that it took her a long time to find her way out. One room led to another, and another, each filled with a Byzantine, hysterical splendor.

When she finally stepped out the back door, she encountered an enormous, cloudless blue sky. The blue was of such intense, absorbing interest that for a long time she could not look away from it. Unlike the hysterical splendor of the rooms—which upon study revealed even more inextricable patterns—this blue only persisted in itself, growing more and more deeply one color. Then she noticed that from horizon to horizon, about two feet above the ground, flew winged creatures, birds of all descriptions—hawks, robins, eagles, hummingbirds, finches, doves, and owls. And though they were of different kinds, they were all pure white and flew silently in one direction, their wings beating in a slow, noiseless rhythm. They converged into a single point on the edge of the horizon, plunging into a hole in the rim of the sun.

Winnie didn't know what the dream meant, but it felt like an omen, resonating with significance. It called for interpretation, yet apart from the phantasmagoric images themselves, nothing communicated—it was a billboard of an empty color.

Winnie finished her second piece of buttered toast and checked the calendar next to the refrigerator. She tried not to notice anything but the scribbled notes, but couldn't help seeing more. Her birthday, October 17, stood out like a face in a crowd and she filled with anxiety at the sight of it. She tried to squeeze off this faucet of worry, but having a family meant everything. She felt she would never be complete without children. Nothing, it seemed, could cancel the divine design that caused her to need them. Even as a child she had wanted children, and as the age of thirty-five approached, stalking her like the expiration date on a can of mushroom soup, it became harder and harder to wait for the time when God would give her a real family. Because if she became too old to have children, that would mean God did not intend for her to have them. But that was impossible. It had to be. It was written in Scripture.

To arrest these alarming thoughts, she returned to her attic bedroom, sat on her bed, and brushed her long brown hair, feeling the hypnotic tug of the bristles and watching her thin hands working. But another unwelcome thought informed her that her hair extended to her waist, and even below, for only one reason: her hair was a vow, a promise she kept to herself, a defiance of the fashions of the world and a commitment to never cut it until she had a child of her own—someone to love without reservation. Her thoughts, her hair, everything about her spoke out against the submissive and accepting person she believed she should become.

Downstairs again, in the office behind the kitchen, Winnie prepared for the evening Bible study, jotting down some of her more relevant thoughts on the second chapter of First Timothy. Two phone calls interrupted her, one to ask if she had seen Ora Good's casserole dish, and one to remind her of a scheduling change for Faith Committee.

At nine-thirty she changed into brown corduroy pants, a cream shirt, and a pair of brown loafers. Like most idealists, she did not bother looking at herself in the mirror before leaving. She tossed her purse over her shoulder and drove to the Orchard Grove Home in Grange.

Stopping at the nursing station to check if any of her people had changed rooms since her last visit, she went to the common room, where three staggered rows of occupied wheelchairs waited. Holding her Bible open before her, she talked for ten minutes about the mansions Jesus prepared for His friends, followed by a group prayer. Then as the nursing staff wheeled her congregation out of the room, she stood in the hallway and shook hands with each one, smiling into their faces even if they were sleeping.

Nancy Droomiker waited for her in room 445, staring from beneath the heavy, pressed sheets with enormous eyes.

"Good morning, Nancy, how are you doing?" she asked, seating herself in the chair beside the bed. Nancy was, as she knew, not doing well. Her whispered speech came with great difficulty, and to spare visitors the discomfort of listening she pretended to have nothing to say. At ninety-six, her body had decided to slowly, methodically shut down.

Winnie opened her Bible and read from Luke, where she had left off the week before. It was a familiar passage, and the older woman's pale lips silently mouthed the words as Winnie read them. Fifteen minutes later, Winnie planted a kiss on Nancy's forehead and said a prayer.

"I'll see you next week," she said, stepping out the door.

In room 423 Elizabeth Shelton contemplated Winnie with total disregard, as though she were a quart of air. "Hello, Betsy," Winnie said, knowing that what the nurses called dementia would prevent Betsy from responding in any normal way. "I wanted to stop in and say hello before I left this morning. I saw your granddaughter Casey the other day. She is certainly a pretty girl. I think she said she was in the fourth grade this year. I understand she enjoys playing soccer, and I'll bet she is an excellent athlete. She sent this card, which I'm going to put right here on the nightstand. One of the aides can read

it to you later. I hope you remember me—Winifred, the pastor of
the Words church. Your son and daughter-in-law, George and Janice,
attend there. You did too, not that long ago. One of the pews still
has your name on it. It's toward the front, which means it's still in
good condition. You know how people will do anything to avoid sitting in front. Well, I see my time is about up, so I'd better be going.
Let's pray before I leave. Dear Heavenly Father, thank you for the
life of Elizabeth. We know we can trust You because You told us
You will never forsake us. Please help Elizabeth to remember who
she is, if that is Your Will, and if not—if You are the Only One to
know who Elizabeth is—may she find peace in some other thoughts.
Give health and courage to Elizabeth and her family and bless our
prayer, for we ask it in the name of Jesus. Amen."

In the hallway, she spoke briefly with Reverend Winchell from
the Grange Congregational Church. As he talked to her in a professional, lecturing tone, he frowned, and Winnie suspected that he did
not approve of women pastors, or at least of women pastors wearing brown corduroy pants.

Walking out of the nursing home, Winnie looked at the sky and
was immediately reminded of her dream from the night before.
The blue seemed intensely and especially blue. On the sidewalk,
she lingered for a moment, going over the errands she had to run in
town. The air had turned cooler and she wished she had worn a coat.

It was from this point forward that Winnie, for years to come,
would review in her memory every thought and action, looking for
some way to explain what later happened. She walked to her car,
drove to the Piggly Wiggly on the corner, and purchased groceries—
no frozen items because she did not know how soon she would be
back at the parsonage. She walked across the street to the hardware
store and bought five twenty-amp fuses to replace the ones that
burned out when the washing machine, furnace, and refrigerator all
came on at the same time. At the bakery she selected three doughnuts and a small, round loaf of bread. She deposited her salary check
at the drive-through window of the bank, withdrew fifty dollars in
cash, filled her car's tank with gasoline, considered purchasing a
lottery ticket as a visual aid for Bible study, but was momentarily

possessed by a demon of frivolity and bought a package of red gum instead.

Her next stop was at the home of Muriel and Don Woolever, an old couple who lived outside Grange. Don had a heart condition that severely limited his ability to get out, and Muriel still suffered from a broken hip.

When Winnie knocked on the farmhouse door, no one answered. She checked the garage and after finding it empty she scribbled a note on a piece of paper and taped it to the front door.

While she was backing her car out of the driveway onto the road, Winnie wondered where she would end up if she drove south on the road instead of north. She had never continued past the Woolever's home. And because of the leaves blowing from trees like torn brown parchment pages and thin ribbons of steel-gray diaphanous clouds stretching out of the horizon in trails of lost grandeur, Winnie drove south, following the winding road between irregular stretches of oak, birch, and pine.

The blacktop changed to gravel and the road narrowed, not well traveled. There were no houses. Neither were there signs of telephone or electric service.

The road narrowed again. She climbed a steep hill, turned left, then right, and descended into a valley marsh.

Cattails, skunk cabbage, wood asters, and thick-bladed grasses rose out of standing water on both sides of the road. There were few trees taller than hedge height, with the unsightly, bowl-shaped nests of herons lodged thickly in them. Three deer stood knee deep in a shallow pool, eating floating vegetation and staring at her car in wide-eyed disbelief, water streaming from their narrow, delicate mouths.

Still she could see no houses, driveways, or mailboxes. She drove over a narrow bridge with wooden planks, rusted iron sides, and a hand-painted sign in orange letters, EIGHT TON LIMIT. The wooden planks thumped loudly against her tires. On the other side Winnie parked next to a stand of sumac and returned with a doughnut to stand on the bridge above the little stream.

Not wanting to get her clothes dirty, she refrained from sitting on

the planks and leaned against the iron railing. The clear, cold water
ran beneath her brown shoes and she ate the pastry with great satisfaction after discovering the filling to be custard. Overhead, a skein
of geese flew in a disorderly V-shaped line, calling in hoarse, plaintive
tones. Once again she was reminded of her dream from the night
before. Checking her desire to eat the remaining portion of her pastry, she tossed it into the water as an offering of thanks and watched
it float downstream and around a switchback. Crisp autumn wind
moved through her thin shirt, touching her skin. A sugary buoyancy
filled her stomach. She contemplated both sensations on her way
back to the car.

As she climbed behind the wheel she was startled to feel her
name spoken. "Winifred." She climbed out and turned back to the
bridge, hoping to find someone behind her. She was alone. But she
was certain of having heard her name spoken in a clear voice with
throaty personality. It had felt to her like the voice of her mother,
yet not hers, a voice she knew yet couldn't place. Most of all, it had
resembled her own voice speaking without the usual interior echo—
from the outside. She walked back to the bridge, stood in the middle
of the planks, and listened.

Once again she heard her name spoken, this time in its more familiar appellation: "Winnie." Accompanying the sound came the sense
of someone beside her, behind her, before her, around her, someone
she couldn't see and couldn't touch, someone whose presence was
intensified through the absence of anything to attribute it to.

The feeling of buoyancy she had earlier experienced in her stomach delightfully changed and spread through the rest of her body. She
felt light enough to float. It seemed as if the breeze moving across
the marsh could carry her with it. She held this feeling for a moment
and then realized something very uncommon was happening. The
grasses in the ditch appeared to be glowing. The red, cone-shaped
sumac tops burned like incandescent lamps in a bluish light unlike
any she had ever seen yet instinctively recognized. And the pleasure
of recognition—discovering the familiar within the unknown—
comforted her with its stillness. She looked at her hands and they
seemed to be lit from the inside, her fingers almost transparent. The

light glowing within the grasses and the sumac glowed within her, within everything. They sang with her through the light, jubilantly, compassionately, timelessly connecting to her past, present, and future. Boundaries did not exist. Where she left off and something else began could not be established. Everything breathed.

She understood her predicament: the world, experience, sensations, memory, time, and dream could not be separated. The realizations taking place were not taking place "inside her," but all around, everywhere. The problem lay not in establishing the objective truth of what she perceived but rather in establishing how the truth had come to be perceived—how otherness had been obliterated. She participated in being looked at as much as looking. She was not simply having a vision of something; she was something in a larger vision. A Great Omnipresent Looking had turned upon her and she looked through it. The whole world participated in awareness.

The miracle of consciousness, the hiding place of God, split open like a fruit too large for its peel. Time lost its linear appeal and assumed the form of the wholly holy. Events, forces, and mind were the same thing, creatively at work. The world and the Kingdom of God became factually identical; each existed one in the other. The sun reflected from the clouds in avenues of colored ideas. The contradiction of conceptual antagonists stood side by side, making sense. The solitary miracle of Pure Grace held everything else inside it, wonder and peace. Death stood before her and she recognized it—a mere shadow cast by life, not a separation; the breathing of life bound it up as shape binds substance.

She walked down the embankment and into the stream, where the cold rushing water swirled around her ankles, calves, knees, and thighs in such a happy, embracing manner that tears filled her eyes. The water was alive. And as her sense of herself as an autonomous individual migrated into everything around her, her sense of isolation and loneliness merged into belonging. She found her true home and her true home found her. There was no "other" place. The grasses were part of trees, part of the smallest organisms in the water, part of the water, part of the worms in the soil, part of the soil, part of the air, part of her. All were constantly changing into and out of each other. And all of these were part of God, that infinitely small and infinitely large spirit that loved her, whatever she was, whenever she was, without reservation, and the realization of this love brought the numinous splendor of divine, mobilized thoughts flooding through the world. It felt like waking from a nightmare of harsh and brutal illusions into welcome beyond measure. A banquet of celebration had risen up inside and around her—more and more life, larger, richer, and more joyful life.

A white pickup came clanking down the narrow road, thumped and rattled across the little bridge, and came to a stop not far from Winnie's little car. A man in a work coat climbed out and stood for several minutes looking between Winnie's opened car door and Winnie in the creek. He climbed down the embankment and walked along the edge of the stream.

"Is everything all right?" he asked.

"Oh yes," said Winnie, the water rushing around her.

"Are you sure?"

"I've never been surer of anything in my life."

"You're crying."

"If I am, it is different than you think."

"I was afraid you might be having some trouble. My name is July Montgomery and I farm in Champion Valley. That cold water will ruin your health."

"If only you knew how little those things matter."

"You're probably right," he said, and sat down on the bank beside a honeysuckle. "Come out of the water—just for now."

But Winnie didn't move. She didn't know what to say. This was the most important time of her whole life, but its importance was unspeakable. Words hadn't yet been invented to talk about it. What now filled her was understood through a long chain of lucidity that would break if she spoke about any single link. Nothing, yet everything, had changed.

The stranger sitting on the bank was no exception—he also glowed from the inside. She could feel both his kindness and his sorrow radiating from his face—feel it as her own. But she couldn't explain.

"We're all together all of us all," she said. "You're in here too."

"In where?"

"In here, in God."

"I don't believe in God. What's your name? Do you live around here?"

"You don't believe?"

"I'm afraid I don't see any sense in that kind of thing."

"What kind of thing?"

"God, churches, praying, and heaven—that kind of thing. My wife went to church for a while, but for myself it never made sense. Did you say you lived around here?"

"Where I live is not important. The only thing that's important is this."

"What?"

"This."

"I don't know what that is."

"Not 'that,' this."

"Is there a phone in your car? I could get it and you could call your husband perhaps, or a friend or relative."

"Why are you concerned with such small things?"

"I'm just a small person, I guess."

And just when she felt her heart breaking from not being able to communicate what she was experiencing, he seemed to understand. He looked at her and he somehow understood. Something in his experience connected with hers and he felt it.

She walked out of the water, took off her brown loafers, and sat next to July on the grass, her corduroy pants soaked nearly to the waistline. Her ankles and feet were bright red splotched with white. He wrapped his coat around her shoulders.

"That isn't necessary," she said.

"Probably not, but it makes me feel better."

"I don't understand how anyone can not believe in God," said Winnie. "What else can satisfy our desire to at once understand and love?"

"Never made any sense to me—a man in the sky writing laws, judging actions, and deciding fate."

"Oh no—not that god. Did you think I was talking about that god?"

"I guess I did."

"Not even the old me could believe in that god. I mean I tried, but I couldn't. That god died a long, long time ago, if it ever existed, which I seriously doubt."

"Which one were you talking about?"

"You know—the only real one. Oh, how impossible this all is."

Tears continued to run down Winnie's cheeks. July handed her a fairly clean handkerchief, but she handed it back without using it.

"Words are meaningless," she said. "The truth dies before it fits into them. Language lacks the capacity to hold anything real. It serves an utterly different master. What's really real is a home words can't get into or out of."

"Not everyone is capable of seeing the things you see," said July. "Some of us have been too deeply hurt."

Another vehicle, a station wagon, came from the north. It slowed to walking speed and came to a complete stop in the middle of the bridge. A window rolled down and a woman's shrill voice called, "Winifred, is that you? Pastor Winifred?"

Winnie stood up.

"That's Muriel and Don Woolever from my church. I'd better go see them. It's my job. Don is probably back from visiting the doctor and I need to check on him. Muriel sounds anxious."

"I could tell them you're busy, if you want more time."

"No, that's all right. It's been nice talking with you."

"Keep my coat."

"You're very kind, but no thank you," she said, handing it back. "I must be going. Where did you say you lived?"

"On a little farm outside Words, on Highway Q."

Winnie put her wet shoes back on and climbed up the bank. After speaking for several moments with the old couple, she climbed into her car, turned around in the road, and followed them north.

July put on his coat and went back to his truck.

THEFT

I N THE GRANGE PARKING LOT IN FRONT OF THE BRICK OFFICE BUILD-
ing of the American Milk Cooperative, Cora climbed into a car
with Alice Hobs, the neighbor who drove on Mondays, Thursdays,
and Fridays. They heard a tire squeal and looked toward it.

Grahm turned off the road, raced across the lot, and pulled in
front of them before they could leave, coming to a pitched stop. A
small scream came from Alice, and both women stared wide-eyed
through the windshield. By the time Cora recognized him, Grahm
was out of the car and halfway to them, three chrome-colored balloons in one fist and a handful of cornflowers in the other.

"It's all right!" she shouted at Alice, who was searching frantically
for the lock to her door. "It's my husband."

"Happy birthday," said Grahm, opening the door and thrusting
the flowers toward his wife.

Cora climbed out, accepted the gifts, and stood looking between
her husband—his hair wet and uncombed, his shirt half out of his
pants—and her children sitting without seat belts in the front seat.
"Happy birthday!" said Grahm again, and Cora burst into tears.

"For Christ's sake, Grahm," she yelled. "What's wrong with you?"

At this signal, Alice slowly backed away from them and drove out
of the lot.

"I thought we could go out for dinner," said Grahm. "It's your
birthday."

"Why does everything have to be *like this*? It's pathetic, Grahm.
Why can't anything ever be nice?"

They drove to the Red Rooster Restaurant and ordered meals
that included a trip through the salad bar.

Seth and Grace were happy to be eating out, and even happier to
be inside a public building where the censure of strangers prevented

their mother from continuing to yell at their father. As she watched them running in and out of their booth, playing with the silverware and salt and pepper shakers, and marking up the paper placemats with the Crayons the restaurant provided, Cora felt herself relaxing.

"Who's milking?" asked Cora.

"Wade," said Grahm.

"We can't afford to hire people to do our work," she said. "And Wade's on probation."

"I've known him since he was a boy."

At home in the driveway, the children bolted from the car and fled into the house. Grahm and Cora remained in the front seat, looking into a rapidly darkening sky.

"I just wanted to—" began Grahm.

"I know," said Cora. "It's not your fault. I'm just so tired. They're trying to make me quit. They hired a girl just out of high school and they're giving her a lot of my work. Today, Phil pretended to be unable to find the new application forms, which left me with nothing to do for over two hours while that new girl made out the reports. They're trying to make me quit."

"It's not worth it. You should resign."

"We need the money and the health insurance."

The screen door banged shut on the front of the house. Seth and Grace stood on the porch, looking at the car. Their expressions caused Cora to go to them immediately. Grahm went to the barn to pay the neighbor and send him home. Minutes later, Cora found Grahm in the milk house.

"Someone was in our house," she said in a breathless whisper. "The papers are gone—all of them. They found the box in the up-stairs closet. I don't think anything else was taken."

They ran inside and silently set about putting everything back in order. Hoping to keep Grace and Seth from knowing that their home had been violated, they pretended nothing out of the ordi-nary had happened—as though natural forces were somehow ca-pable of spewing out the contents of cabinets, drawers, and closets. As they worked they knew that the thoughts Seth and Grace might entertain to explain the disorder—such as their father going through the house in a fit of rage—might be even more detrimental than the pretending, but they couldn't help it. The truth hung heavily in their chests and they couldn't imagine speaking it to their children. Their privacy had been spoiled, their sacred place defiled.

After they finished putting the house in order, Cora remained upstairs with Grace and Seth while they did their homework. Grahm called Wade to see if he had seen anyone.

"Hell no, Mr. Shotwell, I didn't see anyone all the time I was over there. And you've got to believe me—I had nothing to do with whatever happened."

"I know that," said Grahm. "I never thought you did."

Grahm called the police and at about ten-thirty met two men from the sheriff's department in front of the milk house and together they walked across the driveway, under the tamaracks, and onto the porch. Cora joined them. The officers inquired after the robbery. One of them wrote with a ballpoint pen into a fat, leather-bound pad of paper. Strapped to their waists hung a number of other lumpy, leather-covered objects, and their brightly enameled badges reflected the porch's orange bug light. Despite their laconic professional manner, Cora could tell they did not regard the theft of papers as a very serious crime.

"Were the doors locked?"

"We don't have keys anymore," said Grahm. "After they were lost we never bothered getting new ones."

"You should always lock your home," said the officer with the pen. "Doesn't your insurance require locked doors?"

"We're between policies," said Cora.

The policemen said they would return the following day and interview neighbors. Information sometimes turned up in this way, leading to a "solution." But they did not sound optimistic. When the car left, Grahm and Cora assumed they would not see it again.

Grahm returned to the barn, threw down hay for the cattle, and freed a stuck drinking cup where the lever releasing the water into the small basin had become corroded. When he returned to the house, all the lights were turned off. At first he thought Cora had gone to bed, but after kicking off his boots and stepping inside the living room he saw her darkened figure on the edge of the sofa.

"I'm frightened," she said.

"I have a rifle somewhere in the attic," said Grahm.

"What are we going to do?"

The following morning, unable to sleep, Grahm got out of bed even earlier than usual, filled the manger with hay and ground feed, and went out to bring in the cows, his boots crunching on the frozen grass. A clear sky lit his way, and he found the animals huddled together in the northeast corner of the field. The dog ran around them in circles, nipping at their back legs, nudging them out of cud-chewing sleep, herding them toward the barn. Eager for grain, they did not resist.

Grahm breathed deeply, his breath white in the cool air. He listened to the wind moving through the trees, then the sound of a door closing. Over the sharp rise, an engine started, followed by the sound of tires on gravel, moving north. He watched as a gray van climbed over the hill.

Two hours later the milk truck arrived, and standing next to Grahm the driver drew a sample of milk from the bulk tank. He inserted litmus paper into the bottle, and it immediately turned color, indicating the presence of an antibiotic.

"Sorry, Grahm," he said. "We have to discontinue anyone contaminated twice in the same year, and this has been twice in less than three months for you."

He took another sample. Once again, the test showed traces of antibiotics.

"Sorry, Grahm," the hauler said. "I'll take one in for the lab to analyze, but I'm afraid I can't accept your milk. And unless the lab test shows something different—and it won't—you'll have to find another plant."

"Someone's putting antibiotics in my tank," said Grahm.

"That may be, but I can't take your milk."

After the truck pulled out of the yard, Grahm stood looking down into twenty-five hundred pounds of ruined milk—milk that couldn't even be fed to his calves for fear of killing the bacteria lining their stomachs.

He went to the house and met Cora, who was hurrying to her car. "See that Seth eats something before the bus comes," she said. "And give them money to pay up their lunch account. And don't let Seth leave his coat behind."

"Have a good day," said Grahm.

Later that morning, Cora was fired.

VISITOR

L ATE AT NIGHT, RUSTY CAME UPSTAIRS, UNDRESSED, AND HUNG his clothes over the back of a chair. He crawled into bed beside Maxine as unobtrusively as possible, slowly relaxing the muscles in his legs in a manner that sometimes seemed to reduce the pain in his knees.

The darkness of the room surrounded him like an ocean. Maxine's breathing came steady and strong, comfortable and wide, a smooth, rolling, migrating sleep.

Rusty lay blankly awake, aspirating in choppy, nervous breaths, hovering outside the borders of contemplation, an onlooker to his own thoughts.

Memories of the day danced in and out of plans for tomorrow and scenes of knee replacement surgery. But the wandering thoughts continued to return to the young Amish boy standing in the shadows behind the woman with big feet, regarding him with suspicion. As the memory repeated again and again, it filled Rusty with revulsion and contempt, lacking all proportion to the place the boy had played in the events of the day.

He tried to avoid returning to the memory of the boy, but could not. To give himself peace, he attempted to exercise some compassion, forgiving him for not having shoes, for his shabby, ill-fitted clothes, a cloistered life that rendered the outside world fearful, and the coarseness of the big woman with the broom. But he could not. The image of the boy returned to him, and as it did, he felt increasing hatred for him. His legs began to hurt and he sat up in bed, waking Maxine.

"What's the matter, Russell?"

"My knees," he said.

"You need that operation."

"Maybe and maybe not. Right now I need a pill."

In the medicine cabinet Rusty could find no aspirin. Instead, he found a prescription given to Maxine six months ago after dental surgery, and he took three tablets. But he resisted returning to bed, afraid the same thoughts would find him again.

Downstairs, he carried a cup of hot tap water with a squeeze of lemon into the living room, sat on the sofa, and sipped the sour liquid in the darkness. The lemon had a soothing smell. He thought he saw something moving, an animal perhaps, in the moonlit farmyard. He went to the window but could not make out the shape. It was cold near the glass as he stared through it, trying to see something that lacked definite borders. To keep the pane from fogging, he held his breath. Something seemed to move from one minute to the next, near the barn. He watched until his legs hurt enough to force him back to the sofa, and he remained there until he could feel the painkiller working.

Then he saw it again, and returned to the window. This time he was confident that he was seeing something. It moved from one place to another, like an animal, rushing quickly ahead five or six yards, then freezing for several moments before continuing to another shaded area. It advanced from beyond the barn, under the gas tank, beside the lilac bush, and onto the front lawn. As it came closer, its shape grew more defined, and by the time it crossed beneath the clothesline to crouch in the row of mums at the edge of the garden, he could see clearly that it moved on two legs, like a child.

Rusty backed away from the window and assured himself that he couldn't be seen. He had turned on no lights downstairs.

The shape continued coming forward until it stood just beyond the window—a boy, dressed in patched overalls, with naked shoulders, barefoot. Rusty froze as the child pressed his face to the window, his eyes searching and the palms of his hands against the glass.

Then Rusty saw his hat—a hand-sewn leather hat, without a bill, with fur lining and oversized earflaps. The sight of it calmed his breathing. It was the kind of hat that no one had worn for sixty years. It was the kind of hat that could not be worn. It was the same hat Rusty had worn for three winters until his mother had given it to his younger brother, Carl, and Carl had worn it until one of the dogs chewed it beyond mending. At the recognition, the searching expression on the boy's face changed into a smile, showing several front teeth—teeth that were perfectly white, untarnished by his later smoking.

Rusty moved forward and the boy backed away from the window. When Rusty took a step closer, the boy retreated again. Rusty went to the back door, opened it, and stepped into the yard. The cold grass bit into his feet. The boy backed further away and they looked at each other. The boy took the hat off his head and stuffed it into his overall pocket. Then he turned and ran silently, effortlessly between the mums, beneath the clothesline, across the barnyard, disappearing into the darkness beyond the barn. Rusty raised his hand as if to call him back, then returned inside.

In the kitchen, he heated a saucepan of water and poured it over two heaping spoonfuls of instant coffee. He added cream from the refrigerator and sugar from the cabinet and seated himself at the table. The hot mug warmed his hands and he drank deeply, staring into the steaming liquid. His memory, stretched like an elastic band almost beyond its limit to include the many paths his life had taken, snapped back to its normal position, where it had first been imprinted. He remembered the little unpainted house where he had grown up, above the quarry, north of the logging road along the river, five miles from the town of Domel. He could smell wood smoke curling from the chimney and hear the jeering of crows as they fought over a place to sleep in the pines. The stars poked through the darkening sky above Tinker Hill. He remembered—for the first time in decades—the dirt path worn around the side of the house, the goat pen and the root cellar door that usually stood ajar, a face-wide slot of absolute blackness opening into the heart of the unknown. He could smell the outhouse near the mulberries and hear his father's dogs running through the timber along the ridge.

Consuming these memories like a starving man at a banquet, Rusty fought to reclaim his past, in handfuls. He could remember the sound of the neighbor's wagon clattering on the logging road, the clopping of mule hooves, the sight of a yellow moon through the cottonwoods along the river, and the demonic noise of cats in the dump. He stood outside their little home, pumping water from the shallow well, looking at the sky, wondering how fireflies could make fire. Like primeval cathedral bells his mother's voice called and he ran to the front door, pulled the metal latch, and entered. Warmth from the iron cooking stove touched his face. Comforting fumes from the kerosene lamps filled his senses and the room flickered and swam in golden light. He ran across the dirt floor, packed as hard as concrete, and climbed up on the rough wooden bench beside Carl. Across from them, their older sisters, Nora and Elsie, sat in girlish anticipation of eating from bowls of hot biscuits and gravy, winter squash, squirrel fried in cornmeal, and great foamy glasses of warm, sweet milk. His sisters looked at each other and giggled, enjoying some secret feminine game from which he and Carl were thankfully excluded. Under the table, Carl's pet raccoon looked up at Rusty, its masked face providing fatal mockery to any explanation of life that did not allow for a wild designer of deep, unbearable ideas.

Rusty drank all the liquid from his mug, then put on more water to boil. He stood beside the stove, waiting for the little bubbles of air to rise from the bottom of the pan. Memories continued to march through his consciousness, connecting him to parts of himself long buried but still alive. As wraiths of steam silently rose from the surface of the water, he could feel the milky veil that had for so long prevented him from seeing himself clearly dissolve. He poured hot water into his cup and prepared for a long and difficult task—the assembling of bones. He began to feel whole, and it hurt.

STRAIGHT FLUSH

THE HORNED OWL STOOD OUTSIDE THE TOWN OF LUSTER ON the edge of a cornfield, a sprawling steel-sided building with concrete floors and low ceilings. The band Gail Shotwell played with, Straight Flush, drew some of its largest crowds here.

Inside, the main room contained the bar, pinball machines, video poker, dartboards, booths along two walls, and a dozen tables that could be pushed together to allow for dancing. The adjoining room housed a walk-in freezer, grill, and an overhead backlit menu in lettering so small and covered with grease and smoke stains that it could not be read. Those who tried to decipher the words—by cleaning their glasses, standing up and squinting—merely succeeded in signaling to everyone else that they had never eaten there before. The owners, John and Betty Hornshee, hired a band to play on the second Friday night of every month, and people came from a wide area to listen and dance.

On this night, Straight Flush's van and trailer were parked near the side entrance as its four members unloaded equipment through the double doors. Gail carried her bass and amplifier inside, then returned to help with the rack-mounted amplifier, CD player, equalizer, mixing board, effects, microphones and stands, monitors, fogger, lights, and scaffolding. They assembled the equipment on a six-inch-high plywood stage opposite the bar, made from pallets.

Behind the counter, John Hornshee passed two mugs of beer to a middle-aged couple wearing denim jackets, straw-yellow cowboy hats, and boots. Two men in their mid-twenties in T-shirts and blue jeans drank bottled beer at a booth in the corner, absorbed in conversation. A tall, mustached man, late thirties, walked through the front door and called loudly to the owner, with whom he was obviously well acquainted. He was dressed in black denim jeans secured around his waist by a softball-sized Harley-Davidson buckle, and a sweatshirt with large black lettering: SHIT HAPPENS. He exchanged friendly insults with the owner all the way across the room, settled on one of the bar stools, and poured a can of cola into an ice-filled eight-ounce straight-sided glass. Four salesmen ambled into the grill area and ordered meals from Betty Hornshee. A short, muscular bartender in an ironed white shirt and tan pants hung up a leather jacket behind the bar and with obvious satisfaction began arranging a double row of hourglass-shaped glasses on the counter before the mirror. John Hornshee broke open a stack of quarters and dumped them into the cash register with a loud rattle.

Gail helped the keyboard player lift the speakers onto mounting poles on either side of the stage. Jim was in a hurry, hoping to eat before they started. They would play successive forty-five-minute sets followed by half-hour breaks until closing time at 2:00 a.m.

The owner carried two more bottles of beer to the men in T-shirts and on his way back to the bar explained to Gail and Jim that each band member could have three free drinks during the evening. Jim thanked him and hurried off to order a medium-well steak. Gail tuned her bass. Buzz, the drummer, and Brad, the guitar player, plugged cables into the back of the mixing board and selected CDs to load into the player for breaks.

By 7:30 the equipment was ready. Because the television above the bar had burned out in a recent lightning storm, Buzz and Brad carried their first drinks out to the van to listen to the Packers game on the radio. Jim waited in the next room for his steak. They didn't start playing until 8:00.

Gail sat at the bar and sipped from a tall glass of beer. Someone dialed up a Barbara Jean song on the juke and Gail tried to imagine playing in her band, standing on a stage with the charismatic black-haired singer in some faraway city filled with smart, fun young people who appreciated art and were devoted to good music. In the middle of this imagined scene, Shit Happens came over and hit on her, and a little while later the bartender did as well, so she carried her beer to a booth along the wall where she was harder to see.

More people kept coming in, and she watched them. Some she

knew, but most she didn't recognize. Because strange men often approached her, wanting her—not for herself but because of some advertisement for sexual activity that she broadcast by virtue of simply being female—she also tended to see strangers not as individuals but as representatives of types. It was as though people did not walk around in the world as themselves, but as examples of kinds of people, the majority of whom they had never met.

Over there stood a farmer, for instance, and farmers, like her brother, were, or at least had been before their recent economic demise, the rural elite, the established order—landowning gentry whose values and lifestyles more or less set community standards. Very few farmers would come into the tavern tonight, and those few who did would be young, single males. They would stand along the wall, goggling at her and watching the women dance. They would drink hurriedly and leave. Their farms, present or future wives, families, and mainly their sense of themselves demanded more from them than could be shared for very long with a local tavern.

The tall, neatly trimmed guy in the corner looked like one of those educated suburbanites who during the last twenty years had moved into the area for the clean air, lack of crime, and cheap land. Private people, this type also did not, as a rule, frequent taverns: the music was too loud, the food too fatty, the smoke-filled rooms too carcinogenic, and the supply of bottled water too limited. For entertainment they returned to the city for concerts in civic centers, stadium sports, foreign films, and pasta served by male waiters in nonsmoking restaurants.

The nervous little fellow in a suit staring at her from the end of the bar had a reputation of some kind to protect. He wouldn't stay long either, or drink much. His kind were frightened of the increasingly severe laws against drinking and driving—fines, loss of driver's license, public humiliation through mandatory education classes, community service, and jail. These tougher laws had been devastatingly successful in convincing the timid to find private places to drink and were more than anything else responsible for the shrinking number of existing bars and the even smaller number of working bands. Those with reputations worthy of degrading didn't do their serious drinking in local taverns.

But for the most part, the people coming in were of a type so familiar to her that she didn't know what to call them—men and women carrying pitchers of beer from the bar, calling out to each other as though they were in an open gymnasium, some dressed in durable finery and others completely unwashed. They lived in trailers, rented or heavily mortgaged houses, and rooms above storefronts. They worked on construction crews, as field hands, janitors, clerks, part-time plumbers, unlicensed electricians, short-run truck drivers, house cleaners, waitresses, secretaries, cooks, and gardeners. They found employment in factories, motels, lumberyards, garages, stockyards, packinghouses, breweries, grain elevators, and coal plants. They plowed snow, collected garbage, shoveled gravel, poured concrete, guided tourists, sold vegetables out of pickups, trained horses, made crafts, painted barns and houses, repaired automobiles, welded pipe, and fixed small engines.

They were connected to nature and routinely picked wild berries, hunted mushrooms and ginseng, gathered hickory nuts, dried herbs, canned meat, dug up endangered wildflowers, shot ducks, geese, grouse, rabbits, squirrels, turkeys, deer, coyotes, and bears. In some societies they might be called peasants, *fellaheen*, the rural poor, survivalists, bohemians, the underclass, proletariats, Bubbas, self-taught intellectuals, back-to-the-land socialists, right-wing gun nuts, rubes, and dumb-ordinary people—terms of derision that so accurately conveyed the horror their lifestyle instilled in the middle and upper classes.

Their mere presence seemed to imply an overt rejection of Puritan conformity, corporate culture, and status in general. Their unpremeditated way of life constituted a form of social disease that, if it spread, could emasculate the economy, undermine social ranking, and unravel tradition. They did not properly respect or take care of material things, demanded that liberty extend further than the freedom to own property, and at all times reserved the right to abandon whatever they were doing and do something else. They mistrusted all levels of government and rarely voted. They were the same people Plato feared would scuttle his Republic, Aristotle denounced as enemies of the Chief Good, and Augustine longed to shut out of his City of God. They were sensualists, easily distractible, mining every experience for the passion it would yield and moving on.

They streamed into the tavern in anticipation of joining something unpredictable, tribal. They bought their first drinks, clustered in small groups, and waited for the room to fill with smoke, throbbing music, and jostling spontaneity, carrying them to a mental state they could not reach alone. Some, the watchers, found their places along the walls, from where they would not budge the entire night. Others, the talkers, sat closer to the bar. The dancers, not caring where they sat, found themselves sitting at the big round tables near the open floor.

Gail went out to the van and strapped a pair of red leather chaps over her white jeans, stuffed her feet into snakeskin boots that came up to her knees, and tugged at the shoulders of her red silk shirt. She tied the braided strings of the Stetson beneath her chin and told Brad and Buzz it was time to play.

TESTIMONY

After her epiphany at the creek, an urgent need haunted Winifred Smith. A largeness had entered her life that did not wish to be contained. Not only had she come face-to-face with the universal source of all goodness, she had sat beside someone on a creek bank—right beside him, almost touching—and participated in a genuine conversation about heartfelt concerns that really mattered. Neither of these things had ever happened to her before, and it seemed as though she had entered a new civilization whose rules were being established along a different order. When she closed her eyes she could still remember both the Light Within and the weight and smell of the warm old coat that the man on the bank had put over her shoulders.

Returning to the parsonage that evening, she put her groceries away, straightened up the kitchen, and tried to read a book but could not be contained within the pages. As soon as she read one sentence, the memory of it leaped out of her head, leaving her with no historical context to begin the next. A huge, nearly humming quiet surrounded the bed she was sitting on.

She had to talk to someone. She put on her jacket, walked briskly through Words, and knocked on the Brasso sisters' front door. Violet's car was not in the driveway and Winnie listened as a progression of collisions announced Olivia's advance inside. Finally, the knob turned and the door opened a crack.

"Come in," said Olivia, in her wheelchair.

"Thank you," said Winnie. "I hoped I'd find you here."

"Sit down," said Olivia, backing out of the way and colliding with an old credenza. "Take your coat off. Violet's gone into town."

Winnie seated herself on a wooden chair with sculptured arms and a crocheted cushion cover. Olivia parked across from her and asked if she wanted something to drink.

"No thank you," said Winnie. "Do you know someone named July Montgomery?"

"I don't really know him but I understand he lives out of town on a small farm," said Olivia. She folded her hands and regarded Winnie with some caution; the preacher's deep breathing and excited, glowing cheeks seemed to portend something not yet evident.

"He is such a nice man," Winnie informed her, as though she and July were old friends.

"Many think so," said Olivia, "though no one knows very much about him. He lives alone."

"He mentioned being married."

"I think he was at one time."

Both sat for a short time in silence, listening to the distant, crackling sounds of the police scanner in another part of the house.

Then Winnie told Olivia everything, beginning with when she left the nursing home and how the blue sky had arrested her. The tiny woman listened with her hands clamped together to keep them still, her nearly useless legs hanging like matched clock weights out of her organdy dress.

Winnie grew more and more animated as she talked. Her fingers, hands, and arms never stopped gesturing. She shifted positions, leaned forward and back, tossed her long hair, and altered the expressions on her face. She changed the level of her voice, sat on the edge of her chair, and from time to time sprang to her full height to emphasize how Pure Spirit—which was not a metaphor—had caused her to become part of everything, everywhere. She took off her shoes and socks to show how her feet, ankles, and calves had been red and blotched white from the cold water, declaring, "I didn't feel anything but the love of all creation." She held her hands in front of her face to demonstrate how obvious the unadulterated truth could be.

"If only I could explain it to you!" she cried. "My name was spoken, clearly, out loud. If only I could show you what it all means. If only you could believe me when I say it's true! There is no way out of this world, but there's a way in. She or He or whatever we must call this perpetually sustaining force is inside everything—only that's not right either because this is everything. Our separation is one not of distance but of closeness. Nothing could be so near. Our isolation comes from constantly wanting to be with, when in fact we are in. So many of the old ways of thinking are simply wrong, wrong, wrong."

Olivia listened. There were many reasons to be suspicious. Everyone—especially the faithful—needed to maintain a robust skepticism. In this age of profiteering, all a person had to do was watch a half-hour of television to understand how life's most treasured moments could be ransomed to sell underwear.

Olivia had heard many accounts of divine intervention and answered prayer—declarations by people whose health or circumstances had suddenly improved, their habits reformed and characters changed. She had heard that God interceded in business deals, final exams, wars, baseball games, and wallpapering projects. And she had listened to hundreds of sermons on "obeying God." But this was the first time someone actually claimed to have heard the Divine Voice.

God spoke to people in the Bible, Olivia knew, and for that reason the Christian vocabulary was replete with words like "listening to," "hearing," and "speaking." But it was generally assumed, though seldom commented upon, that following the destruction of King Herod's temple in the year 70 the Divine Voice had generally discontinued talking out loud. People now "heard" God through a particular flavor of their own thought and "listened" by reading Scripture passages over and over. Sensory hearing had mostly been left to those as likely to see Elvis as to hear Christ.

As for visions, in a similar manner this phenomenon had been relegated to less-advanced countries with fewer institutions into which visionaries could be suspected of finding a happy home among others needing professional care.

Christians, of course, talked all the time about having "personal relationships" with Christ, but these relationships, Olivia understood, involved feelings, moods, motivations, intuitions, and inspirations. They were relational qualities, not experienced in an objective sense, and the word *spiritual* had pretty much been invented to refer to them. In fact, as more than one modern thinker had noted, the nature of the divine was uniquely subjective. Spirit had no objective manifestation, and as much as people wished to come face-to-face with Everlasting Beneficence, they had to be content with less.

Yet the longing for something else, something better and more satisfying, had not diminished, only the areas in which people felt they could legitimately look. Even the most ardent believers were now compelled to confine their religious urges to narrowly circumscribed venues—church and prayer. They did not cease to desire ecstatic experiences, but often felt resigned to postponing them until the afterlife, when natural laws would be less strictly enforced. They thought it prudent to delay supernal gratification until a time when they would not be interrupted by a scientific culture that didn't approve.

Needless to say, Olivia knew more than a little about epiphanic experience. Her study of Christianity included many books written by mystics and the even more numerous books written about them. She knew the difference between transcendent and immanent revelations. In the former, individuals encountered a preternatural personality, in the latter the symbiosis of life. Winifred Smith had apparently experienced both.

Olivia also knew that such revelations were the Holy Grail, the Pearl of Great Price, the highest value in the economy of faith. True communion was not only an important room in the universal church; it provided the foundation. Epiphany was the holy ingredient around which the church fitted all its theological clothes—the genie in the bottle.

"Did you smell something like sweet almond?" she asked, knowing a sense of smell should never figure into an authentic, numinous experience.

"I cared nothing for sensations," said Winnie.

"How did you know this was not an illusion?"

"Compared to it I was an illusion myself."

"How did you know it was God and not some lesser principality?"

"I do not know how, but I could not keep from knowing."

Winnie exhibited all the genuine signs: lack of hubris, sense of

awe, frustration over the limitations of language, and the contradiction between her exaggerated mannerisms and the purported
peacefulness she attempted to describe. There was also a profound
melancholy—a cloud of despondency over having to return to the
normal world, the gloom of exile. At one point she wept into her
hands, exclaiming, "I can still feel the feeling leaving."

There was no doubt. Winifred Smith had stumbled upon the
Presence of God. She had been chosen.

"You must be very careful in what you say," said Olivia, interrupting Winnie as she told about July Montgomery, the farmer who had
sat beside her on the creek bank and touched her soul. "You must
guard your words like a dragon guarding her cave. There is no telling
the damage you can do with a loose tongue."

"What do you mean?"

"You must prove worthy of the trust placed in you."

"I can try," said Winnie.

"You must always explain your experience in terms familiar to the
church and the traditions of the church. You can't be talking about
God and Christ outside those limits."

"But those are old and this is new!" complained Winnie.

"Foolishness," said Olivia. "New is only old rearranged. Now heat
some hot water and we will discuss this further. Violet keeps the tea
in the high cupboard; the cups are to the left and the pot is under
the sink. We must decide when to tell the others. A small setting is
best, perhaps at midweek Bible study. I'll make sure Violet can have
me ready so you won't be alone. You must not make the poor word
choices you've made here tonight. Others won't be as forgiving.
They'll think you're a prideful heretic. And before you do anything
else, put your socks and shoes back on. I'm uncomfortable with
nudity and informality of all kinds."

As it turned out, however, the little group gathered at the Words
Friends of Jesus Church for prayer and Bible study on Wednesday
night was not critical at all. The usual eight attendees sat in the
middle pews twenty minutes early, catching up on local news.

Violet pushed Olivia inside and parked her in the center aisle.
Because Olivia's health seldom allowed her to attend services other

than on Sunday morning, and then only sporadically, her presence caused a heightened sense of expectation. And due to Olivia's inclination to speak at great length on any subject, the group expressed their worried anticipation by constantly shifting postures and recrossing legs.

Winnie, her face glowing, walked to the front. "I have something to tell you," she said, standing in a long green skirt, a white blouse buttoned tightly around her neck. With her eyes darting from one old face to the next, she began to describe her experience.

Soon, April Wilson asked where, exactly, this had taken place—a stream, creek, or river?

Lyle Fry asked what stream it was.

Winnie said it was down the road from Don Woolever's house.

"Which way?" asked Lyle.

"South," said Winnie.

"Oh, I know where you mean," said Lyle.

"That's Mule Creek," said Ardith Stanley. "At least that's what we called it. People fish there."

"My husband, Floyd, used to fish there," said Norma Hinkley. "It used to be a good trout stream. A lot of suckers, though."

"You can eat suckers," said April. "I can remember Mother cooking them. The whole house would smell, but we didn't mind. We were so hungry we could eat anything."

"It wasn't like it is now," said Ester Thrit. "Just having some kind of dessert was a treat. At Christmas the folks used to go into town and come back with nothing but a box of oranges. Those oranges tasted so good. Not like the oranges they have today."

"They're the same oranges," said Pauline Evans. "They have to be. It's genetic."

"All the same, they're not the same. They put dye in them now to make them orange. But they're not as sweet."

"I tried to grow oranges once," said Lyle. "The tree grew, but fruit wouldn't set on."

"If all of you don't be quiet, Pastor Winnie won't be able to have our Bible lesson," said Margaret Holdsung.

They stopped talking and patiently waited for Winnie to begin the Bible lesson for the night—a continuation of last week's discussion of Second Timothy.

Winnie and Olivia looked at each other. Olivia smiled an assurance that she knew the importance of what had happened, and Winnie began the Bible lesson.

A PRIVATE HEAVEN

B Y 1:00 A.M. SIXTY PICKUPS, CARS, AND VANS WERE CROWDED HAP-
hazardly into the Horned Owl's parking lot and along the road
in front of the cornfield. As some departed, more arrived. Despite
the cool autumn air, six men and three women in shirtsleeves
drank beer around the raised hood of a bright green custom car,
the engine bucking, roaring, and sucking air. The tattooed youth
behind the wheel smiled knowingly, his shirt rolled up to his shoulders. Three men urinated into the rows of corn as two middle-aged
women took turns riding around the building on a Harley-Davidson
motorcycle. A couple argued loudly next to the front door, where
light, noise, smoke, and heat rolled into the night.

Inside, the band was midway through the final set. The main
amplifier had been turned up to compete with the tumultuous din
of shrieking, laughing, and howling. Twenty dancing couples were
interspersed with travelers passing between the bar and tables, carrying drinks. A layer of smoke, colored blue, green, and red by the
band's blaring lights, hovered beneath the low ceiling.

The evening poised somewhere between as-good-as-it-will-get
and closing time, and everyone tried to maximize his or her advantage
before all advantages expired. For some this meant pushing the spirit
of a discussion beyond the usual boundaries, and a fistfight broke
out between two clean-shaven men in knit shirts, broken up by bigger
relatives in work jackets. Three bartenders hurried to supply beer,
cigarettes, and change to a steady flow of outstretched hands. A man
in a baseball hat fell over backwards, where he remained, laughing,
on his back as others stepped over and around him. The mating
component of dancing became more obvious. Single men openly
approached the remaining available women, who were noticeably
less guarded, less coy than earlier in the evening. In the middle of the

room a short brunette in a halter top and shorts climbed onto a table and danced to rhythmic applause without moving her feet. A pitcher of beer spilled. Glasses broke. Three young men huddled together at the bar and appeared to be working up courage to approach Gail at the end of the set. Marijuana and other illegal substances passed freely among friends, and friendships were easily joined.

Earlier in the week, Gail had practiced several new bass riffs, more complicated than anything she'd tried before, with string-slapping and a flurry of fast, double-string crescendos. During the next applause break she asked the drummer if she could have a solo on the last song.

Buzz looked up from his stool, took both drumsticks into one hand, and drank the last of his whiskey sour. "Hell, I don't care." He hollered at the keyboard player, "Give Gail a verse just before the chorus—at the end. We'll all back her."

The first part went well, all the way through two phrases. The dancers at once recognized the new style. Several started clapping and whistling. Then the guitar player hit a wrong chord and the dissonant notes invaded the rhythm. Gail overran a fret and the keyboard player backed out of his chord progression too early. Soon, none of the musicians knew where the others were, and the whole enterprise was quickly falling apart. The living melody was dying and everyone in the room knew it.

At this juncture, a party of large people sat down, opening a line of sight beyond the dance floor, and seated in a booth along the wall was July Montgomery. Across from him sat a woman with short, jet-black hair, her eyes flashing like blue diamonds. Sipping from a bottle of water, she stared at Gail as though from out of a vision, and Gail recognized the regal, olive-colored face from her CD: Barbara Jean.

Gail's mind exploded. She made a heroic effort to second-guess her first impression and convince herself that the person in the booth was not Barbara Jean. What would she be doing sitting in this shabby place with that old farmer? It couldn't be true.

But no one else could look *that* perfectly serene yet frighteningly beautiful. No one else could take up the whole room in that way. Gail's memory of her voice and the airy heights of ecstasy attained

through listening to it enhanced Barbara Jean's physical appearance
to the point where she looked mythic—a modern day Helen of Troy
for whom ten thousand expendable rubes like Gail would gladly sac-
rifice their lives just for the privilege of sitting next to her.

Gail watched in horror as Barbara Jean's splendid mouth curved
into a cruel smile, and she turned away from the stage in a movement that succinctly communicated both frivolous amusement and
dismissal.

There could be no doubt: the world had conspired to humiliate
Gail in front of the only person in it who mattered. All the forces of
evil had been mustered to reveal her in an apoplexy of aesthetic collapse. Her mediocre band was crashing and she with it. She had been
mercilessly undone, mocked and ridiculed, cast into an open pit.

In her moment of free-falling humiliation, Gail looked down
at her fingers as they plucked ineptly at the thick strings . . . and
thought they had a rather nice appearance. They were slender without being too thin and functional but not utilitarian. This judgment
led to a further thought: she might be defeated, as all people eventually would be, but never conquered. There may be better people in
the world and all of them might have a talent denied to Gail, but
fundamentally it made no difference. No one would ever stand over
her and gloat. The light might go out of the world, but even darkness had rules. She could feel the dancers moving, the noise, heat,
and smells, and she welcomed their combined spirit. This was her
element: she was an entertainer.

Her finger curled around the volume knob on the front of the
bass and turned it up. She tossed her head, stamped her foot, stepped
forward, and cried into the microphone something between a rebel
yell and the scream children make when they're starting down the
steep side of a roller-coaster run, where joy and fear jump into one
expression.

The scream reoriented the other musicians toward the deep sounds
marching out of the bass amp—the familiar notes leading up to the
chorus. The drummer slammed his cymbals together; the keyboard
player pounced with all ten fingers on the black and white keys, and
the guitarist hit a high, quivering seventh chord. All four leaned into

the microphones and finished the chorus, nearly drowned out by the crowd's drunken roar.

At the conclusion of the set Gail did not look up, pulled the bass from around her neck, and set it inside the case. She and Brad took the speakers down while Jim and Buzz went to the bar for drinks. She carried her amp out to the van.

Already, the parking lot was half empty, the night cooler.

"Hello, Gail," said July. "Gail, this is Barbara Jean. Barbara Jean, this is Gail Shotwell."

"Hello, Gail." A hand with a small turquoise-in-silver ring on the second finger extended toward her, its grip firm and brief.

"Hi," said Gail.

"Look, I'm going to visit the corn rows," said July. "I'll be back in a minute."

"Men love to piss outdoors," observed Gail.

"All men aren't the same," said July.

"To women they are."

Gail's eyes met Barbara Jean's and the ceaseless industry of her irises made Gail look away. The magazines said she was forty, but Gail was sure she wasn't that old.

"You play and sing well," said the woman. "I wish I had a recording of that scream."

At first Gail thought she was being made fun of, but the older woman's expression reassured her. Then she couldn't find anything to say. All she could think of were stupid things like "You can hear me scream anytime you want," "What's that odd chord in 'Shades of Sorrow?'" or "Where did you get the ring?" She finally gave up and just said, "Really."

Barbara Jean laughed, as though she understood everything about her. "Let's go inside, Gail. You've been standing for over an hour. Let me buy you a drink."

"I guess we really messed up that last song."

"It happens. Your keyboard player was so drunk it's a miracle he could stand up."

"How do you know July?"

They sat across from each other in a booth near the bar. Gail leaned forward, resting her forearms on the table. She was experiencing some success in looking into those oceanic blue eyes without self-consciousness, and this surprised her. Barbara Jean crossed her legs under the table and pressed the small of her back against the wooden booth, folding her hands on her lap. A small turquoise earring was almost completely hidden beneath her glossy black hair.

"July sold me some hay for my horses. I have a summer place not far from here. He asked if I wanted to hear your band."

"I can't believe I'm sitting here with you."

"Why?"

"Because it's unbelievable. It's like being in my own private heaven. Drat, I've still got this stupid hat on."

Barbara Jean laughed in a sudden burst of melodic delight, showing her teeth. She leaned forward and touched Gail's hand. "What did you say, darlin'?"

"This dumb old hat—I forgot I was still wearing it."

"No, before that—you said 'drat.' My sister and I used that word when we were little. It was the only way to swear without being spanked by our parents, and now I can't get rid of it. I didn't think anyone used it but me. I'm always embarrassed when it comes out of me."

"No."

"Yes."

"Where did you grow up?"

"On a Thistlewaite County sheep farm on the other side of the Heartland Reserve."

"I don't believe it."

July Montgomery returned from outside and sat with them for several minutes before announcing he needed to return home. There was a freshening heifer he should look after. He asked Gail if she could make sure Barbara Jean had a ride home.

Gail's heart stopped beating as she nodded her head. No power on earth could prevent her from getting a car to drive the woman sitting across from her home. Nothing was too great a price to pay for that privilege. The two of them alone in the front seat—

"I better go too, it's late," said Barbara Jean, rising out of the booth and standing next to July.

"Wait, can I get you something else to drink?" asked Gail. "I'm sorry, I forgot to ask before."

"I'm afraid the bar's closed," said July.

"They'll sell to me. I know they will."

"I'd better be going," said Barbara Jean, smiling. "It's been nice meeting you, Gail. Bring your bass over to my house some afternoon when we're practicing."

"You've never had an electric bass in your band."

"True, but when you're finished trying new things, you're finished."

Once again, Gail could think of nothing to say. *You're finished* seemed to mean so many things, and before she could respond Barbara Jean had left with July, and Gail watched the old white pickup leave the parking lot.

She returned to the booth to review everything that had just happened, to linger inside what remained of the event until it had been completely exhausted. With some effort, she could still feel the older woman's touch on the back of her hand and see her white teeth inside her laugh. She wondered how long it had been since she'd experienced such supreme joy. She felt twice as alive, twice as good, twice as important as she had only minutes before. A candle moved about in a room that for too long had been empty and dark.

But the new light also allowed her to look around, and hanging on the walls were memories of earlier times when this same joy had proved neither reliable nor beneficial. Feeling alive, good, and important had only served to make her vulnerable.

She didn't know where Barbara Jean lived and didn't believe she really meant what she said about playing with her. The wild felicity Gail experienced was not mutual, not understood.

Several men came over to her booth and she drove them off with a withering stare.

In the remaining hour before leaving, she added to the band's bar tab. By the time they had loaded all the equipment in the trailer, she could entertain only one clumsy thought at a time, as if she were balancing a nickel on the point of a pin.

On the drive back, she asked Buzz to pull over and she threw up in the ditch.

"Never drink without eating," said Jim, holding her by the shoulders.

"Shut up."

WORK BEGINS

RUSTY SMITH ARRIVED AT THE HOME OF ELI YODER ON MONDAY morning, the tops of the trees glowing from early, reflected sun. Thick billows of smoke rose from the chimney, white against the sky, and Rusty smiled at the thought that they had just built the fire.

"Probably went out overnight," he said to himself. He remembered winter mornings in his childhood after the stove had gone out during the night—how the house filled with smoke before the chimney warmed up, the metal sides popping and groaning as yellow flames licked the cool inside.

A corner of a blue window curtain turned up momentarily. The back door opened and Eli stepped outside with two youths, dressed identically, carrying lunch pails and wooden toolboxes.

Rusty rolled his window down.

"This is Isaac and Abraham," said Eli.

Rusty nodded.

"You boys ride in back," said Eli, and the youths clambered behind the cab. Eli handed them his toolbox and lunch pail. "Did the lumberyard deliver the materials?" he asked.

"Yup," said Rusty.

On the way through Grange, Eli said, "If you don't mind I need to stop here by the garage. I got shoes to pick up."

"They sell shoes at the garage?"

"No, the man who lives behind the garage repairs shoes."

Rusty pulled in the drive and Eli got out of the cab. "You boys stay here," he said, and the youths sat down again on the truck bed.

Rusty watched as Eli knocked on the back door of the stucco house and disappeared inside. He felt awkward sitting in the cab with the boys in back. He also wondered what the man who lived inside the stucco house looked like and how he happened to be a cobbler. Rusty's uncle had once owned a shoe store. Rusty and his brother, Carl, stopped there on the way home from school. He remembered the sounds of belt-driven sewing machines and tack hammers striking brads. It had always seemed dark in the shop, but this only added to the place's appeal.

Without knocking, Rusty followed Eli inside the house and found him in a workroom off the kitchen, holding a lumpy paper sack. Rows of shoes and boots stood on shelves along the wall. Other leather items, including a child's riding saddle and a leather-covered chair, were also in the room. Strips of flypaper dotted with sticky, perished flies hung from the ceiling next to the windows.

"That smell," said Rusty to the bearded man behind the card table. "What's that smell?"

"Mink oil."

"Of course," said Rusty. "I remember that smell. I'll be damned. Mink oil. My uncle owned a shoe store. When did you get to working on shoes?"

Ten minutes later Isaac and Abraham came inside looking for their father.

"Told you boys to stay in the truck," said Eli gruffly.

"Not their fault," said Rusty. "Cold out there. We'd better get going—plenty of work to be done. I'll bring those boots over sometime."

Work on the Smith house continued through the week. Rusty worked too, as much as he could, replacing the lower portions of siding. He also made numerous trips to the lumberyard for more materials.

He was impressed with Isaac and Abraham. It seemed remarkable that boys their age could pace themselves like grown men. Though they talked back and forth—usually in German—they remained focused on the project at hand and were most concerned with gaining the approval of their father, who watched them at all times. They employed Rusty's saws and drills with practiced proficiency.

After three days, Rusty began to relax. He could see the likelihood of the work being completed by the end of the month.

But Maxine did not relax. As her mother and sister's arrival came closer, she became more anxious, and no corner of the house was safe from her worried inspection.

"You'd think the queen and all her court were coming," Rusty told Eli as they replaced a rotten piece of siding.

"Women feel strong about their mothers and sisters," said Eli. "And their mothers and sisters feel strong about them."

At first the Amish ate their noon meal sitting on the bench beneath the oak tree. But Maxine soon had them at the kitchen table, so she could heat their coffee and soup on the stove. It troubled Maxine that the boys drank coffee, and she lectured them on the ills of caffeine in adolescent development at the same time that she filled their mugs.

Eli, Abraham, and Isaac remained guarded around Maxine. The formality that normally characterized their interactions became almost ritualized in her company. The more Maxine attempted to put them at ease, the stiffer they became. It was as if eye contact with her had been forbidden—something that passed unnoticed by Rusty but was quite irritating to Maxine.

She was also troubled by the amount of fat in their diet, judging by the items they pulled from their lunch pails, and took it upon herself to inform them of what modern nutritional science had to say on the subject. This led to one of the very few times when Rusty had words with her.

"Leave them be, Maxine. Leave them be. You can't be telling people what they can eat. Look at 'em, they're thin as posts—all of 'em. They're a sight better off than most of our people. It's part of their way. Leave 'em be. And as for the coffee, I used to drink coffee with my brother when we were those boys' ages and it never hurt us."

"Russell, you're five-foot-five and your nerves are completely shot."

"If you don't leave 'em alone, we'll eat outdoors."

At the end of the week Eli handed Rusty a slip of paper with the hours he and Abraham and Isaac had worked, in pencil. Rusty asked if he should pay the boys separately and Eli said no. Rusty gave him a check.

"I wonder if you could go by the bank on the way home," said Eli. "I need to deposit some of this."

"No problem," said Rusty.

"I should also say that we won't be here on Monday or Tuesday next week."

"Why not?"

"We have other things to attend to."

"Whoa," said Rusty, shaking a cigarette from his pack. "We've got to get this done. I told you that."

"I know. But we have other commitments."

Rusty inhaled deeply. "Well, I suppose a couple days won't matter so long as you know the situation I'm in."

"I know it," said Eli.

But later that night when Rusty told Maxine that the workers would not return until Wednesday, her face turned white.

"What other commitments?"

"I don't know."

"You didn't ask them? Russell, my mother is coming and we—"

"Maxine, I know."

"They haven't even begun the work in the basement. We can't have those humps in the floor, Russell. We can't have it."

"I know that, Maxine."

"Did he promise to complete the work on time, or not?"

"I think so."

"Either we've got a commitment or not. Which is it? Are you sure he knows how important this is to us?"

"Yes."

"You didn't tell him, did you?"

"I did."

"I knew this would happen. I'm going to have to get up on those ladders and paint the house myself."

"No you won't."

"My mother and sister are coming in less than three weeks and we're not anywhere near ready. I have the house to clean and the meals to plan and the Lord knows you're little help."

"I do the best I can," said Rusty.

"Well maybe this time it won't be good enough, Russell. Maybe this time it won't be."

The Amish returned on Wednesday and worked through Saturday. Rusty borrowed several heavy jacks from the lumberyard, and with wooden beams taken from Rusty's barn they lifted the southwest corner of the house and began replacing rotten floor joists. The task proved unexpectedly difficult, and on Sunday there remained gaping holes in the foundation, through which wind, a wild cat, fox, coyote, or wolf might enter the basement during the night.

Early Monday morning when Rusty went to pick up the Yoders, no one came outside. He smoked two cigarettes then knocked on the door. The heavyset woman in bare feet opened it.

"Where's Eli?" asked Rusty.

"Gone."

"The boys here?"

"Gone with him."

"When they coming back?"

"Don't know."

"Look, I'm Rusty Smith, and—"

"I know who you are."

"Eli never said anything about not coming to work. My house is resting on blocks and there's nothing but tarpaper covering most of the roof."

"Ella come down sick. Took her to the doctor in the buggy."

"Who's Ella?"

"Eli's wife."

"Who are you?"

"Eve."

"What's wrong with her?"

"Might send her down for treatments."

"Down where?"

"Iowa."

"Iowa! What treatments?"

"Stomach treatments."

"I wish you people had phones," said Rusty, rubbing his forehead. The woman continued looking at the ground, without expression.

"Look," said Rusty, "which doctor did they take her to? I'll go over there."

LETTER TO THE EDITOR

CORA SHOTWELL CALLED THE WISCONSIN DEPARTMENT OF Agriculture, Trade and Consumer Protection to check on the hearing date for her complaint against American Milk, only to learn that a hearing had not yet been scheduled.

"At the conclusion of the first stage of the department's investigation, depending on the findings of the investigative staff and the seriousness of any allegations which may be pending either during or at the completion of the process, an administrative hearing can be convened at the request of the department or at the request of an interested party only if allegations of wrongdoing are possibly felonious and then the case may be referred for determination to the A.G.'s office depending on the specific protocol of the administrative code."

"Is there going to be a hearing or not?" asked Cora.

"That will be determined following the committee's final investigative report."

"When will my papers be studied?"

"I'm not certain which papers you are referring to but I can assure you that a formal investigation such as we are now completing is altogether rigorous and thorough and because of our licensing and regulatory oversight of all Wisconsin milk plants, both private and cooperative, the issues within our purview relating to procurement, testing, processing, labeling, packaging, sale, and distribution of milk and milk-based products will become fully transparent, the requisites both exhaustive and current, and all appropriate and relevant materials will be compiled, sealed, and duly examined in accordance with department procedures relating to the administrative review."

Cora found Grahm cleaning the barn and told him, "We need a lawyer."

"We've done nothing wrong. We're not hiring a lawyer."

"Then we have to show the papers to someone other than your sister."

The person they chose was the son of a neighbor. They did not know him very well, but he had worked in the Luster Police Department for a number of years. Cora got the phone number from his parents, called him that evening, and arranged a meeting.

In the morning, they copied fifty pages of documents at Kwik Trip and put them in a manila file folder.

Lester Rund waited in the restaurant booth next to the window, wearing his uniform. They sat across from him and Cora dropped the thick file on the table, causing several heads to look up from their lunches. She explained how the papers had come into her possession, told Lester about the burglary of their home, their visit and phone calls to the department, antibiotics in their milk, how she had been fired for no reason, and their fears of being watched. She explained how they had reported the milk tampering to the state department, which sent a man to look around the farm and did nothing more.

"What do you require of me, Mr. and Mrs. Shotwell?" asked Lester, paging through the folder.

"We hoped you'd know what to do," said Cora.

"We at least want you to keep the papers in a safe place somewhere—so you can say we gave them to you," said Grahm.

"I'll show them to the sheriff," he said.

At home, Cora and Grahm began composing a letter to the editor. They had a lot to say, and they disagreed about how to say it. Grahm thought they should first point out that this was the United States of America, where justice and fairness were every citizen's right. Any government agency that did not treat its citizens fairly was evil. It was the government's job to make sure that individual rights were never taken away, and a co-op's job to market milk fairly so the dairy farmer—its rightful owner—could make enough to live an honorable life. But when the farmer—who by definition had less power than a giant co-op—could get no help from his government when his rights were violated, then what protections did anyone have? Once evil had taken hold, no limits applied. The Constitution and the Founding Fathers were dedicated to the principle of justice for all, but if these were just empty words and *no justice* prevailed, then American soldiers had given their lives for nothing. Veterans' widows would have no comfort if the cause of their husbands' dying—which at one time had been the light and hope of the entire human race—had been corrupted.

Cora thought it best to stick to the facts.

"These *are* the facts," said Grahm.

"We just need to write down exactly what happened."

"That's not enough," said Grahm. "First we'll explain who we are and what we believe in. We've always been hardworking and honest, never spent a day on welfare, never been arrested for anything. We love America as much as we love our farm—we're just doing what's *right*. We speak the *truth*. And we're not afraid."

"Those things can't be written down, Grahm."

"They can. I've written most of them right here."

"They're matters of the heart. You can only know those things by knowing someone firsthand."

"Other farmers will know what we're talking about."

"We're not writing to other farmers. We're writing to protect ourselves. Then no one will harm us because it won't do them any good because the truth will already be out."

"I'm not afraid of them."

"Grahm, it doesn't matter if we're afraid or not. We have to just go ahead and do it."

They checked with the newspaper on its letter policy and only then compromised about what to put in the letter.

It was astonishing how little could be communicated in 250 words or less; it was like trying to put on too-small shoes. They were barely able to introduce themselves, describe where they lived, name their children, tell how many cows they milked, how many acres they farmed, and how long the farm had been in the family. Grahm banged his fist on the table out of frustration. When chore time came he abandoned the project to Cora and walked to the barn.

Cora continued writing and rewriting, interrupted only by the arrival of the school bus and Seth and Grace's frantic search to find something to snack on before disappearing upstairs. With great sadness she crossed their names out of the letter in order to eliminate half a dozen words and two commas.

The final draft still contained 370 words, but looking through old issues of the newspaper confirmed that several published letters had exceeded the suggested size. She typed it, put it in an envelope, and attached a stamp.

Placing the letter in the mailbox and closing the hinged metal door gave her an uncomfortable feeling. The action seemed dangerously irrevocable. After the mailman picked it up there would be no way to undo the act. The whole world was about to turn its attention on them: an elephant smelling an ant. They would be thrust into a public arena of movie stars, gangsters, politicians, and war crimes perpetrators. Their telephone would soon be ringing off its hook, the mailbox filled with letters from strangers wanting to become friends or kill them.

She could sympathize with her husband interpreting the threat in a physical way. It seemed so tangible, at least for a person like herself who suffered from stage fright and could remember feigning sick in order to stay home from school to avoid giving a speech. Whatever malady it was that made attention-from-many radically different from attention-from-few, she suffered from it.

But she had committed herself.

Days passed, and after she had searched the paper many times, the letter finally appeared, reproduced exactly as she had written it, even with one misspelled word followed by "(sic)", with their names and address directly below. Above their letter was one about the need for prayer in schools and beneath it an auction notice.

To the editor—

Our Thistlewaite County dairy farm has been in the family for over 150 years. My husband's grandfather was a charter member of American Milk Cooperative way back when it was Winding River Cheese and we have always shipped to them. Four years ago I began working off the farm for AMC as a secretary and assistant

*bookkeeper at the branch office in Grange. I got regular raises and
promotions. In the performance (sic) of my duties I discovered
AMC was cheating farmers, lying to the government, and selling
contaminated milk. I made copies of papers that proved all these
things and called the Wisconsin Department of Agriculture, Trade
and Consumer Protection to inform them. The very next day our
milk tested positive for antibiotics, but we are becoming certified
organic and use no antibiotics. An inspector came out from the
Division of Food Safety and we said someone put antibiotics in our
milk. He said he would "make a report" and we never again heard
from him. We lost our insurance. We were then called into DATCP
and told NOT to bring our papers. Not very long later, someone
broke into our house and stole the papers out of the upstairs
closet. We called the police but they found no evidence. Later, our
milk again tested positive for antibiotics and AMC canceled our
contract. This time we took a sample to an independent laboratory
and they confirmed the antibiotic gentamicin, one we have never in
our whole lives and the lives of my husband's parents used on the
farm. A short time later I was fired from my job at AMC because
I would not pick up the branch manager's laundry on my lunch
break though they said it was for something else. To Whom It May
Concern: we have many more copies of the shipping records, lab
reports, and tax forms and have given them to very important people.
We are now shipping to a different milk plant and it will do no
good to harm us because DATCP has begun an investigation and
everything that is now secret will be made known. Woe unto those
who sin in the sight of God.*

    Cora and Grahm Shotwell
    Hwy Q, Words, Wisconsin

Cora expected the telephone to begin ringing that day. Instead, a
policeman arrived—one of the same policemen who had investigated the burglary. He politely handed her a notice to appear the
following day with her husband before an administrative judge at
the Wisconsin Department of Agriculture, Trade and Consumer
Protection.

The following day they left for Madison, and Cora took with them the Madison newspaper. On the front page began a three-page article featuring the American Milk Cooperative. The CEO, Burt Forehouse, grinned out of a half-page color picture surrounded by packages of butter and cheese, gallon jugs of milk, and bags of milk powder. Next to him stood the governor of Wisconsin. The text explained how AMC had grown from a "horse and buggy cheese factory started by hardscrabble dirt farmers before the days of milking machines, pasteurization, bulk tanks, and refrigerated trucks" into a prominent international business. There was another picture, on page two, even larger, of the twin Holstein statues on either side of the entrance doors at AMC's headquarters. On page three was a picture of "Burt's homeroom," an office with rows of computers, awards on the wall, and dozens of smiling employees.

Directly below the picture, it read, "'A major player in the global marketplace,' said Burt Forehouse. 'Farmers can be proud of what they've built here. Wisconsin dairymen began this business, stepped up to the plate and hit a home run. They were never satisfied with just being good. They demanded to be the best. They saw the challenge of national and international competition and responded to it. We're second to none in value-added milk products, and first in returning to our farm patrons the highest quality of services.'"

When he was asked to comment on the less attractive aspects of his successful career, Burt Forehouse said, "Without a doubt the most difficult part of my job is having to tell a farmer—one of our patrons—we can no longer pick up his milk. It deeply saddens me to let someone go, and we try in every way to work with our less progressive farmers to help them adjust to the high standards demanded by the consuming public. But there are always a few who can't make the transition from the old ways to the new economy. Some just can't take hold of the tools of new technology. In the twenty-first century they still believe they can farm the way their grandfathers did before science learned what we know today about eliminating contaminants at all levels of production."

In a state building in Madison, Cora and Grahm were shown into a room with a nearly bald judge sitting behind an elevated bar, a black robe drawn securely around his neck. There was also a uniformed officer and five other men sitting at tables, but the Shotwells did not know if they were judges wearing suits, or lawyers, or who they were. No one introduced them, and the judge and men seated at the tables continued reading from papers.

After five or ten minutes the judge read Cora and Grahm's names and asked them to step forward. The uniformed officer held open the little wooden gate separating the seating area from the other half of the room and they passed through. Cora let her arms fall flat against her sides and Grahm put his hands in his pockets. The judge explained that a departmental investigation was under way, and that he was asking everyone to refrain from making statements about matters relating to the proceedings.

"What does that mean?" asked Cora.

"It means not to talk about this case or anything related to it."

"Not talk about it to whom?" asked Cora.

"To anyone."

"Anyone?"

"That's right."

"Not even each other?"

The judge took a breath of impatience, rubbed his neck, smiled, and said, "Yes, even each other. This will seal the proceedings while they go forward and protect everyone involved. My ruling on this is final and any breach of it will be referred to the magistrate for immediate prosecution in the district court."

"I don't understand this," said Cora. "How can I not talk to my husband?"

"Oh, you can talk to your husband," said the judge, folding his hands and smiling in a fatherly way, "you just can't talk about this case."

Grahm glared at the judge, his hands squeezed into fists inside his pockets. He felt small. He looked around the room and wondered why everything he knew seemed irrelevant here. His understanding of animals, plants, soil, machinery, chemicals, medicine, carpentry, plumbing, his family, and people in general—all became obsolete in this room. Everything here seemed pointlessly formal, like a bad dream. The judge wore a black robe, but why? Was it a requirement? And if so, who made it a requirement? Who decided on the color?

Why did he sit behind an elevated counter? Were the carpenters given instructions to build a counter so high and wide—like the measurements of the altar in Solomon's temple? What would happen if the counter were two inches too short, or too tall? Would that undermine his authority? And if not, why was the judge so far up in the air? Did the elevation have something to do with dispensing justice? Grahm shuddered to think of the poor souls who had stood in rooms like this and had their lives taken away from them, were severed from their families and friends and everything they understood through Rube Goldberg machinations they did not comprehend. And though the judge smiled at them and tilted his head to the side, no warmth came from his eyes. He had never even introduced himself, never said anything like, "Hello, I'm Jim Shabatz. My wife and I live in the house across from the park. We have two grown children. I was assigned to head up this hearing. My grandparents used to farm and I spent time on the farm as a boy. We've called you in because we needed to include you in this thing and I hope the traffic wasn't too bad driving in."

"Excuse me, sir, but this doesn't seem right," said Cora.

"Trust me, it is," said the judge.

The uniformed officer then held the little wooden gate open again and in no time at all Cora and Grahm stood looking at each other in the parking lot.

"Do you believe this?" asked Cora.

Back at the farm, they ate lunch at the kitchen table.

"We need a lawyer," said Cora.

"We can't even pay our bills," said Grahm. "We haven't done anything wrong. And if we needed a lawyer the judge would have told us. Aren't they required to do that?"

"That's just it—we don't know."

There was a knock on the front door. Lester Rund was not in uniform, and he stamped off his boots before coming inside. Today was his day off, he said, and he carried the manila envelope under his arm.

"I'm afraid I can't keep this, Mr. and Mrs. Shotwell. I showed it to the sheriff and he advised me to return it."

"Why?"

"He said that keeping it could negatively involve the department and complicate an investigation taking place in another agency. So I'm returning this to you. If there is some other way that I could help I'd be more than happy to, and I hope you won't hesitate to get in touch with me." He then paused a moment before leaving, and said, "I hear we're supposed to get some snow."

FIRE IN THE FIELD

IN PREPARATION FOR WASHING THE INSIDE OF THE REFRIGERATOR, Maxine carried all the frozen food from the freezer compartment down to the basement chest freezer. Then she cleared out the compartments. She found many things to throw out—some on the compost pile behind the barn; the rest she put in the pen with Rusty's old white terrier.

At around noon she answered the telephone and was asked by an operator if she would accept a collect call from Mr. Russell E. Smith. She agreed, astonished by the request. In over forty years of marriage she had never accepted a collect call from her husband.

When he didn't speak, she said, "Russell, is everything all right?" and she encountered a long pause.

"Maxine," he said.

"You'll have to speak up, Russell. I can't hear you."

"I'm in Iowa."

"What are you doing in Iowa?"

"We come down with Ella."

"Who's 'we' and who's 'Ella'?"

"Eli's wife."

Rusty had driven Eli, Abraham, Isaac, and the boys' mother to Dubuque, Iowa, because of a stomach problem. She apparently had a history of seeing a doctor from there—some herbal practitioner (they had no medical insurance). Other Amish families lived in the area and Russell said he would drive them around until they found a place to stay. Then he was driving back home. He'd return to pick them up whenever Eli's wife improved enough to come home.

"Did all of you fit in the front of the truck?" asked Maxine.

"Abe Lincoln rode in back," said Rusty.

"Abe Lincoln?"

"That's what I call Abraham. He don't mind."

"When will you be back home?"

"Soon as I get there."

"Do you have a map? Where are you?"

"Just across the river. It's not that far. I didn't want you to worry."

"You be careful, Russell."

Maxine sat down and slowly drank a large cup of coffee.

The house was not going to be finished in time.

Rusty arrived home at around five. She saw his truck disappear into the barn, then heard the lawn mower running and watched him mowing along the edge of the fence, the white terrier limping alongside. It was after dark before he came in.

"What took you so long to get home?" she asked.

"I had to go over to Eli's house and leave off a message for his mother-in-law."

"How will you know when to go back and get them?"

"They'll call from a store phone. You should see the casino they built up on the river."

"Why were you at a casino?"

"I wasn't *there*—I saw it from the road."

Work on the Smith house did not resume until Thursday, and rather than progressing it seemed to Maxine to go backwards. In order to splice in the new joists in the basement it was necessary to remove part of the floor in the guest bedroom. Despite an effort to salvage the oak tongue-and-groove flooring, pieces were broken. And the two-and-a-half-inch boards—common in older homes— were no longer popular enough for the lumberyard to keep them in stock. Also, the old flooring ran thicker than modern flooring, so extra time would be needed to shim up the new stock—when the order finally arrived—to the level of the rest of the floor. In addition, the new boards would have to be stained and finished to match.

The holes through the floor in the guest bedroom provided an unobstructed view of a dank corner of the cellar, and by standing at just the right place you could see all the way through the foundation and into the yard.

Maxine tried to reconcile herself to the bitter truth that the house would not be completed for her mother's visit. The only question that remained was how much of the damage could be patched over. Old wood shingles covered the yard, and parts of the roof were still protected only by tarpaper. The siding presented a quilt-work of every conceivable surface—splotches of light gray primer next to new trim boards, and, worst of all, exposed insulation. From the road it looked like a rural slum.

And her optimism was not bolstered when one evening she drove the Amish workers back to their home while Rusty looked for more siding at the lumberyard. The sight of the Yoders' mostly unpainted farmhouse and completely unpainted buildings gave her little reason to think people who lived amid such conditions would have any concern—other than a mercenary interest—in improving the appearance of other people's homes. They didn't share her values.

When Rusty returned home he discovered Maxine in the front yard picking up wood shingles and putting them in a tin wheelbarrow. He found a grass rake and assisted her, building a burn pile in the field north of the barn. As they worked, big flat flakes of snow began to fall like shredded gauze around them. The flakes—some as large as silk moths—drifted aimlessly in the wind before gently landing, fitting themselves to the contour of ground, and dissolving without a trace of moisture.

Though it was clear there would be no accumulation, Maxine regarded the sight as a harbinger of doom, a signal that the relentlessness of time would soon bring deep winter. The yard would be covered in snow, icicles hanging from bare trees, the ground as hard as concrete and owls arching forward on twisted branches beneath a silver moon, searching the white, barren land for the bodies of mice moving toward the gaping holes in the Smith foundation. Destiny could be neither diverted nor delayed; it marched forward like glaciers down a slope. And though she knew the meandering, porous gobs of falling snow possessed an intrinsic beauty, it was of a mocking kind.

"I hate to see it snow," she said.

"I know," said Rusty. He crumpled up an invoice from the lumber-yard, poked it beneath a piece of wood on the corner of the pile, and lit it with his cigarette lighter. The calico-patterned flame disappeared under a worn, grooved shingle. A sudden trill of smoke curled upward and a bright yellow flame leaped into the pile of dried-for-a-century oak and cedar.

Though it was early in the evening, it soon grew dark. Maxine went inside to make supper while Rusty gathered another load of shingles and dumped it on the burn pile. He remained in the field stirring the fire with his rake, the snowflakes falling around him. Looking into the flames reminded Rusty of when he and his brother had hunted in the woods above the old quarry. They had always built a fire to sit around as the dogs worked the coon up trees.

While he was watching red-orange sparks rising into the dark sky he remembered the sound of the dogs, their voices sharpened to a hysterical pitch by trait breeding, far in the timber. He remembered the thrill of anticipation as he and Carl took up their rifles and ventured away from the fire, following the distant howls, into the woods.

Maxine called him inside, and they ate in silence.

After watching the news, they went to bed.

At one o'clock in the morning Rusty became convinced he would never be able to sleep, climbed out of bed, and dressed. Maxine woke up an hour later, put on her robe, and went to look for him. Walking from room to room, turning lights on and off, she finally saw the small, bright spot of fire in the field north of the barn. In the back yard she found him filling the wheelbarrow with shingles.

"It's the middle of the night, Russell."

"It's light enough to work."

"Let the workers pick them up—it's hard on your knees."

"The workers aren't coming in the morning, and my knees are fine."

"What do you mean?"

"The Yoders aren't coming today. They have a community work day—helping some new Amish family move into the neighborhood. I didn't know how to tell you."

"Come inside. It doesn't matter."

"Maxine, we aren't going to be ready."

"It doesn't matter. My family will just have to see us the way we are."

"But this *isn't* the way we are," said Rusty.

"Come inside, Russell. It's starting to snow again."

"I'll just finish up this part of the yard."

A NEW SONG

GAIL SHOTWELL WOKE UP IN THE MIDDLE OF THE NIGHT. SHE tried to go back to sleep but a feeling-idea she could not quite identify attracted her attention and she carried it downstairs.

Her house seemed different in the dark, softer and more intimate, and she avoided turning on the lights. The cool air felt especially clean against her skin, and beyond the windows several stars focused on the sleeping earth like faraway telescopes. She opened the refrigerator door and an oblong box of blue light silently expanded.

She sat with a can of caffeinated cola at the kitchen table and thought about the feeling-idea again. Its only definite character, as far as she could tell, seemed to be an unusual mental disturbance—an emptiness with the power to draw her into it.

Then a memory from her childhood replaced the emptiness: standing under the tamaracks beyond the porch, her father coming toward her, tears running out of his eyes. He said her school friend Georgia Wood had been killed by a Jersey bull. He took her hand and they went in the house.

This memory was replaced by another, in which her brother gave her a ride in his first car. They drove all the way into Luster and bought two root beer floats. When they drove home it was after dark, the moon so bright that Grahm turned off the headlights.

Gail looked at her hands and the feeling-idea returned again. This time she knew what it was: a song—a melody trying to come out. Acting on the urge to free it, she located her bass and began searching for notes that related to each other through the same emotional quality as the trapped feeling inside.

Such an inspiration had never really visited her before. Not like this. Though for as long as she could remember she had heard music in her head—life-sustaining, sorrow-repairing music—the tunes were never her own. She only remembered them.

This was different. The feeling inside her had never been expressed before, yet it longed for expression and had chosen Gail to accomplish the deed. It was jiggling out of the primal psychic strands of whatever memories and passions made her. She had been chosen, and though she couldn't quite hear it yet, she felt the inspiration trying to make a sound through her. It wished to be born. This newness, or rather the compelling urge to make something that would later become new, had mysteriously lodged in her unconscious, and it ineptly yet vigorously signaled to her conscious self. This new song would be like no other. She felt like a small child again, sitting in a room of adults and yearning to find a way to tell them that most of what they said was wrong, to correct the folly in a beautiful way.

Three cups of coffee and hundreds of notes later, the imperial round-faced clock on the wall announced a quarter to eight. Robins, blackbirds, and finches moved around outside in the morning light. She had fifteen minutes to get to work, and, consequently, would be late.

"Drat," she said, thinking how unfortunate it was that deadlines could be so easily ignored; they would be so much more useful if they prompted compliance sooner, instead of saving all their nagging force to spend on the last few moments.

As she rushed into her work clothes she promised herself to return to the rescue mission later, and she buried the feeling-idea in a safe place in her memory where she could find it again.

Her old convertible bumped, rattled, smoked, and flew as well as it could into Grange; she ran across the asphalt lot and into the side door of the plastic factory. The punch meter greeted her with a whirring noise and she exchanged a few short comments with people on their way to the front office. At her workstation, she draped an olive gray apron over her neck and began shoving squares of warm plastic into small cardboard boxes.

Within an hour misgivings arose. The sound, sight, and smell of the hot machines hammered mercilessly against the song that was still trying to come out. The grim resignation on the faces of the other workers made it difficult to keep in contact with her inner self.

During morning break she drank a soda with five others from Packing, increasingly unsure of the possibility of staying at work. The possibility soon nose-dived when her future song informed her of a chord progression that might serve as a ladder for getting the rest of it out. And the attending excitement was irrepressible.

At eleven thirty-five Gail went to the main office and complained of being too sick to keep working. There was simply no way she could go on.

"You have no more sick days left," the man said.

"I can hardly breathe," said Gail.

"Go see a doctor, and get a note proving you were there."

On the way home, another piece of her song broke through—a lyric. As she imagined particular chord changes, a phrase jumped into her mind: "More than wonder, more than love." She leaned over and popped open the glove compartment, searching for a pencil and paper to write down the words and chords, fearful she might not remember them. The dashboard's inner compartment looked like the inside of a Dumpster, and due to not watching where she was going she forced a blue Chevy onto the shoulder of the road. The driver honked.

"Drat," said Gail, steering back to her side. Finding nothing to write with, she parked in front of a tavern and hurried inside, borrowed paper and pencil, and bought a glass of beer. In a corner booth she set to work, frequently sipping from the glass and gnawing on the eraser in moments of deep concentration.

"Hello, Gail."

"Oh, hi, July."

"Mind if I sit here?" He was carrying a cup of coffee and an egg sandwich, wrapped in oiled paper and resting on a white plastic plate.

"Sure, I'm leaving, though. I'm writing a song."

"Not working at the factory today?"

"No."

"Can I hear it when you're finished?"

The front door banged closed and three men dressed in farmer clothes came in.

"Maybe. Sure. I have to leave now. This place is getting too crowded. I've got to go home and try this out."

"I'm glad you're writing a song. You probably don't remember this, but many years ago when you were little you and your friend Georgia Wood used to walk from Georgia's house to the creek on the other side of my farm, and while you walked you often sang songs together. I don't know how to say this, but your voices, they sounded as close to angels as anything I ever heard. You've got music inside you, Gail. And Barbara Jean said the same thing that night after hearing you in the bar. Can I look at what you have?"

"No, it's not finished. And besides, I have no idea how to do this, I mean the right way. These scribbles, no one else could understand them. I've never done this before."

She gulped down the remaining beer in her glass and rushed through the room and out the door.

At home, the sound of the bass helped jog loose more of the song and she worked on it all that day and into the night.

FINISHING UP

THE DAY BEFORE MAXINE'S MOTHER'S VISIT, ALL THREE YODERS were on the roof laying new shingles and pounding roofing nails. Rusty had gone to the lumberyard. Maxine cleaned out the kitchen cupboards, replacing the contact paper on the shelves. As she worked she reviewed the meals she had planned. The radio on top of the refrigerator was tuned to a classical music station, and every time she climbed up on the stool to gain access to the high cupboards, she looked out the window. Along the state highway cars moved slowly, and Maxine watched for Rusty's truck. A weather report noted that a storm front moving out of the Dakotas had headed north instead of west and for that reason milder weather was predicted.

On the highway a black buggy pulled by a team of bays turned the corner onto the blacktop and headed toward the Smith house. This was not an unusual sight, and Maxine paid no attention as she wrote "ginger" onto her shopping pad. The next time she climbed onto the stool and glanced outside she saw two more buggies in the distance. These also turned onto the blacktop.

When Rusty returned in mid-morning from the lumberyard with the new tongue-and-groove flooring, there were ten buggies and four wagons standing behind twenty horses in his yard. In the wagons were assorted tools, boards, and ladders. A dozen Amish were on the roof, hammering shingles. Two other Amish nailed flashing into place around the chimney. Others wielded paintbrushes from ladders at varying heights around the house. Still others handed sacks of mortar and boards back and forth through the holes in the foundation as they worked to remove the jacks. Though Rusty did not actually count, more than thirty identically dressed men appeared to be attached to his house. Three or four young boys ran back and forth from the wagons, fetching tools and carrying messages between the adults. Among them was the boy Rusty had first seen in the Yoder house. A salt-and-pepper-bearded man walked over and asked in an abrupt manner, "That the flooring?" Rusty nodded as the man busily gathered up the wooden bundle and carried it away.

Inside, Maxine was frantically making coffee and sandwiches, which covered every inch of the kitchen table—lunch meat, egg, tuna fish, leftover meatloaf, and peanut butter.

"Russell, go down to the basement and bring up all the canned pickles you can find," she barked. "Thank goodness I bought a month's worth of bread. And look in the freezer for something else to put in the sandwiches. There's ham somewhere."

"Since we didn't invite them, maybe we don't have to feed them," said Rusty.

"That's all the more reason," said Maxine.

But before he got a chance to go into the basement an Amish man walked right into the kitchen and said, "Excuse me, but we're going to need more paint. It's drying about as fast as we put it on."

"Right behind you," said Rusty, and they went outdoors.

It was well after dark before all the work was completed, including the floor in the guest bedroom. Eli himself had overseen the staining and finishing, making sure the new portion of flooring matched the old. Before leaving, the Amish picked up the rest of the trash in the yard and threw it on the burn pile in the field.

Driving the Yoders home, Rusty said to Eli, "Give me a fair figure for those men. Nobody is working for me for nothing."

"Nobody expected to," said Eli.

Rusty lit a cigarette and said, "Maxine appreciates it."

"Yup," said Eli.

"You people are all right," said Rusty, "despite your religion."

"Jha," Eli laughed, "but it's because of our religion that we're all right."

When Rusty returned home the yard light illuminated Maxine,

pushing the tin wheelbarrow from one horse dropping to another, loading it with a scoop shovel.

"I'll do that," said Rusty. "You go on inside. It's been a long day and you'll probably need to be calling your mother and sister about the trip."

SNOW

I T BEGAN TO SNOW—NOT HEAVILY, BUT PERSISTENTLY. DRIVEN like powdered fog from the north, a dry, weightless snow arrived in Thistlewaite County with a nearly audible sigh, an empty, barren whisper that Upper Midwestern farmers recognized in the marrow of their bones and meteorologists detected through their digital instruments as the kind of snow that could get bad.

A stationary cold air mass perched above Wisconsin. It lingered there for several days, until, like the Owl of Minerva, it stepped off its frigid crag, opened its monstrous shadow wings, and came south, squeezing water out of the air. By nightfall, Thistlewaite County had accumulated three inches of new snow and temperatures across the state soon fell below zero.

Another several inches arrived the following day. The screen on the front porch of the Shotwell farmhouse presented almost no barrier at all, and the tiny flakes drove freely through the woven aluminum diamonds, accumulating in foot-deep drifts in the corners, the sloped ridges as perfectly formed as bell curves drawn by mathematical monks. Similar equations were plotted in the corners of windows—illustrations in crystalline grace and concave solitude.

The temperature continued down, while the land, layered with whipped-egg-white frosting, presented overwhelming evidence that Magnificence could be lavishly, wantonly squandered. Horizon after horizon of monolithic, wind-sculpted splendor rolled and unrolled, never to be witnessed by a single breathing soul, an extravaganza of extravagance.

On his way to the barn in the early morning, Grahm brushed the snow from the thermometer on the porch, the red liquid shrunk to the hairlines below minus fifteen.

Too cold to settle, compact, or fuse, the jagged flakes waited, zillions of them, yearning to be called into duty by ever-changing patterns of wind. More snow fell and temperatures continued falling, until from one end of Wisconsin to the other people repeated, "It's too cold to snow."

During the next night, temperatures plunged to minus twenty and the air turned outer-space sterile, without a trace of color or smell.

But the denizens of Thistlewaite County were on the whole resilient to these periodic reminders of the Ice Age. The local culture in fact required a certain amount of snow and arctic temperature to freeze-dry bacteria and retain Wisconsin's unique blend of vegetation, wildlife, and human temperament. Natives to the county had grown up with iced inconveniences. Others, lured into residence by summer vacations, marriage, college acceptance, work, or happenstance either adjusted or fled after their first encounter with blistering cold and the hypocrisy of neighbors who called out to each other "Cold enough for you?" and complained without ceasing but refused to sleep in. It was not a place for those hoping for an easy, tropical, unplanned existence.

Banks, stores, gas stations, and other enterprises remained open. Snowblower, chain saw, gasoline, battery, jumper cable, antifreeze, starting fluid, birdseed, snow pants, shovel, salt, soup, and popcorn sales boomed. Urban and suburban homeowners grumbled but removed snow from their walks twice a day. Ice-fishermen bore deeper to reach water. Homeowners with wood-burning stoves swelled with satisfaction as they wedged oak, maple, elm, and ash logs through firebox doors, content as squirrels with their long-sightedness and as happy as accountants with frugality. In taverns, all television sets were tuned to weather stations and bartenders commiserated with customers sitting in insulated vests on stools, numb to the insight that they could have stayed home. Farmers chipped away ice in drinking cups and water tanks, fought with frozen pipes and trough cleaners. They milked cows in barns heated by circulating blood. With dump buckets on the front of their tractors they cleared lanes for the milk trucks.

School superintendents, like Norse gods, stubbornly refused to yield to students' perpetual prayers for a snow day, unwilling to schedule unbudgeted days in the spring. Janitors squirted graphite into outside door locks. School bus drivers ran orange extension cords out of their houses to engine heaters. Humidifiers pumped water back into the desert air of the more modern homes, yet occupants still woke up in the middle of the night to the rifle shots of already-dried timbers shrinking further. Plumbers, furnace repairmen, and fuel delivery drivers had less sleep and made more money at this time of year than at any other. They prided themselves on their subzero resourcefulness, but it was nothing compared to that of the road crews—small armies chosen, trained, and outfitted for this one contest, who dug into hoarded mountains of salt and sand, eager to prove their indispensability.

But even these people knew when to surrender, and this storm provided them with an opportunity to exercise that yielding judgment. Night temperatures fell below minus twenty-five and the air assumed a lung-biting quality that tasted like isopropyl alcohol. Even habitual joggers stayed indoors, restlessly running in place. Snowdrifts grew so large in places that small villages could be hidden beneath them, and road crews began to admit they were falling behind. So many commuters with cell phones were stuck along the interstate that the plastic buttons on the Highway Patrol switchboard became permanent rows of lights. Weather bureaus broadcast statewide travel warnings. On the borders of Wisconsin, airplanes balked and circled, waiting for clearance.

Churches, senior citizen and day-care centers, Lamaze classes, parks, and government buildings were the first to announce closings. Local radio stations devoted nearly all their ad time to public service announcements, as advertisers requested that their companies' names not be associated with the obstruction of vital weather information.

Mid-morning, the first public school in Thistlewaite County announced it was sending students home early. After a moment's hesitation—a token rebellion against the inevitable—other schools followed the domino theory of school closings until all the county schools announced early closings.

The Grange schools, like most, selected a noon closing time in order to meet the minimum requirement for a statistical day. After lunch the students climbed noisily into the buses, and drivers with deep worry lines inched into the blowing snow.

It took Seth and Grace a full two hours to get home. Theirs was the next to the last stop, and they were so glad to get off the bus that the cold air actually felt good. In addition, a momentary lull in the storm created a still and magical interval between the mailbox and the house, and they kicked at the drifts with their boots and ran in circles to see their footprints in the virgin snow.

Inside the house, they ransacked the cabinets for treats, found a box of chocolate chip cookies and a half-eaten bag of potato chips. A soda completed the menu and they settled down at the table. Their father outside somewhere and their mother still waiting tables at the restaurant, they devoted themselves wholeheartedly to arguing over whether they should eat the entire box of cookies. Grace won, saved half of the second row, and put them back in the cupboard. Then she went to the bathroom. When she returned Seth had eaten the rest. After she yelled at him sufficiently they decided to test the sledding on the hill behind the barn. They dressed in their barn clothes, pulled stocking caps over their ears, and went outside.

The lull that had existed when they got off the bus still reigned, and the tracks they had made coming in were as fresh and crisp as when they had made them. They found the sleds and pulled them into the barn to look for their father.

They could not find him and abandoned the sleds to look for cats in the milk house. With the dipper they drew out a pint of cream and put in into the bowl. But the bigger cats wouldn't let the kittens get any, so they found jar lids and fed them separately. Then they carried the kittens up into the haymow and built homes for them to live in, but they ran away. After that they recovered their sleds, carried them down between the rows of standing and lying-down cows, and went out the back door of the barn.

The snow was deeper here—way above their knees—but it was light snow, and walking through it was not too difficult. The sled runners sank in too far, however, and they decided they'd have better luck with plastic saucers. So they left the sleds inside the barn door and went back to the shed. They could only find one saucer, and Seth pulled Grace behind him to the barn. Surprisingly easy to pull, the red saucer glided smoothly along the top of the snow. They went through the barn again and resumed their expedition back to the pasture hill. Grace walked behind Seth to avoid cutting her own path, but because her walking was easier Seth made her pull the saucer.

They stood beneath the lone burr oak at the top of the hill and looked down into a palatial wasteland of whiteness flowing to the creek and the woods beyond. In places, the drifts had giant rounded tops. Just to their right ran a valley of snow leading between two high snow mountains—a tunnel of purity yearning to be spoiled.

The ride down was faster and even more fun than they had hoped, and at the bottom they plunged into a drift that nearly buried them both. Laughing, they started up the hill and paid no attention when more snow began to fall and a northeastern wind stirred through the tops of the trees.

REMEMBERED LOVE

A S THE SNOW CONTINUED TO FALL ON THE WORDS REPAIR SHOP, Jacob Helm became discouraged. His work room filled with heavy metal things of all sizes and shapes, impatiently waiting to be fixed. Anxious people bundled in heavy coats, hats, earmuffs, wool scarves, and insulated boots kept bringing in more. The whole world, it seemed, was breaking down—frozen cars, tractors, snow-blowers, chain saws, generators, snowmobiles, four-wheelers, space heaters, and every other petrol-powered modern invention intended to make life easier.

Several levels below full consciousness, a useless passion quarreled against Jacob's well-being. He could feel it, relentlessly striving to pollute his thoughts. Machines could be fixed, returned to their functional state of health, but why? To what end? What purpose justified mechanical purpose? Why should things be repaired if the lives they were meant to enhance remained empty?

Last night, he'd heard the cougar again—its cry even more threatening in the thin November air. The bold, screaming challenge had pierced his sleep, and out of the gap ran a thread of unwelcome wakefulness. The beast's mere existence crowded upon his own. Its tracks encircled his house. It demanded something from him, a response. But he had none to give.

He sent Clarice home and closed the shop in the early afternoon. His jeep was completely covered with snow. He swept it off with a broom and drove over drifted roads with round sides. At the entrance to his driveway, he lowered the plow on the front and carved another ribbon of snow from the long, narrow, winding, white trough leading to the house.

He put the jeep in the garage and waded through the deep snow toward the house.

Inside, the temperature had dropped to around fifty degrees, and he ate a bowl of vegetable stew. Then he retired to his living room with a bottle of bourbon. He collected the newspapers and magazines scattered on the upholstered chair and sofa, shoved them into the stove along with several logs, and set them on fire. Seated before the open door, he watched the flames spread and reached for his pipe and tobacco.

A booth of cured aroma seeped out of the pouch and surrounded him. He transferred clumps of bark-colored tobacco into the deep, curved bowl, poking and pressing each layer against the blackened interior sides. When he was finished, the moist, spongy column almost rose to the top.

Striking a match and holding it above the bowl, he sucked the yellow flame into the tobacco, where individual strands crinkled to red life, accompanied by a frying sound. When the entire top glowed, he tossed the match in the stove and leaned back in his chair to lubricate the top, bottom, and sides of his tongue with oily, narcotic smoke.

The stove's heat lulled him further; he swallowed an inch of bourbon from the jam jar and opened the photograph album resting next to the chair. There, pictures of his wife stared back at him from six, seven, and eight years ago.

I shouldn't think of her as "my wife," he thought. After all, she was no longer a person, no longer anything—her picture a signpost to nowhere. Yet she lived in his memory, continuing to persuade, exerting her undying influence over him while she herself—in all her insubstantiality—remained impervious, unchangeable, frozen in a relationship that only yielded in one direction.

The memory-worn pictures were not just images on glossy paper, but catalogs of personal memorabilia, cross-referenced in numbing detail. Looking into the resemblance of Angela's former face released museums of intimate, elemental facts about him. She, or rather her image, had become a symbol for *him,* an earlier version, the Younger Jacob—a person for whom he now felt envy and even resentment over having been cut out of his inheritance.

By looking at her picture Jacob perceived the gulf between what it felt like to be alive now and what it had felt like to live six, seven, and eight years ago. Through her picture he acknowledged that his present experiences were no longer as fully endowed. His goals no longer called to him as loudly, and the sequenced paths leading to them were not nearly as well lit. He once knew how to move through the forest of mornings, afternoons, and evenings, following the trail of his desires without hesitating or looking up, the field upon which his expectations unfurled as clear as an unbroken sky. Now, he shared no mystery with anyone and the adventure had become a job.

The outline of Angela's ankle above a brown oxford reminded Jacob that time itself had passed differently six years ago. Each minute had contained the possibility that an invisible door would soon open and Unmediated Truth stare back at them. Fully exposed, the gates of perfect understanding would open and he and Angela would fold into each other with a surrendered whimper.

He looked away from the album and closed his eyes, as though protecting them from the unbearable glare of memory.

Her illness had driven a wedge between them, interrupting their sacred dialogue, the source of his joy. How he missed that vital center—talking, touching, and living one life in two parts. The disease persisted until what she most longed for she could not share with him at all, and their citadel against the outside world was finally breached, ruined. His final request—that she allow him to accompany her in death—was denied, and after the denial a pledge exacted, an animal resignation to continue, perhaps not fully, not well, but to go on, like a broken machine.

Everyone told him he would get over it. Time would heal. He believed it himself and pictured a future in which his endowment would be restored, his full inheritance come through. He would start living again and feel the resurgence of good things returning. He believed in this hope and, soon, this belief became a promise. Thoroughly convinced by the promise, he even began to imagine how grateful he would feel when it was fulfilled.

Months and years passed and he still did not get over her death, and Jacob began to feel not just broken, but violated. The promise made to him—by himself and others—had been broken. Each day betrayed him to the next as each minute nurtured the bitter root of

betrayal until the only trace of his earlier hope had been wrapped
in an anger over its irrecoverable loss. And there were times, many
in fact, when it seemed the only way to remain alive was to remain
alive angry.

As the tobacco burned lower in the bowl, the smoke became less
sweet, acrid. The stove insisted in an increasingly strident voice that
he sit farther away from it, and when the pipe finally went out he did
not bother to relight it. He scraped the ashes and charred tobacco
onto a piece of paper, tossed the paper into the fire, and closed the
cast iron door.

DESPERATION

A T FOUR O'CLOCK BONITA AND CORA HUNG THE CLOSED SIGN in the front door of the Red Rooster restaurant. Cora passed through the same door fifteen minutes later, leaving Bonita, who lived in town, to finish closing up.

It was already dark. Despite the bitter cold, the truck started, and before she was out of town the defroster made inroads in the frosted windshield. Soon, an expanding dome of clarity allowed her to sit upright and the assiduously whirring heater granted her the privilege of taking off her thick wool gloves.

The pickup's headlights did not penetrate very far into the blowing snow, a situation made worse by her inability to suffer the dizzying sight of warp speed interstellar space travel whenever she attempted to use the high beams. But traffic stayed light, the yellow lines along the side of the state highway were visible in spots, and road crews had recently plowed. Other cars, she noticed, also drove on low beams, and there was a ghostly, ship-in-the-fog quality when she met oncoming vehicles—a noiseless, ethereal encounter with floating lanterns.

Moving at about twenty-five miles an hour, it took Cora almost forty-five minutes to reach the county road leading to the farm. She turned off the state highway, drove a short distance, and stopped the truck. The road before her had not been plowed—or not recently enough to make any difference. The path before her was not a road at all but a rolling plane of snow with only two barbwire fences to break the vast white continuity. Between those two fences, some-where, were two deep ditches and two miles of Sand Burr Road. She took a deep breath, checked to make sure the truck was still in four-wheel drive, manually shifted into low gear, and inched forward, hoping to be able to stay an equal distance between the fences.

A short time later she stopped again, deciding that this was insane. Fences could never be relied upon to tell where roads were. And her memory of the contour of the ditches led her to believe that when one tire found its way off the road the steep sides of the ditch would turn every effort to pull it out into an illustration of tar-baby futility. Her only chance, she decided, was to go back and continue down the state highway to Hutch Road in the hope that it had been plowed.

But just getting back to the highway presented a problem. She could not, of course, turn around, and the truck's backup lights were useless. She climbed out to look behind her, only to climb back in and say, out loud, "What was I thinking?" She reconsidered her options: going forward, backing up, or staying where she was. The last option seemed the least attractive—freezing to death would happen as quickly in the ditch as sitting in the road. Might as well try something. Backing up seemed the better option, because if she got stuck it was better to be stuck closer to the highway.

She assumed the direction her tires were pointed in—if she didn't turn the steering wheel—would lead her back along the tire tracks that had brought her here. Her headlights would hopefully show if she were following the tracks.

It worked, though she climbed out five times to check behind her. She reached the place where the road widened and intersected with the highway and then found herself moving again to the left of the comforting yellow markers, meeting the friendly sight of fellow travelers carrying lanterns.

Cora turned on Hutch Road and saw fresh tracks to follow. After a mile and a half without incident, she turned onto Wilson Road, which ran more or less parallel to the wind and had not drifted over, and later turned onto Sand Burr again. This time she only had a quarter mile to inch forward, emboldened by the possibility that she could—if she had to—walk the rest of the way down Q.

Finally, she identified her snow-mounded mailbox, pulled into the drive and into the shed, and hurried through the deep snow to the house.

The warmth of the kitchen soothed her. She took off her coat and boots, threw away the empty potato chip and cookie packages that were on the table, and the soda can. She assumed the children were in the barn and wondered what to make for supper. Even after staring into the refrigerator she had no definite ideas, so she decided to change out of her uniform and think about it in more comfortable clothes. Upstairs, while pulling a sweatshirt over her head, she wondered again about Seth and Grace, and she went down the hall to look in their rooms. No lights. She again assumed they were with Grahm in the barn and made a conscious decision to not be angry about the bag of cookies.

In the kitchen again, she noticed the clock—six fifteen—and looked out the window. The snow blew so thick she could not even see the lights along the side of the barn or the vapor light on the utility pole. Her imagination filled with stories of farmers frozen to death between barn and farmhouse—lost in a blizzard, unable to tell which direction to go.

She decided to go out to the barn. She took the foot-long flashlight from the tool drawer, but because of its inefficiency in penetrating the blowing snow, she went carefully from the porch to the tamaracks, from the trees to the fence, from the fence to the shed, from the shed to the milk house.

Grahm was milking when she found him, wedged between the all-white Holstein and the one with only three milking tits. Though it was sixty degrees warmer in the barn, the breath from the cows still misted in front of their wide, wet noses.

"Trouble getting home?" asked Grahm.

"A little, and I'm glad I had the truck."

"Barn cleaner froze up again. Did you hear the weather?"

"No. Where're the kids?"

"Haven't seem 'em."

"They're not out here?"

"No. They aren't in the house?"

"No. Did they do their chores?"

"I told you, I haven't seen them. I thought they were in the house. I saw the school bus go by, around two o'clock. I was in the shop. They must be home."

"*Grahm, they're not in the house.*"

"Did you look in their rooms?"

"Of course I looked in their rooms. They're not in the house. Their coats and boots are gone."

"Maybe they're in the haymow."

Cora climbed up but knew as soon as she stepped off the ladder that they were not in the mow. It was dark and cold.

"Cora," called Grahm, his voice anxious.

He had found the sleds that Seth and Grace had abandoned in favor of the plastic saucer resting against the door leading to the pasture.

They opened the back door and immediately the wind slammed it shut. They opened it again and with the aid of the barn lights and the flashlight saw the rounded trail leading away from the door, tapering and merging into level snow after several feet.

Cora began calling into the blowing snow, knowing that even from fifteen feet away she couldn't be heard.

"They're out there," said Cora.

"We're not sure," said Grahm. "Let's look again in the house."

They went to the house, but did not find them. Cora called the police and ambulance, but neither gave assurance they could reach the farm before morning.

On the way back to the barn they stopped in the shed, where Cora remembered, or thought she remembered, seeing the sledding saucers. Both were gone. They went through the barn to the machine shed, and to the shop. Cora was growing hoarse from calling into the blowing snow.

Back in the barn, they stood again by the opened back door and looked out.

"If they're at the sledding hill we'll never find them," said Grahm.

"They could have tried to get back," said Cora. "They could be just a little ways away, lying in the snow."

"They could be almost anywhere," said Grahm.

"They're out there," said Cora. "I know it. I'm going." And she started out.

"Wait!" shouted Grahm. "Wait!" He ran through the barn, and

when he returned he was carrying a hundred-foot length of hemp rope. He tied one end to the door and the other end around Cora's waist.

"I'll lead the way," he said, "but don't let go of me."

They waded into the dark squall.

Deeper behind the barn, the snow was well above their knees, mid-thigh in places. The flashlight was good for only about eight feet, and Grahm moved it from side to side as they waded forward. The wind bit through their clothes, and ice covered the front of the scarves wrapped around their heads. Both tried not to think, focused narrowly on a shared belief that at any moment the flashlight beam would discover the hooded forms of Grace and Seth walking toward them out of the cold.

The blizzard hissed, groaned, and roared in the sky.

Cora felt the rope tighten around her coat. She pulled Grahm backwards and he almost fell on top of her. They'd come to the end of the run. It seemed hopeless. Seth and Grace could have been standing close to them, ten feet to either side, and they would have walked past them.

"We can fan out, move to the sides!" shouted Grahm into the ice covering Cora's scarf. "Let me take you back first. You've got to keep your strength up."

"No!" she shouted back.

Together they walked in wide arcs, judging their position relative to the door by the direction of the cord leading away from Cora's waist. After completing each arc, they came toward the barn another two yards, coiled another loop of rope, and headed in the other direction.

By the time they were back inside the barn, the flashlight had gone out and Cora could no longer feel her feet. They closed the door, shook the ice from their scarves, and sat, exhausted, on bales of straw. A short time later Cora got up again, the rope still around her waist, and said, "I'm going back."

"It's no good," said Grahm.

She went out. Grahm fell in behind her, leaving the barn door open so the light would shine out ten feet. Without the flashlight, they could barely see their hands before their faces. They slogged forward and Cora continued calling into the howling wind. At the end of the rope, Cora called again, listened, and called again.

Grahm had a bad feeling and was quickly getting an even worse one. They were exhausted, their feet and hands numb. Each effort proved more difficult, every motion less sure, less controlled. They were stumbling, falling. As they lost strength—and they were losing it quickly—their mental faculties would also fail. Soon they wouldn't be able to keep thoughts in their proper places. Their sense of hope was becoming linked with their physical desperation. They thought—Cora thought—that as long as they kept floundering through the snow there was hope. The obvious conclusion was to continue until they fell over and froze. They were losing the ability to make reasonable judgments about the risk involved, the likelihood of succeeding, and the possibility that their children had not gone sledding at all.

"Let me try to find another length of rope!" shouted Grahm.

And then what Grahm had been afraid would happen, happened. Cora fought with the cinch around her waist, pulled the loop of rope up over her head, and placed it in Grahm's hands.

"No!" he shouted, and she turned and walked into the snow. A moment later she was gone, replaced by blizzard.

Grahm was alone, with nothing but a frozen rope that attached him to his barn.

COMPLETING THE CIRCLE

G RAHM STOOD ALONE IN THE BLIZZARD, HOLDING THE FROZEN rope connected to the barn, to safety, and to everything he had known prior to this moment. His hands and feet were completely numb. In a clear, calm, and unified vision, he saw his past life—not only everything he had done but everything he had hoped to do. He saw his goals and his dreams in perfect detail. He saw his beliefs, things he could not know for certain but still held true, as clearly as pictures drawn on paper. He saw how his personality had been formed, how he had taken what he had been given and with the help of both longing and loathing fashioned from it a way to be. He saw how he had failed at, succeeded in, avoided, and delayed the challenges he faced. He saw his old friend Fear standing near him, protecting him from both real and imagined harm. He saw his parents and understood how they were a part of him and he a part of them. He saw his sister's fierce spirit burning out of their childhood like a wild torch. He saw his land when his parents and grandparents farmed it, and before it was a farm, when the Singing People walked across it on their way to the river, carrying their children. He saw everything he had ever known and ever hoped to know. He held his life in his hands, let the rope fall away, and rushed headlong into the blizzard. The void welcomed him, and three or four steps later his gloves found the back of Cora's coat and he pulled her toward him. They fell backwards into the snow and got back up.

"The tree," he yelled. "The oak tree at the top of the hill! It should be straight ahead."

They plodded forward, side by side, connected to each other at arm's length, Grahm's right glove holding Cora's left, with their other hands extended into the black blowing. The cold was now numbing their whole bodies. They fell, got up, staggered forward, and fell again. Their sense of time became distorted as eternity wrapped around them. Their thoughts blurred. They went on and on until they could no longer feel the cold. Then Cora screamed. Her right hand had brushed against the side of the burr oak. She guided Grahm toward it and they felt their way around its thick, gnarled trunk. Cora tripped and fell away from Grahm. Grahm reached down for her and found a plastic saucer; under it was one of his children, then the other, lying at the base of the tree. A renewed strength whistled through Cora and Grahm as they lifted their children's limp bodies over their shoulders.

Freezing now seemed inconsequential. The storm lost its inner strength and seemed to only be pretending to be cold, faking fury. They had found the tree, found their children, completed the circle. If they died now they would die together, which was not like death at all. Death was separation—living while their children froze. That possibility no longer existed. It was gone. What they had now bore no resemblance to death, no matter what happened. Only life extended beyond them. Together they could live in the void if need be, forever. Together they could do anything.

They began walking toward what they hoped was the barn, carrying their children over their shoulders and clinging to each other with their free hands. The wind, Grahm noticed, was now behind them, no longer blowing crystals of snow into their eyes.

They tried to keep in the trail they had made on the way out, but this was impossible. The best they could do, Grahm decided, was to keep the wind blowing against their backs, and though blizzard winds could not be depended upon to blow consistently in one direction, it provided their only compass.

Apparently it was not at all good, and once again Cora encountered something solid. A barbed wire along the fence separating the pasture from last year's cornfield ripped open the sleeve of her coat. At the end of the fence, they knew, waited the machine shed. Once again, a bugling strength sang inside them—a soundless sound that communicated with the numbness in their limbs—and Grahm carried both children as Cora guided their way along the fence until they came to the wooden post at the corner.

From here they continued to the machine shed, from the shed to the barn, to the toolshed, from the shed to the wooden fence, from the fence to the tamaracks, and from the tamaracks to the house.

Cora stumbled upstairs and returned with blankets while Grahm peeled the coats, boots, and frozen clothes from Seth and Grace. Both were listless, their speech slurred. Grace could hardly keep her eyes open, and could not stand on her own. Cora wrapped blankets around them and set them side by side on the couch next to the space heater, like human cocoons.

Standing over their children and beginning to relax, Cora and Grahm took off their own coats and boots and unwrapped the ice-encrusted scarves from their faces. Their hands shook. Holding her head, Cora began to cry and could not stop. Grahm sat on the floor next to the sofa and realized he couldn't feel any part of his body. When Cora stopped crying she sat beside him. Their limbs hurt as feeling slowly returned. They looked at each other like people who had just found hell's door ajar and walked out, and did not know what to say. Nothing seemed adequate.

"Not bad for two people who can't take hold of the tools of new technology," said Cora.

Grahm looked at her. Then he smiled. Then she smiled. They began laughing. They laughed until they could feel jabbing pinpricks in their hands and feet. They laughed until it seemed they couldn't breathe. Then Grahm sobbed for several minutes, blew his nose, and they laughed some more.

"That's funny," said Grahm, and they laughed again.

The family thermometer still did not register the temperature of the children, though both Cora and Grahm hit the lowest rung, ninety-four degrees. Outdoors, the wind stopped blowing. The weather station said the storm had moved southeast, toward Chicago. Cora commanded her body to stop shaking, and she began to move around. The home health manual explained that two degrees an hour was as fast as a body could raise its own temperature and carbohydrates were the best things to eat for quick heat. She warmed some fresh milk, boiled water for tea, and began frying doughnuts, the children's favorite.

Grahm sat at the table, watching Cora. The dough fizzed and crackled when she placed in the hot oil.

"You did it," said Grahm.

"We both did it," said Cora.

"It was you," said Grahm. "It was you."

Grahm felt his strength return as he warmed up, and at a little after midnight, worried he could hear the cows bellowing from the pressure of milk against their udder walls, stepped outside. By then the air was almost calm. He *could* hear his cows bellowing. He put on his coat, stepped off the porch, and headed toward the barn. In the distance, a siren. From the windows in the milk house he watched as the township snowplow, followed by an ambulance with lights flashing, came up Sand Burr Road and onto Q. They pulled in the drive and four men and three women ran into the house.

The children were fine, with only frostbitten ears and fingers.

That night Grahm and Cora both slept, without dreaming, like stones.

The following morning, temperatures climbed above zero. After milking the cows—two hours later than usual—Grahm looked out the back door of the barn at the expanse of snow leading into the pasture. No signs remained of the trails they had made, no trace of what had happened the night before except the end of the rope attached to the barn door. It ran a short distance and disappeared into high, level snow.

In the machine shed he cut a length of snow fence, carried it through the snow, and placed it in a circle around the oak at the top of the hill. To the fence he wired a wooden sign: WARNING: NO-ONE HARM THIS TREE, GRAHM SHOTWELL.

Then he went to the toolshed.

Grahm found the pipe bomb he had made but not yet found a way to use, set it in the vise, pulled out the fuse, unscrewed the end cap, and poured the powder out on the shed floor. He struck a match and tossed it onto the dark pile of powder. Lacking containment, it flared briefly in a bright, white *phooost*, filling the shed with smoke and the smell of sodium nitrate, carbon, and sulfur.

Outside, he could hear cars moving along the road at an almost-normal speed. The storm had passed.

FAMILY

MAXINE DROVE TO THE MADISON AIRPORT AND RETURNED in the afternoon with her sister and mother. The trip took longer than expected because the flight had been delayed due to hazardous winter weather. Rusty met them in the driveway, took the walker from the trunk, and helped his mother-in-law fasten onto it.

"How does it feel to not farm anymore, Russ?" asked his sister-in-law Marjorie as she walked carefully along the path shoveled through the frozen yard in her heels.

"I keep busy," said Rusty.

"Yes, Maxie tells me you're quite industrious. Do you still have all those dogs?"

"Only one."

"Did you paint the house or something?" asked the old woman, looking hard through her thick glasses.

"A while back," said Maxine. "Be careful there, Russell. Watch her hands going through the door."

"Nobody paints anymore," said Marjorie. "Vinyl siding has done away with all that. I don't think there's one painted house in our whole division. Vinyl's cheaper in the long run and much nicer."

"Did you remember my bags?"

"Yes, Mother, we've got them in the car. Russell will bring them in."

"Doesn't smell quite like I remember," said Marjorie.

"The animals are all gone," said Maxine.

"Well, thank goodness for that. With all the other inconveniences you put up with, you should at least have fresh air."

As they entered the kitchen, the old woman asked again about her bags and Maxine reassured her that her bags were in the car. Rusty parked the walker next to the table and Maxine set out glasses.

"We have fruit juices, milk, and soda," she said. "What would you like, Mother?"

"Fruit juices?"

"Yes, orange, grape, grapefruit, and vegetable juice."

"What kind of soft drinks do you have?"

"Just about any kind you can name."

"Oh my, I'm afraid I can't name many. Nothing for me."

"Nothing for me either," said Marjorie. "I'd forgotten what an older kitchen this was. You don't even have a microwave."

"I'm afraid not," said Maxine. "We don't have a place to put one, and Russell can't see a need."

"Really, Russ! You've got to get with the times. I couldn't live without a microwave. Nobody really *cooks* anymore. Nobody has time for it."

"We're just old-fashioned," said Maxine.

"Where's my room?" asked Marjorie.

"Are you sure you won't have something to drink?"

"Do you have a downstairs bathroom?"

"Right around the corner."

"Did you remember to bring my bags?"

Rusty went to the car to retrieve the suitcases. As he pulled the luggage from the trunk, a shiny black Ford Expedition with tinted windows and a license plate reading MOVEOVER pulled into the drive with a blast of the horn, announcing the arrival of his daughters, sons-in-law, and grandchildren. The two families had ridden together from Chicago. They bailed out beside him, and his daughters carried his grandchildren into the house after learning that their grandmother and aunt were inside.

"Where should I park this baby, Pops?" asked Drake, referring to the Expedition.

"You can park it in the barn," said Rusty.

Drake surveyed the distance to the barn. "On second thought, I'll just leave her here for right now. We won't be staying overnight. This way I can keep an eye on her. We've got rooms rented."

"Maxine planned on you staying here."

"I know, but we don't want to put you out. And anyway—you

know—the swimming pool is a big feature. We also want to go to the Dells tomorrow and check out some of those water slides. I suppose you've been there many times."

"No."

"How 'bout them Packers!" shouted Tim. He was the younger of the two and, as Rusty recalled, a sports enthusiast.

"How about them," said Rusty.

"Looks like they might pull it off this year."

"Hike!" sang out Drake, and the two young men jumped in the air and pretended to run forward with footballs tucked under their arms.

"Here, we can take those, Pops," said Tim when Rusty began carrying his mother-in-law's bags across the yard.

"I've got them."

"No prob-lem-o," said Drake.

"Hike!" they both shouted again and ran around hunched over as though carrying footballs. Drake tossed the diaper bag between his legs and Tim threw it to him as he ran toward the house.

Inside, the younger grandchild cried while Brian, age three, ate cereal with milk and sugar. Maxine seemed to hover from one place to another, like a spider on a thread.

"Sit down, Maxie," said Marjorie. "You're making the children nervous."

"There's no reason you can't stay here."

"Ashley didn't sleep in the car," said Elizabeth over the cries of her daughter. "Maybe I better go upstairs and see if I can put her to sleep."

"Brian slept most of the way—and he's hungry," said Rebecca.

"Did you remember my bags?"

"Yes, Mother, your bags are here now. Russell, put them in the guest room. Drake, what would you like to drink?"

"We brought beer," said Drake.

"I told you not to bring the beer in," said Rebecca.

"I know," said Drake, "but your parents don't mind—do you, Pops? Everybody needs a little refreshment."

"I just don't know how you can live without a microwave. But I guess that's the way it was years ago. Right, Mother?"

"We didn't have microwaves," said Blanch. "We hardly had a pot to piss in."

"Oh, please!" said Marjorie. "Let's not have any of that crude language, Mother. You make it sound so unpleasant."

"Well, we didn't," said the old woman.

"As I remember," said Marjorie, "we were one of the more re-spected families."

"Tim, take that bowl away from him—he's spilling."

"Here, I'll get that," said Maxine.

"Hike!"

"You two go outside if you're going to horse around," said Elizabeth. "Now you've got her started again."

"Who else wants a beer?"

"I'm going to take her upstairs."

"Use Rebecca's room. Marjorie's staying in yours."

"Oh great, I've got to climb all those stairs."

"You can share Mother's room if you'd rather."

"No thank you. No offense, Mother, but privacy is a commodity you can't be without these days. It's the main reason homes are so much larger than they used to be. Living on top of each other like this is no longer civilized."

"You girls were always spoiled."

"Did you hear that, Maxie?"

"Tim, I told you to take that bowl away from her."

"What are you *doing,* Maxie?"

"I'd better get the roast in the oven."

"Does old Mrs. Jackson still live down the road?"

"She's not that old," said Maxine. "She still lives alone, though she uses crutches now. She still has a big garden."

"No, you can't watch television, Brian. We're not here to watch television. Maybe you'd like to tell Grandma what you did at day care. No, you can't watch television."

"Anybody know who's winning the game?"

"I'll just check," said Drake, disappearing into the living room, followed shortly by Tim.

"Russell, you'd better show them how to work the television."

It was in times like these that Rusty most regretted his retirement. In earlier years his work had humanely limited the time he spent with company. He felt trapped. It seemed unnatural to be in the house—with company—in the middle of the day. The television playing in the afternoon had profoundly unwelcome associations: one of his daughters home sick from school, visiting people in the hospital, the invalid sister of a salvage yard owner who knew the names of all the soap opera actors. As for sports, Rusty could not remember ever watching a game from beginning to end and sincerely hoped something would come up to prevent him from sitting through this one. Sports were for people who didn't have enough work to do, and now he found himself among them.

Sitting stiffly in a recliner next to Tim and Drake, watching football, Rusty entertained the same question that social situations always posed for him: Just who's paying for all this? Before his retirement this question had an answer—he was. Some people could talk and watch television and do nothing all afternoon because others were working.

Of course there were people all over the world who sat around talking, drinking, eating, and watching television, and there was nothing really *wrong* with that, but while they sat around other people worked. Both were necessary. Society was glued together by one group sitting around and another group doing something useful.

But now everyone had money. Even discounting all of his and Maxine's savings, his Social Security alone could cover the expense of the next couple days of sitting around. In addition, Tim and Drake, though barely thirty, were employed by large corporations and made more money than he had ever dreamed of. Everyone had money now, and sitting around, loitering, had become a way of life. His grandchildren were being methodically instructed in how to enjoy living while doing nothing.

And it wasn't just the expense. There was also the lingering feeling that everyone in the house unwittingly engaged in something slightly immoral, disreputable. Only he, Rusty, remained aware of it, and felt the need to counterbalance them, redeem them, by having something else to do.

Maybe only older people like himself could understand the need for work, real work—the sanity that comes from keeping busy.

"Fourth down!" yelled Tim. *"Punt, you suckers!"*

"Hike."

Rusty wondered what his brother, Carl, was doing, and resolved to try to find him.

ENVY

O LIVIA LAY IN HER DARK ROOM WITHOUT SLEEPING. OUTSIDE the window she could see a thin sliver of moon nailed against the sky. The house was quiet except for Violet putting things away in the kitchen, and Olivia felt lonely.

She remembered her childhood—much of it spent with her mother, who had fretted over Olivia's poor health. She remembered countless doctors and "cures." They had once driven all the way to St. Louis for a jar of something that looked like muddy water and tasted like mold. One year she had taken "light therapy," lying in her underwear beneath a very bright light with special, healing filters. She had improved slightly during her teenage years and had even attended Haviland College in Kansas, an interval that now burned in her memory with particular clarity. Her Independence: extravagantly merry years filled with making her own decisions and feeling normal. But it did not last. Long before graduation, sickness forced her to return to Words, to the bed she lay in now.

As their health declined, her grandmother and then her mother went to live with Violet in Grange. Aunt Leona came to live with Olivia and her father, and her aunt took care of her for nearly ten years. Then Violet moved back to Words, and a few months later Aunt Leona went to live with one of her daughters, she said, but Olivia knew better. Violet forced her out—her ways and Violet's conflicted. Violet refused for anyone else to care for her father, who lived until that Day of Great Sorrow, eight short years ago.

Never once had anyone wondered if Olivia would find someone outside the family to love. Of course she wouldn't. And no one had ever wondered—since her mother died—if anything extraordinary or even interesting would happen to her. Of course it wouldn't. Normal people had things happen to them, but the only things happening to Olivia originated from the befuddled machinations of her own body. She happened to herself. She hardly existed except as a project of Violet's. She would never be like heaven to someone else—only a charitable activity for earning the right to get there.

As Olivia lay in the dark thinking, she realized that, unlike Pastor Winifred, she had never really had something important to say. When she talked, people's eyes glazed over, as though they were beginning a long train ride through Iowa and Nebraska with nothing to eat and nothing to drink and nothing to read. No one expected God to actually show His Favor to her, to let her into His Hiding Place. His Grace would never ever be available for Olivia other than in the general way all people share it, like ants in a bag of sugar. The Lord had never touched Olivia.

She listened as Violet finished cleaning up the kitchen. Then, from across the hall, she heard the brushing of teeth. As the rapid swishing and sloshing continued, a feeling gave birth to an idea inside Olivia. It might have amounted to nothing more than a passing thought, a notion entertained briefly before falling asleep but after Violet had climbed into the bed across the hall, followed by the sounds of sagging springs and heavy breathing, other sounds had come into Olivia's room. Her neighbor beyond the hedge began playing her bass, and the deep tones filled the night air. The low, melodic phrases haunted Olivia, encouraged her to entertain her new notion, turn it over and over, make it into something more real, nurture it into a plan.

The following morning when Violet prepared to leave for town, Olivia said she wasn't feeling well. She would stay home and write a note to Nancy Droomiker in the nursing home.

After Violet left, Olivia called the bank where she had a savings account that had been started for her thirty years ago. The account had been increased in tiny amounts, sometimes from an auction or other sale, sometimes from a family member worried about her future, and in later years from the money left over from her supplemental security income.

Yes, the account was still there, she was assured, earning interest per annum, safe as a bug in a rug.

Next, Olivia had to get the hatbox down from the top of the tall cabinet in Violet's bedroom.

It wouldn't be easy, mostly because of the woven throw rug at the foot of Violet's bed. Throw rugs were fine for rolling straight over, but when turning was required, her wheelchair's swiveling front wheels had an uncanny way of picking up folds and trapping her between two insurmountable humps of fabric.

To solve this problem Olivia took the broom down the hall with her. She also had a gripping device for picking up small objects from the floor.

With the broom, Olivia pushed the rug under Violet's bed, giving her just enough room to navigate to the bureau. Here, she used the broom to work the hatbox to the edge of the bureau top and topple it over. As it fell, it turned upside down. Olivia's mind emitted an audible shriek when the papers inside—curved upward on the corners from years of lying in a cramped container—skidded across the floor. Some of them slid under the bed.

"Ha!" said Olivia, a sound more like a bray or a bugle note than a laugh. "You will not prevail."

With the broom she guided the overturned hatbox toward her until she was able to catch it and place it securely on her lap. Then, still using the broom, she maneuvered the papers within reach of the fingers of her long-handled reacher. She dropped many in midair before they made it to the hatbox, but she kept working.

The box prevented her from leaning far enough ahead to reach those papers directly before her feet. So she backed out of the room, down the hall, and into the kitchen. She left the hatbox on the table and returned to the bedroom, backwards. Faced in this direction, she was able to reach the box top and two of the three papers still remaining under the bed—including the deed to the house. These she held in her teeth while she inched the last piece of paper toward her.

Then Violet's car pulled up next to the house.

As quickly as she could, Olivia went to the hallway and, working the broom behind her, attempted to pull the rug from under the bed and into its flattened position. It was impossible. She had to be pointed in the other direction.

She left the broom in the hall and wheeled to the kitchen, where she put the remaining papers in the box. As Violet walked up the front ramp, Olivia, inspired with frenzy, put the box in the oven, closed the door, and opened the refrigerator. The cold air made contact with the sweat pouring from her forehead.

When Violet came inside, she found her sister attempting to reach a pitcher at the back of the refrigerator.

"Land sakes!" said Violet. "You'll have milk all over the floor. Here now, look at the state you've got yourself in. You're sweating like a butcher. Come out of there."

"I want to get it myself," said Olivia. "You go out and bring in the mail."

"It's too early for mail," said Violet. "The snow slows them down."

"I heard him. Go out and get the mail."

"All right, all right, but first let me get the milk. And look at this—you've got cereal all over the top of the stove."

"Get the mail!" shouted Olivia, summoning her most despotic tone of voice and allowing Violet to peek momentarily into her underground cavern of caged anger, which both sisters were dedicated to keeping tightly sealed. "I can get the milk myself."

Violet put her coat back on and went outdoors.

Olivia sped down the hallway, recovered the broom, entered Violet's bedroom (facing forward), and straightened the rug. Then she tossed the broom into her own bedroom and returned to the living room just as Violet came back in.

"Anything?" she asked.

"No. I told you it was too early."

"You can get the milk," said Olivia. "I couldn't reach it. And I'm sorry about spilling the cereal."

"I'll fix us some tea," said Violet. "Here, let me push you. Are you ever sweating! You must have fever."

During the next several days Olivia telephoned Byron and Pauline Roberts, who later invited Violet to supper one week from Saturday evening, without Olivia. Violet tried to beg off, but they would not be placated. They insisted she needed a break from her caretaking duties. They would be having fried chicken, and they suggested that Violet bring one of her special pies.

The following day, Olivia asked to be taken into Grange to have her hair done. While she was in the beauty parlor there, she sent Violet on an errand to Wal-Mart and wheeled across the street to the bank. She met with Louis Brinkle, who could remember when his father had handled the Brasso family loans.

Olivia took the deed to the house (bequeathed to the two sisters by their mother but placed in Olivia's name at the time of their father's death), out of her handbag.

"Should I assume this loan will be for a similar purpose as your last?—which I believe was, let's see, fifteen years ago, for porch and roof repair."

"You could make that assumption," said Olivia.

"Then I might at this time caution you, Miss Brasso, that the amount of the loan we discussed on the telephone is substantial in relation to the income of both you and your sister."

"Oh, I quite understand," said Olivia, "but there is no need to worry." She took out her recently updated savings book and passed it over.

"I see," he said, thumbing through the small pages with professional ease. "My sense of fair play now advises me to advise you that it would be better to withdraw the funds from this account and save several points of compounded interest. Why take out a mortgage when you have the needed assets in your savings account?"

"My savings account has sentimental value to me," explained Olivia. "My mother and father started it and I have never once made a withdrawal, as you can see."

"Very well. Then we may begin," said Louis. "How would you like the money?"

"In cash," said Olivia.

By the time Violet returned from Wal-Mart, Olivia was back at the beauty parlor, curls from her hair lying all over the floor.

Three days later she withdrew all the money from her savings account and put the entire amount—in one-hundred-dollar bills—into a plastic shopping bag along with the cash from the loan.

When Saturday arrived, Violet assumed Olivia would want to be left in her bed with the head cranked up to its semireclined position. This was customary, with all of Olivia's necessities—telephone, books, crafting supplies, television remote, and police scanner—in easy reach.

But tonight Olivia wished to remain in her wheelchair, fully dressed. "Someone may come," she said.

"That's not too likely," said Violet, who did not want to have to undress her when she came home. "It's been quite a spell since we've had unexpected visitors unexpectedly."

"Just the other day Pastor Winifred came over," said Olivia. "You can never tell."

"I still think you would be more comfortable—"

"You don't think anything of the kind," snapped Olivia. "Why don't you just say that it's too much trouble for you to get me ready for bed when you're tired?"

"Don't start that."

"If it weren't for me you could—"

"I won't listen to this, Olivia. I've heard it before—how you've ruined the lives of our whole family. If you want to stay in your regular clothes, that's fine."

When Violet put on her coat and opened the front door, Olivia was still dressed in her brown print dress and laced shoes, in her wheelchair before the television in the living room.

"I shouldn't be so very late," said Violet, looking back at her sister and marveling at how remarkably small she was. "The last time Byron showed slides, everyone fell asleep after the first wheel."

Violet closed the front door behind her, carrying a hot peach pie inside a covered pan.

Olivia picked up the telephone and a half-hour later the Countryside Taxi Service arrived. The driver, wearing a heavy gray scarf over an unzipped leather jacket, pounded his gloves together to keep his hands warm as he waited for Olivia to open the door.

"Please take these out to the car," she said, holding out her handbag and a plastic shopping bag, "and then return for me."

Olivia taped a note to the front door and he pushed her down the long ramp leading from the porch.

"Nice evening," remarked Olivia.

"Yeah," said the driver. "Will you require assistance getting in the car?"

"Yes," she said. "And I will also require assistance getting out of it."

Though he easily could have set her eighty-nine-pound body on the back seat, he nevertheless allowed her to guide his assistance so that she played the major part in making the transition. Then he folded her chair and put it in the trunk.

In no time at all, she was riding into the starry night. The interior of the cab smelled of cigarette smoke and other coarse, earthy odors, not unlike the inside of her uncle's old jacket in the hallway. From the back seat, the headlights seemed tightly focused, stretching way out in front of the hood like a tunnel through a forest.

SEEKING HELP

A MOVEMENT OUTSIDE CAUGHT JACOB'S ATTENTION AND HE cracked open the kitchen window to better listen. The moon, partly hidden by clouds, provided a murky light and the trunks of trees appeared black against the snow. A moving sliver of light winked out of the darkness, accompanied by low, unintelligible murmuring and the sound of breaking snow.

Stepping onto the back porch, Jacob watched seven men emerge from the timber on the hill. They wore hooded jackets with leather gloves and carried several wooden crates between them. Most were bearded—members of the militia.

"Hello, Jacob," said the first, turning off his flashlight.

"Hello."

"We brought a couple older M60's for you to check over." Four men came forward, setting the wooden crates heavily on the porch floor. "They're still packed in grease."

"I've been pretty busy lately, but I might have some time next week," said Jacob. "Hope you're not in a real hurry." He went inside and returned with the half-full bottle of bourbon. "Cold out here. Want a drink?"

His visitors, in heavy green jackets, sat on the open porch and passed the bottle and glass between them, their breath misting before their faces.

"Nice place you got, Jacob," said the leader, Moe Ridge, a large man with a graveled voice. "Private. A man can do what he wants here."

"That's the idea."

"I suppose you've heard about that killer cat—chewed up some cattle yesterday."

"I heard they were feral cattle."

"Cat's a killer. Some people put up a reward. No one's safe as long as it's around."

"Maybe not."

"We want a computer system at the camp, off-grid, satellite link— something like what you have here. Can you set it up"?

"I'll need to know how much you can afford to spend," said Jacob. "Also depends on what you want to do with it."

"We may not have much time, the way things are going in this country." He took a long drink and passed the bottle and glass to the man sitting next to him. "Damn government."

A sweeping arc of headlights moved through the trees in the east and the men stood up, drinking the last of the whiskey. Someone had turned off the road. In the distance several dogs barked.

"You've got visitors, Jacob," said Ridge, handing back the empty bottle and glass. "You should come to one of our meetings. Next Friday night some men from Iowa and Missouri are coming to talk about forming a national federation, an alliance. More and more men realize it won't be long before someone must take a stand for the principles this country was founded on. We're meeting in Snow Corners."

"I'll keep it in mind."

"Thanks for the drink."

"You're welcome."

Jacob watched as the men walked out of his snow-filled back yard and into the dark timber. When the sounds of the approaching ve- hicles grew louder, he stepped off the porch and walked out to greet two pairs of slow-moving headlights nodding and lurching along the winding, narrow lane through the snow.

July Montgomery climbed out of his white pickup and stood holding a grocery sack. Behind him parked a newer pickup with dual back wheels. A small man limped forward, not recognizable in the dim light.

"You know Rusty Smith," said July.

"Hello, Rusty."

"Yup."

"Hope you're not busy, Jacob. I brought some of that fancy coffee they sell at the health food store, doughnuts, and cigars. What's in these crates?"

"Nothing important," said Jacob. "Come inside."

The three sat by the stove, drinking the coffee.

"Rusty has a problem," said July. "He wants to find his brother and hasn't seen him in—how many years?"

"Sixty," said Rusty Smith, poking an unlit cigarette into his mouth, his face as wrinkled as a baked apple.

"I told him I knew someone with a computer who could probably find him on the Internet."

"I thought you had your own computer," said Jacob.

"That's what Rusty here thought, and I do, but I don't have Internet service—too much advertising."

"Go to the library," said Jacob. "Genealogy questions are routine."

"Nobody likes going into libraries," explained July.

Rusty took the cigarette out of his mouth and placed it behind his ear. "I'll pay you," he said.

"Librarians are trained—"

"I already told him you'd do it," said July.

"It might take a while. And I'll need as much information as you can give me."

"Give him your paper, Rusty."

Rusty took a folded piece of lined notepaper from his pocket and handed it to Jacob.

"Not much here," said Jacob, staring into the scribbled words. "Too many people have this last name."

"Do what you can," said July, passing the bag of doughnuts around.

"I'm going," said Rusty.

He went out and the sound of the truck in the snow faded.

July bit into a doughnut. "You don't seem quite like your usual self," he said.

"I'm not," said Jacob.

"How about a game of chess?"

"No thanks."

"What's this?" July asked, picking up the photograph album.

Jacob quickly leaned forward in his chair, as though to take it away from him, then sat back again. "What's it look like?" he said.

"This a picture of your wife?"

"Her name was Angela."

"Tell me about her."

"I'd rather not."

"Do it anyway."

Jacob lit one of July's cigars and talked about her.

THEODYSSEY

O LIVIA SAT IN THE BACK SEAT OF THE RURAL CAB AND TRIED
to relax. The driver seemed competent enough, despite an
alarming disposition to occasionally take his right hand completely
off the steering wheel and rest it along with his entire right arm on
the top of the front seat.

After about ten miles Olivia ceased worrying that she would be
identified by someone standing along the road or looking from a
window with binoculars.

The problem, as she understood it, lay in her limited experiences—
her confinement. There had been too few opportunities for God to
show favor to her. She had to be available, in a place for God to do
His Work.

It wasn't that God didn't love her. It was that she, Olivia, had
never put herself into a place where the myriad ways through which
God communicated favor could reach her. All her life she had waited
for God to seek her out, heal her body, and give her a new life. But
waiting for God's Grace to knock on her door hadn't worked, so
now she was going after Grace. She would follow her theodyssey
wherever it led.

It was, as Saint Augustine had so succinctly pointed out, a problem
inherent to time. In each successive moment, something brand-new
came into existence while something old died away, simultaneously.
Something from the past continued; something else perished. Christ
appointed those things He wished to continue, as well as those He
allowed to discontinue. To know if one had His Blessing, one needed
to place oneself at the cutting edge of time—to find a situation that
could not help signaling approval or disapproval, continuance or dis-
continuance. She needed to take a chance.

Failure, for Olivia, had gradually become inconceivable. To fail

would mean God did not maintain control, which simply could not
be true, and even if it was true—the abysmally small possibility that
everything right and good simply wasn't—then what did she have
to lose? The risk of failure could only be weighed in a universe of
meaningful value, but if God didn't exist and life had no value—if
time had no divine edge and things just happened willy-nilly—there
was nothing to risk.

The only real danger lay in giving doubt a fair hearing.

At the entrance to the Lake Delton Casino, the driver helped
Olivia into her wheelchair and she paid him with a single bill taken
from the plastic shopping bag.

"Wait," said the driver, coming back out of his cab and stopping
her just before she entered the building. "Let me take you back
home. I don't think this is a good idea to be here alone. I've seen this
before. Let me at least call someone."

"Get behind me, Satan," said Olivia and wheeled through the
automatic doors.

Inside, a large man in a very red jacket greeted her with a smile.
She rolled past him and sat for several minutes in the lobby, looking
into the great, pavilion-sized room.

She had anticipated the blinking colored lights and carpeting, but
the cleanliness surprised her. There were no smoke-filled rooms,
at least that she could see, nor half-shaven men in green sunglasses
hunched over tables served by lascivious women with much of their
legs exposed. They had a cafeteria, though, with cloth napkins.

People streamed in and out of the front doors. Some went straight
into the casino, others moved toward the cafeteria, restrooms, and
Indian gift shop. If anything, older people were in the majority, and
she saw several other people in wheelchairs.

Olivia assumed it would take some time to become oriented.
Gambling took many different forms and she was unfamiliar with
them all. Raised in a family that believed playing cards with faces had
been purposefully designed to undermine the plan of salvation, she
had gleaned what little she knew of gambling from television, which
of course never explained anything.

She found a glass panel on a wall with all the pertinent state laws and rules spelled out in detail. Pamphlets explained how the games worked. And there were the many friendly employees determined at every change of her direction to assist her.

She purchased a small bucket of quarters and parked herself before one of the gambling machines. The coins slid into the shiny, welcoming slot in a pleasing manner, and in a very short time the machine released several handfuls of quarters that rattled to the bottom, accompanied by electronic bells. The quarters in the bottom chute were too numerous to fit back into her bucket, so she did as she saw others doing and played them from where they were. Soon she had lost all of them and nearly her entire bucket as well, but then the machine let loose another internal rain of coins and she was back to almost where she had started.

She stretched and rubbed her neck. The nearby clock read nine-thirty.

It didn't seem possible. She had been playing for over an hour. Time had sped up. A woman with a black string tie and red jacket asked if she would like something to drink, but Olivia shook her head, gathered her quarters, and went deeper into the casino.

She found a roulette game, and after buying a hundred dollars worth of "chips," Olivia learned there were a variety of bets that could be made. Each bet—referred to as a "transaction"—was accomplished by putting a chip, or several chips, in different places on the table. All involved guessing in which slot a ball tossed onto the moving wheel of slots would end up. There were thirty-six numbered slots, eighteen red and eighteen black. There were also slots marked o and oo.

You could bet on the ball coming to rest on a certain number. If the ball came to rest there, you won thirty-six times whatever you bet. Or you could wager on the ball stopping on any red- or black-numbered slot. You could also bet on a number and a color, or a color and a group of numbers.

The mathematical probabilities, or odds, for each type of bet were clearly explained in the pamphlet. And though the print was fairly small, there was no further attempt to disguise the fact that the odds stood against the player. This seemed commendably honest, like the sheet of contraindications in a box of prescription drugs.

There was a commotion behind her. Bells rang and lights flashed. Several people hurried toward the noise and Olivia followed them. A woman about her own age stood next to a very large slot machine with tears streaming down her face. The machine accepted hundred-dollar tokens and the flashing on the blinking plastic window read $$$10,000$$$. The woman could hardly stand up, and several strangers came to her rescue. "Way to go," they said. "Congratulations."

"I did it," she said, shaking and sobbing. "I walked by this machine and I just knew. I knew. I just knew."

"You did it!" others said, hugging her, letting her cry into their clothes. "You did it. Good for you."

After the woman stopped crying momentarily, the people congratulating her went away. She took the winning token from the machine, carried it to the cashier's booth, and went to another slot machine with a bucket of quarters. Olivia followed her and watched as she played, intermittently sobbing and holding her hands against her face, then placing another coin in the slot.

Olivia returned to the roulette table and played for nearly an hour without significantly winning or losing anything.

She began to think about the numbers and the wagers. It occurred to her that a dollar could be bet on, say, the ball landing on a black slot. If you lost, you could double the amount of your bet. No matter how many times in a row you lost, as long as you kept doubling your bet, when you finally won—and you would have to win sometime—you would be ahead one dollar.

She tried it and after three spins won one dollar. In this way you could always be assured of going home a winner, so long as you continued playing long enough. You might not win much, but you would not lose.

Her next insight into gambling came with the realization that the numbers—themselves—were meaningless. She noticed that the players around her avoided betting on a particular number after that number had recently won. But this made no sense, she reasoned. The winning number would as likely repeat as not. If the number sixteen, for example, won five times in a row, the chance of its winning on the next spin remained as good as any other number. Similarly, if the number five had not been a winner for a long time, it should be no more likely to find the little white ball sitting in its slot after the next spin.

The problem was with people. When they were faced with decisions, they felt compelled to find reasons for making them. Numbers that corresponded to birth dates and other special occasions came to be thought of as "lucky." In addition, numbers were sometimes believed to have charm (threeness or twelveness, for example), when in fact they were empty mathematical symbols. Even more strangely, people sometimes felt they had a relationship with a certain number—a shared affinity, a mutual caring—which made pet ants seem sensible in comparison.

All of this seemed possible because people knew in their hearts that everything happened for some reason. About this they were right, thought Olivia. But they were wrong in assuming they could know the reason. Only God knew why things happened. He had set the universe in motion, hung the stars, and caused inert groupings of molecules to spring to life. The lonely, He comforted. Those who trusted Him, He never failed. And though He did not think for His favorite people, He could influence their choices if they paid close attention.

Olivia went to the cashier's booth, converted all her money to chips, and returned to the roulette table. She played with faith, and in less than fifteen minutes lost more than forty thousand dollars.

It didn't seem possible. She looked at the other players at the table. They met her eyes briefly and disappeared, not wanting to share in her bad luck.

Olivia backed away from the table and pushed herself slowly down the rows of slot machines to the lobby. She did not know what to do next. She had fallen through the basement floor of her life and now found herself in an utterly unknown place. She looked at the clock and realized Violet would be at home—back inside the house

Olivia had just lost to the bank. She looked through her handbag but didn't have a quarter to call.

She sat in the lobby until after midnight, waiting. She assumed they would make some provision for the ruined people left inside at closing time; but when she finally asked someone, she learned the casino stayed open twenty-four hours a day, seven days a week.

This also seemed impossible. How could any place stay open all the time? Yet in this new place where she found herself, anything and everything could happen. The supernatural safety net that had always protected her had been taken away, and she continued to sit in the lobby.

Over the next several hours, the shame, horror, and stupidity of what she had done became well documented in her mind. At two-fifteen she went outside, hung her purse around her neck, and began pushing herself through the parking lot toward the highway.

FEAR

WADE ARMBUSTER KEPT A CUSTOM AUTOMOBILE IN HIS FA-
ther's machine shed, under a gray car cover. Most of the
year it just sat there, surrounded by tractors, plows, rakes, forks,
skid steers, fans, and other machinery. He had provided his most
treasured possession with multiple layers of peerless green lacquer,
into which he could stare as though into a still pool of water, and an
interior of rich, oiled leather. With the hood open, the car smiled like
an extrovert with new braces. He considered it a work of art more
than a machine, though functioning was one of the requirements of
machine art.

Sometimes in the middle of night he would slip out of the trailer
beside his parents' house to the darkened shed and unwrap it, pulling the cover from the fenders as if he were pulling clothing from
rounded hips, heels, and shoulders. Then in the illumination of a
single bulb in the rafters, he stood back and gazed, sometimes for
hours. The interlaced shadows, curves, lines, and colors seemed in
some primitive language to reveal more about himself, about passion, about life, than he could fully explore.

He viewed it from different angles, never able to fathom the
whole, each new view a separate avenue of insight. The genius of
the black and orange flames on the front fenders—the perfection of
the frolicking waves conforming to the contours of the hood—held
a secret that promised to open soon.

On this cold winter night, Wade climbed inside and sat behind
the wheel, where a row of darkened gauges looked up at him, mute,
shiny, and spotless. He turned the ignition to On and listened to the
hum of the small electric motor in the trunk, pumping racing fuel
to the carburetors. He stepped on the accelerator twice and turned
the key. The massive engine groaned loudly, painfully again and

again, and then came howling to life, the sound reverberating from of the building's steel sides. A cloud of fuel-rich exhaust loomed up behind.

At every touch of the accelerator, the motor responded—as quick as a sliver. He turned on the parking lights to illuminate the little green bulbs in the housing of the gauges and surveyed the quivering needles that reported on conditions inside the engine. After assuring himself several times that all was well, he armed the nitrous oxide injectors and touched the toggle switch mounted on the gear shift lever. The engine coughed, spit, and filled the shed with an acrid mist. The nitrous tank was frozen. It was winter. He'd forgotten about that.

Wade revved the motor several more times to clear the ports and turned it off, climbed out, and shut the driver's door. He stepped back to admire the car from the rear and felt almost good enough to go back to bed. Everything seemed just right. Unlike much of the rest of his life, this part, right now, seemed in good order.

But then he noticed something he didn't like and drew his tattooed hand over his closely cropped hair. He spit on the concrete floor, rubbed his neck, and stepped several feet to the right, hoping to correct the impression.

There it was again, an angle of the car that did not look good. Plain, homely. He spit again and stepped back. He'd seen this before. It had always bothered him about the car and was part of the reason he'd bought another set of alloy wheels—to compensate for the sagging quality of the trunk. Something looked too heavy, bulging, old and fat, coarse and crude.

He closed his eyes and attempted to rid himself of the impression through a condemnation of it—as though some momentary spirit of ugliness had entered the shed from the outside, making his beloved the branch upon which the black witches jabbered.

It was the right car, he insisted, often pictured in magazines. It turned heads. He had consulted experts. Many of them. Last year he'd won prizes at car shows. People often looked at him with envy streaming from their faces.

But when he opened his eyes the evil twins were still there: banality and vulgarity.

He experienced fear. What if this was not the right car? What if he had overlooked a critical part of the vehicle's intrinsic nature—something that could never be lacquered over, sculpted away, softened by files, sandpaper, and polish, or offset by a view of the massive, chrome-plated differential? Was there something inherently wrong, subtle yet terribly flawed, that he had overlooked?

The only way now to prove to himself—to find out for sure—that he had the right car, was to drive it. He rolled aside the steel door on the front of the building and climbed behind the wheel. Driving at this time of night violated the narrow conditions of his parole, but he couldn't help himself. Once this kind of internalized fear appeared, it imposed restrictions on the choices he could make.

Fear, more than anything else, had to be listened to. It was the only true guiding principle. Without fear, life would be impossible. And when all the unneeded, superfluous thoughts and feelings were eliminated—the slate of experience wiped clean to the essence of sensation—there would be nothing left but fear. Guarding the palace of oblivion, it stood alone. Without fear, human life had no direction, a moth with one ragged wing.

The engine came instantly back to life and he drove through the opened door. Outside, the three-inch exit pipes did not seem quite so loud, and Wade attempted to creep through the farmyard without waking his parents—a hopeless ambition. Due to the pitch of the camshaft and the stall converter, slow speeds were difficult. The staggered lurching, surging, and gasping that so delighted those attending car shows, drag strips, and rallies now proved a liability. The engine died three times before he reached the road, and his parents' bedroom window on the second floor lit up like a warning light in the sky.

Once he was over the little hill to the north of the farm, he shifted into second gear, cracked the throttle, and felt the joyous thrust of acceleration pressing him back into the seat.

Turning onto the deserted state highway, he left twenty yards of parallel rubber stripes on the concrete before settling into a level hundred miles an hour. The night was clear, the engine now warm, and the heater began to circulate leather-softening air. All of the windows of the houses he drove past were darkened.

His sense of *rightness* returned. The steering felt tight, the motor and exhaust sounded just as they should, and the hood and fenders in front of him seemed perfect. Everything was in its proper place. He turned the radio on, loud, and drove several miles along the deserted highway.

As he approached town, a few cars began to appear—old guys in pickups and station wagons going home after the bars closed. He saw some younger people, two small guys in a rusted Honda, a long-haired, heavyset fellow pumping gas into a SUV.

At the traffic lights he turned right to avoid the police station and drove away from town toward Highway 87. He could cross over into Thistlewaite County and return home.

He felt bad about his parents. They would be worried. His mother probably waited for him in the trailer. His father—in the final throes of losing his farm—would interpret this as one more overwhelming failure that he could not prevent.

More cars appeared on the side streets, old guys.

Ahead on the left, the casino parking lot was only about a quarter filled. He could see a woman in a wheelchair pushing herself in front of a row of parked cars. Several rows away three young men climbed out of an old Camaro. Two were about his age. The driver, the biggest, was older, maybe thirty-five. They left the doors of the Camaro open. From the way they walked, Wade knew something was going to happen. Their breath froze in front of their faces, giving them an animal-like appearance.

They met the woman, and one of them grabbed the handbag around her neck and attempted to run away. But she refused to let go. In the struggle she was pulled from the chair onto the parking lot. But she still would not let go.

Wade did not think about what he would do. He did not feel a sense of duty, outrage, or anger. He did not feel anything. He simply turned into the parking lot and put his foot to the floor. His back tires burned a rubber arc toward the line of parked cars, coming to a stop fifteen or twenty feet from the youths and the little woman still holding onto her handbag.

Wade climbed from his car and looked at the older man. "I'd leave that woman alone if I were you."

"Would you," said the bigger man, walking toward Wade.

"I would," said Wade.

"Maybe you should mind your own business, motherfucker."

"Maybe not."

Wade had been in a number of fights during his twenty-eight years. The latest, begun outside a restaurant and ending up inside, resulted in a six-month parole. In all of his other fights—until the actual fighting started—he had been fearful. The possibility of being a coward had terrified him.

But now he was not afraid. He had actually been more fearful, in an overall sense, before he had seen the three get out of the Camaro. As soon as he pulled into the parking lot, all vestiges of fear vanished.

In short, he couldn't remember ever feeling so good. He wasn't worried about what he looked like, whether he belonged there, whether someone would think he looked like a hillbilly. He simply knew what to do.

The bigger man prepared to swing but Wade hit him first, knocking him momentarily off balance. It was a good punch and he knew he would win if he was given the opportunity to continue. Wade landed another solid blow, knocking the other man down, then stepped to the side and shouted at the man holding the purse, "Let go of that."

Then three things happened at once. A brick hit the side of Wade's head, the handbag was ripped from the woman's hands, and another car pulled into the parking lot. It sat a safe distance away, the headlights shining at them and the horn honking.

The three ran back to the Camaro, jumped inside with the handbag, and sped through the lot.

Wade ran to the small woman, lifted her from the pavement, ignored the overturned wheelchair, and hurried with her to his car.

Holding her in his right arm, he opened the passenger door and set her on the custom leather seat. Then he joined her inside. "Don't worry, Ma'am, we'll get it."

The two of them sped after the tiny red taillights half a mile down Highway 87.

REUNION

R USTY SMITH LIMPED INTO THE WORDS REPAIR SHOP ON WEDNES-
day afternoon, and Jacob handed him a manila envelope with
"Carl Smith" written on the outside.

"I'm afraid it isn't very good news," he said.

Rusty stared briefly at the envelope, shoved it underneath his
arm, and took out his billfold. "How much I owe you?"

"Nothing," said Jacob. "It didn't take long and, well, any friend of
July's is a friend of mine. But don't tell him that. He's not sentimental, if you know what I mean."

Rusty, who as far as sentimentality was concerned made July
Montgomery look like a Polish grandmother at Christmas, surveyed
the shop. "Is that for sale?" he asked, pointing at a red four-wheeler.

"No, that's in for repairs."

Rusty stepped inside the craft shop, walked down the aisles,
and bought three small quilts, each marked at twenty-two dollars.
"Don't give me any change," he told Clarice, handing her four twenty-
dollar bills.

At Eli Yoder's farm he pulled in the driveway, scattering chickens
and bringing the dog to full, vocal life. Rusty walked to the house
over the lumpy narrow path stamped into the snow and knocked on
the door. The large woman opened it.

"Here," he said, handing her the quilts.

"What's them for?" she asked.

"Them's for you," he said, and walked away.

In the basement of his farmhouse he sat on his milking stool, lit
a cigarette, and stared at the name of his brother on the envelope.
Then he tossed it on the floor beside him, finished the cigarette, and
lit another.

The stair door opened.

"Russell," called Maxine. "Russell, are you down there?"

"Yup."

"Are you smoking?"

"Not really."

"When you come up, bring your work clothes. I'm starting a load of laundry."

She closed the stair door and Rusty opened the envelope. The obituary inside had been copied from an Appleton newspaper. His brother died several months ago. Preceding him in death were his parents, Nona and Frank, and his two sisters, Nora and Elsie. He was survived by his one daughter, Winifred.

No mention was made of a brother.

There were more papers inside the envelope, but Rusty did not read them. He lit another cigarette and straightened his left leg, hoping to change the focus of pain in his knee and clear his mind of unwanted thoughts. Ten minutes later he gathered an armload of dirty clothes and climbed the stairs. Maxine opened the door and he carried them into the laundry room.

"I'm going out to the barn," he said.

He stopped at the dog pen, and the giant white terrier crossbreed came slowly out of her house and looked at him. "That's okay, old girl. You don't have to get up. Go back to sleep."

He continued to the barn. A bitter March wind knifed through his jacket and he stood for a while in the snow, listening to the cold. The horizon of trees drew a ragged edge against the milky sky, an uneven zipper. High overhead a pair of crows beat wings in rhythm, then one branched off to the east as the other continued north. Rusty resumed walking, making fresh tracks in the white, crusted surface.

The barn doors were frozen shut. He kicked one free and dragged it through the icy snow until a slot large enough for him opened up.

Inside, he put away several tools that were lying on the bench, hanging them in their proper places along the pegboard.

Don't make no difference, he thought. They're dead. Knowing it didn't change anything. Not one pale sliver of the real world had changed.

He walked deeper into the building, into the long room where the cows had been milked. The stale smell of cow hide and manure still lingered here. Stanchions rose out of the concrete in two skeletal rows. Iron sentinels. In the dim light the whitewashed walls turned gray, the massive oak beams in the ceiling outlined by long troughs of shadow.

The empty room magnified the silence, and the shuffling sound of his boots against the concrete dissolved into it. He sat on a plywood box next to a window and stared into the woods in back of the barn. Dark trunks like black marble pillars rose out of the snow.

He looked through the window for a long time, until the light faded from the afternoon and the inside of the barn had become as dark as a tomb. Dead, he thought. All dead and lying in the ground, and I'm the oldest. Doesn't seem right. A bottomless error.

The wind rattled the frame of the window.

Cold in here, he thought, lighting a cigarette and struggling to his feet.

Then he heard a sound and his heart stopped momentarily, sharpening his attention to a fine point. He dropped the glowing cigarette and squashed it. In the haymow above him something moved.

Walking in the loose hay.

Heavy.

Human heavy.

In his barn.

Hiding.

A faint sound, a groan.

Silence again.

Utter silence.

Rusty eased back onto the plywood box. He sat very still, looking from time to time at the ladder leading to the mow, which could hardly be seen in the darkness. Twenty minutes later as he rose again to leave, a loud clamoring, scrabbling sound came from the far end of the building.

More movement above in the hay.

Heavy walking.

Then nothing.

Rusty crept out of the barn, leaving the slot in the door open and following his own trail in the snow to the house. In the basement he loaded his rifle and shoved a flashlight into his jacket pocket. He ignored Maxine, who opened the stair door and announced that dinner would be ready in a short time.

Halfway to the barn, he stopped.

People desperate enough to be hiding in privately owned, unheated barns would probably be capable of some violence if they were threatened. Just what did he intend to do?—carry the rifle up the ladder, shine the flashlight around, and take aim? His knees would give out before he reached the top.

He went to the garage and drove away in the pickup.

Five miles later July Montgomery opened his front door and invited Rusty inside his small kitchen. Rusty refused.

"I need your help. Someone is in my barn. I heard 'em. I need you to climb up there and find out who it is."

"Sure, Rusty," said July, buttoning a long-sleeved cotton shirt around his undershirt. "Step in here while I get ready. I just finished milking and took a shower. Want a cup of coffee?"

"I'm in a hurry."

Rusty stepped just far enough into the kitchen to close the door behind him.

July sat at the oak table and pulled a pair of white socks and brown boots over his feet and a short time later followed Rusty home in his own pickup.

Maxine came out to greet them when they pulled in the drive, and Rusty told her to go back inside. "I've got something in the barn to show July."

Rusty took his rifle from behind the front seat and they walked together across the snow.

"You got any lights in there?" whispered July.

"Not in the mow."

"Maybe whoever you heard is gone now."

"Not likely. I don't think they know I heard 'em."

"Maybe we should turn on all the lights that work, make a lot of noise, and come back in an hour."

"I need to know who this is," said Rusty.

"Maybe it's someone you don't know."

"Then I want an introduction."

"Have they been taking things?"

"Maybe, I don't know."

"Perhaps you were mistaken about what you heard."

"I wasn't."

When they reached the barn their whispering grew even more guarded. They went to the ladder leading to the haymow and Rusty handed his rifle and flashlight to July. "Take these," he said.

"I'm not carrying a gun up there," said July, looking at the square hole in the ceiling with apprehension.

"Why not?"

"Probably shoot myself."

"I'd take the gun if I were you."

"Well, you're not," said July, accepting the flashlight.

He climbed up. Nearing the top, he announced in a loud voice, "Okay, I'm coming."

Rusty leaned against the wall, bolted a cartridge into the rifle's chamber, and watched as July crawled through the hole above him. He saw the flashlight turn on, pan out, and disappear. He heard July walking through the loose hay.

A short time later, July returned and climbed down, quickly.

"Let's get out of here."

"What do you mean?"

"We should leave."

"Why are you still whispering? What did you find?"

"You've got a cougar in your haymow, Rusty—a big one."

"What's he doing up there?"

"How do I know what it's doing there? But it wasn't too happy about having a light shined in its face."

"Here, take the rifle up and shoot it."

"I'm not going to do that."

Then they heard a sound above them, moving heavily in the hay toward the hole in the ceiling.

Rusty shouldered the rifle, aiming up the ladder.

"I've heard a cat is a hard thing to kill and a wounded one is

extremely dangerous," whispered July. "I think we should come back
in the daytime."

"What's that damn cat doing up there?"

When they left the barn, Rusty closed the front door, scraping it
across the snow. Walking back to the house, he said, "I never heard
of a cougar in a haymow."

"You don't use your barn much. It's a long way from the house
with timber right behind it. I guess if there was a first time for a
cougar in a haymow, it might as well be yours."

"Still don't make sense."

"Some things don't. You want me to come over in the morning?"

"No. I'll take care of this. You want some supper?"

"I'd better get home. I had some things I needed to do tonight.
Thanks anyway."

"What color was it?"

"Black. Why?"

"I just wondered. Look, let's say you don't tell anyone about this.
I mean, hell, don't tell anyone. There's been a lot of talk about a cat
and I don't want a bunch of people coming over here."

"I won't tell anyone."

"How much do I owe you for your time?"

"Forget it, Rusty," said July and drove home.

He put the rifle away in the basement and went upstairs. Maxine
waited for him. The manila envelope rested on the table before her,
its contents scattered on top.

"You want to talk about this, Russell?"

"No. I'm hungry."

"Where's July?"

"He went home."

"What were you doing in the barn?"

"Nothing important. What's for supper?"

At night, lying in bed, Rusty could tell that Maxine was not asleep,
her breathing short, quiet, and controlled. As though to confirm this,
she spoke:

"I know you don't want to talk about it, but I'm very sorry about
your brother and sisters, Russell."

"Yup."

"Winifred Smith is your niece. There's no mistake about it. You've got to talk to her. She has a right to know."

"Yup."

"You know who she is, don't you? She's the tall woman who—"

"I know who she is."

"You want to tell me now what is in the barn?"

"Nothing you need to worry about."

"Then I'm going out there first thing in the morning."

"No you're not."

DON'T GO THAT WAY

O LIVIA'S HEAD HURT AND HER MIND SPUN DIZZILY FROM HER defeated struggle to retain possession of her purse in the parking lot. The countryside came and went with such unconscionable rapidity that it was better not to look out the window. She stared wide-eyed at the stubble-headed young man who had grabbed her and crudely shoved her into his car. He sat behind the wheel staring madly into the windshield in front of him while she held onto the door and dashboard and was absolutely certain she would die. The sounds of the motor and radio alone were enough to kill a person. And what had the lunatic said before he'd abducted her?—something about not worrying? "Don't worry, Ma'am . . ." She assumed this was a bit of black humor, perhaps something tattooed kidnappers with blood and jewelry all over their faces often said to their hapless victims before they smashed their cars into steel girders going one hundred and seventy miles an hour in the middle of the night. Since she had so recently lost all of her and her sister's money in a casino and joined the world of the damned, she had not expected it to be inhabited. But apparently it was.

The little red taillights of the car ahead turned onto another road, and her driver tromped on the brakes—an action that almost planted Olivia inside the glove compartment.

"Better put on your seat belt, Ma'am."

More black humor, she assumed, and she gripped even tighter to the door and dashboard as the car skidded through the corner and resumed its bellowing, wrenching acceleration. The idea of strapping yourself inside seemed like closing the lid on your own coffin. At these speeds, when the end came there would be nothing left of the car or anything inside it but several wagons of rust dust. She considered praying, screaming, weeping, and pleading all at once,

but instead felt a more instinctive expression taking place as urine
flowed out of her as freely as freedom itself, through her dress and
onto the soft, clammy seats.

Everything inside the car seemed appropriately designed to resemble hell—black, red, and chrome—with some kind of jewelry
in the shape of a skull hanging from the rearview mirror. A little
demon with a red beard and oversized revolvers was mounted on
the gearshift.

The car ahead of them—much closer now—turned another corner, and once again her kidnapper went into a braking skid that required all her strength to keep from being thrown out of the seat.

More accelerating, tire screaming, and engine noise.

The car ahead turned again, this time down a snow-covered
gravel road, leaving a white cloud behind it. But this did not make
the slightest impression on her crazed kidnapper, who of course
drove into it without thinking about the inevitable consequences of
driving as fast as mechanically possible without the benefit of sight.

They continued like this for what seemed like a mile or more,
then faint red lights could be seen through the billowing snow as the
car ahead turned off the gravel road and onto another highway, with
her suicidal driver right behind it.

Soon they were so close to the car in front that Olivia was sure
they were going to hit it, and then, to her utter and complete astonishment, they did. The imbecile sitting next to her rammed right
into the car ahead, denting the trunk and busting out one of its
taillights.

A little further down the road there was a loud *crack* and a ragged
hole appeared in the upper middle of the windshield.

"Those bastards shot my car!" shouted her driver, rolling down
his window with a manual crank.

This statement provided vital information to Olivia. Combined
with the fact that her kidnapper had just rammed his car into the one
they'd been following, she felt pretty sure he was chasing them, and
not simply trying to keep up. Perhaps, despite dressing and looking
and talking alike, they were not all in this thieving and kidnapping
business together.

Then, while he was driving with one hand, and sometimes only a single finger, the young man beside her reached under the seat, withdrew a short, fat, thick gun with two enormous barrels, held it out the window, and fired twice. The sound was so incomprehensibly loud that Olivia had nothing to compare it to. It made the sounds of the engine and radio seem like the purring of kittens. It more resembled a solid blow to the head than a sound, and afterwards she could near nothing at all.

Ahead, the car's remaining taillight had been extinguished, and there was a trunk-sized hole in the back window. Through the ragged opening she could see the backs of three heads. One of them turned toward them and threw something that slid over the trunk and landed in the road. Her driver ran over it and stomped on his brakes.

This time she *was* thrown to the floor.

There, lying on a black rubber mat that smelled of something resembling furniture polish, she conducted a quick assessment of her new circumstances and felt surprisingly safe. The dashboard created a little roof over her head and the partially sequestered ambience seemed almost reassuring.

From her more secure home, she felt the car come to a stop. The madman next to her moved his long legs, opened his door, and ran into the night. Then she was alone for a while, and when he returned, he had her handbag.

"I got it, Ma'am," he said proudly, reaching down and lifting her back onto the seat next to the fat gun.

Olivia could not hear what he said because her head was still ringing from the shotgun blasts. But she recognized her handbag as well as a triumphant smile beaming from the driver's bejeweled face. And while she was looking through the hole in the windshield at a single star in the sky, she came to a clearer understanding of what had happened.

In the farmhouse down the road, a light came on, then two more. The front door opened and a man in pajamas stood in it. Much farther down the road, over the distant horizon, came two police cars with lights and sirens.

"Oh fuck," her driver said. His face turned white and she could feel his fear like a wind blowing. "Fuck," he said again. He buckled her into her seat, closed his door, turned around in the road with a shriek of tires, and roared off in the opposite direction. When they reached the gravel road, he turned down it, just as the police cars reached the house with the man in the doorway. One of the cars stopped. The other continued after them.

At least this time we can see, thought Olivia, as they hurtled down the gravel road and over a little bridge she hadn't noticed before. It occurred to her that perhaps the young man had taken this road in order to raise enough snow-dust to prevent his license plate from being read. It seemed unusually thoughtful for someone who was completely insane, and her estimation of him inched slightly upward in the animal kingdom. At the stop sign they turned right and she noticed his hands shaking. Again, she could feel his fear. After another mile he braked hard again and prepared to turn left.

Olivia's hearing was returning, and as sounds began to reach her again she noticed she no longer felt as though she would die immediately. Well, that wasn't quite true. She still felt certain of perishing into the afterlife at any minute, but for some reason she was becoming accustomed to the feeling. Sensing the fear of her driver had a mitigating effect on her own, as though only so much terror was allowed in any given enclosure.

"Wait!" she shouted. *"Don't go that way.* I have a scanner at home. They always catch people going that way. Go straight ahead and take a right, then take the next left. You can't outrun a police radio."

Her voice seemed authoritative for her size, and Wade obeyed it, continued to Highway H, turned right, and sped to Willow Creek Road.

"Turn here," commanded Olivia. "There are plenty of curves and hills on this road. It ends up on the ridge, where you can go three ways." Wade braked, and at the intersection Olivia rolled down the window and hurled the shotgun into the snow-filled ditch.

"Damn, what did you do that for?"

"You can get it later if you really need it."

They continued for several more miles, around corners and over hills, following the illumination of their one unbroken headlight.

"Turn into that drive up there," shouted Olivia.

"*What?*" shouted the frantic driver.

"Turn at the mailbox. Hurry. The Rasmussuns are on vacation. They left this morning. Park behind the garage, behind the house."

Panic oozed from every pore on his face as he turned into the plowed drive. Behind the house in the snow-filled yard, he turned off the engine, lights, and radio.

Suddenly they were sealed together in near-total darkness, surrounded in every direction by a silence as overwhelming as the earlier din of engine and thundering music.

Olivia could hear him breathing.

The sirens grew louder and louder and then flew past them toward the ridge roads.

"You can't walk?" he asked.

"Not a step."

"I guess you pretty much need that wheelchair."

"Pretty much," said Olivia.

"These people on vacation?"

"Yes, until next month. They went to the Holy Land on a trip sponsored by CUC—Christians United in Christ."

Outside they could hear more sirens, and as they continued listening three more mechanical insects flew past the house. Fifteen minutes later two more passed, one from each direction, moving slowly, with searchlights stretching into the countryside like probing yellow tentacles. Both continued without stopping.

"If they catch me I'll go to prison," said Wade.

"No you won't," said Olivia. "You can tell them what happened."

"It wouldn't matter what the fuck I said. I've been in trouble before. I'm on parole."

"I see," said Olivia. "Well, as long as we're making confessions, I'm afraid I've peed on your car seat."

Wade laughed—a sound that in some ways troubled Olivia more than anything else so far. "Hell, that doesn't matter," he said. "But we'd better get you into some dry clothes. My grandmother had trouble with that like you can't fucking believe. I took care of her for three years."

Wade reached for the ignition to start the car.

"Don't do that!" shouted Olivia. "They'll catch you for sure if you leave now. With shots fired there's no telling when they'll give up. You have a hole in your windshield. And that man at the house probably got a look at your car."

"Can't just stay the fuck here. If I don't show up at seven o'clock at the cheese plant they'll call my goddamn parole officer. And we got to get you some dry clothes. Folks are probably looking for you."

"That doesn't matter," said Olivia.

"We can't just sit the fuck here. Look, I know someone two or three miles down the road. I'll run over there and be back as soon as I can with his truck."

"That won't work!" shouted Olivia, frightened by the idea of being left alone. "All these families along here have dogs. We'll borrow the Rasmussuns' car. The Mitchell family drove them to the airport. I'm sure they won't mind. It's in the garage."

"How are we going to start it?"

"The keys are probably in it. They wouldn't have taken them to the Holy Land."

"Are you sure you know these fucking people?"

"You can trust me."

"I have no choice."

"True, you don't, and thank you for not using that f-word."

Wade was gone for what seemed to Olivia a long time—enough for her to wonder if he had decided on his foolish plan of walking to an acquaintance's house. When he returned he crawled in beside her and said, "The garage is locked."

"I guess you'll have to break a window," said Olivia.

"I'm not breaking a window."

"Then carry me over and I'll break the window."

"I won't do that either."

Then a light came on inside the house and a silhouette stood in the window, a telephone pressed to one side of its head.

They left hurriedly.

"I thought you said there was no one home," said Wade, accelerating at open throttle down the blacktop.

"It looked like Florence Fitch. It would be just like her to stay in someone's house when they were gone, snooping around under the pretense of looking after the place."

"Oh fuck, there's no way out of here," he cried as the end of the dead-end road loomed ahead.

"Quick," said Olivia. "Stop swearing and turn in here."

"Where?"

"In the driveway."

"Who lives here?"

"Who cares—it goes back into the woods. Hurry, the police lights are on the ridge."

Wade turned into the lane running between the trees.

At the end of a very long and curved driveway, he pulled up next to an odd-shaped log house. Still in a panic, he looked out the window, surveying the windows lit from an inside light. Then he saw someone standing on the back porch holding a machine gun, and cried, "Get down."

Wade threw his body like sack of potatoes over Olivia.

She lay there for an unthinkably long while, half on and half off the seat, his weight pressing against her in a warm, heavy, and unfamiliar way. Finally she decided there could be no reasonable explanation for why they were doing this and she said, "Get off me, you big lug."

When Wade sat up again the man on the back porch had left the machine gun on the porch floor and was now standing next to the car.

"What are you doing here?" he asked, looking inside. "Oh, hello, Olivia."

"I'm not Olivia," said Olivia, trying to look like someone other than herself by frowning and smiling at the same time.

"Of course you are," said Jacob.

"If she says she isn't, she isn't," said Wade, who didn't know who she was.

"Is that the motor from July Montgomery's toolshed last summer?" asked Jacob, listening to the idling engine.

"Yup," said Wade proudly.

"Aspirated engines have a distinctive sound," said Jacob.

Sirens were descending from the ridge.

Wade gripped the steering wheel to keep his hands from shaking. "Fuck," he said.

Jacob noticed the smeared blood from Wade's face on Olivia's blouse. "What's going on here?" he asked.

"Pay attention," said Olivia to Jacob. "We need you to understand a whole lot of things in a whole little time. First, we're completely innocent. Second, those police cars don't know that we are innocent. Third, this will likely be one of the places they suspect that people who they think aren't innocent but are in fact innocent might be hiding. We need your help. Please."

Jacob listened to the sirens, then ran to the garage beside the log house, backed his jeep out, and drove down the drive. Halfway to the road, in the narrowest part of the lane, he turned the motor off, climbed out, and lifted the hood.

Several minutes later a patrol car turned off the road and followed the drive as far as the jeep. A policeman climbed out, his searchlight fastened on Jacob.

"This your place?"

"Yes."

"Live here alone?"

"Yes again."

"What's your name?"

"Jacob Helm."

"Having trouble?"

"Battery keeps shorting out."

"Kind of late to be working on it."

"I need to get to work in a couple hours."

"We're looking for a fancy car, green or light blue, loud motor. You see anyone tonight? Anyone come by here?"

"Sorry, no," said Jacob. "Say, can you use your government radio to call someone for me?—I mean the one in your car. I'd sure appreciate it."

"Call who?"

"My cousin in Grange. I've got the number here."

"Why? Is this an emergency?"

"I need to get this jeep running. Here's the number. If an old woman answers, don't talk to her, just ask to speak to Frank. If a man answers it will probably be Frank, and if it is Frank, ask him for Lenny. When Lenny comes to the phone, tell him Jacob, that's me, wants the battery—the one the old woman has stored in the back of the shop next to the tarp and paint—the one with the side terminals, not the other one. He'll know which. And tell him to—"

"Sir, I haven't got time for this. You can walk back to your house and use your own phone. You have one, don't you?"

"Of course I do."

The patrol car backed along the drive to a place wide enough to turn around, then returned to the road.

Wade parked his car next to the log house, and Jacob offered to help carry Olivia. "I've got her," said Wade, and placed her on the front seat of Jacob's jeep.

"I'll bring it back before daylight," Wade said.

"I'm not going anywhere today," said Jacob. "Bring it back in the evening. And you better order a new windshield for your car, and a headlight."

After Wade and Olivia were back on the highway, they met a squad car, then another.

"Should we pick up the sawed-off?" asked Wade.

"Not on your life."

On Highway 87 they stopped at a roadblock.

"We're looking for a green or light blue car," said the patrolman, pointing his flashlight in the jeep's open window, past Wade and straight into Olivia's face. "Wonder if you folks have seen or heard anything."

"Nothing dangerous, I hope," said Olivia, touching her face with both hands and opening her mouth into an oval shape.

"Dangerous enough, lady. Keep your eyes and ears open. Let us know if you see something."

"We will, officer," said Olivia.

He waved them on.

"It's a good thing he didn't look at the other side of your face," said Olivia. "Your eye is almost swelled shut. He would have wondered about that."

In the casino parking lot, Wade put Olivia's wheelchair in the back of the jeep.

They drove through town.

Wade asked if she would like something to drink.

"I've had quite enough fluids passing through me, thank you."

"How about something to eat?"

"I don't have any money. I lost everything at the casino."

"I have money," said Wade.

"I guess that would be all right."

"What would you like?"

"I don't know," said Olivia. No one outside her family had ever asked her what she wanted to eat, and the astounding novelty of this seemingly ordinary question had a strange attraction. "How about a sandwich?"

"Damn good choice," said Wade. He pulled into a convenience store and rushed inside. When he returned he had two refrigerated turkey sandwiches, with lettuce and tomato, in shrink-wrap, and potato chips. They ate in the parking lot and continued eating as they drove toward Olivia's home in Words.

"My name is Wade."

"I'm Olivia."

Several miles passed.

"Excuse me, Ma'am, but I really want to thank you. I mean I don't think we'd be here without, well, you. I mean I don't think I'd be here. You're real smart. And, well, this might sound stupid, and it probably is, but this has really been a good night for me. I feel very good about tonight. Very good."

"Remember to take good care of this car," said Olivia. "Nothing can happen to it, do you understand? Nothing. Not a scratch or a dent or a blemish of any kind."

"I understand, but it's already kind of beat up."

"There's my house—the one with all the lights on."

"You know," said Wade, pulling over and stopping momentarily, "I'd like to, I mean, damn, Ma'am, I would like to see you again, if you'd consider it. You're really cute. Would it be all right for us to go out together?"

At first Olivia wondered how the eye closest to her could see anything at all. Then she smiled and tried to think while the undiluted meaning of what had just been said began dissolving all her rational thoughts. She fought against his words and what they were doing to her, gave up and felt alive, good, and important. Her lungs, she noticed, were breathing in more air than usual. "What exactly did you have in mind?"

"I don't know. What would *you* like to do?"

"I don't do much of anything, I'm afraid," said Olivia. "My life is one of almost complete inertia."

"Then maybe you could come with me to a dogfight."

"A what?"

"I went to a couple and they're very, well, they're just very damn cool. They train these dogs to fight. They're special, fighting dogs. You bet on which ones will win. The owners and breeders meet in barns and other places—never the same place. I mean it teaches you something about human nature."

"You mean it teaches you what human nature *could be.*"

"Yeah, something like that, but I'd really like it if you'd go with me. I never have anyone to go places with."

"That settles it," said Olivia. "We'll go together."

He parked in front of her house. Fourteen people and three cats came onto the porch and watched as Olivia and the youth in the jeep finished eating the potato chips in the bag. Then Wade took the wheelchair out of the back, set Olivia in it, and pushed her up the ramp.

"This is my new friend," she said. "Tell them your name."

"Wade Armbuster. Glad to meet you."

The crowd parted and Wade pushed her inside. Then he came back outside, climbed into the jeep that looked just like the one belonging to the owner of the Words Repair Shop, and drove away.

Olivia rolled into her bedroom.

After Violet had sent all her neighbors and friends away and called the police to tell them that her missing sister had been found, she followed her.

"What's going on here, Olivia?" she demanded. "We've been worried sick about you, just sick we've been worried."

"I'm afraid I've had a little accident," said Olivia. "I need a bath and some clean clothes."

"Land sakes, your dress is soaked! Where have you been? It's four-thirty in the morning!"

"It's a long story, and not an entirely pleasant one. You should prepare yourself, Vio. I'm afraid we're homeless."

MEASURING UP

F INDING HIS CHILDREN IN THE SNOW HAD A PROFOUND EFFECT
on Grahm Shotwell. Closed ski runs opened in his mind, and
down them rushed convivial thoughts, eager to evaluate his circumstances. They insisted that something new and significant had occurred the moment he let go of the rope and followed Cora into the
blinding snow. He had taken a leap of faith, with a giant emphasis
on the leaping part, because when the rope fell from his hands, he
remembered with perfect clarity, he had had faith in nothing. He had
simply stepped forward.

Yet that decision, lacking assurances and convictions of any kind,
had been cause for the most important action of his life. The fact
that his children were now alive seemed too big to contemplate. And
even if he and Cora had failed, the ineluctable principle upon which
they had acted would have remained unblemished. The still, small
voice had to be obeyed, even when it was so small and still as to be
unintelligible.

The implications of this seemed both monumental and vague,
and his brain—on fire—sought to understand what had happened
to him. It could mean that some unknowable Spirit ruled the world
and directed his actions, or perhaps that he had simply been lucky.
Or it could mean that when he was confronted with life-threatening
situations he should cast reason aside and depend on his unassisted
instincts. Or that the deep connection between him and his wife
and children in some way determined how things turned out. Or it
meant that the avoidance motive—fear—should be ignored in all-
important matters.

The Room of Vital Wisdom may be empty, he thought, but that
should not prevent us from going inside.

Weeks later, Grahm still remained exhilarated, as if he had come downstairs in the middle of the night and found the game of life arranged like chess pieces on the kitchen table, with his color enjoying a clear advantage.

Nothing seemed impossible now.

He would prove to himself and to anyone else paying close attention that he was worthy of Cora, whose unwavering courage had allowed her to step into the blizzard without a safety line first. Compared to hers, his role had been that of a mere disciple, a follower. Something was needed—some action to show that they could stand side by side.

He found July Montgomery in the field behind his house, forking manure out of his New Holland spreader in the middle of the afternoon.

"Chain break?" he asked.

"Frozen apron. It always happens when they're full," said July, breathing heavily.

"Here, let me help. Your age is showing."

"You must want something," said July.

"I do," said Grahm, taking the pronged implement and jabbing it into the remaining manure and straw in the spreader, lifting it onto the steaming pile on the ground. "I want you to come with me to American Milk's annual meeting."

"I thought you were organic now and weren't shipping to them."

"I'm not. That's why I need you to go with me—so I can get into the meeting. And I think you know more about these things than I do."

"What things?"

"Annual meetings."

"Does this have something to do with the letter you wrote to the newspaper a while ago?"

"I guess it does, but my wife wrote it."

"You won't be listened to," said July. "Nothing controversial gets into annual meetings. Co-op employees and dignitaries outnumber farmers four to one. Everyone dresses up. They turn up the heat and serve a heavy meal—with alcohol—so everyone is half asleep before the meeting begins. All the real business is done in executive sessions.

Even the financial report, if there is one, is not discussed. There'll be over five hundred people inside the building and the farmers who come will mostly be those sitting on the board, or who used to sit on the board, or are related to board people—old gents who own farms but never get their own hands dirty. The rest come for the food. It's like any large corporation—the big boys know if they can't control the annual meeting, they can't control the company. Their lawyers set the rules accordingly. It's worked for thousands of years: those with power keep it."

"I have a copy of the bylaws and it says every annual meeting must have a time open to the membership. It's in the charter."

"Of course it says that, but it doesn't work that way."

"Will you go with me?"

"It's a bad idea. You won't be listened to. Spring will be here soon and there's a lot of work ahead. It's a long ways up there."

"Please. I can't go alone."

"Yes, I'll go. Now give me back that fork," said July. "You're doing it the wrong way."

"Thanks," said Grahm and turned around to walk away.

"Wait," said July. "Do you remember a long time ago—when you were very young, maybe twelve or thirteen—you were clearing brush on the piece of ground your father bought. Do you remember? You were hardly big enough to lift the chain saw and were cutting sumac along the road. It was getting dark and you had almost half an acre of stalks lying on the ground."

"I remember you stopped," said Grahm. "I'd never seen you before. We stacked up the dead wood and made a fire."

"Yes. And the sparks rose into the sky like nothing either of us had ever seen before."

"I remember," said Grahm.

"I just wondered if you did," said July.

THE MEANING OF TRUTH

T HURSDAY AFTERNOON AT THE CASINO, BRIAN LEASTHORSE CAR-
ried a briefcase of invoices into his office and set it next to the
computer. He took off his jacket, loosened his tie, unbuttoned his
cuffs, sipped from a half-empty cup of coffee, and looked out the
window at the construction site at the other end of the parking lot.
He added the last of the coffee from the smudged glass pot, hoping
to raise the combined liquid temperature to an acceptable level. He
took another sip, thought about making a fresh pot, and resigned
himself to the lukewarm, bitter beverage. With a last look at the
clock on the wall, he sat at the computer, opened the briefcase, and
began entering numbers into a spreadsheet.

As he began to flow into his work, successfully ignoring the reality of three or four hours before he could go home, the telephone
rang. It was Security. Someone wanted to see "the manager."

"Call Personnel," said Brian.

"They don't answer. Clarence says they're at a convention or a
seminar or something."

"Get Stover."

"Stover's in the Cities with the Cartbuckle lawyers."

"I don't have time for this."

"Somebody's got to talk to her. She's making a lot of noise."

"Where's Shirley?"

"Shirley didn't come in today."

"Fine. Send her up."

Brian took a long, terrible drink of coffee. He stood up, stretched
to relieve the pain in his lower back, put on his jacket, and passed his
hands lightly over his glossy black hair. He didn't like dealing with
customers. Well, that wasn't exactly true. Years ago, when he worked

in Security—his first position with the casino—he'd enjoyed it. Back then, hours had passed with loitering, amiable ease.

Through his office door he saw a woman step out of the elevator at the end of the hall. She looked ordinary enough—thirties, as slender as a heron with a bright yellow blouse and dark, nearly floor-length skirt, perhaps wool. A column of autumn brown hair, very long and very straight, fell behind her shoulders, even lower than the handbag hanging from her right shoulder.

After leaving the elevator she hesitated, took several steps, and steadied herself by momentarily touching the wall. Then she assumed a new posture. Her neck and head rose out of her yellow collar perfectly erect. She straightened her shoulders, drew her arms to her sides, turned, and marched toward him with an almost militant resolve, her long skirt flapping around her thin legs.

Her physical features were soon eclipsed by her expression, as though she was possessed by a single grand idea. Her face had "that look," and without knocking she walked through the doorway and stood before his desk.

"Can I help you?"

"That is my sincere hope."

"I'm Brian Leasthorse," he said. "Would you like a chair?"

"No thank you," said Winnie.

"How can I help you?"

"By returning the money one of my people lost here a short time ago—all of it, please."

"'My people?'" said Brian, smiling broadly.

"My people," repeated Winnie, her narrow, freckled face glowing with purpose, "are the people in my church. I'm the pastor of the Words Friends of Jesus Church, forty-five minutes west of here. One of my ladies, Olivia—she lives with her sister, Violet, in a house inherited from their parents—was here in a wheelchair. Violet is a widow and Olivia a spinster and lifelong invalid. Violet is in her sixties, if not older—I don't know for sure because it seems impolite to ask. Olivia came here last Saturday night—in a taxi, as near as we can tell—with more than forty thousand dollars. She lost every

penny. That money was all she and her sister had. I assume you have
a refund policy."

"Refund policy?"

"Yes, a provision for giving the money back."

"I'm afraid we don't have a policy like that," said Brian, shaking his
head solemnly and looking straight into her eyes. "But I can certainly
commiserate with your situation. I'm sure those ladies are nearly
inconsolable. It must be very difficult in your position."

"This isn't about me," said Winnie, who stared back without blinking, and Brian looked away. "This is about something that should not
have happened—an *evil* that can now be corrected."

Brian was astonished at the impression the word made upon him.
It seemed so raw and distasteful. Evil? "Are you sure you wouldn't
like to sit down?" he asked. "I know the area you live in. It's beautiful
there. For three or four years I've had my eye on a particular piece
of wooded land that I'd like to own around there. Why don't you
sit down?"

She shook her head and her long hair responded in waves.

"Would you care for a cup of coffee in the cafeteria?"

"I never drink coffee," said Winnie, "and I would never eat or drink
anything inside a gambling establishment."

"I see."

"Are you really the person in charge?" asked Winnie.

"I am today."

"It's hard to believe you don't have a refund policy."

"This isn't a clothing store, Miss—?"

"My name is Pastor Smith. Perhaps I haven't explained the situation well enough. See, Violet has taken care of Olivia for over ten
years. They have nothing but Violet's Social Security and what little
money Olivia saved through the years from family gifts. They own
about a dozen dresses, wear sweaters through the winter to save
heat, and drive back and forth to the grocery store in a twenty-year-
old automobile. Olivia, who hardly ever leaves her house, took out
a mortgage, withdrew all her money from her savings account—in
cash—and came here while her sister was visiting a neighbor."

"I don't see what this has to do with anything."

"Are you listening to me?" asked Winnie. Her voice did not rise, but grew more intense. "I'm telling you the truth. Olivia took all their money, including a substantial loan, and brought it here in the middle of the night. She lost it all at your gambling tables."

She pulled papers from her handbag. "Violet got these from the bank. See here—this is the exact amount. I've circled it. It's proof."

Brian ignored the papers. "I do wish you'd sit down, Pastor," he said.

"I prefer not to," said Winnie.

"This is a business," said Brian with a nearly imperceptible sigh. "We run a business here."

"A gambling business," said Winnie.

"These books—" Brian motioned toward a shelf of hardbound volumes and loose-leaf binders. "These are the laws of Wisconsin as they pertain to our business. They regulate everything we do. We can't turn on a light switch without the approval of the governor, the Wisconsin Senate, and the Board of Indian Affairs. We pay a gaming fee, pay federal, state, and local taxes, and employ over a thousand people who pay federal, state, and local taxes. Inspectors and auditors visit us routinely and we are, in addition, accountable to the tribe that owns all our assets. This is a business like any other."

"You may be a business," said Winnie. "But you are certainly not a business like any other. What is your product?"

"Entertainment," he said with weary courtesy. "For the glad chance of winning money, people spend money. It's good entertainment."

"It may be entertainment," said Winnie, "but not good entertainment."

"To each her own," said Brian.

"I'm afraid I'm not making myself clear," said Winnie. "*A crippled woman* came here in a *wheelchair* around eight o'clock several Saturday nights ago and *lost forty thousand dollars*. That money was *all she and her sister had*. She was not one of your 'high rollers,' had never gambled in her life, did not have anyone to advise her, and did not even have a ride home. I do not think she was *entertained*, and in six or seven months she and her sister will have *nowhere to live*. All this is the *absolute truth*."

"I do not doubt your sincerity," said Brian.

"Then give their money back."

"I can't do that. It's not as though we have a room full of cash here. Our revenues pay the salaries of our employees, and the electricity, heat, and insurance; they pay for the hotel currently under construction and all the people working for the contractors. We have investors who trust us with their investments. The tribe has schools, clinics, and dozens of community programs that directly depend on this casino. And the circumstances of many reservation families are far worse, I might add, *far worse* than the circumstances of the women about whom you speak. I do not have the authority to refund money. No one does. Taking money from the casino would be against the law."

"God's law is the only important law," said Winnie.

"God's law is unfortunately not recognized by the Wisconsin Gaming and Licensing Commission," said Brian.

"You're not hearing what I say," said Winnie, her face still possessing the look of righteous certitude. "These sisters are—"

"Stop," said Brian. "It won't do any good for me to hear that again. We have reached an impasse. You think if I understand something specific and personal about these women that it will make some difference. But it doesn't and it won't. We can't detain everyone who walks through the front doors and ask if they can afford to come in, and we certainly can't turn handicapped people away. Would you have us stop customers in the parking lot and accuse them of gambling with money they cannot afford to lose?"

"But it was a *mistake*," said Winnie. "Your reservation families may indeed be living in regrettable circumstances and no doubt injustices were committed that contributed to that, but it's never right to victimize one person in order to make up for another's prior victimization. As decent people we are responsible for only those misfortunes we have influence over, and you have influence over this one. It was a tragic mistake and you can correct it."

"People are free to make mistakes with their money. It was no

more a mistake than if this woman had paid forty thousand dollars
to attend a fund-raising dinner at the Democratic headquarters."

"I'm sure *they* have a refund policy."

"I'm afraid you are very, very naive—and I don't mean that in a
negative way," said Brian.

"What I'm saying is quite simple," said Winnie. "It is *wrong* for
you to keep these ladies' money. I know it's wrong and you know it's
wrong. I'm asking you to give it back."

"Try to see this from our point of view, Miss—."

"Pastor Smith, and don't say 'our' when it's really you."

"Pastor Smith, there is no difference between this and your friend
purchasing forty thousand dollars worth of stock just before its value
falls."

"This wasn't an investment and it wasn't a rational decision," said
Winnie. "It was a *mistake.*"

"If your friend had won forty thousand dollars I doubt you would
be here today attempting to give it back."

"Then you don't know me, because I would be here in that case
as well, if I knew anything about it. You simply don't understand. I'm
telling you the truth but you can't accept it."

"It's not the truth we disagree about," said Brian. "It's the meaning of it."

"The truth only has one meaning," said Winnie. "It commands us
to act charitably toward each other."

"It's curious how this truth only moves in one way," said Brian,
for the first time breaking his formal manner. "There was no similar
truth when *your people* were moving here from Europe, slaughtering
my people, taking the land for yourselves. Apparently no compassion-
ate truths applied then. But as soon as one of your more vulnerable
citizens walks into an Indian casino, the truth comes jumping out."

"Violet and Olivia had nothing to do with the many crimes against
Indian people, present or past."

"They have certainly benefited from those crimes."

"Should the sins of the fathers be suffered by the daughters to all
generations?"

"No, but neither should those sins be dismissed. Like it or not,

Pastor Smith, we live in a collective society. The treaties and compacts that allow for some Indian nations to operate casinos and lower your taxes are like any other laws: they are based on general principles. They allow for certain public behaviors—in this case gambling—in the belief that it will, on average, benefit society. In some individual cases the permitted behavior may be detrimental; that is unfortunate, but it cannot be avoided if the general benefit is to continue.

"It's the same with speed limits on highways. The overall benefit of higher speed limits is offset by the death of some individuals who might have lived at slower speeds. A person whose friends have died on the interstate can lobby to have speed limits reduced, but she cannot complain that some injustice has taken place—because at the time the law was enacted it was assumed that there would be, regrettably, more deaths due to higher speed limits."

"I'm afraid your analogy has snared your feet," said Winnie. "If my friends were to die while driving on an interstate highway I could not complain of an injustice, but if it were in the power of the highway department to restore them to life, they would. They don't have that power, but you do. You can correct an instance of two individuals falling through the cracks in the general benefit."

"I've told you I can't do that. It's as impossible for me as for the highway department to restore life."

"Anyone can plainly see why the highway department cannot restore life, but no one, except you, can see why Olivia's money cannot be refunded."

"It's not in my power."

"Of course it is. If you were so inclined, you could easily write out a check for $43,241.53. You could do it. It would be in your power. It's only the goodwill you lack."

"A moot point."

"Well, I hoped to not have to go into this, but you have forced me," said Winnie, taking a deep breath and standing even straighter. "All right, I'll tell you everything. Last fall I had a vision, an epiphany, and I saw God, or She saw me—however you wish to say it."

Winnie became more animated as she talked, her arms and hands moving. "I should not have done it, but I had no one else to tell. So

I told Olivia and, well, I guess you can imagine what an impression it made upon her—she being an invalid. Anyway, she thought she would give God a chance to bless her through a monetary sign."

Brian sat down in the chair across the desk and put his head in his hands.

"So you see, it was really my fault this all happened. I sinned through my blindness to the effect I was having on another person. You have no idea how deeply I regret it. I should have known better, but now at least you can see what happened. Olivia felt unloved and she acted out of ignorance. The devil made her think God hated her, and to prove this was not true she came here."

"'The devil'?" said Brian without looking up.

"Call it whatever you like—the dark psychological agency that makes us think the worst of ourselves and others. I don't care if you prefer another word. Words mean nothing to me, absolutely nothing. She came here not to win your money, but to find God's love. It was a theodyssey. So, in actuality, she wasn't seeking entertainment, as you say, but looking for God in the wrong way and in the wrong place. It was a mistake—one in which you are not in any way to blame, except that you temporarily ended up with the money that had been provided for Olivia and Violet to live on."

Due to her impassioned talk, her hair had become mussed. To correct it, she shook her head and the straight brown locks re-arranged themselves again, falling like water behind her shoulders. And as she turned, he could see that her hair fell far below her waist. Her eyes darkened and the glow that had earlier projected from her face virtually beamed into the room.

"So, now you have all the facts," she said and smiled for the first time, her white teeth gleaming.

Brian stared up at her and tried to ignore his mounting sexual desire. The look of triumphant dignity on her face—God, how appealing! Her advocacy for her church members colored every expression in a tenderness that should not—in the best of worlds—have conveyed a sensual content, but it did. She actually believed her intimate narrative would convince him, and this was so extraordinarily endearing he felt himself becoming aroused. She seemed so childlike, and though the qualities of children—in women—were supposed to be indefinitely detoured from the paths leading to the house of adult—male—carnal pleasure, they nevertheless connected in the bright intersection of her smile.

His imagination began to suggest several wonderfully improbable vignettes of the immediate future and what her neck might flow into beneath her collar, how her hair might feel to touch, which he struggled to push out of his mind, but not without an audible groan of remorse. Why, he wondered, do we minute by minute create a world in which the things we most spontaneously desire are forbidden? Why do we continually create places celebrating the values we most despise, where a man will type numbers into a computer all afternoon—without questioning—and defend his company's right to keep the money of a cripple to a woman he longs to love?

"I don't know where to begin," said Brian. "Won't you please have a chair?"

"No thank you."

"In the first place, laws hold our society together. They are the organizing principles. Personal possessions are everything—the essence of what we are—and it is *our money now*. When the money belonged to your friend, she had the laws on her side. But a legal contract was made—admittedly a high-risk contract, but a contract nevertheless—and the money passed into our hands. It is our money. The arguments you keep making are not legal arguments, and legal arguments are all that matter."

"To the contrary," said Winnie. "We can never fully place our trust in the law. You know it in your heart. The law always kills. As human beings we have the obligation to transcend law through mercy. If we all had to live by the law, we would all be condemned— all of us. It is only by showing compassion and mercy that we create a better world."

"This world is the best it can be."

"It isn't. I know it. It could be so much better."

"This is my job."

"But it's *not right*," said Winnie, and her smile dissolved. Also, the

light that had been shining from her face faded as she understood—
with a sense of personal violation—that even after she had revealed
the whole inner truth, her petition was going to be denied. She felt
diminished.

Brian, seeing her light dimming, felt his sexual interest replaced
with a growing emptiness. And as the emptiness grew, he became
angry.

"I would personally like to be able to give the money back," he
explained. "But I can't."

"Oh, you can," said Winnie. "But you won't."

Brian realized the words taking shape just beneath his tongue
were something like, *If you smile again with that look on your face and
love me, right now, right here, with the same passion you feel for your God,
I'll give the money back.*

"I'm sorry," he said. "I won't do it."

"Then I am sorry for you," said Winnie. She turned around and
marched out of his office, down the hall, and into the elevator, the
ends of her hair bobbing up and down.

Brian took off his coat and drank the last of the cold, bitter coffee.
He shuddered, faced his computer, and resumed entering numbers
into the spreadsheet.

Winnie walked out of the elevator on the first floor and into the
glittering main room. She stood for several minutes looking to her
right and left, then went to a long table with a roulette wheel. She
gripped the wooden underside, thought of Jesus overthrowing the
money changers, closed her eyes, prayed, felt a newfound strength
enter her body, and lifted.

Bolted to the floor, the table didn't budge.

She stepped back several feet, sighed, threw back her hair with a
toss of her head, and walked out of the casino, assisted by a man in
a red suit who opened the door for her.

In the parking lot, she climbed into her tiny yellow car and felt
overwhelmed by a horrible loneliness. She fought against it, tried
to pray, but was soon weeping over the immense gulf separating
how society should be from how it was. The absence of benevolence

permeated everything. She felt completely shut out of the world of people—excluded.

You stop it now, she commanded, wiped her face with a tissue paper, started the car, and drove out of the lot.

A FRAGILE BALANCE

T HE WORDS FRIENDS OF JESUS CHURCH TOOK UP A COLLECTION to keep Violet and Olivia Brasso in their home. But the worry that they might be subsidizing gambling losses had a moderating effect on the normally generous congregation, and it wasn't as large as Pastor Winnie hoped—only sufficient to meet the mortgage payments for three months. The donation also had to be taken in secret—collected in a red, heart-shaped box that had once contained individually wrapped cream chocolates—because of the embarrassment Violet would feel if she knew about it.

The box, containing a little more than six hundred dollars, was quietly given to Olivia, who for reasons unknown to everyone felt no embarrassment at all.

Olivia simply defied understanding since returning from her night at the casino. From that moment forward she insisted on having the police scanner on twenty-four hours a day. She called Rachel Wood to inquire after her cousin's pilgrimage to the Holy Land, when it was known that Olivia and Janice had never been fond of each other. And during Wednesday night Bible Study Violet reported that her sister had ordered library books about fighting dogs and the Wisconsin probation system, topics she had never before shown interest in.

And the situation inside the Brasso home—between the two sisters—became far from stable. Tempers flared like pressure-sensitive bombs placed at strategic locations around the house. Even a sullen expression could trigger an explosion. But that was to be expected. The fragile balance between full-time caregivers and full-time care receivers, as everyone knew, required more deep-breathing concentration than most people were capable of.

A dependent person like Olivia, by her very existence, created burdens for an independent person like Violet. She did not have to speak or even clear her throat to have a place in Violet's mind, where she steadily lived like an unruly flame on the edge of a continent of long, dry grass. Every creak in the night, every cough, odor, drip, click, groan, whimper, and sigh found resonance. Even complete silence—especially complete silence—could not be trusted, and Violet's vigilance had been honed to such acuity she frequently found herself weighing the vertiginous qualities of silence to determine if she needed to walk down the hall and check again.

But Violet's concern for Olivia was matched and perhaps even exceeded by Olivia's preternatural awareness of Violet. The only remaining bulwark standing between Olivia and the county home was the all-too-human figure of her older sister, and to not be aware of everything about her was equivalent to a pet not knowing where its food came from.

Even in her sleep, Olivia knew, exactly, Violet's whereabouts. From the confinement of her wheelchair or bed—day or night—Olivia deciphered the language of stirring, occupied space and could tell if Violet was in her bedroom, sitting in the living room, or at the breakfast table.

Kitchen drawers and dining room cupboards uttered distinguishing sounds when they moved. Each piece of furniture had its own voice, wood-groaning in response to shifting weight. Each door latch possessed nuance and personality. Each light switch snapped on and off with a unique tonal decay. Footsteps in the hall differed from footsteps in the dining room as clearly as oboes differed from clarinets. The sounds on the second floor—where Olivia had not visited since the days when her father had carried her upstairs—she remembered with undiminished precision. Even the boxes and crates in the upstairs storage room—a room she had never, ever been inside—made familiar faces when they were moved. They were part of Olivia's world, and like all world travelers, she guarded their places inside her.

And when Violet was out of the house, Olivia lived like Moses adrift in a basket, waiting, waiting, waiting. And though she might also be occupied with other things—important things—those other things were like minor skirmishes in the larger revolution against the time separating her from the satisfying safety of her sister's presence.

The more intimate aspects of their life together further complicated this ballet of proximity. Ancestral blood and long, deep associations related them and they interacted through narrowly prescribed footpaths, each path worn shiny smooth by the need to avoid dangers on either side, where unsleeping family demons crouched, ready to spring. A false word or gesture could bring to howling life an ancestral civil war of ritual meanings in which hundreds of thousands had perished but neither side could ever confidently claim victory.

Olivia's very life depended on Violet's good graces, and she well knew the boundaries of her own desires, though she frequently did not—to her own regret—always keep within them. She understood not only *when* to ask for a glass of water or a ride into town, but also *how* and *why*. She tracked her sister's changing moods like a flower following the sun.

As for Violet, she had, to be sure, made a heroic choice to care for her sister. It took sterling courage to stand against the prevailing notion that those who care for others do so because they lack the superior qualities needed to excel in the marketplace of personal achievement. The pervasiveness of this demeaning judgment—known only to those who have stood against those snarling winds—seeped into every corner of popular thought and accounted for, Violet thought, the main division between the "church" and the "world."

The "world"—meaning the world of embodied ideas and spirits—insisted on the rule of individual rights and freedoms, and anything that curtailed their full expression was seen as illegitimate insurgency. The "church"—meaning the world of disembodied ideas and spirits—insisted on the rule of personal duty and mutual, deferential obligation. For the "church," the curtailing of individual rights and freedoms was not just desirable but fundamental. The two civilizations viewed each other with uncomprehending hostility, and Violet remained ever watchful for signs of enemy advancement.

For these reasons it was absolutely necessary for Violet that Olivia be of high moral quality. Whenever Violet was convinced of this—that Olivia was worth it—she felt content with her life. But whenever she became unsure about whether the burden she carried served some heavenly purpose—if the scales of eternal justice might balance more evenly with Olivia sermonizing and hurling insults at strangers from a bed in the county home—then her life became more difficult.

And so the delicate counterpoise between Violet and Olivia suffered greatly when Olivia returned home covered in urine in the care of a violent-looking young man after gambling away their life savings. And it didn't help when days later the crude fellow returned and took Olivia away again, only to return in a loud green vehicle with hell's flames rendered in perfect detail on the front fenders, the two of them sitting inside, eating something from a shiny bag and laughing like wicked children.

Two days later—when Olivia announced that she had agreed to go with Wade to the dogfight the coming weekend—Violet said she would refuse to dress her.

"Of course you will, Vio," said Olivia. "You know how much it means to me."

"That's what concerns me," said Violet. "You've lost your mind mostly. Why would you have the slightest interest in going to a dogfight where they fight dogs?"

"Now, we already talked about that, remember? I agreed to tell you where we were going if you agreed not to judge."

"I'm going to refuse to dress you for your own good. You have no business in a place like that. It's against the law and that's bad."

"Plenty of things are against the law, Vio," said Olivia. "Freeing slaves was once against the law."

"Oh, just stop it, Olivia. Just stop it. That old slavery thing can't be brought up every time a person wants to do something against common sense. This is just the opposite of that. The current laws need enforcement, making stronger, not changing them. Those poor dogs need to be rescued and given a real chance to have a happy life."

"That's what I'm talking about!" said Olivia. "This is my chance to be happy."

"If you're not happy it's your own fault. You have a perfectly good life and there's nothing on earth wrong with it."

"Yes, I know I do, but you have a life too and it's so very much bigger than mine. This is my small chance. Please don't prevent me from taking it. Please, Violet, you'll get me dressed."

"What kind of person takes a poor crippled woman to a dogfight? Indecent is what it is, Olivia, indecent."

"Don't be so harsh, Vio. He's young and I'll admit he doesn't think through things as well as you or I, but that's the very definition of being young. He has a good heart."

"I don't trust you."

"I know I made a mistake. I know that and I've admitted it—how many times? I'm really sorry, Vio, but God will take care of us. See, that's what I learned. God will take care of us."

"What you mean is I will take care of us. But I don't know how I'm going to be able to. We can't continue much longer."

"Yes, of course, Vio, and I'm forever grateful for you, but God will take care of us."

"He was doing a good job of it before you gambled away all the money He provided for us to live on. And now, not ten days later, and that's a very short time, not long, you want to go to a dogfight."

"Jesus would have gone to a dogfight, Vio," said Olivia. "He spent His entire life ministering to those on the margins. He called tax collectors, lawbreakers, and lowlifers to be His most trusted friends. Jesus would not refuse to attend a dogfight. He loved all people."

"The question is if Jesus would have dressed his delusional sister so *she* could attend, if He had one, a sister. And no is the real answer. No."

Finally, Olivia frowned until her eyebrows nearly touched and said sternly, "I'll never forgive you if you don't dress me, Violet."

"Yes you will, when you see I was right you will and you'll see."

"I won't ever."

"Yes you will."

"I won't and you know I won't. You know how long I can hold onto things. You may someday forgive me for losing all our money, but you know in your heart that I will never forgive you if you don't get me dressed this weekend."

"That's unfair," said Violet.

"I know it," said Olivia. "But I'm that way. I'll hate you until the day I die."

Violet remained silent, communicating her surrender.

"Thank you, Vio," Olivia said. "I'll never forget you."

"Yes you will," said Violet. "But you have to promise to tell me everything."

"Oh, I will," said Olivia.

INSURGENCY

G RAHM SHOTWELL AND JULY MONTGOMERY DROVE TO THE Twin Cities in Minnesota. The parking lot of the Asmythe Convention Center was nearly full. Two large men in blue blazers checked July's patron number against a computer list and allowed them to enter the cavernous room. A thick maroon carpet covered the floor.

They sat at the only unoccupied table in back and listened to the roar of hundreds of plate-clattering spoons, forks, bottles, glasses, china cups, moving chairs, conversation, and piped-in country western music.

Mostly old and middle-aged adults, dressed as though they were expecting to meet Dolly Parton, sat in groups of ten and twelve around circular cloth-covered tables. They toasted each other with frosted glasses, called for more food, laughed, shouted, and walked back and forth from the bathrooms. A line of elevated tables with co-op officers and honored guests sat in front. July pointed several out to Grahm, including a former U.S. secretary of agriculture, the Texas chairman of the House Ag Committee, a syndicated farm economist, and a radio talk-show host.

Cameramen from the three local news channels were setting up beneath the elevated podium, aiming black-shrouded lenses on tripods into the open space behind the microphone, joined by farm journalists and their smaller cameras. Waiters better dressed than July and Grahm served platters of steak and creamed potatoes, soup, mixed vegetables, salad, fruit, Colby cheese, butter, and fresh warm white rolls. Waitresses in peach-colored makeup, black skirts, and pressed blouses drove stainless steel dessert carts between the tables. The temperature was stifling, rapidly dissolving the ice in the water glasses.

Grahm thought it seemed odd that farmers should be so uncomfortable dining; after all, they produced the food. But the tables with working farmers were easily identified. Accustomed to out-of-doors grappling with bulky objects, noisy machinery, and natural elements, they appeared ill at ease indoors, shy in making eye contact, clumsy with their forks, spoons, and cups, and overly loud in talking with each other. Conflicting habituation could be read in their faces. Because it was late afternoon—chore and milking time—they were restive; but because they weren't working and their stomachs were full, in a warm room, they should be sleeping, and they blinked, yawned, and grimaced to keep their eyes open.

The farm women, nearly starved for anything resembling higher culture, demanded more from the occasion than it could possibly yield. With eyes as white as freshly peeled hard-boiled eggs they inspected the jewelry, hair, and clothes of the other women, tasted each morsel of food disapprovingly, strained to hear conversations from neighboring tables, worried about wrinkles in their faces, and frowned at their husbands to sit up straighter in their chairs.

Grahm at once realized the problem he faced. The feasting roar—a room filled with well-dressed revelers and dignitaries seated at elevated tables; gold watches, new shoes, and relaxed smiles; white tablecloths; music, waiters, and copious platters of food; television cameras and spoon-dropping farmers and their scowling wives—was the Immortal Engine of Progress. Only the material out of which the engine's cogs were fashioned had changed in thousands and thousands of years. The gears themselves moved in exactly the same direction and manner.

Ah, to be included at the table of people whose backs did not ache and feet were not swollen, whose nurtured capacity for merriment so exceeded all unpleasantness that the bass notes of living could be blithely ignored. This was the real human technology that from time immemorial had driven small farmers off their land and muted the howl of those caught in the gears. In the scramble to secure a place at the banquet—at least for their children—the cries of those run over by the Engine of Progess could scarcely be heard. Their own desire to be within the halls of leisure left them without sufficient volume to complain. The celebration of prosperity was so deafening, the intoxicants so strong, who could stand against them?

While the feasting continued, speakers walked from the elevated table to the microphone, their amplified voices wafting out over the room. The specific content of their short speeches was not important, only mood, cadence, and style. The Texas representative spoke of the need for farmers to become "global players on the world scene," to "work hard, work smart." The syndicated economist praised "the crude but infinite wisdom of the farm market" and congratulated those present for being "ship captains in the new economy." The talk-show host condemned the "socialist agenda of rabid environmentalists" while extolling those "dedicated to achievement, quality, and economic freedom." The former secretary of agriculture told of "government bureaucrats who couldn't tell a Holstein from a spotted camel" and the need to restore the United States to a station of "honor, integrity, and excellence" in the eyes of the world. "You are the real leaders," he said, "plowing furrows into the future."

At each ornamental phrase the room erupted in applause. Even the working farmers—those without immigrants providing the labor on their farms—sleepily pounded their rough hands together, happy to be seen supporting the expressed sentiments. Their farms mortgaged to the furthest reaches of liability, their milk prices at historically low levels, they still did not wish to be impolite or run counter to community goodwill.

The emcee finally introduced the American Milk Cooperative manager and chief executive officer, Burt Forehouse, who carried the microphone around in front of the podium. Confidence radiated from every inch of his short frame and three-piece suit. American Milk had enjoyed an exceptional year, with record high revenues, and everyone present had "made it happen." He said they were all "partners in building a world-class dairy industry." The American farmer "can outproduce, outperform, and plain outfarm anyone, anywhere, anytime. We have always been the best, we will continue to be the best, and anyone who doesn't think so can kiss my ass." And for the sake of the government bureaucrats referred to by the former secretary of agriculture, he held up a picture of a Democrat donkey.

The room exploded in laughter and applause, which took a full minute to subside.

"Now, let me take some questions."

The cameramen went back to their tables, satisfied they had made copy.

A young man seated at a table near the podium eagerly raised his hand and asked, "Has the acquisition of Lakeland Cooperative added to AM's competitive position in the East?"

"You'd better believe it," said Forehouse. "With Lakeland we now have a fluid stream into the New York milk shed, with potential for flows into other New England markets."

Another question from the same table: "How important is the new Illinois drying plant?"

"I'll let our economist from Illinois field that one."

The dairy economist at the elevated table explained how diverting excess milk supplies during flush periods into world markets was critical in avoiding cheese inventory and price volatility. The Decatur plant, he explained, would facilitate asset allocation and expand opportunities in efficient procurement and marketing diversity.

"With all the talk in Congress about trading with China, what is the export potential for dairy products?" asked a woman at another front table.

"You might say there are more than a billion reasons to sell cheese in China," said Forehouse.

More laughter and applause.

Grahm, his dinner untouched, his face pale and his hands shaking, stood up from the table. He exchanged a last, furtive look with July.

"Sit down," cautioned July, giving the only advice he could offer. "This is a mistake."

As Grahm walked around the tables, chairs, and dessert carts, it became apparent to many that he was not simply another person on his way to the bathroom. The fearful, glassy stare, for one thing, did not bode well for the uninterrupted flow of congeniality. As he walked, a hushed whispering grew up around him. At about midway, Burt Forehouse spotted him and began closing his remarks.

"I want to thank all of you for coming to help us celebrate another successful year," he said. "Please feel free to continue eating and talking with your neighbors and friends. The bar will remain open for another hour, I'm told, and—"

"I have something to say," said Grahm, coming to rest directly beneath the podium in the middle of the abandoned tripods, his voice uneven but loud. "My name is Grahm Shotwell. Somebody has been contaminating my milk, breaking into my house, and threatening my wife, and I think you know something about it."

The room grew absolutely silent.

"*You* are responsible," said Grahm, pointing his finger. "What you're doing isn't right and you know it."

"I have no idea what you're talking about," said Burt Forehouse. "I've never seen you before in my life."

"You're not as smart as you think," said Grahm. "My grandfather was a charter member of American Milk. Years ago, it was an honest co-op. The farmers here know we're being cheated now. We don't know how you do it and we don't know what can be done about it, but we know there's crooked work going on. As for me, I know what you did to my family and I have the papers to prove it."

"That's a damn lie," said Burt Forehouse.

The security guards standing by the three exit doors moved forward.

Grahm took a piece of folded paper out of his pocket, unfolded it, and began to read from the letter Cora had written to the newspaper.

After the first sentence, recognition flickered in Burt's face. "You're breaking a judicial restraining order!" he shouted.

This statement proved unfortunate for Forehouse. Had he refrained from making it, Grahm would have remained without support and the six guards would have taken him away. But it was now clear that something—something unknown but nevertheless real—lay behind Grahm's actions.

A farmer in a jacket too small for him stood up and lumbered forward. Of unknown origin, perhaps a descendant of Chaldean giants, he easily moved the obstacles in his way to either side. His ponderous gait bore witness to a lifetime of bodily resignation. And it wasn't just his size that sought to define him, it was also his determination to insert himself into the breach, as though he had some familiarity and perhaps even fondness for places of simmering violence.

Standing beside Grahm and looking directly at Forehouse, he said, "Let him talk." Then he turned his wide body to face the approaching security force.

Inside the space of a single thought, the fragile alliance between those prospering from the farm economy and those actually farming weakened and in some cases cracked. A dozen farmers from nearby tables stood up—nine men and three women—and came forward, forming a small phalanx between Grahm and the guards.

The guards stopped and Grahm continued reading from his letter.

"We can't hear back here!" someone shouted from the back of the room.

The large man in the small jacket clambered up on the elevated stage, stretched out an enormous hand, and took the microphone. Then he climbed down and pointed it at Grahm. "Start over," he said. The cameramen and journalists rushed to recover their equipment and capture an unobstructed shot.

When Grahm finished reading the letter, ending with, "Woe unto those who do evil in the sight of God," another thirty farmers rose to their feet and joined those already standing in applauding. Most did not completely understand what the letter referred to, as they had not entirely understood the speeches, but they endorsed the sentiment.

"Thank you, Mr. Shotwell, for your concerns," said Burt Forehouse. "As you know, the issues you speak of are under departmental review. As a farmer-owned cooperative we try to avoid this kind of litigation because its legal costs come out of general revenues, which hurts everyone—especially our pay prices. But you have a right to your day in court, even when your case lacks merit. This is America, after all. So let's move forward and get back to our—"

"Thank you," said Grahm, not knowing exactly what to say next, but remembering when the rope slipped from his hands. "I'm glad you want to return as much money as possible to the farms. Keeping that in mind, how much does this cooperative pay you?"

"My salary is commensurate with those paid by other competitive businesses."

"That's not what I asked," said Grahm. "If this is a farmer-owned cooperative, as you say, how much are the owners paying you? I mean, all the money I got paid last year for my milk—every dime— is on record and anyone can look it up. So how much are you being paid?"

"I'm not allowed to give that figure. It's proprietary."

"See, that's just what my wife said you'd say. But how can a farmer-owned co-op have proprietary information that's not available to the farmer owners? When my grandfather and his neighbors founded this co-op, there were no secrets written into the charter."

Burt Forehouse stood behind the podium and watched fifteen Minneapolis police officers enter through the exit doors. Unlike the unarmed security guards, they had helmets, holstered guns, and polished black clubs. They took the microphone away from the giant farmer and escorted Grahm, July, and three others out to the parking lot.

"You're free to go," one officer said. "But don't come back here."

That night at the restaurant, the voice of her husband leaped out of the overhead television. Cora dropped a bowl of vegetable soup into the lap of a salesman from East Moline who was sitting at the counter.

The Channel Three footage from American Milk's annual meeting was pared down to thirty seconds, and the portion chosen to represent Grahm was this: "That's just what my wife said you'd say. But how can a farmer-owned co-op have proprietary information that's not available to the farmer owners?"

"I'm sorry," she said to the offended man, offering him a handful of napkins. "It slipped."

"You stupid idiot, look at me!" shouted the man as he stood away from the counter. "You're going to pay for this. These stains will never come out. I can't believe it."

"I'm sorry," said Cora.

"Sorry doesn't cut it. Look at this!"

At the end of the counter, Wade Armbuster stood up and walked forward.

"Look at this! You clumsy fool."

"I'm sorry," she repeated.

"Shit!"

"Watch your mouth," said Wade.

"Wade, this isn't necessary," said Cora. "We can fix this."

"Get lost," said the offended salesman. "This doesn't concern you."

"It does, because I'm the guy telling you to shut your mouth."

"Wade, go sit down."

"Nobody's going to talk to you like that, Mrs. Shotwell."

"Go sit down, Wade. Please go sit down."

"That's right, hillbilly, go buy another nose ring before you get hurt."

At home, Cora waited up for Grahm. Seeing the headlights turn into the driveway, she met him in the yard. They talked in the kitchen.

"I wish you'd been there," said Grahm, his face glowing. "Afterwards, in the parking lot, farmers kept coming over to talk. July and I stayed two hours. You wouldn't have believed it, Cora. They're on our side. There are families all over this country who feel just like we do. They know the system is against them, that things aren't right, and they're having a meeting up at Snow Corners in a couple months and they want us to come."

"Who's 'they'?"

"Folks like us. People who are tired of having other people wipe their feet on them. They're forming a group to fight this corruption."

"Grahm, we don't have time to be going to meetings. And the judge told us not to be doing anything like that."

"That judge can go to hell. I mean it, Cora. We're not alone any longer. Others are with us. We've been pushed around long enough. It's time to start pushing back."

"You can't push a judge."

"You were right, Cora. I didn't see it before. You were right to

stand up to them. They don't know what the right thing is anymore.
The evil runs too deep. And there's no such thing as justice without
people standing up and demanding it."

"I got fired tonight," said Cora.

"Why?"

"I dropped a bowl of soup on someone and he got angry and said
some things. Wade threw him through the front door. Cut him up
pretty bad. I tried to stop it but I couldn't."

"Wade did that?"

"I tried to stop it."

"I hope he at least gave the poor fellow a chance."

"Not really. Wade doesn't look as strong as he is and I guess the
guy just wasn't thinking clearly."

Grahm laughed and his teeth flashed. "You got fired?"

"The salesman demanded they fire me because I wouldn't tell
them who beat him up, I mean after Wade ran off."

"Good, I never liked you working there."

Cora laughed. "It was kind of funny, Grahm. He told Wade he
should go buy another nose ring before he got hurt and Wade said,
'Here, I'll give you mine if you think it will help you any.' He unclipped it and handed it to him. I mean it was kind of funny if you
took the time to think about it."

"You're kind of funny yourself, Cora."

"I am not."

"And beautiful and smart."

Grahm blushed and they looked at each other in a way they'd
almost forgotten how to look at each other. Cora smiled as Grahm
moved closer to her. All of a sudden she was no longer tired and
there were still several hours before morning.

Later, upstairs, Cora said, "Grahm, you've got to promise me you
won't go to that meeting up in Snow Corners."

"I can't promise, Cora. I'll do anything for you, but I can't promise that."

SLAUGHTER

SOMETIMES IN THE THEATER OF WINTER, A DAY WILL APPEAR with such spectacular mildness that it seems the season can almost be forgiven for all its inappropriate hostility, inconveniences, and even physical assaults. With a balmy sky overhead, melting snow underfoot, and the sound of creeks running, the bargain made with contrasts doesn't look so bad: to feel warm, one must remember cold; to experience joy, one must have known sorrow.

Winifred Smith took the opportunity afforded by such a day to invite Violet Brasso to join her in a picnic lunch at a local park. Violet accepted the invitation—glad to have a social event away from her home—and agreed to meet her there after some errands she needed to run in Grange.

The bright, warm afternoon slowly made inroads in dispelling Winnie's lingering discouragement over her encounter at the casino several days before, and as she drove her little yellow car toward the park she felt better and better. Amoeba-shaped pools drained from snow drifts lay along the shoulders of the road, in the ditches and fields, and though spring was not here yet, it could be imagined.

Occasional glimpses of grass were a heralded sight after so many months of winter. She thought how fat green blades of lilies and crocuses would, in time, be plunging up through the chocolate ground, putting winter to rest. She loved the sight of new plants growing among clumps of snow, happily swelling upward like prisoners released from casks of brown ice, holding no grudges. Mushrooms would be popping up, and there was absolutely nothing she loved better than finding mushrooms. It was a way of leaving the world of people and merging with the laced unconsciousness of nature.

She turned off the main highway in order to drive on back roads, over fields still mounded high with rolling acres of whipped cream.

Great globs of heavy, melting snow fell from tree limbs, splattering on the road like buckets of watery paint.

Arriving at the county park, she drove up the steadily rising hill to the picnic area, where five picnic tables, the snow now gone from their horizontal surfaces, had been planted in a high, snow-covered field near a grove of poplar.

She contemplated the thawing stillness of the deserted park and the white-throated birds flitting along the edge of the woods. Carrying the picnic basket, she walked through the snow to the tables and began laying out lunch.

In the distance she watched Violet Brasso's old Buick coming up the hill. It did not appear to be running well, and after it turned into the park the engine died when it was about fifty yards away. Winnie walked down the road to help the older woman carry her basket.

"Land sakes," said Violet, struggling with arthritic difficulty to climb out of the car. "Troubles seem to be finding me troubled lately. The repairman said I should have something done—I can't remember what it was, do something in the motor—and I guess he was right."

"I can take you home after our lunch," said Winnie.

"I know, dear, but someone needs to come get my car."

"There's an emergency phone by the utility shed. Here, give me that basket. Up we go."

They walked to the phone booth and while Violet placed a call Winnie carried her basket and thermos to the picnic tables and continued to set out lunch.

"This was such a good idea," said Violet after she had joined Winnie. "You don't even need a jacket. Nature has such healing powers, and, land sakes, we all need healing."

They sat for a long time, just looking. The ubiquity of the mounds of snow—everywhere shrinking imperceptibly—expressed a sublime, musical crinkling that could almost be heard and seen in the clear air.

"Oh no, I left the cake in the car," said Violet.

"Let me go," said Winnie.

"It's on the front seat."

Winnie walked down the blacktop and noticed buds beginning to swell in the tops of branches, the sky holding them in its blue grip.

She could not find the cake inside the Buick and called back to Violet.

"Look in the trunk, dear."

Winnie found the keys sticking out of the ignition and opened the rounded truck, where a Bundt pan rested next to an assortment of clothes, garden tools, and quilting supplies.

A jeep turned into the park, climbed the hill, and stopped behind her. A man dressed in a disorderly way came out of it, his bristled, tired face smudged, carrying a toolbox.

"Hello," said Winnie, not looking directly at him.

"I told Violet to replace that filter," he grumbled, and walked past her. As she closed the trunk, he opened the hood.

Winnie carried the cake up to the picnic tables.

"My lands, I forgot the lemonade too," said Violet. "It's in the back seat on the floor behind the driver's seat. There's hardly a single thought I can think to keep hold of anymore and I don't think I know anymore where my thoughts go."

Winnie returned to the car just as the man was closing the hood and wiping his hands with a rag. The smell of grease surprised her with its sweetness.

Winnie found the thermos of lemonade and followed him toward the picnic tables. His back seemed wider, she thought, than backs usually were, but she couldn't be sure, and his feet plodded through the snow as though he didn't care where he stepped, his tracks ragged and uneven. Pointed strands of hair jutted out from beneath his cap like black flames.

"Will it start?" asked Violet.

"It will start. Your fuel filter was plugged." He took from his pocket a cylindrical piece of grimy, rusty metal and blew into it as if it were a referee's whistle. "See, it's stopped up. Here, you try," and he offered it to Violet and Winnie, wiping his mouth on his sleeve.

"No thank you," said Violet. "Please, stay and share our lunch. Pastor Winifred, this is Jacob Helm. Jacob, this is my pastor, Winifred Smith. Do you know each other?"

Two heads shook.

"Come on, Jacob," said Violet. "Sit down, sit down."

Jacob looked into the distance, as though viewing all the things he would rather be doing, then grimaced and sat down, continuing to rub his thick hands with the rag.

"Jacob lives in a log house in the woods, over by Cemetery Road," explained Violet. "He owns the craft shop."

"That's nice," said Winnie.

"How did you make out at the casino?" asked Violet in a quiet voice, passing paper plates around.

"Not well," said Winnie. Her face darkened with memory.

"I told you there was no good use going over there," said Violet.

"I hope you didn't lose much," said Jacob, smiling at Winnie in a bored manner.

"I went there on a personal matter," said Winnie. "I do not gamble."

"I meant no offense," said Jacob. "I don't gamble either."

"No offense taken," said Winnie. "Do you have principled objections to gambling, or do you come from a secular humanist perspective?"

"I have no objections to gambling," said Jacob, accepting a paper cup of lemonade. "It just seems a waste of time."

"How pragmatic of you," said Winnie.

Jacob drew the cup of lemonade toward the same mouth that had earlier blown into the grimy cylinder and a frown captured Violet's face.

"Before you drink that," said Winnie, "I think we should ask a blessing on our meal, if that's all right."

"Fine," said Jacob. "Should we also hold hands?"

There was a long pause.

"Are you mocking me?" asked Winnie.

"Of course not. I was under the impression that people often hold hands before they pray. I don't know."

"Excuse us," said Winnie, and bowed her head. "Our Heavenly Provider, please bless this food You've provided and teach us Your Everlasting Ways in the Name of our Lord and Savior Jesus. Amen."

Jacob ate the cheese and cucumber sandwiches, potato chips,

apple slices, and homemade vanilla pudding and cake, while Winnie sipped sparingly from her hot tea, noticing that Jacob had refused her beef and noodle soup as well as her potato salad.

From beyond the poplars—down the hill—came muffled, sporadic shouting. The shouting grew more distinct, until individual voices could be distinguished, followed by the sound of branches breaking. Then the high-pitched whine of small-bore engines. The sound of breaking branches grew louder and soon Violet, Jacob, and Winnie saw the shapes of large animals running toward them through the trees, followed by the sound of the engines and shouting.

At first it seemed to Winnie that they must be very large deer, as they leaped over bracken, through the snowdrifts, and around trees, picking their paths with quick, wild cunning. But she soon saw that they were cattle—five young steers and a somewhat older heifer. Behind them, men on snowmobiles shouted at each other and attempted to drive the animals south.

The young cattle reached the edge of the wood and stared at the picnic tables, open field, and road, their nostrils flared like dark trumpets, water dripping from opened mouths and their eye sockets rimmed with terror. The steers plunged forward into the waiting snow, crossed the road, and jumped the fence at the edge of the park. They continued into the adjacent field, where stalks of corn stubble poked through the snow. Again they looked almost like deer as they effortlessly cleared the next fence, hardly resembling the clumsy and ponderous movements of domesticated cattle in feedlots. The heifer followed, but due to her larger size she stopped at the four-foot fence and looked around in a moment of fearful indecision.

Three snowmobiles emerged from the woods and with much shouting the riders continued toward her. The animal again considered the fence, and then rather than run on the road—the choice of animals accustomed to human-made paths—plunged back into the field, running downhill and away from the picnic tables. Soon the snow became too deep to run in.

One of the snowmobile riders stopped next to the picnic table and the other two riders caught up to the floundering animal as she struggled helplessly in the deep snow.

"Sorry to disturb your meal," said the man from beneath a hooded sweatshirt, turning his engine off.

Thirty yards downhill—near enough to hear the breathing of the animal and her frantic attempts to lunge out of the deep snow—one of the men climbed off his snowmobile. He pulled a carbine from under the seat and with the head of the heifer raised in fearful defiance, shot her. Her body slumped to the side and she lay fallow in the snow.

The sound of the rifle seemed to silence the park, driving the birds out of it. Winnie stood up and held both hands against her cheeks as tears ran down her face.

"Sorry to disturb you folks," repeated the farmer. "But once they get off on their own there's nothing to be done. They don't have any sense. When they run down like that in the snow they suck moisture up their lungs and die of pneumonia in a couple days. There's nothing you can do. Those others—the younger steers—we'll have to shoot them with ought-sixes from a distance, I guess. Who knows how long they've been living out like this? They must have gotten through the fence and the hired men didn't count them missing. It's a wonder the mountain lion didn't get all of them."

In the open field below, the men took out long knives, cut the throat of the heifer, and began carving her up. A circle of dark red spread into the snow.

Tears continued to run from Winnie's eyes. "There's no way you can justify this," she sobbed. "You have no right to treat an animal that way."

"Can't let the meat waste," said the farmer.

"No living thing should be run down and shot."

"People got to eat," said the farmer.

"You should at least feel sorry," yelled Winnie, her anger darkening her face.

"People got to eat," he repeated calmly.

"There are laws against hunting in a public park," said Winnie.

"You'd be wrong about that I'm afraid, Ma'am," said the farmer.

"Pastor Winifred, sit down," whispered Violet.

Winnie, however, stepped away from the picnic table and shouted at the farmer. "Owning animals doesn't give you the right to be cruel. If anything, ownership should make you more protective. Have you no conscience?"

"Sit down, dear," said Violet, embarrassed by her behavior.

Below them, the hired men filled large clear plastic bags with chunks of bleeding flesh, stacking them beside the snowmobiles in the snow.

"What kind of man are you?" shouted Winnie.

"People got to eat," repeated the farmer.

"Actually," said Jacob, "people don't have to eat meat. I don't."

Winnie was quiet for a moment, then whirled around to face Jacob, her eyes burning with rage. "That's not the point!" she screamed. "We're not talking about that. We're talking about being reverent and humane, not your own self-righteousness!"

She ran through the snow to her car and drove away.

"I'm sorry," said Violet to the farmer. "I'm not sure where she grew up, but I suspect it was in a city."

"No offense taken. I'm sorry it had to happen this way."

"Lester, you didn't have to shoot the animal in front of her," said Jacob. "Those steers—the ones that got away—how much are they worth?"

"Not a lot, I guess," said the farmer.

"I'll buy them," said Jacob. "How much do you want to leave them alone?"

"Can't do that," said the farmer, starting his snowmobile in a cloud of oily smoke. "They get in the neighbors' crops. Everybody knows they belong to me, Jacob."

He joined his hired men.

Violet and Jacob finished their lunch and Jacob helped her to the car. He returned for the baskets and other containers. The Buick started on the first try and after leaving the park Jacob and Violet went in different directions.

FIGHTING DOGS

W ADE ARMBUSTER PLACED OLIVIA ON THE FRONT SEAT OF HIS pickup, put the wheelchair in the back, and drove away from the Brasso house with Violet watching from the unlit window in the upstairs storage room.

"Thanks for writing to my parole officer," said Wade when they reached the state highway.

"I was happy to do it," said Olivia, clicking her seat belt into place. "I hope it's all right if I bring a camera."

"I'm not sure that's a good idea," said Wade.

"Did you get your car put away?"

"Yes, it's back in the machine shed. Jacob helped me with the windshield. You want to get something to eat afterwards?"

"I guess it depends. When does this event start?"

"It starts as soon as enough people and dogs get there and ends after there aren't any more dogs to fight. There's a truck stop not far from where we're going."

"A truck stop," repeated Olivia, relishing the sound and the attending idea. "What a perfect place for people riding in a truck."

"I brought some blankets," said Wade. "It can get cold at a game. You want one now?"

"No thank you. I've got on plenty of clothes."

Wade turned off the state highway and onto a northbound blacktop. The distance between houses grew longer and longer. A floating oval moon and canopy of stars were visible in the east.

Crossing the county line, the blacktop deteriorated and the old pickup clattered loudly over each bump and pothole. They drove through Snow Corners, a tiny village on the edge of a pine forest. Of the two dozen homes only one appeared lived in, and for Olivia, who studied each passing attraction with supreme interest, the single window of light held haunting enchantment.

Wade drove between two towering walls of thick black pines, the feathered branches blotting out the light of the night sky. Olivia breathed deeply, savoring the smell of Christmas as it mingled with the odor of antifreeze and burned oil wafting out of the heater.

Several miles later, Wade turned at an intersection marked by a rag tied around a road sign and drove downhill, deeper into the forest. Near the bottom, he slowed and searched along the road. Another rag—tied to a stick shoved into the ditch—marked a drive. Wade turned in, put the truck into four-wheel drive and continued forward, following earlier tracks made in the snow, the branches of the pines on either side of the narrow lane almost touching. Soon, a cattle gate blocked their progress: KEEP OUT, PRIVATE PROPERTY.

Wade stopped before the gate and turned off the headlights. Then he turned them on and off twice. As though formed from the forest air, a stooped figure in a snowmobile suit emerged from the trees, dragged the gate to the side, and with a thick gloved hand motioned them forward. Olivia watched him with the wonder of a cat watching a mouse—or a mouse watching a cat.

They followed the narrow lane further downhill, pine limbs brushing audibly against the sides of the truck. At the base of the hill the lane turned left and spit them out of the forest into a large clearing, where the welcome light of the moon reflected brightly across the surface of snow. In the middle of the clearing, twenty or twenty-five vehicles, mostly vans and pickups, were wedged around an unpainted barn. Homemade wooden crates and wire cages sat in the back of many trucks, but all that Olivia could see were empty, with the exception of one large white lumpy shape. Smoke billowed from a metal chimney at the side of the barn, and a single lantern hanging from the side of the building marked the entrance.

Wade parked as near to the door as he could and set Olivia into her wheelchair. The air was cold and he threw a blanket over her lap. The snow was deep, and because of the front casters on her wheelchair, he wasn't able to push her through it, so he pulled her backward to the hard-packed path. An unseen pair of arms rolled the door aside and a woman sitting on a stool held out a coffee can. Wade pushed two ten-dollar bills into its open mouth. Quick as a flash, the woman's big, nimble hand dove into the can, plucked up one of the tens, and handed it back to Wade.

"No charge for wheelchairs," she said, smiling a missing-front-tooth smile. "They bring their own seats."

Originally a horse barn, the building had stalls along three sides and a large open area. Thirty or forty people stood and sat on bales of straw around a chicken-wire pen.

"That's the pit," Wade told Olivia and pushed her over to inspect the six-sided enclosure, which looked as if it might have been constructed earlier in the day. The arena had been dug a foot into the dirt floor, reinforced with wooden posts, the sides made of chicken wire. Trouble lights fastened to the tops of the posts directed light into the pit, which was about twelve or fourteen feet in diameter.

A dozen men and a few women stood with muzzled dogs on leashes. More men and dogs were in the open stalls. Wood and coal smoke seeped from the seams of a squat, hot-fired iron stove, and many of the spectators, Olivia noticed, had removed their coats. A blackboard on the wall listed the scheduled matches, along with the weights of the contestants: Caesar (58) vs. Wide Mouth (52); LockJaw (67) vs. Lady MacBeth (62); Jake III (45) vs. Iron Bitch (47); White-Eye (76) vs. Vice President Al Gore (81).

Wade parked Olivia at a comfortable viewing distance from the pit and pulled up a bale of straw to sit beside her.

A thin, salt-and-pepper-whiskered man seated at a card table took bets and scribbled names and numbers into a notebook. Before him, an opened leather suitcase served as a cash register. Standing behind him and to the side of the blackboard an enormous blond youth kept his hands shoved deeply in his jacket pockets. Despite the lack of any official designation, badge or sign, his purpose was clearly enforcement.

Olivia drank in the sights, smells, and sounds like a woman dying of thirst. Hoping to make herself look less like an invalid—and also because she was too warm—she removed the blanket Wade had tucked around her and folded it neatly on the bale of straw next to Wade.

"Most of these dogs look like American Staffordshire terriers," she said.

"We call 'em pit bulls," said Wade. "Or just bulls."

"That's a slang expression," said Olivia. "It dates from when the English used dogs to bait bulls."

"I wondered about that," said Wade.

"They seem fairly docile," said Olivia, who imagined that dogs bred for fighting, like horses bred for running, would be nearly uncontrollable. But the mostly mottled, shorthaired dogs sat next to their handlers like any other pets, and even in some cases, she noticed, wagged their tails when people petted them or talked to them.

At the same time, she noted, they weren't like most other dogs. Wide, square heads and necks; small eyes, tiny ears, muscled shoulders; short, bowed legs and inscrutably blank expressions gave them a unique appearance, emphasized by heavy leather muzzles and oversized collars.

"That's what makes 'em so cool," said Wade. "They make excellent fighters but very poor guard dogs. It's their breeding. They don't bark much and generally like people. When they're used as guard dogs they sometimes get stolen. They'll climb into anybody's car. It's just other dogs they don't like. It's bred into them."

"What?"

"The game—the fighting instinct."

It was a curious notion, Olivia thought, the idea of breeding behavior as opposed to physical features.

"What does that mean?" asked Olivia, pointing at the handwritten No Coon sign hanging below the blackboard.

"Raccoons aren't allowed," Wade explained. "Some people always want to see a raccoon tossed in the pit with a small dog. They fight like hell when they're cornered. It's because they're wild. It's what they try to breed into the bulls—to put the wildness back in 'em that was earlier bred out. When a coon is thrown in the ring, either it or a dog is going to die."

"You said bulls like people. That's not a wild trait."

"I know it doesn't make sense, but that's the way it is. Whatever makes the bulls good at fighting each other also makes them like people, I mean generally. Some of the other game breeds aren't like that—the bigger ones—but they don't, pound for pound, make as good fighters."

The first match, Caesar versus Wide Mouth, began when two men led their dogs into the pit and took off their muzzles. Caesar, a brown five-year-old male, six pounds heavier than his brown three-year-old opponent, struggled to get at the other dog. The younger dog waited patiently for its collar to be unfastened, but when it was released it charged the bigger dog, jaws snapping. Wide Mouth—the bitch—met the assault, and they merged into one ball of snarling canine fur, limbs, and teeth.

Five minutes later, both dogs were covered with blood. And though the wrestling, snarling, and biting continued undiminished, even Olivia could tell which dog had the upper hand. Caesar, the older dog, dominated. His larger size contributed to the unbalance, but he also seemed more dedicated. The younger dog, in comparison, seemed hesitant, confused, fearful, trying to protect herself—defensive. When she bit, she did not hold on with the same tenacity.

In the next few minutes both dogs showed signs of exhaustion, but the male's superiority became increasingly apparent. The future of the contest soon became inevitable and the judge—a small copper-skinned man wearing a jacket with "Joe" sewn into an oval patch above the left pocket—blew a whistle.

"Hold off!" yelled the female's owner and both owners rushed into the pit and separated their bloody animals. Afterward, Olivia noticed, the dogs were shaking, and the defeated female hung her head and limped out of the pit. Caesar, however, strutted out of the gate with a prideful, smug expression—to the delight of many onlookers, who clapped, pointed, and smiled at the blatant display of celebrated victory.

"People like that," whispered Wade.

A dozen gamblers rushed forward to collect their winnings from the card table. The thin, whiskered man counted bills into waiting hands, observed by the giant blond youth, his small, deeply recessed blue eyes expressionless.

The volume of sound inside the barn increased. Like a first round of drinks, the fighting had loosened everyone up, releasing shouting, laughter, and persiflage. There was movement to study the dogs scheduled for the next fight and place bets. Cigarettes and cigars were lit and fresh pinches of chewing tobacco packed into cheeks. The dogs in the room grew more anxious. The stove door was thrown open, blue smoke belched into the room, and chunks of coal the size of muskmelons were tossed inside. More jackets were taken off.

Olivia was beside herself. Though she had tried to anticipate what a dogfight would be like—through library books, *Dog Lovers* magazine, the World Book Encyclopedia, and her focused imagination— she was completely unprepared for the impact it made upon her. The savagery of the animals left her quivering in her limbs and breathing through her mouth. It was repulsive, sickening, terrifying, pathetic, and shameful. At the same time it was exhilarating, riveting, and, oddly, fun. She identified with both the winning and the losing dog, and felt as though she had just won, and lost, the most critical contest of her life. Her heart beat fiercely and she felt like crying, shouting, lecturing, and laughing, all at once.

She turned to Wade with an ashen face and said, "Christ forgive us, they fight like people, if people had only their mouths."

"I told you it was cool," said Wade, who was also somewhat ashen, though trying to appear nonchalant.

"It isn't cool, Wade," said Olivia. "It's horrible."

"I'm sorry, do you want to leave?"

"No. I don't know. It's ghastly."

"Do you want to place a bet?"

"I'm no good at gambling."

"How about a cup of coffee? They got cream."

"No."

Olivia tried to clear her mind. She studied the other people in the room, both condemning them and drawing on their brute strength. She breathed deeply and closed her eyes. It was as if she had opened a familiar door and found, just inside the wallpapered room amid antique furniture and hardbound editions of classical literature, a hideous creature devouring handfuls of rotting meat and smiling at her as though they were related. She understood now why some people relished dogfighting and others abhorred it. She also understood, perfectly, what "game" meant. It was as Wade had said—the quality of wildness, the blind inability to compromise or surrender.

But for the love of Saint Francis—the contradictions! It was almost too much to bear. Olivia found herself sitting in a roomful of Neanderthals who so honored the vital spirit of living that they willingly broke laws in order to glimpse a reflection of it. They were so much worse (through their unregenerate lack of compassion) and so much better (through their reverence of courage) than educated humanitarians. It was a maze of incongruity. The benighted willingly climbed down into the cellar and paid homage to the Monster of Survival living there, while the enlightened—with whom Olivia usually identified—refused to acknowledge their homes even *had* basements, let alone savage instincts living in them.

As though to nullify any possible generalizations to be drawn from witnessing her first dogfight, the second match was over in a matter of seconds. In this contest Lady Macbeth, the smaller of the two dogs—a long-haired mongrel bitch somewhat resembling a collie—sunk her teeth into the male's shoulder, gave a lunging shake, and turned the pit bull over on his side. When she let him up he ran to the other side of the pit and jumped the chicken wire. The whistle blew and people rushed forward to collect their winnings and bet on the next match.

Olivia watched seven matches, most of them less than fifteen minutes long. One lasted about half an hour and ended in a tie, with both dogs exhausted and bleeding, carried out of the pit to the cheering of the onlookers.

As the night wore on, Olivia's surprise over discovering a basement in the collective soul of animal-kind gradually abated, and the fascination-in-horror of making eye contact with the monster living below—due to its single, banal stare—grew wearisome.

Olivia's introspective habit of sifting through the sands of her emotions, a process acquired over a lifetime of bad health, set to work.

The winnowing process rendered a hard, cold analogy. Suppose more powerful creatures, like Greek gods, wanted to worship the vital living force through the eugenic cultivation of savage human features—the breeding of genetically cornered animals—to hoot and holler over mortal combat from the immortal safety of their cloudy bleachers. What would be her judgment of that?

Wade noticed the change in Olivia's attitude and said, "Maybe we should leave."

"Yes," said Olivia.

But then the main door opened and along with a cold blizzard of air came a huge man with a shaved head in a brown trench coat, leading a waist-high black dog so large and fearful-looking that its appearance silenced the entire barn. The creature felt the attention of the room and a low utterance curled from its massive throat—a growl descending into and beneath the registers of human hearing. This animal not only was a different breed, but also seemed a different species.

The woman at the door, still seated on her stool, held out the donation can, but the man waved it aside.

For the first time in the evening the blond youth by the blackboard moved. He walked around the pit, took his hands out of his pockets, and pointed at the advancing man. "You and your dog aren't welcome here, Orville."

"It's a free country, Junior. But if I'm breaking some law, call the police."

"Don't come closer," said the blond youth, looking not quite as large as before.

The man stopped, pulling the giant dog to heel with a single tug on the chain. "All right," he said. "Take it easy. I just thought you'd want to see a real dog."

"The last dog you fought was drugged, and you refused to call it off after the match was over," said the blond youth. "We've got rules and you're not welcome here."

"That may be, Junior. But it still seems that in a room full of such great dogfighters there would be one, just one, willing to fight a real dog."

"That's a black Tosa," whispered Olivia to Wade. "They're a Japanese breed with a lot of mastiff in them."

"I know what it is," said Wade.

"I'll say it again," said the youth. "You're not welcome here."

"I see. But if I don't leave, well, that would be interesting. I mean, here I would be, unwelcome, but still here."

The youth reached into his jacket pocket and another low growl rolled out of the giant dog.

"Keep your shirt on, Junior. You there—in the wheelchair. Wouldn't you like to see a real dog fight? I mean isn't that what you came here for? Well, Ma'am, what do you say?"

"Your dog is too big," said Olivia. "Anything over one hundred and fifty pounds is generally considered—by most experts—too slow. And I agree that rules should be followed."

"Well, there you have it," the man bellowed. "From the mouth of a cripple. My dog Cannibal is too big and slow. So why won't anyone put a dog up against him? Why is everyone afraid? Come on, lady, tell them again why they have nothing to fear."

Wade rose to his feet and picked up a length of two-by-four lying on the floor. "Back off," he said, stepping forward.

"Wade, get back here," shouted Olivia.

A short man in coveralls limped out of a horse stall along the wall and called out, "Damn it, Orville, shut your yapping mouth. I've got a dog outside."

"Then you better leave it there. But if you have the nerve to bring it inside I'll give you five-to-one. I'll give everyone in this room five-to-one. And that includes you, Junior." He pulled a wad of bills out of his trench coat pocket and held it above his head as he walked over to the card table.

Several men rushed forward to bet and the man in coveralls went outside to get his dog. The youth resumed his position beside the blackboard.

Wade sat on the bale of straw next to Olivia and explained, "Orville and Rusty Smith have hated each other for a long time. Years ago one of Orville's dogs with gunpowder shoved up its ass killed one of Rusty's."

"A grudge match," said Olivia.

Rusty returned from outside with an old white pit bull crossed with European mastiff—by far the biggest animal in the room with the exception of the Tosa. The dog was battle-worn, its face and neck scarred from a lifetime of fighting. One eye cocked to the side from vertical purple gash, and a large piece of her left ear was missing. A section of jowl was also gone, leaving several teeth—including an upper fang—exposed.

"That's Trixie," said Wade to Olivia. "She's been around a long time. I never heard of her losing a match, but Rusty said two summers ago that he wouldn't fight her anymore."

Olivia looked at the white dog and felt an immediate kinship. The beast walked beside the limping man with such dignity and poise, ignoring the other dogs in the room as if they didn't exist, her scarred head held high. Without a muzzle or leash, she kept her good eye on her owner and climbed onto the scale to be weighed as though she had done it many times before. Her weight was recorded on the blackboard at 142 pounds, the tosa's at 176.

"I want to bet on that dog," said Olivia and drew six hundred dollars out of her denim dress. The bills smelled faintly like cream chocolates.

"I thought you were no good at gambling," said Wade. "Trixie's too old and there's too much of a weight difference."

"You shouldn't discount the advantages of age so easily," said Olivia.

"I'm just telling you what I've seen. There's a reason Orville's willing to give five-to-one."

"That man's a bully and a braggart," said Olivia. "I've seen men like him all my life. He would do anything for attention."

"All that talk might also be sucker bait," said Wade. "And Rusty couldn't resist it."

"Are you going to bet for me or do I have to do it myself?"

"And get us some coffee," added Olivia. "Looks like it will be a while before we get to the truck stop."

When the two dogs were brought inside the enclosure, the pit suddenly seemed too small. Trixie sat down next to Rusty with an almost tired expression while Orville took the muzzle and harness off Cannibal as he paced and growled. Then both men stepped out of the pit and closed the gate. The barn grew silent, and at Orville's signal, the black tosa leaped forward, met in midair by the white bull.

The screaming crowd came to its feet, but the noise could not compete with the great snarling inside the chicken-wire enclosure, where it sounded as if all of Satan's demons had been turned loose. As the dogs wrestled to get hold of each other, they pressed forward until they stood on their hind legs.

This stance gave the advantage to Trixie's lower center of gravity, and she succeeded in obtaining a mouthful of dewlap. But her purchase on the loose folds of skin proved impossible to maintain, and she only tore off a rat-sized portion of hair and flesh before the larger dog was on top of her, biting the top of her head and neck. By the time she escaped, her partial ear was completely gone and blood flowed freely over her head.

The size of the dogs added to the drama. Knowing a person would be torn to pieces in an unarmed fight with either one of them heightened the tension. It was an atavistic reminder of a time when the human niche in the world was by no means secure.

The fighting in the pit continued for almost forty-five minutes, until the dogs faced each other, heads lowered, necks and shoulders dark with blood, covered with open wounds. A final lunge from the tosa backed Trixie up against a post, where the black dog finally got a grip. And though she continued to fight, she could not free herself and soon lay in the dirt, struggling helplessly—providing an equally clear but less attractive glimpse of Wildness in Defeat.

The judge blew the whistle, but the tosa did not desist, even after Orville had entered the pit and covered his trench coat with blood attempting to pull him off. When he finally succeeded, Cannibal gave a final, victorious bark at his prone opponent, but no sound came out. He tried again, straining, opening his giant mouth and forcing air through his throat, but only a gasping wheeze escaped. Orville fastened the muzzle and harness into place and led Cannibal out, a signal for the winners in the crowd to rush forward and claim their cash.

When Rusty stepped into the pit, Trixie raised her head and attempted to climb to her feet. When she could not, she looked up at her owner in shame.

"That's okay. Good girl," said Rusty, falling to his knees. But the old dog was so embarrassed over losing the match and being unable to get up that she looked away, avoiding him.

This was too much for Olivia, who apprehended at once that the old dog wasn't fighting out of an inbred fraternal aggression or from some expressed feral gene, but out of devotion to its owner. She wheeled over to the edge of the pit.

"You there," she shouted. "You there! How dare you!"

"I seen you give the boy money to bet," muttered Rusty, stroking the dog's head.

"Yes, but you knew she didn't have a chance against that dog. You knew it and still made her fight."

"I didn't know she would live," said Rusty, looking up at Olivia, his eyes unexpectedly soft. "I thought he would kill her clean. She's filled with arthritis and cancer. I thought if she could die doing what she was bred up to do and not suffer any longer . . . She can hardly get up in the morning. Who'd guess she would last this long? She even punctured his lung, damn near beat him."

"You fool," said Olivia and threw the blanket over the chicken wire. "Wade, go in there. Cover her up. For the love of God get her out of there. We're taking that dog home."

"She won't live," said Rusty, spreading the blanket in front of the dog.

"You were wrong once and will be again," said Olivia. "If ever an animal had a soul, that one has."

Wade and Rusty lifted the white terrier onto the blanket and carried her out of the pit. Outside, they laid her in the back of Wade's pickup.

"That your older sister?" asked Rusty. "She's really cute for a cripple."

"Nope, she's my girlfriend. You sure it's all right—her taking your dog?"

"Trixie deserves a woman like that to die with," said Rusty. "I just couldn't figure out what else to do with her."

"You could have put her to sleep," said Wade.

"What kind of way to die is that?"

Back inside, Wade pushed Olivia toward the door.

"Wait," said Rusty. "Take this. Those cuts will get infected." He placed on Olivia's lap a large can of tan powder with green flecks. "It's antibiotics mixed with minerals and herbs. Put it in her food. Take some yourself. Who knows, it might help."

The woman at the door answered a short crackle on her walkie-talkie, and after listening to another crackle jumped off her stool and yelled, "Three patrol cars and two cage vans just drove through Snow Corners."

A stampede of men, women, and dogs poured through the front door. Wade tossed Olivia into the cab and the wheelchair into the back with the dog. He followed other pickups and vans across the clearing and plunged into the narrow lane through the forest to the black-top, the pine branches slapping with dark, leafy violence against the windows.

A half-hour later Olivia asked the waitress at the truck stop, "Do you have any meat scraps for our dog?"

"Sure, how many you want?"

Olivia poured some of the tan and green powder on top of the scraps and Wade carried them outside. Then he returned and they sipped coffee and waited for their meals to arrive.

"I hope you got a place to take that dog, 'cause I can't take her home with me," said Wade. "My parents get one look at that animal and I'm in real trouble. They'll call the police."

"Your own parents would call the police?"

"Yup."

"Why?"

"It's hard to explain. Mostly it's because they're so beaten down. Dad's losing the farm and Mom's given up. They keep thinking if they do what they think everyone expects of them, everything will work out."

"They think convention will protect them," said Olivia.

"Yes, like all their troubles come from having overlooked some rule. They think being extra-good citizens will make something miraculous happen, save them from each other and losing the farm. It's bullshit."

"Why do you stay with them?"

"Dad couldn't get all the work done alone, and Mom—I don't want to talk about them. So, did you have an okay time so far tonight?"

"I've never had such a night as this, so I can't compare it to anything. It's been both lamentable and outstanding."

"Good," said Wade. "I liked it too."

"Wade," said Olivia, blushing, "can you help me get to the bathroom? It's that coffee. This is embarrassing, but my sister will kill me if I don't come home dry."

"Hell, Ma'am, that ain't anything. And you should know that nothing about you could ever embarrass me. Shit, the more I see of you, the better you get. I'm not kidding. Come on." He lifted her out of the booth and carried her in his arms. On the way to the women's bathroom, a middle-aged couple at the counter stared at them.

"Get used to it, motherfuckers," Wade snapped.

"Wade!" said Olivia sternly, then burst into laughter, losing control of her bladder.

The living room lights were on when Olivia returned to her home in Words. Violet sat in the middle of the couch watching television and stood up when they came in.

"Hello, Vio," said Olivia. "We took your advice—what you told us to do—and rescued one of the dogs. Will you please go out to the truck with Wade and help carry her inside? I'll get some newspapers to put down on the carpet. Hurry, because Wade has to get home soon, and I have so much to tell you."

THE THIEF

A	FTER SEVERAL MONTHS, THE LAST PIECE OF GAIL SHOTWELL'S
	song fell into place. She connected a microphone to a tape
recorder and sang into it, then played it back. Several words didn't
sound right, so she tried again. Then the bass was so loud that it
drowned out her voice.

When she finally had a satisfactory recording, she drove it over to
July Montgomery's small farm, ran an extension cord from the milk
house into the main part of the barn, and played it for him as he
milked his Jersey cows.

"Play it again," he said. "And turn up the volume."

July closed his eyes, nodded his head, and said he thought it was
the best song he had ever heard.

"You're just saying that," said Gail. "It's not that good."

"It is," said July, his arms, clothes, and boots splotched with dried
dirt, lime, and antiseptic. "When I listen to it I see pictures in my
head, and that means it's very good."

Gail unplugged her tape recorder and drove home.

For the next two weeks she took as much work as she could get at
the plastic factory, paid most of her overdue bills, and thought about
asking Barbara Jean to listen to her song.

Gail had driven past her summer home several times, just to look.
Each time she had been disappointed because the house sat so far
off the road that almost nothing could be seen or even imagined
about the way the popular musician spent her time. At the entrance
gate, two stone pillars stood on either side of a concrete drive, with
globe lights suspended from iron chains. The tall, four-board fences
had been painted chalky white, something people with expensive
horses often liked to do. Once, Gail had seen someone in the front

yard—a dark speck in a patch of green—but could not even tell if it was a man or a woman.

Barbara Jean had invited her to practice with her band some afternoon, but did that mean she could just show up on any afternoon? Did "some" mean "any"? It had been a long time since last October—half a year. Had the offer expired?

She thought about calling, but that seemed like a bad idea.

Finally an especially bright, warm day arrived and Gail—after working a night shift and spending the morning in a tavern—felt her confidence soaring somewhere between feeling invincible and feeling lucky. She drank another beer and drove out of town.

She navigated between the stone pillars at the road and two long rows of white fence. In back of the house was a garage and parking area with two sports cars parked haphazardly next to each other, as if they had been randomly dropped from the air. Further back were several small painted buildings, a horse barn, and a John Deere tractor with several bales of hay in the loader. A miniature donkey stood on its hind legs, drinking water from a stock tank. Gail parked beside the sports cars and took small satisfaction in the fact that although her coupe was sixteen years old, dented and rusting around the fenders, at least it was a convertible.

The clay-red house seemed modestly-sized—larger than her own but smaller than many modern houses—and she pushed the doorbell. It made no sound that she could hear. The door opened and a woman of about thirty-five said hello. She was tall and as slender as a wand, her skin blacker than night. Her shaved head shone like oiled gunmetal. She wore sandals, khaki pants with many pockets, and a blouse with every color of the visible light spectrum.

"I'm Gail Shotwell. Barbara Jean said I should come over some afternoon, and, well, here I am."

"Bee Jay isn't up yet," said the woman, looking at the bass case resting on the concrete step. "But come in. We played in the Cities last night and things are a little slow around here. I'm Yesha. You want a cup of coffee?"

On the inside, the house seemed enormous, or at least the kitchen did. A long wall of crank-out windows spilled sunlight onto hanging pans, polished marble, and a glossy, brown-tiled floor. A large vase of garden flowers sat on the table in the corner.

In the middle of the sun-soaked kitchen, a woman with a complexion resembling lacquered porcelain sat at the counter on a tall stool, drinking a glass of orange juice. Her eyes were pale, pale blue, her hair curly white-blond, and she wore loosing-fitting white capris and a white top. Her bare feet leaned together at the soles, embracing at the toes.

Both women appeared to be about ten years older than Gail, and she at once began building a psychic bridge over the Age Ravine that separated them, trying to seem older. Then as soon as she noticed she was doing it, she stopped.

"This is Monica," said Yesha. "Monica, this is Gail."

"You play percussion," said Gail, and Monica smiled wearily.

"I hope you like strong coffee," said Yesha, pouring Gail a cup of what looked like pure India ink. She put it on a saucer beside Monica's orange juice.

Gail sat on one of the four tall stools and wished she had thought more carefully about what to wear, though this was an old problem for her. She never liked what she wore, and, well, blue jeans with a red button-up blouse ought to be good enough. It's what she wore to work. Her sneakers were a little ragged, however, and she wrapped her feet around the wooden legs of the stool.

"Whoa," she said, and without intentionally meaning to she made a face. "That's strong."

Monica laughed. "People ingest Yesha's coffee at their own risk."

"I like it," said Gail.

Sounds from deeper in the house announced the movements of the owner. From some unknown place, Barbara Jean, wearing a pair of green silk coveralls, walked into the kitchen. Her green eyes focused on Gail, and after a long, uncomfortable moment her face registered recognition.

"I'm Gail Shotwell. We met last fall."

Barbara Jean nodded and Gail felt a new tension in the air. Her presence, even after just waking up, was immense.

"Bee Jay, you want something to eat?" asked Yesha, handing her a cup of coffee. The black-haired woman shook her head, carried the cup of coffee over to the table, and sat next to the vase of flowers.

"You should eat something, Bee Jay," said Yesha. "Let me fix you an egg."

"No eggs," whispered Barbara Jean, sipping from her coffee, and Gail marveled at how mysteriously ambiguous the words seemed. "No eggs" could mean there were no eggs in the house, or that she was hungry for something but didn't want an egg, or that eggs in general were not good for you, or that she was allergic to eggs, or that she wasn't hungry and didn't want an egg or anything else. And the way she whispered the two words—to someone familiar with her whispering—could also mean that she wanted an egg.

Gail began to wish she hadn't come. She could feel her earlier confidence draining away, leaving in its place an anxious emptiness. She'd never even been to the Cities and they were only four hours away. Her life was small, limited, and of little consequence. She also had no experience—outside of immediate family members and occasional overnight lovers—with situations involving people who had just climbed out of bed and were waking up together. It seemed bold to live in such an open manner, and she felt both attracted to the communal informality and unsettled by it.

Yesha opened the refrigerator, took out a bottle of soy milk, and carried it along with a box of cereal, a bowl, and a spoon over to the table. Before she could pour the cereal, Barbara Jean waved her away. "I'm not hungry."

"Gail says she likes Yesha's coffee," said Monica.

"She's a polite girl," said Barbara Jean, and from the tone of the comment Gail knew she was being made fun of.

"I like any kind of coffee," said Gail.

"Are you still playing with that same band?" asked Barbara Jean.

"I guess so," she answered, hoping the fun-making wasn't extending into more personal areas.

"How's it going?"

"Excuse me?"

"How's it going with the band?"

"It's going okay. Look, I'm sorry to just barge in on you like this."

"If I remember, I think I invited you to come," said Barbara Jean.

"Yes, I mean you did, yes, but it's still hard to know when to come, but, well, I have a song and I'm wondering if you could listen to it."

"What kind of song?"

"One I wrote," she said, taking the cassette out of her pocket. "It's called 'Along the Side of the Road.'"

A space of frozen silence opened like a doorway into a hollowed-out glacier. Then just as suddenly, it closed. "Sure," said Barbara Jean and took another drink of coffee. "Let's hear it."

Yesha and Monica followed her out of the kitchen and down a wooden staircase. Gail picked up her bass and followed.

In the center of a large basement room with polished maple floors sat a baby grand, surrounded by an assortment of chairs, microphone stands, amplifiers, musical instruments, and a bar.

Gail handed her cassette to Yesha, and she poked it into a rack-mounted tape player. Within seconds, her song was playing through two black-faced speaker cabinets, and each scratchy imperfection could be perfectly heard.

The young women listened, and before the song finished Monica climbed into the set of drums to play along softly. Yesha hung an f-hole jazz guitar over her shoulder and Barbara Jean stood at the piano, searching for an accompanying key.

"This is a good song," said Yesha.

A private joy rose up inside Gail.

"Play it again," said Barbara Jean, switching to an electric piano.

A woman in a white T-shirt and faded jeans walked out of the stairwell and into the basement room. She was short and younger than the other three, almost as young as Gail, with black hair, black eyes, wide face, prominent cheekbones, and a smooth, copper-brown complection. Gail didn't know if she had come from another room in the house or from outside. Without introduction, she took a fiddle from a case, tightened the bow, and joined in as though she had been playing Gail's song her whole life.

When the tape ended, Barbara Jean told Gail to sing her song into one of the four microphones.

"I'll get my bass," she said.

"Forget the bass for now," said Monica. "Just sing."

She did, and soon experienced something resembling driving a car for the first time. Her voice was no longer just her voice. Its power was enhanced, augmented through a nimble accompaniment that responded instantaneously to her very thoughts. And unlike the Straight Flush, these musicians were wildly inventive, creating ever-new ways of complementing her singing. New rhythms danced in and out of old rhythms. And the lyrical phrases expanded with meaning in the context of the exploring drama of the music.

She'd never sounded so good.

"Let's try it again," said Barbara Jean. "Monica, you sing with her on the chorus."

"It's a little wobbly in the middle," said Yesha, sitting on a wicker chair and plugging her guitar into a tube amplifier.

"There're too many measures in the bridge," said the woman on the violin. "Drop the middle. And that minor doesn't come off the F-chord in the right way. Use the ninth instead."

"Monica, go deep on the end of the chorus—the last line needs to darken. This can work for us very well. It has a huge sentimental core."

"Rita, take a full line solo before the last verse and don't pull off that faraway melancholy. When the 'Leave me along the road,' comes up, use a hammered string.

Gail sang her song again and was again lifted up by the accompaniment, borne away to a place where plastic factories, unpaid bills, human cruelty, flat tires, and leaking hot water heaters did not exist. She was part of a better, more brilliantly imagined world.

She wasn't exactly sure when it happened, but sometime around the second chorus—when Monica's voice found a lower, haunting harmony with her own—something changed. As she sang, Gail listened to the resonant sounds, harmonics, and rhythms, and a bad feeling crept like a thief into her mind.

This new world wasn't hers.

Her song now sounded like a Barbara Jean song.

She leaned into the microphone and kept singing, reassuring herself that the new sound was much better than her own; it was also her big chance.

But it wasn't her song anymore.

The character and mood of the original feeling-idea had been made into something brighter and easy to find. Fleeting images of her mother's face and her childhood friend no longer rose out of the chord changes in the second verse. The hard edge of the song had been softened and its outcry had been nuanced. The smoldering sorrow was now almost pretty, and the spirit beyond wonder and beyond love had been lost.

Gail stopped singing, closed her bass case, took the tape out of the player, and walked toward the staircase.

"Where are you going?" asked Barbara Jean, almost angrily.

Gail stopped and looked into her resplendent green eyes and tried to think of something to say. Nothing seemed right. She could not tell what was happening to her. Trying to smile, she felt a wall of tears building up behind her eyes and she walked up the stairs, through the kitchen, and outdoors.

Her convertible started on the second try and she drove away.

THE UNIVERSAL ACORN

T O PREPARE FOR HER SUNDAY SERMON, WINNIE DROVE TO THE
Grange Public Library. The little brick building often exerted a
calming influence over her; it possessed an almost monastic quality,
free from telephone calls, the smell of food, and visitors. On occasion, it also served as a place of meditation and prayer.

Inside, she sat at the large, spartan desk in the reading room, surrounded by her favorite books of biblical annotation and reference,
and wrote notes on a legal pad. Except for Leslie Weedle, the librarian,
and Maxine Smith, a volunteer, the building was as deserted and as
still as old age. The late-afternoon sun drove through the windows,
illuminating shafts of paper motes and creating a bright, pleasant
pattern on the worn wooden floor.

By 8:30 p.m. Winnie had outlined a sermon based on passages in
Revelation—passages of dreamlike imagery, illuminating the paths
that Spirit often rode through the mind. She closed her notebook,
shut her eyes, and entered deeply into a private thought just before
Maxine placed her hand on her shoulder in an unexpectedly friendly
manner and told her in a practiced, lowered voice that the library
would be closing soon.

Winnie collected her things and went to her yellow car.

The damp evening air chilled her to the bone, and she was fam-
ished. It seemed an eternity before the heater began pouring warmth
onto her feet. She took a shortcut past the cemetery on the hill, driving faster than normal. Then she noticed the long drive heading back
into the dark woods, stopped, backed up, and drove down it.

Jacob opened the door, wearing a gray sweatshirt and dark green
sweatpants, his feet bare, his hair wet and uncombed. He was clearly
surprised to see her, and during his halting greeting Winnie decided
he had forgotten her name.

"I hope I'm not bothering you," she said. "Perhaps you don't remember me. I'm Winifred Smith."

Jacob looked beyond her to the car. "Is anything wrong?"

"No, nothing's wrong. I was on my way home from the library and wanted to stop and apologize for several days ago. I behaved unconscionably and I ask your forgiveness."

"Come in," said Jacob, swinging the door open.

"I can't stay," she said, but stepped inside and stood on a small oval woven mat.

Jacob closed the door.

Winnie felt the warm, humid air surrounding her in such a sudden, ambient embrace that she wondered how anyone could afford to have the heat turned up so high. It seemed like bad stewardship, wasteful, irresponsible, and self-indulgent. It also felt wonderful. The woody interior of the house and the smell of burning wood made it seem as though she had just stepped inside a roasting chestnut.

"You'd better take off your coat," said Jacob. "I'm afraid I forgot to close the door on the stove before I took a shower and, well, it's pretty warm in here."

"I can't stay," said Winnie. "I just wanted to apologize."

"What for?"

"I was angry with you. I don't know why. Well, I do know why but I know I shouldn't have felt that way. It was small-minded of me. And when I said that eating meat wasn't the point, well, it was very much the point—or at least a contributing factor—and I guess I wanted to look the other way so I could remain on my tiny blessed island of self-delusion. So I snapped at you and I'm sorry. I just wanted you to know that I've thought a lot about it and will never again eat meat, at least not meat from cattle. And I'm sorry."

"You were upset, and understandably so. Take off your coat and sit down. I'll make some tea."

"You forgot my name."

"I didn't know whether to call you Winnie, Winifred, or Reverend, but I didn't forget."

"It's no matter. My, is it ever warm in here!"

"Here, let me take your coat. Sit down."

"It's late and I think I've said all I need to. I really can't stay."

She watched him put her coat in the closet, noticing his bare feet, again.

"How about a cup of tea?"

"I don't drink anything with caffeine."

"Then I have the just right kind. Are you hungry?"

"No," she said and scowled because it was untrue.

"You haven't eaten," said Jacob, as though he had momentarily peered into her mind. "Let me get you something. I was just about to eat myself. I have soup, made yesterday. It's ready."

"Listen, Mr. Helm," began Winnie.

"Call me Jacob. Besides, you fed me a couple days ago."

"I'm afraid Violet brought most of the food. She's both a cooking expert and a cooking machine."

Winnie followed him into the kitchen, and with surprising efficiency, for a man, he set out a meal of soup, salad, bread, and cheese on the table next to the computer. "Here, sit down," he said, seating her and returning to the refrigerator for salad dressing. "I apologize for the computer. I don't have another place to put it. Do you take cream or sugar with tea?"

"No thank you. Is this squash soup?"

"I'm afraid so—you don't like it?"

"Yes, very much. I haven't had squash soup for many years and the smell is laden with pleasant memories."

"I hope it won't be too spicy for you."

"That would be impossible," said Winnie.

"Will you ask a blessing before we eat?" asked Jacob, seating himself across from her.

She looked at him suspiciously, but he had already closed his eyes and lowered his head.

"Precious Lord, we ask that it may please You to bless this food to our bodies so our lives may be in the service of Your Kingdom. Amen."

"Amen," said Jacob.

Winnie tasted the soup, then set the spoon down and frowned.

"You don't like it?" asked Jacob.

"Excuse me, Mr. Helm, but I was under the impression that you were not a believer and I don't understand why you would say 'amen' to something you could not in all honesty affirm. I suppose you are just trying in your own way to be nice but there is something terribly offensive in pretending something you do not believe—as though it were an empty formality."

"I apologize if I offended you," said Jacob. "It's not exactly true that I do not believe in God, but it always seems more truthful to deny it rather than allow someone to think I agree with whatever their religious position might be."

"I don't have a 'position,'" said Winnie.

"Then I apologize again," said Jacob. "I'm afraid talking about these things makes me uncomfortable. I only wanted to affirm your request."

"For whom?"

"For you."

"By saying 'amen,' Mr. Helm, you gave the impression you had committed yourself to the service of the Kingdom as well."

Jacob put down his own spoon. "I don't know you well enough to understand what you mean by that, Winifred. I have only a vague notion, so the best I can do is give my consent to your own wishes—for yourself—whatever they are."

"In that case I accept your apology," said Winnie and resumed eating. "I'm overly sensitive about being mocked. It's a weakness of mine, I'm afraid. This soup is quite good. It so much reminds me of my mother. She made this every fall. What joy those memories of her bring to me."

"I have something I'd like to ask of you," said Jacob.

"What?"

"Perhaps we can talk about it after we've finished."

"I really must not stay long. Do you always keep your house this warm?"

"I told you, it was an oversight. Should I open the door?"

"No. It feels so good to be warm. I'm not used to it."

"I suppose you have many people who talk to you about personal things," said Jacob.

"It's not unusual," said Winnie. "It's my 'position.'"

Jacob laughed.

When they had finished eating, he carried their remaining tea into the living room and Winnie seated herself on the edge of the straight-backed chair nearest the door, pulling aside her long hair to avoid sitting on it. Once again, she noticed his bare feet.

"Here," Jacob said and handed her a framed picture of a young woman wearing white shorts and standing in a garden.

"That's Angela," he said. "I mean that *was* Angela. We were married for about five years and she died of pancreatic cancer a while ago—quite a while ago, actually."

"I'm very sorry," said Winnie, feeling the same confusion she always felt when she was given a photograph of a stranger. Was it expected that a human connection could be achieved through the picture alone? It seemed so self-evident that nothing important could be communicated in this way, when all the living parts were missing. Better to show a button from a dress, share a memory, a grocery list—anything but a picture. Pictures were for people to whom the frozen physical outline had some resemblance. Pictures of pure strangers evoked stereotypes. It was a desperate act, like prying a faded photo out of a wallet on the eve of battle and showing it to someone next to you. It made her sad.

So instead of seeing what Jacob hoped for her to see in the picture—his own perceptions of his beloved former wife—what Winnie saw was a pair of shorts that were in her opinion too short for any woman to wear outdoors, too white to be worn in a garden, and too tight for someone in need of some exercise. And from these impressions she attempted to understand how deeply Jacob had felt about his wife. It was maddening.

"I didn't know you had lost your wife," she said, handing the picture back.

"How could you?" said Jacob. "Have you ever lost someone you really loved?"

"I'm familiar with grief, if that's what you mean," said Winnie. "Would you like to tell me about her?"

"Yes, but I'm not going to. Anyway, I was wondering if you might pray for me—I mean if you could. I can't stop mourning. I can't seem to quit. It's gone on too long. Way too long. It was understandable in the beginning, but this has gotten out of hand. I have a gaping absence in my center. It isn't leaving enough of me. I'm surrounded by loneliness and this grieving simply must end."

"I don't know if I can pray for that," said Winnie. "It's not right to stop grieving until you're all done. Grief has its own rules and they must be followed."

"Then pray I finish soon," said Jacob.

"Very well," said Winnie. "That's what most prayers are for—speed." She tossed her head, closed her eyes, folded her hands together, straightened her back, and said, "Dearest Heavenly Mother and Father, hear our prayer. We thank You for all You have given us, especially Your Son and Light of Our Life, and we commit into Your Care the soul of Mr. Helm, trusting You will accomplish Your Work in him swiftly. Amen."

When Winnie opened her eyes she discovered Jacob staring into them. She worried that perhaps he had been looking at her for some time and her earlier fear of being mocked returned.

"Thank you," said Jacob.

"You're welcome."

"Do you think anyone has ever understood why some people, good people, die so young?"

"Probably not," said Winnie. "Sometimes it's best not to ask why. We must accept things as they are."

"You don't," said Jacob, remembering the park.

"I try as hard as I can."

"Shouldn't we strive to change the world, to make it better?"

"Yes and no."

"Doesn't history teach us that real progress only comes through struggle?"

Winnie's expression darkened. She looked at the floor and remained silent. Jacob pursued her. "I can tell you would like to say something."

"I'd better not."

"What is it?"

"I should be going."

"Say it."

"I hope this won't make you think less of me, Mr. Helm, but I don't think 'progress' or 'history' really exist. They're made up. People imagine them to flatter themselves. We live in an eternal present, as does every other living thing. It changes yet doesn't change. We can no more understand the past than we can fly. The idea of progress and history is a product of pure cultural arrogance."

"What a wonderful thought!" said Jacob with a surprised, spreading smile. "Do you honestly think that?"

"I do, but I don't expect you to understand it. So many of my thoughts are nearly incomprehensible, especially to me. But that's something else I must accept. There really is no place for me—no place in this world I belong. And I don't expect that to change."

"I know the feeling," said Jacob.

"You do?"

"Since my wife died I've lived like a ghost."

"A ghost?"

"It feels like I'm never really here, or anywhere. Some part of me shows up to stumble through, but something else is always missing, and the missing part is worth more than the other."

Winnie stared at him, drank the rest of her tea, and put down the cup. Her mind raced from one incomplete thought to the next, looking for one that would both hold her feelings and explain them. She'd lived like a ghost all her life, and was living like one now. She'd come to accept that ghost-living defined the normal, shared human experience. But when Jacob spoke of it, it didn't seem fair, or right. It seemed unnecessary that he should live that way. And if it was unnecessary for him, it was also unnecessary for her, and the compelling immensity of these twin unnecessities caused her to turn directly toward him and meet his eyes fully. When she spoke, her voice came out of her in such a gentle and unsure manner that she hardly recognized it. "Jacob, I experienced Oneness, once," she said.

"What does that mean?"

"There was one time when I didn't feel like a ghost. I experienced the unity of all things, last fall. I felt it and saw it. I want to tell you."

"I don't understand."

"I know you don't and I wish you could," she said, her words coming faster and faster. A glow kindled inside her face. "It would give you the same comfort it gives me. There is a bigger world that holds this one inside it."

"How?"

"The way an oak tree holds an acorn. This world and all we know of it is that acorn, and from inside it we marvel at how such a wonderful acorn universe came to be here, strewn with galaxies and abounding in complexity. For the most part we remain unaware of the branch from which we are hung, the leaves that process the light, the wonderful trunk that connects us to the ground, the roots that burrow after water and nutrients; instead, we calculate the odds of our acorn springing to life on its own, unconnected to a tree. The uniqueness of our acorn world astounds us—when in fact there are ten thousand acorns on our tree, ten thousand trees in our forest, and ten thousand forests. And all the forests and all the trees and all the acorns are only one single thing, grown up from a single acorn. We are not separate, and I want you to know that. We are all part of one thing, and nothing good has ever passed or can ever pass away. There is no way out, but there is a way in, and when one person feels lonely like a ghost it touches us all."

Jacob smiled. "I can't tell you how much I enjoy talking to you. It seems I never talk with anyone, not about anything real. No one I know has anything to say. Let me get you more tea. You have no idea how much this means to me."

Winnie returned his smile, but before she could say anything more, she completed a thought that condemned her in her own mind.

At first it seemed to be someone else's thought, but she soon recognized it as her own and a quick terror found her. She wondered if Jacob had motile spermatozoa.

"I must go," she said, standing up.

"You haven't finished your tea," said Jacob. He stood up and extended one of his thick hands toward her.

Winnie backed up. "I'm sorry. Please, just give me a minute," and she walked into the kitchen area, struggling to gain control over her emotions. *Stop it. Stop trying to make me run away. You always do this to me. Stop it.*

She stood by the kitchen table and slowly began to feel better. She allowed the fingers of her right hand to touch the back of the chair she had earlier been sitting on when she was eating the squash soup, and she concentrated on the sensation. Her anxiety abated as the texture of the wood against her fingertips came into focus. Her breathing came easier.

Then she noticed a corner of notepaper sticking out from under the computer's keyboard, and the handwritten word S-M-I-T-H. The fingers on her right hand continued toward the paper and nudged it out from its hiding place enough to reveal a second word, C-A-R-L.

A cinch fastened around her heart, and tightened. There were ten thousand explanations for how these words could have come to be here, but they were powerless against the raw horror evoked by the sight of them. Questions formed in her mind, but when she tried to consider them they dissolved.

She looked at Jacob and he immediately rose to his bare feet.

"Winifred, what's wrong?"

"I must leave," she said, walking quickly to the closet, taking her coat from a hanger, and noticing a huge military weapon standing in the corner.

She pulled on the door but it did not budge. Her heart beat in her throat. *He locked it.* She pulled again, and again the door refused to open.

"You have to push down, Winifred," said Jacob. "The frame is warped. There."

As soon as it opened she bolted through it, threading her arms through the sleeves of her coat on the way to her car. Her shoes splashed through pools of melted snow.

HUNTING

R USTY CLIMBED OUT OF BED BEFORE FIRST LIGHT AND DRESSED in the same clothes he had worn the night before. He went downstairs, filled a thermos with coffee, and packed two sandwiches inside a paper sack. In the basement he loaded his rifle, pulled his winter coat around him, and walked out beyond the barn.

Starlight streaked raggedly through the sky, a threadbare satin sheet hastily flung over the dark heavens.

He chose a spot overgrown with brambles and brush, with a view of the back of his barn and the slowly descending wooded valley. A stump left over from a black locust harvested for fence posts and firewood served as a stool. From this partially hidden position he could watch the cougar return to or depart from his barn, and shoot it.

As he waited, he drank from the thermos of coffee and thought about his brother.

One memory after another visited him, and Rusty subtracted from them everything that did not bear directly upon his brother, until his recollections of walking to school with Carl, falling asleep in their shared bedroom, and running together through the sandy fields surrounding the quarry yielded only the essential, unmitigated, taken-for-granted feeling of Carl's presence—the steady, minute-by-minute awareness of him.

A cardinal called in the distance and several small brown and white birds flew up the valley, stopped, and moved on. Minutes later he heard another scolding cardinal voice, this time closer, followed by fleeting sounds, the breaking of small branches, crushing dry leaves.

The sounds grew louder and Rusty searched from one side of the narrow valley to the other, trying to locate the source. The muscles in his neck tightened as he realized the cougar was not on the ground at all, but leaping from tree to tree, coming forward in the haphazard and galloping manner of a squirrel. Hidden in the branches, the animal would be hard to see. Rusty slid the top cartridge from the magazine into the firing chamber and nudged the safety into the Off position.

The sounds seemed to be coming mostly from his left, and he half raised the rifle to his shoulder when he saw what looked like a shadow moving through the trees about a hundred yards away. The shadow floated from one limb to the next, gathering more shape and solidity, moving with an unconscious, rapid ease that implied deep familiarity with the valley.

About thirty yards away the large cat jumped to the ground and froze, then looked quickly from side to side. Something like a haunch of venison hung from both sides of its mouth. Its long tail waved slowly from right to left, and it looked at Rusty as though anticipating his presence.

Rusty pulled the rifle snugly into his shoulder and took aim through the iron sights. The color of the animal impressed him. It seemed like nothing he had ever seen before—this kind of bright black. It drew all other colors to it, like water into a drain. The animal possessed a darkness even beyond black, with two glowing eyes as yellow as stars.

The cat bounded forward, covering twenty or twenty-five yards in four leaps. It sprang into the maple growing next to the barn and scrambled up the thick trunk in less time than it would take for a man to run through a room. From one of the limbs, it launched itself onto the barn roof, tearing loose several shingles. It leaned over the edge, leaped again, scrabbled against the weathered barn boards, and disappeared into the small high square window, which swallowed it like a shadow swallowing a shadow.

Rusty lowered the rifle and reset the safety. He didn't know why he hadn't taken a shot. He simply didn't. And to keep from thinking about it any longer, he committed himself to shooting it at the next opportunity. Sooner or later the animal would climb from the barn window, and he would be waiting.

The valley was now saturated with new light, and he took a drink of coffee and bit into one of his roast beef, lettuce, and mayonnaise sandwiches. It had been some time since he'd eaten outdoors and he revisited the experience of food tasting different in the open air. Its flavor changed. Neither better nor worse. Different. Good different. Brightened somehow. He and Carl had often eaten outdoors. His brother, more than himself, had loved natural things, bitterly disliked school and being indoors.

Then Rusty heard more sounds coming up the valley and soon recognized them as boots moving through snow, leaves, and brush. Birds scattered ahead of it, and a human shape finally came into view, walking slowly between the trees, pausing frequently, looking up. A man wearing a light brown leather jacket and khaki pants.

As he came closer, Rusty became convinced that he did not know him: an older man, about Rusty's age, height, and weight. In many ways he resembled Rusty, or rather resembled the way Rusty might have appeared to others if instead of working like a hungry dog all his life he had been born into a family with money and connections, with self-confidence, and had become a professional hunter, acquired the most expensive sporting clothes and a custom-built rifle with a thumb-hole stock, engraved barrel, German laser night-seeing sights, and loaded with 150-grain partition bullets.

As a way of announcing himself, Rusty stood up.

"Morning to you," said the stranger, walking slowly toward him. He spoke quietly, with an almost aristocratic air, and his lips and thick gray mustache did not appear to move when he spoke.

Rusty nodded.

"You must have seen him," he said, inspecting the sides of the barn.

"Who?"

"That cat. Trailed him three times last week. Curious. Each time he comes here."

Rusty thought about his brother. He remembered Carl sitting up one cold night in the middle of winter, feeding the stove. After he'd put a new log inside the firebox, he'd return to breaking open hickory nuts with a hammer, picking out the nut meat inside and storing it in a Mason jar.

"This animal some business of yours?" asked Rusty.

"Some of the folks around here put up a reward."

Rusty thought for a short while about people offering to pay someone to kill an animal that was currently living in his barn and pulled at the bill of his old cap.

"Did you see it?" the stranger asked again, still looking up at the high window in the barn.

"See what?"

"The cat."

"Who are you?"

"Name's Arthur Lode. I understand they call you Rusty."

"Some do."

As though to offer contrary evidence, in the distance the door on the back of Rusty's house banged shut and Maxine called, "Russell, Russell."

"You see it or not?"

"What I saw was someone named Lode walking onto my property. What I expect to see now is him walking off it."

Rusty stood a little to the side, a movement that repositioned the barrel of his rifle so it pointed to the ground directly between them.

The man smiled easily. "Sure thing, old man," he said, turning around. "Only a matter of time."

He walked back in the direction he had come from.

Rusty watched until he disappeared, stood for several minutes longer, and returned to the house.

July Montgomery's old white pickup was parked in the driveway, and inside the house he sat beside Maxine at the kitchen table. They were drinking coffee. July hadn't taken his jacket off, and Maxine wore a cotton print dress with a sweater. The furnace was running.

Rusty joined them. Maxine handed him a clean cup and he poured the last of the coffee from the thermos into it.

"You're not going to shoot that animal, are you, Russell?"

Rusty glared at July and he smiled sheepishly and said, "Sorry. I just assumed you'd told her."

"Don't know yet what I'm going to do," said Rusty. "I don't know why he's up there. It don't make any sense. Nothing for you to worry about, though."

"Maybe it will just leave on its own," said Maxine. "Doesn't seem to be hurting anything."

"That animal's a killer," said Rusty. "It's eaten several steers already."

"We have too, Russell. Does that make us killers?"

"Those steers belonged to someone!"

"Don't raise your voice."

"How does it get into the barn?" asked July, unzipping his jacket.

"Climbs through the upper window in back."

"Tell you what, Rusty. I got to thinking about this last night. We'll wait until it leaves and I'll climb into the mow and close the window—nail it shut."

Rusty drank the rest of his coffee, set the cup down, and said, "He probably won't come out until near dark. I know he saw me and there was someone else tracking him from down the valley. Probably spooked him some."

At dusk, Rusty and July waited for the cougar to come out. Hidden behind a long row of stacked firewood, they talked in whispers.

"Did Jacob find that information you wanted about your brother?"

"Yup."

"Not good news, I take it."

"Nope. How about yourself? Do you have a family?"

"They're gone now."

"Mine too," said Rusty. "I didn't think it would make a difference, but it does."

"I know what you mean, or at least I know it in my own way."

"I've got a niece, my brother's girl. She lives in Words. Didn't know that before."

"You mean the preacher?"

"Yup."

"I met her last fall," said July.

"What's she like?"

"She's the real thing, Rusty."

"What does that mean?"

"It means you're going to like her. That young woman is worth about a dozen ordinary ones. So she's your niece. That's something. Does she know who you are?"

"Nope."

"Want me to introduce you?"

"Nope."

"You're going to tell her, aren't you?"

"I'll do it in my own time."

They continued watching the back of the barn.

"I remember when you came into this area," said Rusty. "To be honest, I didn't think you'd make it."

"I almost didn't."

"You lived in that chicken coop next to the house."

"I couldn't afford to heat the house," said July.

"Anyway, I didn't think you'd make it."

"Shhh," whispered July, and out of the high window in the barn climbed the black cat. It lunged for the overhang, caught it, and pulled itself onto the roof. It stood there for a short while, looking in all directions, then crept down the incline several yards and leaped into the maple. In no time at all it was on the ground and bounding down the valley, stopping frequently to listen and watch.

"Let's go," said July, and they hurried around the barn and entered through the front doors. There was still enough light to see fairly well inside.

From his collection of tools, Rusty handed July a hammer and a handful of nails, and told him that he could pile up baled hay in the mow to reach the window, which closed from the inside.

July climbed up the ladder and Rusty waited below, holding his rifle.

When after a short time there were no sounds of hammering or stacking hay, Rusty called up, "What's going on?"

"Be quiet," came the voice from the mow, and soon after July climbed down.

"What's the matter?" asked Rusty.

"This is a bigger problem than we thought," said July. "There's a mostly grown cub up there. My guess is it crawled in and its mother can't get it out. So she hauls food in for it."

"You mean I've got two wild cats living up there?"

"Yes. The young one may be hurt. Looks like it favors its left front leg, a sprain maybe. Probably came in before it stiffened up. Now it doesn't want to leave."

"Great," said Rusty. "That's just damn great."

SPRING

VIOLET BRASSO'S ADJUSTMENT TO THE GIANT PIT BULL PRO-
ceeded as smoothly as could be expected. Her inveterate fondness for caregiving could not resist the charm of helplessness.

The Brasso dining room was transformed into a single-occupancy
canine revitalization unit where the dog's wounds were routinely
bathed, treated, and dressed. Knowledgeable neighbors paid consola-
tory visits; poultices, special foods, tonics, herbs, and other remedies
were administered. Medicines were sprinkled in with twice-a-day
home-cooked reduced-fat meals, followed by tooth brushing. The
church's prayer chain included the white dog's name in its interces-
sory activity. Olivia called in health updates to Pastor Winnie, who
noted them in the weekly bulletin.

As the animal's health improved, Violet took her for walks around
the neighborhood and the benefits of dog ownership soon became
apparent.

First, there was the companionship. The familiar roads, alley-
ways, and trails took on new dimensions when they were traveled
mutually. And as the dog's stamina increased, their walks became
longer and more frequent.

As these routines were becoming established, spring arrived in
a circus of warm ghosts, each day stealing away another part of
winter. In the shade of the house, the last mound of snow shrank
and vanished. The frozen, lumpy ground softened discretely—first
just the idea of something less hard; then a squeaky, frosty crust;
then a greasy topmost skim followed by shifting layers of gelatinous
instability. Then came ever-deepening mud, and the trees, bushes,
and grasses sucked up the sticky goo through their greedy roots, as
if they were slurping milkshakes up paper straws.

Buds blushed in scarlet as they remembered how to pucker and open along arcades of unfurling branches, creating a new syntactical venue for Blue Skies. Flower daggers stabbed up out of the ground. Frogs, salamanders, toads, and other amphibians performed their annual resurrection, digging out of skin-breathing sleep and throating jeers at the simpler, less ceremonial life forms. Organized gangs of red-winged blackbirds appeared, overnight, congregated in empty trees, and pretended through their gleeful chattering to have always been there. Finally, the drying ground conspired with greening grass to provide the spongy-hard consistency that Violet's feet so loved to feel through her homemade moccasins, and recurring dreams climbed up her sturdy calves as she walked.

With spring came new yet familiar smells, carried in shifting rooms of haunting surmise. And what better way to experience them than in the presence of a creature specifically designed for olfaction? The white dog's nose never ceased its testing, exploratory work.

Violet marveled at how such an enormous animal could become frozen in her tracks, incapacitated by a stray molecule of air-borne interest, staring off into the distance, scanning for a second, confirming trace. Sometimes the short hairs on her back rose up in a row of spikes in response to a scrap of scented worry, and she would plant her front feet as though bracing for another overpowering whiff. Obviously, for Trixie, the primal scene from which all actions arose was not an unresolved parental image but rather a dark theater of pregnant odors—a fragrance of destiny—and Violet sometimes wished to escape the Human Picture Prison and, just once, inhale a plot.

Violet also took delight in walking along paths for years forbidden to her because of the fierce, barking dogs living along them. Now, those same dogs that had once terrorized her sat mutely, warily, sheepishly as they passed. The dogs with doghouses did not come out of them.

Violet also felt more confident encountering some of her neighbors—rough, taciturn men who sat on automobiles, trucks, and lawn mowers, drank beer, honed ax heads, burned trash, and preyed on female neighbors with their eyes.

"Whoa!" said Leo Burley. "Don't bring that animal around here,

Violet. There are laws against those kinds of dogs, and it's missing an ear."

"It's a free country," replied Violet, gripping the thin leather leash while the stolid white dog looked impassively out of her massive head. "Come, Trixie."

And indeed the country did seem much freer with her dog. She could go anywhere, anytime, without fear. And when Violet discovered that the dog liked to ride in the car, she took her on errands, Trixie's wide face taking up most of the side window.

Olivia also grew quite fond of the animal and often insisted that Trixie sleep in her room at night, though in fact the dog preferred to be wherever Violet was. Over time, this may well have developed into an issue of some contention between the two sisters, except that something else soon demanded Olivia's full attention.

It began on a whim.

After consulting briefly with several knowledgeable neighbors about the likely contents of the coffee tin of medicine that Trixie's previous owner had given her, Olivia decided to take some herself. So twice a day after sprinkling the powder into the dog's food, she slipped a heaping teaspoon into her tea along with enough sugar and cream to neutralize the awful taste.

She was not sure why. Perhaps it was just to be ingesting something her sister did not administer, ration, or even know anything about. Not that Olivia had any complaints about Violet's supervision of her medications and foods, which was quite conscientious and competent in a slightly dictatorial and fascist way. Perhaps it was just to be performing a secret ritual. For whatever reason, it continued week after week after week, until the tin of tan powder with green flecks was mostly gone. And absolutely nothing came of it until one afternoon when Violet was out walking the dog.

Olivia had been placed on the living room sofa, a book about schizophrenia among Christians resting beside the telephone on the end table. It was a cloudy day, and the interior of the house seemed unusually gloomy. The police scanner broadcast a conversation about the mountain lion that had been seen on two recent occasions: eating a feral steer, and again in a tree on the edge of the Heartland

Federal Reserve. Apparently its territorial cry—at night—sounded like screaming, and many people were quite alarmed over hearing it.

Olivia turned off the scanner, turned on the lamp, and searched for the bent page marking the end of her last reading. Her toe hurt inside her yellow sock resting on the carpet. She moved it to relieve the ache and found her place in the text.

One paragraph later she set the book down and stared at her right foot, which, she recalled, hadn't moved on her request for over ten years. She tried to move her toes and watched—incredulously—as the yellow fabric of the sock nudged into the air. It was an enfeebled movement, nothing like the arched, clawing yawn of a normal toe stretch wherein each of the fleshy five digits fan out in taut curlicues of wiggling neural freedom. It was only a nearly imperceptible, bony jerk beneath cloth.

But to Olivia it seemed like the Second Coming.

She tried again, and again her mind explained what she wanted to do to her nerves and her nerves carried the idea all the way down south to her foot and the appropriate muscles there listened to the notion, understood at least most of it, and performed a series of contractions. The system worked.

Olivia felt like a member of an endangered species, a seed stored for centuries in an earthen jar finally planted and sprouting.

"Violet!" she cried. "Violet!"

But Violet was nearly a mile away, walking with the dog and looking for watercress along Thistlewaite Creek.

NEW LOVE

J ACOB HELM STARED INTO HIS WOODSTOVE. HE THOUGHT ABOUT
fire and how the fundamental event—the inner working of the
wasting hot disease—was completely obscured by its flamboyant
symptoms. The conjuring yellow, blue, red, and orange flames
danced in fairy rings on the perimeter of the logs. The brown lig-
neous surfaces smoked, blackened, shriveled, cracked, glowed, and
collapsed into feathery dust. But just *how* the woody cylinders had
been rendered to ash remained unseen. The steady progression of
effects was clearly displayed, but the pounding heart of the process,
the cause, thrived in secret.

In the same manner something unseen came alive in Jacob, its
birth announced through an inching movement of imagination.
Staring into his stove, half dreaming and wishing he could fall completely asleep, he began to remember the first assault upon his Great
Sorrow, the vision of the undressed young woman on her back porch
playing a musical instrument. Fleeing from this memory, he returned
his attention to the fire, without success. Then out of the center of
his growing discomfort, a new feeling emerged, drawing all the elements of his consciousness toward it, a single star in a dark sky. As
it moved closer, it assumed a shape of surprising comfort, and after
a short while he recognized Winnie. Soon, the imagined perception
sharpened and he saw her perched on the edge of his mind in the
straight-backed chair in his living room, her knees pinched together
and her eyes narrowing expectantly as she prepared to pray. Her
lips turned down in their corners as though fearful that the words
they were about to release would not faithfully convey the messages
entrusted to them. Her almost comic seriousness, exaggerated by
freckles splashing between her eyes and her sloping cheeks moving
away from her ears, all perfectly remembered.

The willful domination of her upper lip as it parted company from the plump, slightly frivolous bottom lip. Even her slender nose and tapered, vanishing eyebrows somehow embodied her longing for honesty—a sacred mission to be true to herself and loyal to an empyrean principle so cherished, so idealized, she could not imagine it as her own.

He could *see* her, even the nearly imperceptible hairs above her lip that made mockery of the idea that facial hair was masculine. He remembered the slippery glint of teeth when she smiled, the faint smell of dandelions and hay on her breath, and the pure circadian indigo of her voice rising out of her throat and into her dark eyes, where her pupils exuded a continuous overflow of bright black.

Slowly, Jacob turned from the stove, afraid the physical movement might frighten away the rare creature he had stumbled upon. But it remained with him, still and calm. Even as he rose to his feet, he could *see* her, an incorporeal spirit formed from the wedding of sorrow and firelight.

He knew it was love. That ancient vibrating string had only one harmonic, and its joyous aching filled every corner of him.

It had been years since he'd felt the stirring of this unchecked sympathy and it returned like Lazarus marching from his tomb. He paced from one side of his home to the other, glad to be moving but frantic with uncertainty.

Why had this realization come now? It had been days since her visit. It seemed unnatural, unhealthy, even perverted to experience such powerful affection in the absence of its object.

But that was the way of most things, he decided. They happened and were later realized, the visible flames from an earlier, unseen burning. Between the heart deciding and the head knowing, a fugue state. In his case, it had been so long since any message between the two camps had gotten through it had taken several days to clear a path. Now here it was.

He searched his memory for an earlier, less favorable judgment of her, and seemed to remember having entertained strong doubts about her sanity. But the evidence upon which that earlier judgment was based had for some reason been tampered with, and the same traits that had once led him to condemn her now compelled his wild admiration.

There was also room for a thousand colors of concern. Was this something real? What prevented the possibility that some chemical-hormonal eruption had misfired in his limbic system and because of this synaptic accident his reason had seen reason to crown Winnie as the cause?

He needed a hard science to determine if this new way of perceiving Winnie in some way involved the actual Winifred Smith or had strayed like a rudderless ship out of the Feigning Ocean.

How could he know? Real love did not live in a single home; either it lived in two places at once or it did not live at all. It could be neither confirmed nor denied in isolation. Only the object of his new longing could inform him. Self-reflection seemed useless.

He glanced at the clock and didn't care that it was late.

If he heard her voice, he would know—for sure.

He tore through the telephone book.

Smith, Winifred, Rev.

Then he didn't want to dial. This new feeling was the best thing that had visited him in a long, long time, and even if it was wholly imagined, he feared losing it. He did not want to return to the person he was before the feeling arrived.

Yet he also did not wish to be deluded.

He dialed the number and engaged distant ringing. Five, six, seven . . .

"Hello, this is Pastor Winifred." (Muffled, slurred, sleepy.)

"Hello?" (Slurred, sleepy.)

"Hello?" (Sleepy.)

"Hello."

The tiny sound of her voice coming out of the half-inch speaker into his right ear was so assuredly attached to the actual tongue and lips of the speaker on the other end that it beckoned for him to crawl into the telephone line after it. He couldn't think of anything to say and listened until she hung up.

The gavel had struck. It *was* real. The shapeless spirit had been found alive in the world, embodied.

Jacob hung up the phone and immediately wanted to call her back, apologize for waking her, confess his insensitivity, beg her to forgive him, and explain everything that had happened to him in the last half hour. But that seemed like a crazy idea and instead he devoted himself to full-time worry.

He hardly knew her. Any number of things might be wrong with the way he kept imagining the two of them together.

Yet his level of deepest impulse had been engaged. Her voice had reached into him and thrown the switch. He had to see her again, and whatever happened would happen. His compulsion to match his idea of her to her physical presence—to revel in unique particulars, incarnate the mental shape in which she lived inside him, find her soul and contemplate it, speak to it, even touch it—acknowledged no hindrances. His fearful, yearning joy was even more pronounced because he well knew this newly found treasure's terrible worth. He had stood on the bottom rung of this ladder before and understood the implications of climbing higher.

Somewhere, a bargain had been sealed. For the frail chance of knowing her completely, he had recklessly wagered an eternity of need.

He felt alive, important, filled with purpose, his capacity for both suffering and pleasure growing exponentially.

As if to arrest his ambition, Jacob pulled the picture off the wall. But since he had last looked, the photographic image had changed. Instead of holding him in her vise of nostalgia, his wife standing in a garden in white shorts six years ago seemed to wish him a speedy departure. Her smile knew that another, more desperate absence had replaced hers and she seemed well satisfied with her new circumstances, glad to be rid of him.

Even with the picture in his hands, Jacob could still perfectly recollect Winnie sitting like a folded-up butterfly on the edge of a leaf. Her feet pressed together, her back not making contact with the chair, her eyes closed, her lips moving, the scent of something between almonds and lilacs trapped in her long hair. When she opened her dark eyes he could see his own thoughts flashing through them.

He was beside himself and could no longer be contained within the prison of his own house. An inexplicable largeness had entered his life.

Fifteen minutes later, he arrived at the farm of July Montgomery, parked his jeep in the front yard, and banged on the door. When it opened he rushed inside. "I've got to talk to you. I don't know what to do. I didn't think this could or would ever happen. You have to help me."

KEEPING IN ONE'S PLACE

A S OLIVIA WAITED FOR HER SISTER TO RETURN FROM HER WALK
with the dog, she became less excited about discovering a
healthy connection between her brain and her right foot. She had
been trained by experience to be cautious in assessing the possibility
that she might find release from her disease. How many times in the
past had she and others been encouraged to hope that her condition
would improve? Disappointments had followed discouragements
like a caravan of lame, dusty mules.

Never again, she resolved. I've been tricked by hope before.

She would keep quiet until she had something trustworthy to
report.

So when Violet returned with the dog and a bread bag filled with
watercress, Olivia said nothing. Nor did she speak when for the first
time she was able to move her other foot—even when she began to
feel the kind of pain in her lower back, hips, thighs, knees, calves,
ankles, and feet that any person might feel after years of atrophy.

Instead she complained, truthfully enough, of diarrhea, and Violet
took her to the Grange Clinic, where in the privacy of the examina-
tion room she moved her feet for the doctor.

Dr. Fleckmann, an aging general practitioner, arranged for a
week of tests, at the end of which two specialists from Madison
with half the alphabet marching after the names on their shirt pins
explained to Olivia that she had been misdiagnosed in earlier years.
The symptoms commonly associated with multiple sclerosis had
instead issued from an undetected spirochetal bacterium. Prolonged
doses of oxytetracycline, the primary antibiotic in the coffee tin, had
been effective in beginning to counteract it. They recommended a
more narrowly prescribed medication with fewer gastrointestinal
side effects and returned her to the care of Dr. Fleckmann.

Still suspicious of her long-term prospects, Olivia withheld this news from her sister.

But she was anxious to tell someone about the wild possibility of not being perpetually incapacitated, and Wade Armbuster eagerly agreed to protect her secret and assist in strengthening her neglected muscles. Every weekday after work at the cheese plant, he drove Olivia to a deserted county park, and in a secluded glen surrounded by hawthorn and quaking aspen she began the arduous task of relearning how to stand, balance, and walk.

Her rehabilitation was greatly assisted by the exercise of her iron will. Previously confined to the playground of her home personality, Olivia took an almost sadistic delight in forcing her body to comply with her wishes. Fueled by the unholy anger of nearly a lifetime of needless invalidism, she fought to recover her wholeness. She interpreted pain through its secondary attributes and viewed fatigue as an illusion to be overcome. She tasted her own blood, relished the flavor, and improved quickly.

Unfortunately, her physical advancement was so unconscionably rapid that it outpaced her ability to adjust to it. Her thoughts could not keep up. First, there was the anger, and from that cup she drank deeply and frequently. For years she had been imprisoned in beds, chairs, utilitarian clothes, and ugly, oversized shoes, when all she really needed was a common medicine that could be purchased by the pound. All those interminable hours of staring at ceilings and walls, longing for health!

How she hated those memories.

She had been robbed of her youth. And though she might succeed now in winning something back—some last, fleeting taste of normalcy before creaking middle age and eventually imbecility captured her—still nothing could ever save her youth, which, unredeemed, hung about her neck like a murdered child.

Her spoiled past was a terrible thing to contemplate, yet she felt compelled to stare into this fetid heritage as though to find salvation in revulsion.

She felt as if she had spent most of her life imprisoned in a cold cellar only to learn that the cellar door had never been locked. Now, standing in the outside stairwell, she wondered how she could ever walk fully into the bright front yard after her grandmother, grandfather, mother, father, uncles, and aunts had all died waiting for her to come out. Their absence was more palpable than any presence, and it often seemed better to return to the cellar.

To be healed without their gathered approval seemed unthinkable.

There were so many people to hate, beginning with the doctors. Fiends, warlocks and witches of the black arts! Why hadn't they *known* what to do?

She thought of all the people she suspected of blaming her—who looked upon her illness as lack of faith and her infirmity as cowardice. How could she endure the memories of those smug faces? Their condemnation had been so convincing she had even come to fear her poor health was somehow justified—not because of anything she had *done* but because of who she *was*. Feeling bad had convicted her of being bad. She had blamed herself for something she had had no more control over than she had over Earth's orbit.

It was a fucking infection, Wade said.

At night she dreamed that all the violence of Armageddon had been taped to her body and hidden beneath a yellow raincoat. Just when all of Job's friends gathered around to examine her suffering, she yanked the cord and sat bolt upright in bed, her fists shaking, holding back a scream loud enough to crystallize blood sugar for miles around.

And there was one person with whom she was most incurably enraged—for whom there could never be forgiveness, someone who should have known better.

Violet.

The tiny, stemless indigo- and white-blossomed flowers were just beginning to grow, spreading like scattered necklaces through the park's mowed grass, and Olivia was walking on them, crushing them beneath her feet, her muscles and bones growing stronger.

At night, exhausted, she ate meals in enormous proportions, washed down with plastic tumblers of raw milk.

"Land sakes, Olivia, you must have a tapeworm. There's nothing left over for the dog's leftovers."

Olivia's eyes seethed.

"Here now, if your little outings with Wade are going to make you frown all the time so much, then don't go. It's not like you couldn't find something more useful to do. Yes, Trixie, I'll be right there. Don't carry on so. Land sakes, there's not enough hours in the day's hours."

It soon became clear that Olivia had tied a knot she did not know how to undo. Before she was ready for it she had a nearly fully functioning body, yet had said nothing to her sister. She had trapped herself into pretending to be an invalid inside her own home.

The real problem with accepting her new health—the one that kept her lying mute and unmoving while her sister bathed her, dressed her, prepared her meals, washed her clothes, and tucked her into bed—was what she would do about Violet. What would Violet do without her to take care of? Violet needed her to be sick, and she needed to be sick to keep Violet.

Olivia began to fear that Violet, on her own, would discover her secret. She called Dr. Fleckmann to remind him of the confidential nature of doctor-patient relationships and discontinued her afternoon outings with Wade, despite his loud protests. (As her body had grown more functional, his passion for her had increased, and the exercises he devised for her rehabilitation were, well, they were not very helpful.)

She didn't feel she could live without Violet, yet she was sure Violet would leave the instant she learned of her new wellness. Whatever love Violet felt for her surely had more to do with her being sick than with her being Olivia.

She also began to fear the infection would somehow return and any declaration of health could be shown to be false. So it might be prudent to keep quiet a little longer.

Imprisoned in her psychological jail—a fort that had locked out its own soldiers—Olivia had never been so unhappy. There were no longer any safe thoughts, only anger and anger's silent partner, fear. Each night she struggled with these two, weaving them into a fabric that would allow her to walk away from them, and each morning she unraveled the work and set them free.

One night in early June as Violet slept in her bedroom at the end of the hall, Olivia could not suppress a desire to explore the upstairs.

As Violet breathed heavily, Olivia silently rolled through the living room and parked the wheelchair at the bottom of the steep staircase. Wearing corduroy slippers and a bathrobe, she gripped the sturdy wooden banister and drew herself to her feet.

As she climbed slowly, the creaking of boards proved unexpectedly alarming in the otherwise dark stillness, but these moments were offset by the remembered smell of old varnish, mold, stale air, and her grandparents. Memories ignited with each seven-inch rise in elevation. Ten minutes later, standing firmly on the second-floor landing, she inhaled deeply and looked down the hall, where moonlight entered the four-paned, south-facing window. She reached for the light, thought better of using it, and let her fingers trace fondly over the shape of the switch, the edges rounded by repeated contact with the fingers of her family.

Following a dubious faith in wood groaning less near walls, Olivia traveled down the hallway, supporting herself when possible by pieces of furniture and door frames. It was an enchanted journey—a reverie in which the thoughts of her ancestors, remnants of their souls, seemed imbedded in the walls like scribbled prayers tucked into the Temple Mount. Reaching the window, she looked into the moonlit yard and was amazed at how the high view rendered the familiar scene foreign.

She then opened the door at the end of the hall slowly and stepped inside her parents' bedroom, where giant magnolias on the wallpaper greeted her like familial faces from the world beyond. An ocean of loss broke upon the shores of memory and her heart rushed to inform her of its beating. She crept further in and rested her hands on the walnut bed, marveling at its solemn, diminutive size. Now a resting place for old quilts and boxes of craft supplies, the tiny bed seemed extraordinarily incapable of having once held her mother and father, yet the logic of its having done so remained unimpeachable.

Feeling with her hands around the bed, she reached her mother's dressing table. When she was a child, it had always seemed like a personal shrine, and she drifted into the memory of her mother's face—combing her hair, sucking color from a shiny tube of lipstick, and making her eyes dark, her mirrored reflection so serene, so filled with graceful dignity, so unapproachably goddesslike that Olivia despaired, even now, of finding a maturity of her own.

She removed the rolls of fabric from the embroidered stool, carefully set them on the floor, and seated herself before the mirror. In the dim light she could only make out the outline of her head, where tufts of hair curled outward like dark flames. Behind her, the magnolia faces loomed larger than life, and in an instant of unpremeditated bravery she reached out and turned on the lamp.

The plastic-against-metal *click* exploded the room in fulgent light, and Olivia, unprepared, noted three instantaneous events. The glare could not be contained in the room and raced out of the window and crashed against the oak tree in a blaze of bright leaves; her eyes looked owl-like into their own reflection; and she heard Violet's bed making noises in the room below. She reached to turn the lamp off and succeeded only after knocking a cardboard box to the floor, where it landed in a solid *phalummmp.*

Olivia closed her eyes and prayed she would not be discovered. She confessed to every sin she had ever committed, knowingly and unknowingly, and promised never again to disturb the dead.

When she heard footsteps mounting the stairs she did not know where to turn; her heart was beating so loudly she could hardly listen. She thought of hiding beneath the bed but was sure there was not enough room. Besides, what was the point? Her empty wheelchair sat at the bottom of the stairs like a neon arrow pointing upstairs. There was nothing she could do. What she most feared had passed out of her imagination and into existence. The heavy steps came down the hall and Olivia turned to face them, ready to accept her undying curse.

The door was pushed wider open and the pit bull plodded into the room, looking like a small white cow.

Olivia crept out of the room and closed the door seamlessly behind her. With exacting care, she traveled the length of the hallway and descended the stairs in a seated position, the dog following patiently.

In the safety of her wheelchair, she uttered a sigh of relief that allowed so much of her strength to escape she could barely get back to her room and into bed.

Trixie returned to Violet's room.

MUSHROOMS ARE UP

W INNIE GOT UP EARLY. SHE SET HER CUSHION BEFORE THE east-facing window, lit the candle and placed it on the floor beneath the ledge. Her shawl was in the closet under an oilcloth and she pulled it around her thin shoulders, folded into her ritual posture, and began her morning devotions.

But after closing her eyes she discovered a freshly plowed field of worry. Among other distractions, the sweet smell of furniture oil on the shawl crawled through her landscape of mental images, preventing her from fixing her mind and calming her breath. Her heart beat like a cornered raven's. Shapes howled and thorns sprang from even the most soothing recollections. As though to prosecute her, her thoughts returned again and again to Jacob Helm.

She pulled her shawl more tightly around her shoulders and tried harder. Moving her lips, she carefully considered every syllable of every word of the Twenty-third Psalm, yet even this rigorous discipline could not force her mind to behave. She took off the shawl and threw it to other side of the room but its smell had invaded her pajama top, and like homeopathic medicine it worked more powerfully in diluted form.

Every thought had Jacob Helm beneath it, smiling through his eyes, interested in her, understanding her, appreciating her, respecting her, liking her, his black hair wet, his feet bare, his living room steamy hot.

Maybe if I stop resisting, she reasoned. Perhaps struggle helped the Enemy wax stronger. To end the war, stop fighting. Closing her eyes again, she allowed her attention to follow whatever course it wished, pursuing spiritual victory through surrender.

But surrender, it seemed, had an agenda of its own and this plan came to an emphatic end when she felt saliva climbing up her throat and below, warm and moist, she swelled up like a young grape.

She quickly blew out the candle, left the room, and took a shower. Ever since last fall she had waited for the rest of her New Life to begin, but the one that presently seemed to be emerging couldn't possibly be the one intended for her.

Could individual destinies be mixed up and assigned to the wrong people?

Jacob Helm had called her in the middle of the night, not saying anything, apparently just to frighten her. Even though he didn't speak, she knew it was him. She just knew. And he had her father's name written down next to his computer. These were clearly the actions of a potential stalker.

And even if he wasn't a potential stalker and there was some explanation for her father's name on his kitchen table, what could possibly happen next? Nothing good could ever come from what she felt now.

Downstairs, she combed out her hair, set a pot of water and tea on the stove, and looked into the dim, premorning shapes outside. The back of the church with its two low windows looked like a wide face.

Finished with cording her long flaxen braids, she stared into her brewing tea, decided against drinking it, poured it into the sink, put on her corduroy skirt and jacket, and went outside.

Standing in the front yard felt no better, she discovered, but she soon understood where she needed to be. Her yellow car started with a rattling purr and she drove without headlights into the growing morning light, away from Words, down the valley, over the ridge, through Grange, all the way to the little bridge in the marsh.

This was not the first time she had returned. She had come often and tried again and again to rediscover the epiphanic presence that had once called her name out loud. Yet she found only the barren, empty place—the bottle without the genie. She had even eaten as many as six custard-filled pastries, thinking that perhaps they would help, but they didn't.

She sat on her favorite wooden plank near the middle of the bridge, hooked her arms over the steel railing, her legs dangling over the side. Beneath her shoes the water rushed and murmured along with the industrious chattering of many large, hungry birds and the numb thrumming of insects. She looked into the stream and wondered what would become of her, and added her voice to the others:

"I used to be so excited about my life, Dear One, so willing to be good no matter what—so convinced I would find happiness and peace. But now I spend my whole life taking care of old people who don't know me, don't understand anything about me, don't even like me. I'm lonely and don't know how to stop being lonely. I'm sick of wanting the things I was born wanting and I'm sick of trying not to want them. Mostly I'm sick of me. I want to be more than I am, different than I am, but I can't be. You leave me here alone and it's certainly not safe. There's no telling how I might turn out. My teeth are growing crooked. I'm fraying like an old rope. Must every joy die in a single lick, yet longing last through a thousand banquets? I know I have no right to complain—I'm such a worthless thing—but does that seem fair to You? Why must the puzzle of happiness be so difficult to solve while the twists of grief always grind in the same horrid direction? If You don't want me in Your World why did You invite me in? Why didn't You just leave me outside? Why let me visit if I couldn't stay? Is this a test? What must I do to pass? If being good isn't good enough, how about being bad? I'm so lonely."

She walked to the car, took a pair of scissors out of the glove compartment, and returned to the bridge.

As she cut, ropes of her hair fell into the water.

A noisy vehicle came over the rise. She did not bother to get up and continued cutting until only several ragged inches remained attached to her head. July Montgomery parked his white pickup, walked over, and sat next to her.

"You're out early, Miss Winifred," he said.

"So are you, Mister July."

"Wade wanted to make some extra money, so he's milking for me this week," said July. "It's beautiful here. Just listen to those birds."

"I should be going," said Winnie.

"Wait, I've got something for you," he said and he returned to his truck.

Winnie looked in the plastic bag and her mouth fell open. "Where did you find these?" she shouted, jumping to her feet.

"Around," said July.

"No," said Winnie in disbelief.

"I found them this morning."

"I can't believe it," said Winnie again, handing the bag filled with morel mushrooms back to him.

"Don't you want them?"

"I'll find my own," she said, running toward her little yellow car with the scissors in her right hand.

MAKING BAIL

G AIL SHOTWELL LEFT THE TAVERN IN THE MIDDLE OF THE afternoon and drove home. Her brother's pickup sat in her driveway. Her sister-in-law, Cora, came running out of her house as though chased by a grease fire.

"Where have you been?" Cora demanded, with the same tone she always wielded—one that assumed everything in her life was important and everything else wasn't. "I called your work and they said you weren't there."

"I didn't work today," said Gail. "Why are you here?"

"Grahm's in jail," Cora began, the words flooding out of her. "They came and got him. They just walked into the machine shed and arrested him while he was fixing the skid loader. When he wouldn't cooperate or accept the contempt citation, they put handcuffs on him even though I told them not to. We didn't have anyone else to help with the milking tonight, the kids were at practice and if Teresa wasn't there they needed a ride home, and I had a load of laundry fresh out of the machine, but they just pushed him into the back of the car and drove away. They didn't say anything—just shoved him in the back and drove away. I didn't have time to do anything or call anyone. I wasn't even sure who they were. I mean the side of their car said the sheriff's department and they looked like police, but how can you tell for sure? I didn't think real police would act like that— taking people away when they had work to do. I actually thought when I first saw them that they were looking for Wade because of what happened the other night. That's what I thought when they first pulled into the yard. I thought it had to do with Wade. And I got in the car and followed them and Grahm was hardly able to turn around to check if I was following because of his hands tied up behind him. That must have been uncomfortable. I could tell it was, and they didn't even take the handcuffs off when they pulled him out and pushed him into the building and the district judge fined him a thousand dollars for contempt because they had a video of Grahm at the annual meeting saying all those things that he had been ordered not to say and then when Grahm told the judge that he wasn't going to take it anymore and that this was against all this United States of America was supposed to stand for the judge said he was in contempt again and fined him another thousand. We said we couldn't pay that much and the judge said we either had to pay it or Grahm had to stay in jail for forty days. I asked how we were supposed manage with all we had to do and me looking for a new job and all the work on the farm and not having that kind of money, but I was afraid to go on very far because I thought maybe we'd get fined some more."

"I'm not following all this, Cora."

"I'm telling you just what the district judge said, Gail. Aren't you listening? I'm telling you exactly what he said. Somebody's got to pick up the kids. Somebody's got to milk the cows. We've got all those heifers to feed. I've got to find some money somewhere and get Grahm out of jail. I've got a load a laundry just out of the machine still waiting to be dried. Where were you all day? I've got a job interview tomorrow morning. God, I can't believe this."

"If Grahm's in jail, let's get him out," said Gail. "You can explain on the way. The banks will close soon."

"Do you remember that box of papers we left with you? Do you still have it? Those papers are really important, Gail. Have you been drinking?"

"I know where the papers are."

"You've been drinking. I can smell it. You've been drinking."

"Not much."

"Show me the papers."

"I can show you later. Let's get Grahm."

"No. Those papers are more important. I want to see them with my own eyes." And for emphasis she pointed two fingers at her eyes.

They went inside.

"Where are they?" demanded Cora, as if it was her house and Gail's living in it was an unnecessary indulgence.

"In the closet," said Gail. "They've been there ever since you gave them to me."

But when Gail looked, the box was gone.

"It's gone," she said.

"I knew you'd lose them, you worthless drunken fool!" screamed Cora. "Look again."

"There's nowhere else to look. The box is gone, but I didn't lose them. They're just gone."

Cora burst into tears.

"Come on, Cora, stop crying. Let's go to the bank before it closes, borrow some money, and get Grahm."

"Those papers proved everything!"

"Cora, someone has taken them."

"It's that damn brother of yours," sobbed Cora. "He doesn't have the sense of a goat. At that American Milk meeting he told them everything. He went there and talked about the things we'd been told not to talk about. And he stood out in the parking lot and told a whole bunch of other farmers that his sister had the papers."

"How do you know that?"

"July told me when I went over to tell him not to let Grahm go to that meeting up in Snow Corners."

"What meeting in Snow Corners?

"Someone's having a meeting and Grahm, when I asked him not to go, Grahm said he wouldn't promise not to go, so I went over to—"

"Cora, get hold of yourself." Gail put her arms around Cora, and when the older woman struggled to get away, Gail continued to hold her until she settled down.

"Come on," said Gail. "We'll do it together—one thing at a time. First we've got to pick up the kids, leave them with Bernice, see if Wade can milk the cows, and borrow some money to get Grahm out of jail."

On the way into the city, while Cora explained again everything the judge had said, Gail thought how strange it was to be picking up her brother in jail. Of all the people she knew, Grahm seemed the most unlikely to be there. It was easier to imagine him putting people in jail than being in jail. For as long as she could remember he had been, in one way or another, trying to lock her up. He was prudential. How could the rules of society ever turn against him?—they were too closely aligned.

His entire personality had been manufactured to the exacting specifications of social expectation. His sole pursuit in life always seemed to be the approval of those perceived to have authority, living or dead. His agrarian ancestors had hammered him out like hot steel on an anvil. He had had no life of his own, really—he had been released from the bondage of his grandparents and parents to the servitude of his wife and children without experiencing even a single afternoon of freedom. Even his cows, crops, buildings, and machinery staked him by a short tether.

In some very important ways, she concluded, Grahm had always been in prison. But it still seemed odd for him to be in this kind of prison, built to hold those who refused to accept the voluntary one Grahm had always lived in. For him to be in this kind of prison—it didn't seem right.

The policeman at the desk looked at the bank check.

Cora said, "We would like a receipt for that."

When Grahm was finally brought up from downstairs—where Gail assumed the jail must be—he looked terrible. His eyes did not meet hers. Cora rushed forward to see if the handcuffs had left marks, but he brushed her aside as though they did not know each other.

All the way home, he remained silent. He sat next to Cora in the back seat and even refused to eat anything at the drive-thru.

As soon as Gail pulled in the farmyard, he climbed out and went to the barn.

"You'd better stay here," said Gail. "I'll bring the kids back. Somebody like Grahm should never be like this. It's dangerous for everyone."

THE HEARTLAND FEDERAL RESERVE

NOT EVERYONE COULD FIND MOREL MUSHROOMS. IT WAS HARD to know where and when to look for them, and this unpredictability lent to the fungi an allure of mystery. They were elusive, even cunning in their habits, popping up overnight in secluded nooks to grow unobserved, their tops bearing an unnerving likeness to sponge-brains.

The varied shapes, colors, and sizes added to their appeal. They could leap out of the ground in perfectly symmetrical configurations, their conical gray bodies as small as dollhouse accessories. They also appeared in drab yellow—lumpy, flabby, and grotesque, over a foot tall. In other words, they were wild.

Partly because of these vagaries, morels were highly prized. As condiments, they were considered delicacies of the highest order and in some markets assumed an almost magical status, believed to possess life-enhancing, aphrodisiac properties.

Winifred Smith could find them. Her mother had known how to find them and she had followed in her mother's footsteps. When others would return empty-handed from an afternoon's hunting, Winnie would return—from the same woods—with a filled sack.

She had once found forty pounds of morels during a dry spring in which many hunters hardly found any. Everyone heard about how the trunk of her little car had overflowed. She'd donated them to the nursing home in Grange and the smell of the earthy, rich fungi had accompanied her as she carried them into the basement kitchen.

Some of the home's kitchen workers said it was her natural instinct to find mushrooms—the ability to act knowingly without actually having conscious knowledge.

Others disagreed. They said humans didn't have natural instincts. After the forbidden fruit debacle, womankind had been doomed to remain fully conscious. No more doing things without knowing why they were done. Now, only the lower animals had natural instincts and only God arranged for people to find or not find mushrooms.

Others said it was simply luck, meaning, of course, there were no adequate explanations.

Winnie had her own thoughts on the subject and would have shared them with anyone who asked. For her, morel hunting was a passion. She found more mushrooms because she valued them more. The satisfaction she took in discovering morel hiding places knew no limits. The sight of their Lilliputian gatherings—the moist and mossy conference rooms where they carried on their growing rituals—was like nothing else. No surprise could compare to the sudden recognition of those happy little trolls crouching beneath a fern, staring up at her with the haunting bewilderment of truly wild things. Then after recognizing one, seeing another, then another and another, engaged in their haphazard conformity, delight magnifying delight.

Others simply didn't want to find mushrooms as badly as she did, nor imagine it as fully, or ascribe to it such significance. They didn't begin dreaming of mushroom habitats as soon as the snow melted, and would never consider lying all day in a wooded glen, the sides of their faces pressed to the ground, for the chance of seeing one rise up from the earth—witnessing its birth.

The ways of mushrooms, she thought, were completely different from those of people. It was part of their charm. How many people could you walk by and not even notice—then once you were past them, turn around and because you were looking in the other direction discover them as though they had just materialized? People never acted like that, but morels acted like that all the time. Also, from what she'd read about mycology, and she was careful not to read much for fear of losing her special feeling for morels, they had a marvelous method of reproduction. They propagated through cloning spores. Separate male and female ingredients were not required. They did not need to wait around for pollinating bees or compliant mates to set loose the next generation. They *were* the next generation. Their fertility depended upon simply being themselves, not doing something with someone else. They did not even need to leave the church to be fruitful. They contemplated the drama of reproduction privately, inwardly, and this accounted for, she suspected, their pensive, occult nature. To apprehend a morel was to be in the presence of an alien life form, evolved during the most recent ice age, from yeast.

Horrified that the season had arrived without her, she felt betrayed by her own sensibilities. She hadn't been herself lately. It seemed inconceivable she could have let this happen.

She raced home, parked in the yard, and ran into the parsonage, shedding her clothes. Redressing, she stuffed the cuffs of dark green cargo pants into heavy wool socks in order to keep ticks and chiggers from crawling up the inside, then put on her hiking boots. She feared the socks were too heavy for this time of year but was too much in a hurry to look for different ones. A loose-fitting, tightly knit gray cotton shirt tucked into the pants completed her attire, and she bounded downstairs to search for bread bags.

Winnie knew where she wanted to hunt—a place she had discovered several years ago, deep in the Driftless, ten miles away.

The fragrances of warm spring blew across her face as she sped away from Words.

The Heartland Federal Reserve had been created by government fiat a generation before. Ten thousand acres of rocky, hilly farmland had been declared public domain and stripped of buildings in preparation for damming the Heartland River and impounding an eighteen-hundred-acre recreational lake. The project would be good, it was thought, for flood control and even better for injecting tourism into an underdeveloped county.

Land values had risen quickly as investors bought up potential resort sites. The Army Corps of Engineers began constructing the dam, but not before several environmental groups had gone to court. A temporary injunction halted the project while agronomists and other scientists scrutinized the soil and plants around the dam and drainage basin.

Due to water quality fears, the project was permanently abandoned. The thirteen-million-dollar dam remained as a concrete fossil of foolishness, never impounding a single drop of water. Perhaps to keep it hidden from sight, a seventeen-mile federal security fence topped with three strands of barbed wire was placed around the entire area, which remained, thirty years later, undeveloped and uninhabited. The misfortunes of real estate investors who lost money and farmers who had been forced to sell their farms created a veritable paradise for committed nature lovers. Inside the prohibited reserve one could walk all day and never step on a sidewalk or a road or meet another person.

Winnie parked her car beside the tall fence and stuffed bread bags into her pockets. She walked a hundred yards on the gravel road, beyond the sign: Keep Out Danger Government Property Trespassers Will Be Prosecuted. After a distant vehicle passed beyond hearing, she crawled through an old ragged hole in the fence, hidden by a mulberry bush, and moved quickly into the forest.

It was cooler here, and she felt her body relax as she threaded through the calligraphy of underbrush. She climbed several hills, crossed a shallow creek by walking on stones, clambered over a steep, rocky ledge, and continued along animal trails for another couple miles to a place she had found, by chance, several years ago.

Here, she turned north and crawled through a narrow ravine choked with prickly ash and blackberry, the thorns often tearing through her clothing. Several times she became so entangled that she was forced to retreat and look for another way.

Finally, gratefully, she emerged on the other side, at the opening of a secluded valley protected on all sides by steep, rugged enclosing hills. The earth seemed to have a better smell here; the sunlight held a unique golden color. The air itself felt more filled with oxygen and invigorating ions.

Winnie sat for several minutes with her back against a maple, picking rambarkle out of the tops of her socks. The sun was now higher in the sky and she took off her boots to let her feet air out. She had paid the price for entering her private park and now wished to enjoy it undistracted—rid of every troubled thought. Her breathing slowed down, her moist skin dried, and the thorn pricks stopped smarting. Several red squirrels and a brown thrasher, convinced of

her harmlessness and needing to get on with business, rustled in
the leaves.

She put her boots on and moved forward through ferns, blood-
root, jack-in-the-pulpit, and Indian pipes. She looked for dead elms
with bark still clinging to the smooth limbs—a possible source of
fungi nutrients.

A chipmunk darted ahead to crouch on a flat rock. Behind him
grew a morel, about two inches tall, fat and gray, in perfect condition.
Her spirit soared. The chipmunk scampered off and she surveyed the
area, searching for a vein running up the gently sloping forest floor,
connecting the mushroom by an underground fungal trellis to other
mushrooms.

She saw another morel, then another, leading into a patch of
mayapples. She knelt and reverently worked the first mushroom
from the earth, its cool, hollow, fleshy body pressing against her fingers. It came free without breaking the trunk, with gossamers of dirt
clinging to the root threads. She gathered the others and carefully
approached the mayapples.

Beneath the low, spreading canopy a colony of morels huddled
together like tiny monks in a garden. Sunlight fell in places through
the lattice of watery green, creating a scene of such enchantment that
Winnie sat down to contemplate it more fully. Wonder merged with
beauty, and tears came to her eyes at the sound of a woodpecker hammering on an overhead limb. Approval flooded out of her.

After the moment passed, she gathered up all the mushrooms
and placed them in the bread bag, filling it over halfway.

Her appetite now whetted, she moved toward a place along the
western slope of the valley where she had found the forty pounds of
mushrooms several years ago. It called to her as she moved between
the trees.

The sun entered the late-morning sky, assuming a more somber
nature. She walked around an outcropping of sandstone and found
nothing until she stood in the middle of the sacred spot. Then she
saw a broken mushroom trunk, then another, and another. In a
number of places were pieces of smashed mushrooms, stepped on.

Someone had been here and took them all, and her sense of personal violation soon compounded.

"Winifred," said a voice behind her.

Winnie turned in the direction she had just come from and beneath an enormous oak, dressed in jeans and a tight-fitting white T-shirt, stood Jacob Helm. He held his head high, his black hair as wild as a jay's.

She was so surprised at not being alone that it took her several moments to adjust.

He came ahead several paces, his movements quick and sure. "You shouldn't be here, Winifred."

This seemed like a particularly strange thing to say, she thought. No one should be here—it was a restricted area.

"I think I have as much right to be here as do you."

He moved forward again, narrowing the distance between them. "You shouldn't be here. This area isn't safe."

"Don't come any closer to me," said Winnie, looking at his thick hands—hands that would probably look the same if they were helping her or hitting her.

He took another several steps.

"I told you to stay back."

"Winnie, it's me, Jacob. I'd never hurt you."

"I'll be the sole judge of that."

"This is their practice area. You could be shot."

"What are you talking about?"

He returned to the oak tree, reached around the trunk, and pulled an unseen rope. The movement was accompanied by the sound of breaking stems and leaves. A human figure, a dummy, fell out of the overhead branches and hung suspended in midair, its sewn feet inches from the ground.

"They have targets all over the valley. Someone in here by mistake could get hurt."

"Who are you talking about?"

"This is the militia's practice area."

"Did you pick those mushrooms?"

"Yes."

"You stepped on some."

"I know," he said. "I was in a hurry." The dummy still turned in the air beside him, a featureless, generic effigy. "Are you mushroom hunting?"

Winnie remained silent.

"Look, I'll take you to another place. I found it last year. Then you really must leave."

"Where's the rest of your militia?"

"It's not mine. Moe Ridge is the leader and I don't belong to it. I do some work for them and that's all."

"You called me late one night. I know it was you."

"You're right. After you answered I couldn't think of anything to say. I'm sorry. I know it was late."

"Why would you do something like that?"

Jacob paused, looked at the ground, shifted his weight to the other leg, and said, "I needed to hear your voice."

"That's insane."

"Probably. Listen, you really must not be in here. I can take you to another place to look for mushrooms. It's not far away and my jeep is over here."

"How did you get your jeep in here?"

"That's a secret."

Winnie followed him. The jeep was parked behind several hawthorns and a protecting escarpment of rock.

"I'm not riding in that," announced Winnie, looking at the dented door suspiciously.

"Then we can walk," said Jacob, and they went along a path that was little more than several tire tracks made earlier in the day. After another mile they neared the Heartland River, and Jacob pointed through the trees.

"Over there."

Winnie saw mushrooms growing out of the sloping ground leading down to the water, beneath corkscrew willows and birch.

"Look!" she shouted and ran forward.

They hunted for nearly an hour, without talking, walking along the river and filling up the majority of Winnie's bread bags, which they left along the bank to recover later. Their meandering course brought them to a steep rock wall, where the river spilled down from twenty-five or thirty feet above.

"I didn't know this was in here," said Winnie, watching the falls plunge with a watery roar into a frothing pool at the base of the rocks.

She could feel Jacob staring at her, but when she looked at him, he looked away.

Winnie inspected the rock sides of the falls and they decided to climb up, she on the right and he on the left. The handholds were more numerous on Winnie's side and she reached the top before Jacob did. They sat on the ledge overlooking the valley, the water running beside them. The afternoon sun heated their clothes.

"What happened to your hair?" asked Jacob.

"I obviously cut it," said Winnie, moving farther away from him. "This militia—what do they hope to accomplish by teaching people to hunt each other like animals?"

"I can't speak for them, but I think they want to be prepared."

"For what?"

"For when the federal government finally goes out of control. And you can't really blame them for feeling the way they do."

"Why not?"

"Because many of them have watched their jobs go overseas, their farms be sold out from under them, their parents suffer from diseases they can't afford to treat. And when their children get in trouble for stealing, fighting, or taking drugs, they don't get the same kind of legal help that other people's children get. They're angry about all that."

"Even if the government is corrupt—and for the most part I think governments are always satanic—no one can defeat it."

"It's not about defeating it; it's about surviving."

"Is everyone in the militia unemployed with ailing parents and delinquent children?"

"Of course not, and everyone in the government isn't corrupt."

In the distance they saw several human shapes moving in and out of the covering of trees.

"They're coming," said Winnie.

"We'll collect the mushrooms and I'll take you back to your car," said Jacob. "But we should hurry. They usually hold meetings before their maneuvers begin, but the meetings don't last long."

"How do you know where my car is?"

"I saw it earlier. Come on, let's go."

Then Winnie's own feelings came around a corner and surprised her. She didn't want to leave. She hated the idea of leaving. All the time that she had been sitting on the high rock ledge and listening to Jacob talk about the militia—she now understood—she had been hoping he would explain what he'd said earlier. Because when he'd said that he needed to hear her voice she'd heard something in *his voice* that absolutely needed explaining. She wanted to know if the quality she now clearly remembered hearing in his voice—a quality that both threatened and promised to be a surefire antidote to loneliness—had actually been *in* his voice, or if it was something she misremembered or simply made up. Because if it really had been *in* his voice, then things were certainly different now.

INSIDE THE NEIGHBOR'S HOUSE

A FTER LEAVING SETH AND GRACE AT THE FARM, GAIL RETURNED to Words, parked the convertible in her driveway, and walked across the yard and through the hedge and knocked on the Brassos' back door. She looked through the laced window as Violet's dog came across the living room to a silent, menacing stop on the other side of the beveled glass.

Drat, thought Gail, that face would stop a drill.

Soon, Violet rushed from the kitchen, pushed the dog aside with a sidewise thrust of her hip, and opened the door.

"What a surprise," she said. "Here, get out of the way, Trixie, for land sakes. Come in, come in. What a surprise."

It was the first time Gail had been inside the Brasso home, and with each step more of the interior came into focus. It looked like an antique shop. The only things missing were paper price tags hanging from loops of string, and there were even some of those. Old Age was carefully preserved in the furniture, the artfully organized clutter on the walls and shelves, and the odor of some prehistoric mold culture ingeniously nurtured to withstand modern antiseptic cleaning methods and modernity itself. Passing a doorway leading into the darkened hallway, Gail noticed the lingering smell of cloves, so fragile, lazy, and succulent it frightened her.

A meager breeze languished through an open window, headed in the direction of a metal window fan in the kitchen, directly beneath a framed embroidery of Jesus with hair down to His elbows, holding a very, very woolly lamb.

"Don't mind her," said Violet, referring to the dog. "She's just interested in you. How about a glass of iced tea?"

"Sure," said Gail. "What happened to your dog's ear?"

"Oh, she just accidently lost it. It doesn't seem to bother her, though.

Here, Trixie, come over here and have one of your little sausages. Oh all right, have two. There now, sit. Sit. Good girl. Now lie down, and stay. Stay, stay. Sit, stay."

"The reason I'm here," said Gail, "is somebody took something out of my house. I was wondering if you'd seen anyone."

"Oh my," said Violet, leaving the dog and hurrying Gail into a chair at the kitchen table. "That's terrible. I'd better tell Olivia to turn on the scanner. Oh my. I had no idea, no idea. Land sakes, oh yes, I was getting some tea. Now you just sit right there. Right there. Trixie, stay, stay. Sit, stay. Olivia! You'd better come out here. We have a visitor. There's been a break-in and we're having tea! Sit and stay."

"Maybe she's sleeping," said Gail.

"She's not. She went back to her room a couple minutes ago. She'll be out any second, the dear thing. She's the one who keeps an eye on the neighborhood. I mean the dog and I have little things we're interested in, but the rest we just ignore. I guess I've always been that way. The house you live in, for instance, used to belong to a very private family. They kept to themselves. Everyone wanted to know about them and frequently asked me, because, well, because we lived right here. But I never paid any attention. It just wasn't any of my business why they did what they did, even when it amounted to never paying their fair share. I mean they had plenty of money but people always said they never paid their fair share. Anyway, here's the tea. I should get out the scrapbook and show you some pictures from the old days, if I could just remember where I put it."

"Perhaps some other time," said Gail.

"That scrapbook used to be in the living room in the corner, and as long as it was there I always knew where it was. I mean it was so big no one could miss it. But for some reason it got moved."

Violet went down the hall to check on Olivia and returned pushing her sister before her. She parked her across the table from Gail and set a glass of iced tea before her.

Gail looked into Olivia's face and quickly looked away. She had never seen such a depressed face.

"Our neighbor Gail says something was taken out of her house. She wonders if we saw anything suspicious."

Olivia stared into her glass of tea as though looking at her own death.

Gail wanted to dash from the house, but the dog lay squarely in her path to the door and she was afraid it might catch one of her ankles in its enormous mouth if she tried to jump over it. She nevertheless committed herself to taking the chance if a scrapbook was brought out, or the subject of their hoary religion came up. Everything here seemed so strange. How people could live like this, she couldn't understand.

"Oh, Olivia did that," said Violet, noticing Gail looking at the embroidery of Jesus and the woolly lamb.

"I wasn't looking at that, really, I wasn't," said Gail, afraid the embroidery might offer an entryway into the subject of their religion. "I was thinking what a nice fan you had."

"Oh, thank you. We've had it for a number of years. I can't even recall where we got it. I don't suppose its place of origin will ever be remembered now that it's forgotten. It could have come from most any place, I suppose. Every year we take it out of the storage room and put it in the window. It's just one of those—"

"Father paid a quarter for it at the Drickle auction," said Olivia without looking away from her glass of tea.

"There now, see, I think you're right. Yes, I believe so. My sister has an encyclopedic memory. There's almost nothing she can't remember. Of course being so much younger helps a lot. So, Olivia, have you seen anyone coming and going from our neighbor's house? Have you listened to your scanner? Has there been talk about a break-in?"

"I'm not sure it was a break-in," said Gail. "Nothing was broken."

"All the same," said Violet, filling Gail's untouched glass to the very brim, "if someone comes into your house when you're not home and takes something without telling you, that's a break-in. They don't have to actually break something. Breaking something would be an additional offense added on top of the other."

"All the same," said Gail, "I doubt it would be mentioned on a scanner. It was only a box of papers."

Olivia continued to stare balefully into her glass.

"Well," said Gail, rising to her feet, accidentally bumping the table and spilling some of the liquid from her glass. "I should really be going. Thanks for your help."

"Oh my, you've hardly touched your tea," said Violet. "Perhaps a little sugar will make it go down better. Let me get you some sugar."

"Oh shut up," shouted Olivia. "Just shut up. Can't you see she can hardly wait to get out of here! She doesn't want to listen to you. She doesn't care about our family. She doesn't care about anything but her sister-in-law's papers."

"Olivia! That's rude!" shouted Violet, bringing the white dog to its feet and into a low, protective crouch.

"I don't care," said Olivia. "Of all the bad things that people have done, being rude doesn't even count."

"How did you know they were her sister-in-law's papers?" asked Violet, lowering her voice so the dog would lie back down.

"They were arguing earlier today. Everybody in the whole county could hear them. If the police had voices like that, people wouldn't need scanners."

"Olivia!"

"Yes, I see things that go on, but nobody cares. Everybody is swallowed up by their own lives, and concern for others disappears like crows into the night."

The sound of the metal fan established a lull in the conversation. Gail hesitated, then asked, "Is there something wrong, Olivia?"

"What do you mean?" snapped Olivia.

"You don't look very happy."

Olivia glared at her young neighbor. "What would you or anyone like you know about my happiness?"

Gail tried to discover a response, unsuccessfully. How could people live like this? She thanked Violet again for the tea, stepped over the dog, and left.

TRAPPED BY THE PAST

L YING IN BED AND WATCHING THE MOON OUTSIDE HER WINDOW, Gail felt an alcoholic weight settle on her, making it impossible to sleep. The sky seeped through the window and oppressed her.

She kept thinking about her neighbor shouting at her: "What would you or anyone like you know about my happiness?"

At least there was *some* happiness, thought Gail—or had Olivia only said that to be ironic? And what did she mean by "anyone like you"? Who else was like her? Wasn't she unique? Who was this group of people that she belonged to and Olivia didn't?

Frustrated with her thoughts, Gail got out of bed and went outdoors, into the front yard.

The dark grass was wet and refreshingly cool, and her bare feet felt as though they were walking on chilled lettuce salad. The light from the moon allowed ample vision, and she passed quickly, silently, along the lettuce salad to the cherry tree, about twenty yards north of the house. In the silvery light she contemplated the gnarled limbs curling against the sky and wondered what it would be like to be a tree and permanently habituate a specific location in the out-of-doors.

She heard a heavy vehicle, perhaps a van, rattle over Thistlewaite Creek Bridge. It continued toward Words but did not stay on the main road. It turned, and before long headlights swung into view between the trees lining the lane. They continued a little way further, tires crunching hard on gravel, and stopped. The sound of the motor died and the lights went out.

Then the sound of a door closing—not slammed—followed by silence.

After a short while, she heard footsteps on the lane and she stepped to the other side of the tree, placing its trunk between her and the sound. From there she watched a human figure steal into her front yard, moving quickly, decisively to the front of her house.

Dressed in the blackest of black clothes, it crept beneath a front window and looked in, then moved rapidly to the other window, where it crouched against the side of the house and again stretched to peer inside. The figure then moved to the front door, pressed the side of its black head against the wood, and remained for several minutes, listening. A hand gripped the knob.

Gail watched in horror as her front door was opened just enough for the figure to slip through. Then the door closed, sealing the shape inside.

She shuddered. The situation was almost too appalling to fully comprehend. Her first impulse was to scream, but the more she thought about this, the less sensible it seemed. If there was anything good about her present circumstance it included the fact that she was not inside the house. That fortuity could be quickly canceled by broadcasting her location to the intruder, who could then rush out and find her.

In the pockets of her cutoffs she found several balls of Kleenex, a crumpled receipt from the grocery store, a paper clip, a nickel and two pennies, and a match. She thought of lighting her house on fire, and at first this seemed like a bold yet reasonable plan. She could start the fire and resume hiding. The heat, smoke, and flames would drive the intruder out, and her own whereabouts would never be known.

She could also creep forward, open the front door, slam it, and run away. This plan had the advantage of saving her house, cat, plants, and worldly belongings from incineration, but it also had disadvantages. What if she opened the door and the intruder was just on the other side of it, waiting to grab her?

The safety of her neighbors' house loomed beyond the hedge, about forty yards away, and she thought about dashing over, pounding on the door, and asking to telephone the police.

This seemed the safest plan so far. But it also meant abandoning her house, which didn't seem right. An act of personal defiance was called for. Also, the police might search her house inadequately and leave the intruder inside, concealed in some clever hiding place, waiting.

On the other hand, she could do nothing—just wait for the dark shape to come out again. This would give her a second look at the intruder as well as provide the assurance that he or she was gone before Gail went back inside.

While she was considering her options, she heard her name spoken clearly somewhere behind her, and a throat cleared. She turned and found a very small woman who turned out to be Olivia standing behind her, holding a leash with the white dog on the other end of it.

"Look, Gail," said Olivia, "this is really none of my business, but you really must do something."

"Should we call the police?"

"That person should be afraid of you, not the police."

"We're women," said Gail. "No one is ever afraid of us."

"Still, you can't let people come breaking and thieving into your house and get away with it. Here," and she offered Gail the leash.

Gail went forward, carefully opened the front door, unclipped the collar, and aimed the dog inside. With the hairs along her broad back bristled up like spikes, Trixie walked through the opening.

Gail quietly closed the door and hurried to resume her station behind the cherry tree with Olivia.

Soon, a single shriek followed by many furniture collisions moved through the house, beginning upstairs and coming down. The front door burst open and the dark figure flew outside, its feet touching only the tops of the grasses, followed by Gail's cat, which dashed under Gail's car, followed some time later by the white dog, which plodded outside, lay down in the middle of the front yard, and rested her head on her front paws. The sound of running feet on gravel ended with a slamming door and the sound of a motor. Then a heavy vehicle could be heard clattering over Thistlewaite Creek Bridge.

Gail and Olivia sat on the wet lawn beside Trixie, looking at the moon and listening to night noises.

"Thanks," said Gail. "I guess I'm in your debt."

"I guess not," said Olivia. "I'm so far in debt to everyone and for everything that no one will ever owe me anything. Besides, I can't tell you how many times your music has helped me. When you play your bass at night and sing, well, it's like hearing a human voice from a cell."

"Maybe I shouldn't say this, but you seem depressed," said Gail.

"I am, but it's nothing for you to worry about. My misery will go away as soon as I stop causing it. Every inch of it is my own making. I pray you will never know anything about these kinds of things."

"I do though," said Gail. "It's like trying to outlive yourself, and you can't. We're carved into certain people—trapped by a past that keeps making the future look just like it. Do you want to come inside? I can make coffee. We can talk. My house is always a mess but I have a lot to drink."

"No, I've got to go back before my sister wakes up. She sleeps like the dead between one and three, but after that she's unpredictable. I appreciate the offer, though. You have no idea how much I would love to sit with you in your messy house and drink, but I'm afraid, as you say, my past won't allow it."

"Wait, don't go. I want to ask you something," said Gail.

"What is it?"

"Do you think it's wrong to love another woman?"

Olivia sat in the wet grass and thought about this for a long time, and then asked, "In what way?"

"In all ways."

Olivia sat for a while longer. "Why are you asking me?"

"Because you're here."

"Do you mean wrong in terms of society, the church, the mental health community, or do you mean *wrong* wrong?"

"I don't care about those other things, so guess I mean is it *wrong* wrong."

"Hell no."

"Are you sure about that?"

"Absolutely," Olivia said, and stood up. "Come on, Trixie, we've got to get back before Vio wakes up." The big dog lumbered to its feet and they walked through the hole in the hedge.

Gail tried, unsuccessfully, to coax her cat out from under the car. Inside, she picked up several pieces of furniture and looked to see if anything was missing. As she looked, she found the cardboard box that Grahm and Cora had given her under a pile of clothes in the spare bedroom and then remembered that she had moved it from downstairs to make room for winter boots.

She returned outdoors and succeeded on the second attempt to get her cat to come out from under the car. Inside again, she locked the front door and drove several nails through the back door—which didn't have a lock—and fastened it to the door frame.

As she tried to sleep, robins, blackbirds, and finches were beginning to stir in the morning light.

VALUE

JULY MONTGOMERY FOLLOWED THE WINDING RIDGE ROAD FOR several miles. In the ditches, wild daisies and lilies reached out in blue, orange, and yellow splotches of color. Overhead a red-tailed hawk sluiced through layers of rising hot air, its wings upturned on the ends.

On the road to the old mill, July slowed down while three deer crossed. Later, a bevy of turkeys—adults and young ones—scurried into an open field.

He turned into the drive between the two stone pillars and continued to the horse barn beyond the house.

July found the Appaloosa's stall and carried in the first two bales of hay from the pickup. He broke one open and tossed the end slice into the manger. The spotted horse stuck her nose into the hay, smelled, and chewed. Strands of dried grass stuck out of both sides of her soft curved mouth. "Good stuff," said July, stroking the smooth neck. "I made it myself."

"Bee Jay says you should stay for lunch," a voice said behind him, and he turned toward a young black woman, her head shaved. She wore sandals, khaki pants, and a violet blouse. She reached over the gate and scratched behind the Appaloosa's ear. "I see you found something she'll eat. Poor thing hasn't eaten for three or four days."

"Must have gotten into some moldy alfalfa," said July. "The marsh grass will help."

"So are you staying for lunch?"

"I'm afraid not. I appreciate the offer, though."

The young woman walked back to the house and July continued carrying in the bales and stacking them next to the Appaloosa's stall.

On the last trip he saw Barbara Jean come out of the house and walk toward the barn.

"Yesha says you won't stay for lunch," she said.

"Sorry, but thanks anyway."

"Is that the hay you talked about?"

"Yup."

"Looks like it did the trick," she said, watching the mare. "Where'd you learn about horses?"

"I spent some time in Montana."

"When?"

"A long time ago."

"How much do we owe you?"

"Nothing. The hay belonged to a neighbor and he wouldn't take anything for it when I told him it was for your sick horse."

"I don't like being in debt."

"Say, Bee Jay, did Gail Shotwell play her song for you?"

"Yes."

"What did you think?"

"It was a wonderful song—a little rough around the edges, but very good. I can't work with her, though. She's too edgy, emotional."

July peeled off another slice of hay and set it in the manager. "And you're not?" he asked.

"Of course I am. What I mean is, I can't work with someone like me. She has an attitude and we'd fight all the time. She's also young eye-candy, and that's always trouble in a group like ours. Are you sure you can't stay for lunch? Yesha's a great cook."

"Sorry, I've got too much to do."

Driving away from the horse farm, July continued along the river road and turned into an asphalt drive. It ran uphill toward a brick house overlooking the river valley. He parked in front of the green-house, walked between two long rows of raised flower beds, and knocked on the door.

A thundercloud was growing in the west, and its surrounding steel gray occupied a third of the sky.

"Oh, July," said Leona Pikes, a lively, trim women in her seventies. "Come in. Timothy said you might be coming this week. It's not going to rain, is it?"

"I hope not," said July, stepping inside.

"Tim's on the back porch. I'll bring something to drink. What would you like?"

"Do you have beer?"

"Is a dark Guinness all right?"

"Sure."

July walked through the recently renovated home across polished hardwood floors, over the floral carpet and onto a large, screened-in porch overlooking the boathouse and the river.

Seated in a wicker rocking chair, Tim Pikes looked up from his *New York Times* and smiled, his face finding a few new vertical wrinkles.

"Sit down," he said and lowered the rimless glasses on his nose. He slid the folded paper onto the table.

July sat on the wicker sofa. "I'm here to make the last payment."

"Nearly thirty years," said the old lawyer. "A celebration is in order. Now the farm is entirely yours."

"I want to thank you again for giving me the land contract and all the patience you've shown. You took a chance on me."

"You started out a better farmer than I ended up, July. Leona and I completely failed at farming."

This was mostly true, July knew. Years ago, the bank had begun to repossess the property and everything on it, and had sold off most of the land. The contract with July allowed the Pikes to narrowly avoid bankruptcy. Even so, they had been generous to him.

Leona Pikes arrived with a beer and two glasses of iced tea. She sat next to July on the sofa.

"I hope this won't end your visits," she said. "You used to come all the way into Madison when we were going to law school, and you seem like family."

"You also brought fresh milk, eggs, and vegetables," added Tim. "For several years your visits were the only time during the month when the children had enough to eat."

"You're exaggerating," said July. "I'm afraid I have another favor to ask—a big one. Now that the farm is paid off, I wonder if you could arrange a trust for me. I have some things I want done."

"What things?" asked Tim, sipping his tea. "Leona is more qualified to talk about estate planning. That was more her field."

"First, I want to keep farming as long as I can."

"Of course. It suits you."

July pulled a rectangular piece of newsprint from his cotton shirt and handed it to Leona. She read it and carried it over to Tim, who readjusted the glasses on his nose.

"That's a letter to the editor, written last winter," said July. "And since then, things have gotten worse. I want you to represent them."

"Leona and I are retired," said Tim.

"I've been thinking about this for a long time," said July. "Like I said, I want to keep farming. After I'm no longer able, you or your children can have the farm. I don't have any family."

"You don't have any family at all?" asked Leona.

"Well, that's not exactly true, but the only relation I know about isn't worth a nickel and isn't worth leaving a nickel to. My neighbors are my family, and these particular neighbors need your help."

Tim Pikes looked at the newspaper clipping again. "Shotwell," he said. Then he repeated the name, hoping to dislodge the appropriate memories. "I think I remember Shotwells. Yes. The parents, as I recall, were cruel to their children and worked them like animals—a predilection shared by many of the other local farmers."

Leona smiled and touched July's arm. "I'm afraid Tim hasn't retired some of his earlier habits. Almost anything sets him off. His newspaper usually provides fuel for the rest of the morning. The whole planet, it seems, is simply one endless human rights violation waiting for a legal remedy."

Undeterred, July continued. "I've thought about this a long time. These people need help. Their children, Seth and Grace, are about the age your children were when I first met you. They are in trouble and are likely to get into more. You need to do this for them, and for me."

Leona put down her drink. "When government agencies become entangled in this kind of financial skulduggery—and one is clearly involved here—it can go on for a long time. I'm afraid your neigh-bors would be better off with younger counsel."

"I've thought about this a long time," repeated July.

A man wearing a straw hat and carrying pruning shears walked in front of the porch and opened the screen door. "Sorry to bother you, Mrs. Pikes, but do you still want the dahlia bulbs put next to the roses?"

"Yes," said Leona. "And bring the boat around to the dock. If it doesn't rain, we want to go for a ride this afternoon."

After the gardener closed the door and walked away, Tim turned to July. "I guess the most forthright answer is no. We're retired. But give us all the information you have. We'll make some calls and see what public resources are available. On that basis we can make rec-ommendations. We'll call you in a couple days."

"I appreciate it," said July. "And I guess this would be the time to mention that Grahm Shotwell is against anyone representing him."

"Of course," smiled Leona. "The first healthy reaction to over-whelming odds is to decide you don't need help."

"On top of that, I don't want them to know I have anything to do with this."

The old lawyer laughed, folded his glasses, and pushed them into his jacket pocket. "Of course not, July. Heaven forbid that anyone should know anything about you."

"I just don't want them to know I'm involved," said July. "Like I said, my neighbors are my family, but many of them might not be too thrilled to learn that."

"Foolishness," said Leona. "You hide from people, July. It's an ir-ritating trait. I'm going to start lunch and we want you to stay."

"I'm afraid I have too much to do today, but I'll be back."

When July came to the end of the driveway, he realized that talk-ing with the Pikes about earlier times had temporarily interrupted his plans for the day. A somber mood had been building in him all morning and he could no longer ignore it.

Instead of returning to his farm, he turned left.

At the old mill he parked on the gravel shoulder and assembled the fishing rod beneath the front seat, forcing the form-fitted male end into the female and twisting until the guide eyes lined up. There was a purple lead-head already on the end of the line and he located a bobber and put it in his pocket.

He climbed over the DO NOT TRESPASS sign on the gate and walked toward the stone building standing on the edge of the Heartland River. Inside, the massive grinding mill sat in the middle of an empty room, with bird nests in the rafters, that smelled of sun-warmed masonry. Pigeons flapped noisily through the open windows, raising dust. He went through the room and onto the wooden landing outside. At the south end, the waterwheel's rotting oak slats disappeared into the river.

An old davenport with exposed springs leaned against the stone wall, carried in by other fishermen. July sat on it, looked out over the water, and smelled the oily, fecund odor of decomposing plants and algae.

The current ran in a unanimous direction near the middle. Leaves, small limbs, and clumps of moss floated along at a steady pace. A more democratic variety of currents, swirls, eddies, and back-drifts moved along the banks.

A blue heron flew downriver, its dinosaur head crooking over the water. As the thoughts July wanted to think rose slowly to the surface, he took the chain from around his neck and hung it on an overhead rafter beam. On the end of it dangled the silver ring his wife had made for him.

They were not even twenty years old then, still children—or at least it seemed like that now. Looking at the ring helped focus his attention, leading him into the place he needed to go.

He had loved her completely, without abandon, and after three thieves broke into their Iowa farmhouse one night and killed her, he had continued to love her. He had never gotten over her and he had never tried to get over her. She had introduced him to something that did not go away after she was gone.

And *that* he needed to think about.

He clipped the bobber over the monofilament and slid it five or six feet above the jig, then lay the pole down. He could throw out the line if someone came along.

Where did the real value of life come from? As a child he believed it came from inside him, a by-product of the human machine. Some days seemed worth living and others did not, depending on how he felt, and how he felt depended on the machine inside him. He had been born as a living organism with the capacity to make certain chemicals, and when those chemicals were produced, his experiences had value.

As he grew older, his attitude changed. Things outside him became more important than his machinery's chemical laboratory. Other people, his wife, gave value to his life. She was worthwhile, and if at that time he had been asked where his value came from, he would have pointed to her. The machinery inside him was useless in providing worthwhile feelings without her.

Then, several years after her death, he changed his mind again. He realized that beyond his sorrow, in front of his memories, the same value she had once provided for him was still available. It hadn't gone away, even though she had. They had loved each other and that love was somehow still active. He could feel it, even though she was no longer there. Her influence had changed everything, permanently.

He had rediscovered their love in his neighbors. He felt it when he watched Leona and Tim Pikes struggle to earn law degrees after their failure on the farm. He felt it when Grahm walked toward the microphone at American Milk's annual meeting. He felt it when Jacob pounded on his door in the middle of the night and wanted to talk about Winnie. He felt it when Winnie looked in the plastic bag and ran off to find mushrooms. He felt it when Gail wrote her first song and played it for him. He felt it when Wade said he wanted to move away from his parents' farm to be closer to Olivia. He felt it now as he listened for over an hour to the sound of moving water, as mile after mile of liquid life flowed by the abandoned mill. He needed to feel it, because without it there was no value.

No, he hadn't gotten over her. In all the ways that mattered he was still married—happily married—though he could never explain this to anyone. No one would understand.

July took down the chain hanging from the rafter and put it around his neck. Carrying the rod and reel, he returned to the truck.

Along the road, he met another group of wild turkeys. They looked as though they could be the same ones he'd seen earlier, heading in the opposite direction.

LETTING GO

MAXINE GOT UP AT 4:00 A.M. AND WALKED BEYOND THE BARN to the small lean-to her husband had built on the south side of the woodpile. A light rain during the night had moistened the ground, and the air smelled fresh. A fine mist hovered over the valley and the trunks of the trees were dripping wet. She found him sitting on the army cot, his rifle leaning beside him, in the ramshackle guardhouse he'd built several months ago.

"Thought I heard something," he said, and inspected his watch with a flashlight. "You're up early."

"I couldn't sleep," said Maxine and set out their breakfast: oatmeal with raisins; boiled eggs in the shell; toast with butter, brown sugar, and cinnamon; two six-ounce cans of tomato juice; and coffee. She arranged the meal on two folding trays next to the cot and sat in the lawn chair while they ate.

"Ever notice how food tastes different outdoors?" asked Rusty.

"It's because of the smells," said Maxine. "Most of taste comes from smell."

"I was thinking we might want to build a cabin back here in the woods."

"Why would we want to do that, Russell?"

"For when we felt like getting away."

"Getting away from what?"

"The house and telephone."

"We'd probably want a telephone inside the cabin."

"Why?"

"In case someone called or you wanted to call someone. Oh yes, July Montgomery called last night."

"What did he want?"

"He wanted to know if he could borrow your truck to pull a trailer somewhere."

"What did you tell him?"

"I said you'd never loaned your truck to anyone that I know of and he'd have to talk to you himself. And I also told him that I didn't think your truck was big enough to pull a whole trailer. He said he'd call again."

"How big is it?"

"I don't remember. An average-sized one, I think."

"My truck could pull that like nothing."

A sound came from the direction of the barn and Rusty climbed to his feet and squinted through a space between several logs in the woodpile. He motioned for Maxine to come look.

In the dim morning light, a cougar walked along the roof of the barn, jumped into the nearby tree, and climbed to the ground. It walked forward several yards, turned around, and lay down.

Out of the ground-level door on the back of the barn walked another black cat, about a third smaller than the first. The older animal stood up and they circled each other twice, their tails moving back and forth. The adult ran down the valley. The cub followed, then stopped, turned, and looked directly at the makeshift guardhouse and Rusty and Maxine, and growled.

Then it ran after its mother.

"Beautiful," said Maxine. "It makes your heart sing to see something like that."

"They're finally gone. Now I've got to get that upper window closed," said Rusty.

"I doubt they'll come back anyway, Russell. July was right—the cub was hurt and stayed in the mow until it got better. They won't be back. You can move back into the house now. That hunter you saw will never find them. I mean if they've survived this long there's a good chance—"

"My brother never would have let that son of a bitch shoot an animal on his property," said Rusty. "He had a pet raccoon and used to worry over that animal like it was a person. That's the way Carl was."

"Are you going to talk to your niece now?"

"No. Right now I'm going to eat another boiled egg."

LAWYERS

GRACE SPOTTED THE GREEN CAR FIRST. SHE WATCHED IT MOVE into the farmyard, and a tall old woman climbed out. She seemed momentarily stunned by the heat of the afternoon and walked very, very slowly around to the other side and helped an old man out. He brushed the sleeves of his suit coat, buttoned the front, pulled a briefcase from the back seat, and looked at the weather vane on top of the barn. He moved even slower than the woman did. Grace did not recognize them and asked her brother if he did. Seth was busy nailing a wooden box to a tamarack.

"Never seen them," Seth said. "Must not be from around here."

"They're here now," said Grace, setting down the sack of squirrel bait. Together they ran into the house.

"Can we help you?" asked Grahm, meeting the two visitors in the yard.

"We're looking for Grahm and Cora Shotwell," the old man said, his gray hair parted as straight as a stretched string.

"I'm Grahm Shotwell. This is my wife, Cora."

"Perhaps we could talk somewhere out of the sun," he said.

"Who are you?" demanded Cora.

"The name is Pikes," he said, handing her a business card from his inside coat pocket. "Tim Pikes. This is my wife, Leona. We've been retained to represent you in your dispute with American Milk Cooperative."

"You're lawyers," said Grahm, as though naming a disease.

"We have much to discuss," said Leona.

"You're wasting your time here," said Grahm. "We don't need a lawyer."

"As for the former, Leona and I are uniquely capable of determining the value of our time. Regarding the latter, you are very much in need of a lawyer so perhaps we should get out of the heat."

At the kitchen table, Tim Pikes took a handful of papers from his briefcase and explained, "First of all, Miss Gail Shotwell has asked me to convey an apology for her. The papers she earlier identified as missing and perhaps stolen were in the spare bedroom of her home where she had stored them but subsequently did not remember doing so. They were only recently discovered. She misspoke when several weeks ago she said to Cora that they were no longer in her possession and she regrets whatever confusion this may have caused. You will notice that I have taken the opportunity to look through them, and have brought copies of the most germane."

"She was drinking again," said Cora, frowning.

"That speculation is one of several which Miss Shotwell antici-pated you might offer, and one she does not wish to dispute out of hand. However, it need not concern us now. I see you do not have air-conditioning and I wonder if I could have some bottled water."

Cora looked quickly through the copies of shipping receipts and tax forms. "It's them," she said with satisfaction, smiling in a conspiratorial manner at Grahm. "Now we can nail those bastards to a wall." Grahm returned the smile, then grew self-conscious and closed his face.

Leona laughed. "That's the spirit," she said.

"If we have the papers," said Grahm, "we don't need you. The papers prove everything."

Tim Pikes took off his coat and laid it across the back of a chair. "Mr. Shotwell, proof applies well to mathematics but everything else is a matter of precedent and persuasion. By notifying the agriculture department of the existence of these papers and the illegal practices they serve to record, you've entered a world of litigious grief."

Leona sat at the table. "We've received transcripts of all depart-ment activity as well as the files at the district court, and have drafted a petition to overturn an improper administrative ruling and reopen all proceedings. We've challenged the fine and have prepared a pe-tition on your behalf asking for an injunction to cease and desist

against the cooperative as well as a civil suit addressing the prejudi-
cial termination of your employment. A petition has been drafted
for the removal of the administrative judge assigned to the investigation because of his prior association with the cooperative and other
conflicts of interest, and we have outlined a preliminary petition to
present to the attorney general and district court."

As Leona named the documents, Tim pulled them from the
briefcase and set them on the tabletop, with the blank lines above
"plaintiff" circled in red ink.

"We don't need help," said Grahm. "We need justice, and I'm
beginning to believe that justice is something that means nothing to
the government or the people who work for it."

"Everyone needs help, Mr. Shotwell," said Tim. "And as Aristotle
was fond of pontificating over two thousand years ago, justice exists
only between those who are equally involved in making and enforc-
ing laws. You've offended some very wealthy and powerful people,
and they will do anything and everything to defend their positions
of privilege."

"This is the United States of America," said Grahm, "or at least it
used to be. 'Positions of privilege' means nothing to me and should
mean nothing to judges and lawyers like you."

"Mr. and Mrs. Shotwell, contrary to what you may think, the legal
system was neither founded upon nor designed to reflect the common
decency found in normal human relationships. It primarily works like
the rules for a lunatic asylum. It tries to govern people driven insane
by the inflated idea of their own worth. You've unfortunately become caught up in it, and the outcome is anything but certain."

"What are you saying?" asked Cora.

"I'm saying that if you value your reputation in the community
and want to avoid receiving anonymous death threats in the middle
of the night, including threats against your children, and going to jail
and losing your farm, you should pay attention to us."

"But we've done nothing wrong," said Cora.

"Telling the truth is always wrong if it threatens those for whom
being wrong can never be true."

"Who hired you?"

"Look," said Tim, directly addressing Grahm. "You have a good life here—far better than most. You can work for yourselves, visit with your neighbors, and grow old watching your children become fully conscious adults. It's unlikely you will ever go hungry and you can go to sleep nearly every night in each other's arms. People have no right to wish for any more than that, and if they do they're idiots. A good life is worth fighting for and Leona and I are presently your only way of fighting."

"I don't believe that," said Grahm.

"We understand these problems," said Leona, addressing Cora. "But first, it would be nice to get to know each other better. Our four children and our grandchildren are coming to visit in a week and we'd like for you and Grahm and Seth and Grace to come over for the afternoon. We live not far from here. We're planning on lamb, if that's all right. Tim wants to roast one on an open fire, but that seems extravagant to me. We've never done it before. I'm not sure what we should have to go with it. I'm unfamiliar with lamb. What do you think? We can talk about it later. I'll call."

"There are no guarantees, Grahm," said Tim. "Something can always go wrong, but with our help you have a good chance of winning against American Milk. After several years of exhausting administrative remedies we will finally get into the district court and there will probably be a verdict in your favor, and a fine against the cooperative. Both will be appealed to a higher court and after five or six more years the fine will be reduced to an insignificant amount. But you'll keep your farm and your reputation, and you'll be able to take pride in knowing the good guys won a battle against institution-alized greed."

"We don't have bottled water," said Cora, filling him a glass from the faucet. "Our water was tested, though."

"Who is going to pay you?" demanded Grahm. "We don't take charity."

"We don't give charity," said Tim. "We're mostly retired and can do what we want with our lives. This is something we want to do."

Tim took a long drink of water and Cora said to Leona, "You have four children?"

"Yes," said Leona. "Four children and ten grandchildren. You can meet every one of them next week."

Tim put on his jacket and left a pile of papers on the table, indicating the places where Grahm and Cora needed to sign their names. Then, carrying his briefcase and coat, he returned to the passenger side of the green German car, with Leona holding his arm.

"I don't think we should accept their help," said Grahm, watching them drive away.

"We have to," said Cora. "Under the circumstances, it wouldn't be right to refuse."

Seth and Grace ran downstairs, across the kitchen floor, and outside in urgent pursuit of something known only to them.

Cora went to the stove and continued cooking dinner. She listened to the sound of water coming to a boil, and for the first time in a long while the warm feeling of being safe glowed inside her, a lantern on the edge of a still lake. And now that the subject had been brought into the open where she could examine it—first in the shape of envy and then in the color of desire—she knew her mind quite well: she wanted more children.

RESEMBLANCE

RUSTY KNOCKED ON THE FRONT OF THE PARSONAGE IN WORDS and waited, then knocked again. While he was knocking the third time, Winnie walked around from the back yard where she had been working in her flower garden and asked, "May I help you?" Her hands and forearms were covered with dirt and she held a small trowel.

Rusty took off his seed cap and put it back on, the bill curving low over his eyes.

"Most people call me Rusty," he said, a cigarette bobbing out of the corner of his thin mouth. "Rusty Smith."

"I think I've seen you before," said Winnie, staring at him uneasily. "Doesn't your wife, Maxine, volunteer at the library in Grange?"

"Yup."

"I'm Pastor Winifred. How may I help you?"

Winnie felt an instant and unexplained loathing for the shape and manner of the man standing in the yard. Something in the way he moved, his facial muscles and the attitude with which he stood in his silver-toed cowboy boots, set loose a primordial cascade of neural firing in her lower brain. She instinctually avoided eye contact, hoping to sever the connection between him and her emotions.

"Your last name Smith?" he asked.

"Yes."

"I'm your uncle."

Winnie dropped the trowel and backed away.

Rusty couldn't help staring, recognizing in Winnie—despite her gender and tall, birdlike stature—several unmistakable features belonging to his brother, and these came as some surprise because before seeing them in her, he did not know that he remembered them in Carl. He stepped forward, as though to draw closer to his own memories.

"I'm your uncle—Carl's older brother. We should talk."

"Why?" said Winnie, and again stepped backward, her long legs creating more space between them, separating herself from her memories.

"Didn't know you had an uncle, did you?" asked Rusty. He flicked an ash from his cigarette.

"For years I hated my father," said Winnie. All the twisted and fearful associations that her childhood had locked away in little wooden drawers migrated into the person standing before her. He truly seemed like the kind of man who set traps for others by luring them into despising him, and even as she recognized the bait as bait, she felt herself taking it.

"I'm afraid your father is dead."

Winnie said nothing.

"You're my niece," said Rusty.

"Please go away."

"I should show you something. Will you come?"

"No."

"Yes you will. I can't do this without you, Pastor Winifred. And even if you don't want to cooperate I still need to do my part, don't I? All these years, I haven't been able."

Rusty drove for more than an hour without speaking. Winnie sat on the far other side of the truck seat, staring out the window and concentrating on her breathing. On the north end of the dusty village of Domel, he pulled into an abandoned quarry, steering around pools of stagnant water, rock ledges, and rusting machinery, and parked next to a gate made of steel posts and barbed wire.

"Come on," he said, dragging the gate aside.

Winnie stepped through and they walked uphill.

"There used to be a road here," he explained. "It ran all the way west along the ridge. It's grown over now. Somebody logged off the bigger trees. But the view of the horizon is the same as it was sixty years ago." He stared into it for several minutes.

They continued up the hill, stopping twice for Rusty to sit on a flat rock, rest his knees, and smoke. Scrub oak, sumac, and ash poked out of the sandy wasteland. Near the top, Rusty headed through a thicket of brambles. Winnie followed, and at a place that looked no different from any other place, he stopped and said, "This is it."

"What?" asked Winnie.

"The place we grew up, your father and I. Those foundation stones—that's where the house stood."

"What happened to it?" asked Winnie, noticing five or six irregular stones jutting out of the ground in a ragged line, apparently the only signs of a once-existing homestead.

"Our dad set it on fire one night when he came home from town. He did it on purpose. We were all sleeping inside. One of our sisters woke up and Mother got us out. We stood right here and watched it burn to the ground with everything we owned inside. Carl tried to save his raccoon and was badly burned."

"Did he save it?"

"It burned up in the attic. It was the middle of the winter and we were so cold we stayed here near the fire until some people from town came with blankets and clothes."

"Many people have bad things happen to them," said Winnie. "Some of those things hurt for a long time, but most people don't use them as excuses to hurt others."

"They aren't excuses," said Rusty. "This is the place where Carl and I grew up. It made us. The things that happened here can't be helped and won't be changed, and even if some of them were bad, they weren't *all bad*. So I brought you here to say that however your father may have failed you, he did the best he could."

"I'm in God's family now," said Winnie. "My father can't hurt me any longer."

Rusty leaned against a tree to take weight off his knees. "He did the best he could, and you can't just go off and forget your people. It's not right."

"Your brother's cruelty knew no limits. He left my mother when she was sick. He never had a thought for her, or me, and as much as I live, I live in opposition to him. The most important day of my life was at the foster home when I decided I could make my own life for myself, and I walked away from those memories forever. Talking to you now makes me remember how I used to feel, and I hope to never feel that way again."

"Maybe so," said Rusty.

"You have no idea what it's been like for me," said Winnie. "You can't possibly know what it's like to see a better world—where all living things come together without fear. You can't know what it's like to see that the only thing preventing the Kingdom from coming is a corruption in your own heart, a lie in your own soul, and to know that your only chance to be part of something truly good is to separate yourself from what's inside you. You can't know what it's like to be afraid you can never get far enough away, no matter how long you live, because that unredeemable ugliness is something you've inherited. And you can certainly never know what it's like to go back to the birthplace of that festering terror and get reacquainted. I'm not strong enough to completely forgive him yet, and I don't have to be."

Rusty walked over to the tallest foundation stone he could find and sat on it. "You're mistaken if you think I don't know. What do you think coming here means? I've never been back. I couldn't come before. But you need to know that people do things because they don't know any better. They do the best they can."

"I don't believe that," said Winnie.

"We're related and that's what counts," said Rusty. "If you don't get over whatever it is you think Carl did to you, you won't feel right about all the things you will have to do in your own life."

For the first time since leaving the parsonage, Winnie looked directly at him and said, "Your brother knew what he was doing and he did it anyway."

"It was my fault, much of it."

"What are you talking about?

"I'm talking about Carl. After we moved into town dad drank himself to death. Our mother took in laundry and did what she could, but it wasn't enough. As the oldest, I hired out on a crew that cleaned boxcars for the railroad—they would hire children in those days. I sent money home every week. Later, I worked on a hog farm on the other side of the county, and I still sent money home. But after a few years I stopped going home. I never went back. And by the time I was eighteen I'd stopped sending money. My mother didn't know where I was and that's the way I wanted it. I didn't go back. Carl needed me, but I didn't go back. I didn't."

"Why not?"

"Because I wanted to be someone who could make things right, but I never was."

"How my father turned out wasn't your fault."

"Then you don't understand. We were close. We did everything together and he needed me."

"You were a child yourself," said Winnie.

"Without my help, he did the best he could," said Rusty. "That pretty much ends all I have to say. We can go now."

Their trip back to Words was without incident, except when Rusty laid his pack of cigarettes on the seat between them and Winnie threw them out the window.

"Who made you my judge?" barked Rusty.

"Jesus," said Winnie.

"I'll just buy more."

"Maybe so," said Winnie. "But even if you don't cooperate, I still have to do my part, don't I?"

Despite himself, Rusty laughed. His own daughters had never dared to talk to him that way. As Winnie climbed out of the cab, he again watched the movements of his brother in her.

"I'll see you again," said Rusty.

"Please give me some time," said Winnie. "This isn't easy."

THE COUNTY FAIR

TODAY, VIOLET COULD FEEL HER AGE HANGING ON HER LIKE a heavy coat. In addition to her chest and back hurting, she simply felt old, which didn't exactly hurt but involved negotiating a seemingly endless reiteration of the familiar in order to move between one moment and the next.

When the smoke alarm went off for the third time she took out its battery.

This was an extremely important day, a landmark of late summer. For as long as she could remember, the Words Friends of Jesus Church had gone to the Thistlewaite County Fair, handing out pocket-sized New Testaments and selling pies, cakes, jellies, jams, cookies, and crafts.

Violet's peach pies were famous for their golden crusts and sweet, tropical savor. She always sold as many as she could bake, and more than half the funds raised for evangelical missions came out of Violet's oven. The secret of the filling, once described as "wildly fruity," lay in a special admixture of apricot juice and basswood honey. This year, Pastor Winnie announced they would double the price and she made a new sign: Violet Brasso's Heavenly Peach Pies, $18. "It's for a good cause," she said. "And they're worth it."

It was also the annual meeting of the secular and religious worlds, which for Violet had increasingly come to resemble a war. Each year the army of secularism had grown bigger and stronger, until the Words Friends of Jesus Church's red-and-white-striped booth was the only Christian encampment on the entire grounds.

The fair had changed in her lifetime from a congenial community gathering to an anonymous encounter with people who hardly knew each other. The language of shared piety—the bond that had once glued Thistlewaite County together—had changed, and now there was nothing that resembled a bond of any kind. Their booth had gradually become surrounded by amusements, attractions, and delights with no redeeming value, as if it were tiny Judaea inside the vast Roman Empire.

To the north, the beer tent—nonexistent during the early years of the fair—had grown to the sprawling black canvas monstrosity that now stretched all the way to the grandstand where the raucous bands performed their ear-splitting music. Behind them was the Ferris wheel, from whose dizzying heights the cores of caramel apples, cotton candy stalks, and the sodden remains of Sno-Kones rained down on the top of their booth. (In the previous year corncobs had been added to the airborne trash, and consequently the Farmer's Daughter's Sweet Corn tent and its open tubs of melted butter and quart-sized aluminum salt shakers hanging from rafter strings had been relocated a hundred yards away.)

The arcade entrance stood directly to the south. There, unshaved men with open shirts baited passers-by to bet on throwing dull darts into half-inflated balloons, with made-in-China stuffed animals as prizes. In the narrow alleyway, 4-H youngsters led livestock to and from the show barns, the animals' gleaming, hulking bodies blemish-free except for hard-to-see injection sites near their tails.

Across the dirt midway were the sideshows. Freaks and hawkers. Airbrush artists painting lewd T-shirts. Flea markets selling ormolu trinkets, used pornographic videos, posters, Nazi memorabilia, greasy oil lamps, cheap cigars, antiques, and ordinary rubbish.

Last year, a group of Madison lawyers called something like PROPRE (People Really Opposed to Public Religious Expression) filed a lawsuit to bar the Friends of Jesus Church from participating in the fair but were denied an injunction. They had also attempted to do away with all religious music, clearing the path for a week of uninterrupted C&W, hard rock, and heavy metal. But because of long-standing church connections on the county fair board, this had also failed and the ninety-year-old rule mandating religious music on Sunday held.

This year, the Straight Flush had been hired to play for an afternoon. Though they were normally a country band, they also claimed to know traditional religious songs. Pastor Winnie had at first objected, arguing that a bar band should not even be considered, but after learning they were the only musicians available, she relented.

Violet dressed Olivia in her most attractive summer outfit, but her depression seemed no better. She did not even want to get out of bed. There were holes in the spaces between things, she claimed, and out of them poured an Egyptian darkness.

As Violet baked pies, Olivia sat in the living room, alternately staring through the windows and working to correct her embroidery, which had turned out badly. Apostle John, sitting next to Jesus at the Last Supper, looked like a wolverine. And the more she tried to correct him, the more like a rodent and the less like an apostle he became.

"I'm not going," she said and threw the needlework on the floor.

"Yes you are," said Violet, making room for her fourteenth pie on the crowded kitchen table and standing back to admire the hot, steaming collection.

"I'm not."

"Yes you are. It's unhealthy to stay inside. If you're don't come people will think I'm not taking good care of you. There, only two more to go. Pastor Winnie will be here in an hour to help load these up, and I'm taking Trixie. Do you think you could ride in the back seat?"

"You can't take that dog."

"Of course I can. You remember three years ago when a man shook his fist in Pastor's face? Our booth needs protection."

"Winnie provoked that argument," said Olivia.

"That's not true. Pastor was just defending the Holy Bible—standing up for God's Word."

Olivia scoffed. "She picked a fight and you know it. She can be very truculent when she's in the mood."

"Olivia," admonished Violet, "I don't see any good reason why you can't see the good in good people."

"Oh, shut up."

By the middle of the afternoon all of Violet's pies had been sold. The red jams and oatmeal cookies were also going well. The humidity remained high, but a breeze out of the north helped people stay even-tempered.

So far, there had been no arguments with anyone from PROPRE and the new (and larger) John 3:16 banner could be read all the way down to the miniature ponies. Even Pastor Winnie seemed almost relaxed, and she just looked the other way when a well-dressed couple bought two dozen cookies and a crocheted pot holder and then refused to take a New Testament, which was free with any purchase.

The band was much better than many had feared, playing the standard religious songs with both reverence and skill.

"We should tell them their music is appreciated," said Winnie to the eleven other women inside the booth. "Though I'm not fond of electrified instruments, I think they're doing an excellent job."

"I'll come," said Violet, along with five others.

Winnie pushed Olivia up the midway toward the grandstand. Violet walked beside them with her white dog opening a wide path in the crowd. Five other women, all in their seventies, came behind, leaving the older ladies, Mildred, Amnesty, Florence, and Pauline, to manage the booth.

They crossed in front of the long, crowded beer tent without major incident and had reached the benches in front of the grandstand when the hairs along the white dog's back rose up like spikes. From behind the flea market a bald-headed man with a huge black dog walked toward them, and rather than go in the other direction when he saw Violet's dog, he came straight ahead.

"So we meet again," he said, grinning at Olivia.

Violet said, "Excuse me, please take your dog away from here." She pulled on the leash in an attempt to reorient Trixie.

Flanked by towering speakers, the band hit the first chord of "Leaning on the Everlasting Arms" and sailed into a loud and lilting rendition, with the keyboard player singing the first verse.

A white pickup loaded with sweet corn pulled onto the midway and came toward them. Behind the wheel, July Montgomery was looking for the Farmer's Daughter's Sweet Corn tent. It wasn't where he remembered it.

Trixie lowered her head and began to fight the leash.

The black Tosa bared its teeth and the bald man looked down with a pride bordering on menace. He took a step closer.

The other women from the booth stood in a semicircle near the stage. One of them shouted something to Winnie, but the music was too loud to make it out.

The driver of the white pickup was looking out the side window for the Farmer's Daughter's Sweet Corn tent.

Her attention riveted on pulling Trixie away from the grandstand, Violet could neither hear nor see the approaching truck and was unaware that she was about to be hit.

The band reached the final chord change in the second verse and in a crescendo of amplified sound the drummer, lead guitar, and bass set up the second chorus.

For Olivia Brasso, who could see what was about to happen, horror and urgency conspired to create something resembling timeless tranquility. Inside this inexplicable eternity, she watched Violet at the moment of her disaster, her bones about to be shattered, her flesh disfigured. Struggling with her uncooperative pet, she seemed so old, frail, and oblivious—so helpless, comic, and pathetic in her losing battle to preserve her dignity and at the same time control her pit bull.

And then Olivia became acquainted with the irrational certainty that sometimes causes even cowards to crawl from their lifelong hiding places of their own accord and act as if mortality had no hold over them. As though sprung from a trap, Olivia leaped from her wheelchair, jumped over a low bench, and ran seven paces headfirst into Violet. She knocked the leash out of Violet's hands and drove the heavier woman all the way under the black tent, where they fell together, splattering paper cups of beer across the top of a picnic table.

The pickup continued, with July still looking for the sweet corn booth.

Everyone in the beer tent stood up and applauded.

The blond female could be heard singing the melody, supported by lower, harmonic male voices.

Trixie, twenty pounds heavier than she was six months earlier, tore into the black dog with a joyous ferocity.

The bald man called for help getting the dogs separated but could not be heard over the music.

Tears ran down Winnie's face.

She had seen a miracle.

MAKING OTHER ARRANGEMENTS

VIOLET DROVE HOME FROM THE FAIR WITH HER BLOOD-splattered dog next to her on the front seat. She did not speak to her sister in the back seat. In the driveway, Violet pulled the wheelchair from the trunk and opened it for Olivia.

Olivia hesitated, then shoved the wheelchair aside and walked into the house. Violet followed, pushing the empty chair up the ramp.

"I'm going to hose off the dog," said Violet, and went outside.

When she returned, Olivia had set out tea and was sitting in her wheelchair next to the table, her fingers fidgeting along the edges of her cup.

Violet sat down and sipped her tea.

"Aren't you going to say anything?" asked Olivia.

"The pies went well this year. I was afraid people wouldn't pay the higher price. But they all sold."

"I'm not talking about the pies."

"I'm afraid Trixie may have seriously damaged that other dog."

"I'm not talking about Trixie."

"What should I say?"

"You could have been killed."

"Yes, Olivia, I'm glad you found a way to show me."

Olivia's fingers walked along the rim of her cup. "What are you talking about?"

"The antibiotics and, well, you know."

"You knew?"

"Of course. What did you think? All the things you leave around, climbing up and down stairs at night, exercising in the park, eating like a horse, the muscles in your legs. What did you think?"

Olivia's face turned ghostly, angry gray. "Why didn't you say something?" she demanded.

"You weren't ready."

Olivia pushed her tea away and stood up. "I can't believe this! You knew all along?"

"Of course. What did you think? I've never minded taking care of you. I've always told you that."

Olivia frowned and sat back down.

The dog scratched on the door. Violet let her in and returned to the table.

"Oh, by the way," said Olivia.

"What?"

"I knew you knew."

"Olivia, sometimes you amaze me. Nothing will ever make you grow up."

The dog returned to the door and whined. Violet let her out.

"And by the way," said Olivia as Violet sat down again, "I think this would be a good time to talk about making some changes around here."

"What kind of changes?"

"I want Wade to live with us."

Violet drank the rest of her tea without speaking, her eyes moving from one area of the room to another, as though imagining what they might be like in the future. She carefully centered her empty cup in the saucer and said, "I'm sorry, Olivia, I can't agree to that. It's asking too much."

"Why?"

"I would never adjust."

"Oh, no," said Olivia. "Vio, I didn't mean for him to live *inside* the house. Heaven forbid. That would be intolerable. He will just have his trailer in the back yard."

"His trailer?"

"I told Wade he could bring his trailer here and park it between the garden and the hedge."

"His trailer?"

"Yes, the one he lives in."

"What color is it?"

"The color isn't really important because I'm sure it can be repainted, and he's going to pay us rent for the space. It will almost cover the mortgage payments, I mean almost. And Wade says the co-op is opening a new retail store in Grange and he thinks he can talk to someone and get me a job there."

"Doing what?"

"Selling cheese."

"What color is it, Olivia?"

"The cheese?"

"The trailer."

"I'm not going to say because it can be repainted. Wade is very handy and he can do it. He'll be a big help around here. He can mow the lawn and fix the roof and—"

"What color is it?"

"It isn't the color so much, really. It has a variety of colors. He hired the person who put flames on the front of his car to paint some pictures on the sides of the trailer. And, well, even Wade admits it wasn't a good idea and can be done over."

"Isn't he still on probation?"

"Yes, but I'm sure all that is behind him. He's completely changed. Having him here won't involve any trouble of any kind, I'm sure of it."

"How would he get this trailer all the way over here?"

"July Montgomery is pulling it with Rusty Smith's pickup, tomorrow."

MEETING AT SNOW CORNERS

GRAHM SHOTWELL FINISHED MILKING AND STOOD IN THE BARN doorway, looking into a red-glowing sky and the farmhouse beyond the tamaracks. The cool of evening delayed, it was still hot and humid. Sweat ran from his face and arms. Inside the house Seth and Grace stared into the blue-flickering television. Cora sat beside them on the couch, reading.

Grahm remembered planting the tamaracks, his grandfather holding the saplings in his wrinkled hands and pressing their hairy roots into the earth.

Cora went to the window to stare outdoors.

Grahm backed inside the barn, out of sight.

He turned out the lights in the milk house and drove away in his pickup.

"You're in time for pie," said July, opening the door.

A peach pie rested on the kitchen table. A half-eaten slice sat on a plate before an empty chair. Another slice, uneaten, sat in front of Gail.

"Your sister just brought over a pie. Want some?"

"Maybe some other time," he said, ignoring Gail. "Let's go to the meeting at Snow Corners."

July reseated himself at the table and resumed forking pie into his mouth. "Don't think I can do that," he said. "I'd like to, but it's too hot to go anywhere and I promised someone I wouldn't go."

Grahm glared at Gail.

"Hey, don't look at me, I only brought the pie."

"You said you'd go," Grahm reminded July.

"I know I did," said July.

Grahm stood in the middle of the kitchen while July continued eating and Gail drank beer. When July finished his piece of pie and reached to cut another from the pan, Grahm turned to leave.

"I'll go with you," said Gail, standing up.

"No you won't."

"I'm coming," said Gail. "I'm working on a new song and I need some new ideas. A drive will help."

July let the knife fall back into the pie plate. "All right," he said. "I made two promises and can't keep both. I've got to be back early, though. This will give me a chance to leave off Rusty's pickup."

"Rusty Smith loaned you his truck?"

"It's in the machine shed."

"Better keep Seth and Grace inside the house from now on, Grahm," said Gail. "Religious people are going to go wild when they find out that hell's frozen over."

She and July rode in the dual-wheeled pickup, parked it in front of the Smith house, and climbed in beside Grahm in his older and smaller truck.

They traveled most of the way in silence, the cab surrounded by the muggy darkness. With the windows down, they continued through Snow Corners and into the black pine forest, the hot, sticky air laden with the fragrance of pine sap, which seemed to ooze from the loud, churning hum of insects.

"God," said Gail, "will you listen to that drunken feast. If only I could enjoy something the way bugs love heat."

Fearing she had had too much to drink and not wanting to encourage her talking more, Grahm and July remained silent.

They turned down the narrow lane, branches folding over them like black wings. The steel gate was open and they drove into the clearing, where seventy or eighty trucks, cars, vans, and motorcycles were parked in the long grass around the barn. The lantern at the entrance burned with a hot, hazy light.

A huge youth with small blue eyes met them at the door, his hands in his pockets. When he recognized July he stood aside and let them enter.

The meeting was apparently just starting. Extra folding chairs were being carried out of a horse stall to accommodate the large crowd. By their dress, most appeared to be farmers, but there were also twenty or more men in military-style fatigues and laced boots.

Grahm, Gail, and July found seats in the back row.

In front, three men sat at a wooden table. One stared intently into a notebook, another into his hands. The largest man sat on the far left. The one in the middle—a wiry man in his sixties with neatly trimmed Scandinavian features—inspected the two hundred or more people before him. Seeing Grahm, he spoke to the white-haired man to his left, stood up, and held his arms above his head.

"Can I have your attention," he said. "We need to get started."

In the manner of people not known to each other, the crowd immediately hushed.

"Thank you for coming. As a way of beginning I'd like to introduce Grahm Shotwell. Mr. Shotwell, stand up so everyone can see you."

Surprised at being recognized, Grahm blushed as he rose to his feet.

"This is the farmer many of you heard about from the annual meeting of American Milk. I met him in the parking lot afterwards. Others maybe saw him on television. Mr. Shotwell stood up for rural justice and the police were brought in to keep it from spreading."

Everyone rose, applauding.

Grahm's face burned.

"Go ahead, Mr. Shotwell, say something."

"I didn't come to talk," said Grahm. "I'm here like the rest of you—to listen."

There was more applause as Grahm sat back down.

"Can I have your attention *please*," said the man who just spoke. "Thank you. I'm Bob Finn, the owner of this place, and I've gotten tired of seeing my friends and neighbors driven out of business and off the land. Something needs to be done. I called this meeting to hear from these two men beside me. Maybe we can get something started tonight. So let me first introduce John Bryant."

The man nearest him, wearing a short-sleeved shirt and leather vest, smiled. He appeared to be about seventy. His nearly white hair added an aristocratic flavor to his already cautious appearance. His expression was serious to the point of worried, his voice unusually soft, and the room leaned forward to better catch his words.

"I'm John Bryant," he said. "I farm with my son in Marshall County. Three months ago my eyes were opened for the first time, at a legislative hearing in Eau Claire. It was advertised as a 'listening session,' to hear people's ideas. It was held in the Legion hall, and there were over a hundred people. Representative Flange and his aides sat in front. Everyone was in favor of something being done about milk prices. Representative Flange promised to consider each suggestion.

"I didn't speak because everything had been said two or three times before my turn came. By midafternoon, only several dozen farmers remained. One of the representative's aides thanked everyone for coming and called an end to the meeting.

"I noticed as the farmers left through the front door that a number of others followed Flange and his aides into a smaller room in back. I followed them.

"After about twenty people were inside, someone closed the door. The younger assistants passed around drinks. People were stretching and yawning and joking with each other. I suppose they thought I was one of them, because I was wearing a suit. Anyway, this person beside me—who said something at the hearing about the need for more exports to raise the price of milk—said to Flange, 'So, Ron, where's Chairman Bucruss on the processor pact?' And Flange said, 'He rolled over, thanks to Ralph'—referring to a lobbyist for the Federation of Cooperatives.

"Someone asked who I was with and I said, 'American Milk.' That was good enough, I guess, because they didn't ask me anything else. Turns out they were talking about a deal to raise the quota for imported cheese and milk protein concentrate. Flange's aides said everything was arranged—the shipments of over-quota New Zealand cheese would be covered under the new compact. The milk protein would come in under Department of Defense procurement and not even show up as food imports. When they explained this part, half the room applauded. "Brilliant!" one man said.

"That was my education, you might say. The next day I called my National Farm Organization representative and told him everything. I also talked with the NFO lawyer, and he helped me draw up a petition for a repeal of the compact and a demand that the USDA make regular reports of all imported dairy products. If we get enough signatures, we can force action from our legislators.

"I've taken it around to my neighbors and have more than a hundred and fifty names so far."

The man on the other end of the table waited for his turn to speak. Dressed in fatigues and combat boots, he shifted his bulky frame impatiently.

"My goal is five thousand signatures," said John Bryant, and he held up the petition so everyone could see it.

"Are there any questions?" asked Bob Finn.

"How are you going to get five thousand signatures?"

"Neighbor to neighbor and farm to farm. This is true democracy—the power of the people."

"Who will you present the petition to?"

"I'm going right to the top—the president of the United States of America."

"Didn't he sign the last farm bill, lowering our prices in the first place?"

"You're right. But with this petition—when the president sees that five thousand farmers understand what's going on, that our own co-ops are secretly importing surplus cheese and using it to undercut our pay prices—we won't be ignored. We're taxpayers, producers. We employ veterinarians, feed salesmen, equipment dealers, plumbers, electricians, carpenters, insurance agents, bankers, and many others. The rural economy depends on us."

The man on the other end of the table grimaced and knotted his hands together.

"You mean our own co-ops are importing foreign cheese and ultra-dried milk?"

"Yes, and it's legal. That's what this petition is all about." He held it up again. "We've got to unite around a common goal. We can start with this petition and after we've had a victory we can go on to bigger things, like sponsoring people to run as co-op directors and change the policies of the co-ops."

On the far end of the table, Moe Ridge grimaced for the last time and stood up. The agitation on his face served as his only introduction. He pressed his fists against the tabletop and leaned forward.

"You people have got to wake up!" he said. "Have you worked so long and hard that you can't see what's right before you?"

He walked in front of the table and gestured back at the white-haired speaker. *"This,"* he said, his voice level and intense, *"is futile.* You will grow old and useless listening to this. That petition means no more to the people in Washington than your grandmother farting into her rocking chair."

He began pacing, the veins in his arms and neck pulsing.

"There's *pure evil* staring you in the face and you're afraid to look into its eyes. You're like sheep led to slaughter and people like *this,"* and he gestured again toward the white-haired man, "are the Judas goats leading you into the slaughterhouse.

"Being driven off your farms is a result of planned policies, and if those policies ruin thousands, millions of farmers, it means nothing to those designing them. We don't have true democracy in this country anymore. *Right now* there are people meeting in Eastern Europe—people you never voted for—signing secret trade agreements that will flood this country with cheap milk from Argentina, New Zealand, Australia, Mexico and Europe. *Right now* they are working out the details to bring Russian, African, and Canadian wheat pouring across the borders. *Right now,"* he shouted, "they are acting with the full knowledge and approval of your representatives."

He resumed pacing.

"How do they get away with it? They get away with it the way great liars have always gotten away with lying, by smiling when people carry boxes of petitions into their offices, like ringmasters grinning when circus animals perform in pink costumes. Each signature is proof their deceptions are working, each handshake assurance their manipulations are bearing fruit.

"They depend on you talking to them about democracy, freedom, and equality, when in fact true democracy, freedom, and equality

would end their reign of greed tomorrow. They talk of better education, when in fact an educated public would run them out of the
country tomorrow. They talk about peace and security, when in fact
they are most secure when the country is frightened and confused.
And most of all they talk about personal integrity, because integrity
is something that truly threatens them.

"*You've got to wake up!* There is a group of men no larger than this
group here tonight who already own most of the world's wealth.
Their names are never mentioned in public and you won't see their
pictures in the papers. They don't want you to know who they are,
but through holding companies, trading boards, and interlocking
directorates they control the insurance companies, banks, and investment cartels. They own the Federal Reserve, the Trilateral Commission, the International Monetary Fund, and most of the world's
private prisons. They own the oil companies and the biggest defense
contractors, the chemical and seed companies, newspapers and
broadcasting networks. Their lawyers draft the legislation for your
senators and representatives. They own your so-called president as
surely as you own the change in your own pocket. They determine
whether the Supreme Court will hear a particular case and personally
oversee the activities of the State Department and the Pentagon.

"Yet this gang of robbers want more, and the implementation of
their insatiable designs is forcing you off your farms. There's no appealing to them because there's nothing to appeal to. They have no
community ties, no allegiance, and no faith. They are loyal only to
their own lust for money and power. When their lawyers lay before
them plans to take away your farms and add your families to the
lists of the homeless, they ask only if a quicker way can be found.
They want total control of food production—all of it. They want
to own all the fertilizer and all the seed, the final harvest and all the
equipment to harvest it. They want patent rights on every living
organism.

"They only want two things from you," he said, and held up two
fingers. "Two things. First, they want your hard labor, and they want
it as cheaply as you will allow them to steal it from you. And second,
they want you to be quiet about what's happening to you."

The crowd stared mutely forward.

"Know this: there are plans under way—worldwide plans—to make your children accept, like slaves born into slavery, a lifetime of working for arrogant fools who neither appreciate nor respect them. And when your children remind them of the days when their parents and grandparents owned their own businesses and farms, they will laugh out loud. 'Those days are gone,' they will say. 'You work for us.'

"The time has come, my friends, to look corruption in the eye and not blink. The courts are not there to protect you. They are there to protect the superwealthy *from you*. When did you last hear of the revocation of a multinational corporation's charter because it polluted a community, defrauded the government, or cheated its workers? Is it because the superrich never commit crimes? Is it because the privileged are always good—unlike the poor and working people who fill the prisons? *Do you really believe that?*

"Stop lying to yourselves. Law and order, the police and the Army, are on the wrong side. Being a good citizen should be a sin and bad citizenship an obligation. The people making the laws should never be obeyed and least of all believed. Your government is venal and corrupt, and you should have figured that out a long time ago. The only reason you haven't is that you're afraid of the demands it would make on your honor.

"But I ask you, does God want your children and grandchildren to serve as slaves to wealthy masters, plodding out their lives in crates of worthless space? Is destiny on the side of those idle toads who want to drive you off your farms? Does the Lord form alliances with men who have never worked hard in their entire lives—never once put their whole strength into *anything*—never lost a single night's sleep over a sick animal or the welfare of a child? Would the same God whose Son was crucified for you give victory to those same forces that nailed Him to the cross?

"No! God will stand with anyone who is willing to oppose them, but you *must oppose them*. Stop hoping their conscience will suddenly come alive. It won't. They have no conscience. You must oppose them. When they look at what stands between them and the world they lust after, they must see an open revolution staring back at them, because nothing short of that will ever stop them."

Gail sat in her folding chair, drinking the bottle of beer she brought from July's house, her pupils dilating. She hadn't known what to expect when she'd come, but *this* seemed more unexpected than the Unexpected.

She looked at her brother, who was seized by the momentum of the moment. He leaned forward as though listening to the beating of tribal water drums.

The militia leader continued.

"I know what you're thinking," he said. "You're afraid. You want to believe it makes sense to trust those in authority. You've suffered for so long the outrage of being told things you know are untrue that you wonder how long you can continue standing. You're like trees too tired to hold up your own limbs. You want to believe that behind the mask of democracy there are no conspiratorial faces—only the fair competition of ideas. You're like sheep imagining you've stepped out of the food chain because of the safe pasture you find yourselves grazing in.

"But that can change, and it's changing all across this country as men wake up and prepare to take action. You don't have to live in open conflict with your conscience. You can learn to stop being intimidated. You can learn the tactics of modern warfare so the threat of violence will no longer make you timid. You can learn to be free men again, to assume those massive virtues of your ancestors and stand without shame before them."

Gail watched as her brother's chapped hands clenched together and his head nodded up and down.

"As you train you will begin to see a faint glimmer of something new and hard. You will recognize it as your new self. You were not born to live like sheep waiting to be slaughtered. You can stare back at evil, and the hunted become the hunter."

Grahm shifted eagerly in his chair.

Gail looked anxiously at July Montgomery and he stood up.

"Wait just a minute," he said.

In a single snap of his head, Moe Ridge located the source of the sound, and two pairs of eyes measured each other. July laughed self-consciously as he walked forward, shaking his head, repeating, "Wait a minute, wait a minute."

When he reached the front of the room, he turned and addressed the group.

"Most of what this man says is probably true, but you still shouldn't listen to him."

Moe Ridge walked over and stood close to July, making him look small in comparison, and July smiled again self-consciously.

"The trouble with some people," July said, "is they believe their thoughts are new. They don't think anyone else has ever thought them. Most of us in this room have thought them many times.

"Is there a bunch of greedy fools at work in this and every other country? Yes, of course. Do they often lie, cheat, steal, bribe, intimidate, and murder to get what they want? Yes, they do. Is their propaganda often persuasive and does it convince many other folks to go along with them? Yes again. Does power corrupt? Sadly, yes."

"If you agree with me," snapped Moe, "then join."

"That's just what I'm coming to," said July. "I agree with everything my angry friend here says, up until that joining part. These problems have been around since we first lit a fire in the cave and discovered someone stealing our collection of pretty animal bones with the help of the clan council. But my friend here thinks these problems can be fixed once and for all—right now. Africans couldn't fix them, Egyptians couldn't fix them, Persians couldn't fix them, Greeks couldn't fix them, Romans couldn't fix them, Arabs couldn't fix them, Turks couldn't fix them, Europeans couldn't fix them, but *he* can fix them."

"You're afraid to confront the injustice of a dying civilization," said Moe. "In the days of the founding fathers—"

"Frankly," said July, "I don't give a damn about civilization, dying or otherwise. The only reason we have a civilization is that hardly anyone pays attention to it. Most of us live without trying to change anything. We're content with more important, private things. Myself, I like to farm. If there were something I'd rather be doing, I'd do that. I like farming. I like being outdoors, growing things and feeding animals. I like it. I farm to be farming."

"The tyranny of kings would never have been overthrown without people standing up," said Moe.

"Tyranny still exists. No, my friend, most of the people in this room feel just like I do. We're not here to solve big problems, and we don't really believe in the idea of solving big problems because of the bigger problems that come out of it. We're here to figure out a way to keep farming. The gentleman who spoke before you—he wants me to sign a petition. That's easy enough, so I'll sign it. But you want me to do something else with my life and I simply don't have time for that. As I said before, I like farming. I like going to county fairs, listening to music, and eating my neighbor's pies. None of that involves fighting with anyone."

"You're afraid to stand up for what you believe."

"Whoa there, Moe, I don't doubt your courage and I don't think it's fair to doubt mine. I'm not saying I'd *never* join. Someone may someday figure out how to distribute all good and bad things fairly. Maybe you can do that, find a way for even the most unfortunate people to have the same opportunities as the rest of us. Maybe you can discover how to make sure that only those who truly deserve wealth—or poverty—will have it. Perhaps you can find some men and women who after overthrowing the corrupt fools now in power will not become corrupted themselves. As soon as you find them, let me know. Let all of us know."

The veins in Moe Ridge's neck throbbed.

"I've said all I wanted to," said July. "Thank you for listening." He walked back to his chair.

Moe Ridge seemed temporarily unable to find something to say. The crowd began to murmur.

"I'll join!" yelled Gail, and stood up at the back of the room, smiling her best smile.

Grahm glared at her with a loathing known only to siblings. Everyone looked at her, and because she was one of the few young women in the building, and the only attractive one, they assumed she had been brought in to advertise the militia.

"There's doughnuts and coffee next to the petitions," said the white-haired man.

The crowd climbed out of the folding chairs and moved in several directions, some to their cars, motorcycles, and trucks, a few to join the militia, but most toward the pastry.

Grahm and July signed the petition and carried coffee in Styrofoam cups out of the sweltering building to the truck.

While she waited in line for a doughnut, Gail spoke briefly with Wade Armbuster, who had just written his name onto one of the militia's clipboards.

"Is that your trailer in the Brassos' back yard?"

"Yes," said Wade.

"I saw you join the militia. You must not agree with July."

"Sure I do," he said. "July and I agree on practically everything. We're good friends. He just said all that tonight because he didn't want your brother to join—just like you standing up and saying you would join when you wouldn't. That's okay, I understand that. Grahm has a family and a farm. Big difference is, I'm not a farmer."

On the way out of the building, beneath the hazy light from the lantern, she could hear the insects and feel her new song growing inside her, swelling up with all the sadness, joy, longing, and anger she had grown up around.

THE LOOK OF DEATH

A S THE MORNING RINSED STARS OUT OF THE NIGHT SKY, JULY Montgomery found his cows bunched up along the lower fence and called to them in a chiding voice. They needed little coaxing and fell in behind High Socks, the self-appointed chief of the bovine tribe.

As he followed them in the growing light, July noticed, again, that his pasture was getting thin. The rye, timothy, and couch grass crowded out the alfalfa. He resolved to plow it up in the fall, plant oats or beans and seed a new paddock on the other side of the barn where the soil had more nitrogen. Alfalfa was a nutrient-hungry plant, and four years was about the life span of good pasture—at least in his ground.

Without ever consciously counting his twenty-six cows, July gradually became aware that one was missing. As they lumbered into their stanchions (all but three or four of the younger animals always went to the same places), he knew which one: the white-faced four-year-old that had given birth to an all-black bull calf the year before.

The cows pushed their wide, wet noses into the little mountain ranges of ground feed he had shoveled into the concrete trough earlier, and July returned to the pasture.

He found her on the side of the hill. She was wedged between a willow and the creek. For some reason, she had chosen to lie downhill and hadn't been able to get back on her feet. The dreggy ground was dug up from her doomed effort. The grain and fresh alfalfa in her stomach had reacted with digestive juices to produce methane. The gas had blown her up like a leather balloon, choking off her lungs. She was dead.

The thought of the lonely, desperate struggle to reach her feet and the dumb-animal senselessness of the death brought tears to his eyes—remorse over the suffering and anger over its needlessness. Cows were upright creatures, nearly helpless on the ground. Why couldn't they be more careful?

July got the tractor and dragged her around in front of the barn, where the carcass could be located easily. He called the rendering service (no longer free since two years ago) from the house and returned to the barn.

As he milked, he tried not to think about how death looked. An hour later, still milking, he heard the rendering truck pull into the drive and the cable winch running. He didn't go outside. He would wait for the bill.

His relationship with the animals he raised, kept pregnant, milked, and eventually slaughtered was complicated. He worried over their health and comfort, resented them, appreciated them, pitied them, hated them, and loved them.

East of the barn, July moved a section of electric fence, closing off one paddock and opening another. He drove his herd down the narrow lane between the single strands of bare wire and into the new section of pasture. There, alfalfa rose, uneaten, nearly to their knees. From a distance they seemed to be wading in a green pond.

After cleaning out the barn, scraping the manure off the concrete, hosing it down, sweeping, and throwing lime, July went to the house, showered, and dressed in a clean pair of gray pants and a blue cotton shirt.

At the kitchen table, he drank a cup of reheated coffee, fried an egg, and ate the last piece of Violet Brasso's peach pie. He thought about finding the cow lying by the creek and tried again to push the image out of his mind. The look of death was always disturbing, and he guarded against it. There were many things to do today and it was necessary to keep moving.

He needed to take a load of corn to the mill. The elevator was sticking out of the crib from the last time he'd used it, looking like a tin dragon guarding a keep of yellow gold. He pulled the inverted-pyramid-shaped wagon—the gravity box—around the barn with his Minneapolis-Moline G750.

The tractor was more than thirty years old, which in the modern farming world was something of an antique. Once considered powerful, it had since fallen into the medium range and was in danger of slipping into the small category—shrunk by the trend toward ever larger and more powerful equipment. Still, it possessed a mechanical charm for July, and he had, so far, put up with the inconvenience of hard-to-find replacement parts. The six-cylinder, Oliver-built engine burned liquid propane instead of diesel fuel or gasoline, a somewhat novel feature dating to the gas rationing days of the Second World War. Sporting the optional dual-speed power takeoff and three-point hitch, the tractor was rated at sixty-one horsepower at the drawbar and seventy for the power take off.

July parked the gravity box beneath the neck of the elevator. He backed the tractor near the elevator, climbed down, and coupled the PTO shaft protruding from the rear of the tractor to the conveyor shaft of the elevator. The heavy machinery locked together with a confirming metallic snap. Then he engaged the PTO, commanding a loud clattering as the shaft transferred its turning to the chain-driven elevator.

A cool breeze blew out of the north and he found the grain shovel in the barn. Wanting to keep his shirt clean, he tossed it inside his pickup and put on the long denim coat hanging on the milk-house wall.

The prospect of rain increasing, he quickly shoveled corn into the clattering elevator, thankful for the lightweight plastic body of the shovel. The dried ears rode up the slats of the conveyor chute and dropped into the gravity box, and he watched for the level to rise above the top. When it did, he climbed out of the crib and into the wagon to kick the ears into the corners until there was room for another eight or ten bushels.

Letting himself to the ground, he noticed a pocket of sky that seemed unusually blue in contrast to the growing gray.

The corner of his denim coat brushed against the whirling PTO. The six-sided shaft collected the material, folded it over, and wrapped it up, yanking him down. At the same rate of turning, he moved from alarm to injury, to mutilation, and then to death. The coat was finally ripped from his shoulders and his body fell to the ground.

FINDING JULY

As jacob bolted a carburetor to the cylinder head of a gasoline-powered electric generator, Winnie's car drove by the front of the shop. Several minutes later it went by again. He washed his hands and shouted into the craft room.

"I'm leaving, Clarice. Will you close up?"

"Of course, Mr. Helm," she shouted back.

"Stop calling me *mister*."

"Yes, sir."

Outside, Jacob saw the yellow car disappear around the corner, heading for Thistlewaite Bridge. He ran to his jeep.

A mile down Highway Q, Winnie pulled onto the shoulder and got out. Jacob stopped behind her.

"Are you following me?"

"No," he said. "Well, yes. I saw you drive by and I was ready to leave and wondered where you were going."

"You can't follow me around, Jacob."

"I know that. I do. Where are you going?"

"I'm taking a quart of blackberries to July Montgomery. He probably hasn't had time to find any."

"That's just where I'm going. I need to talk to him about something he left at the shop."

"Is that true?"

"Yes. Go on, I'll follow."

The jeep and the yellow car continued for another mile and turned into the drive.

In the farmyard, a tractor could be heard running and the elevator clattering on the other side of the barn.

"I'll check the house," said Winnie.

Jacob watched her walk away and followed the worn path around the barn. The clattering was louder here and he saw the gravity box parked in front of the crib, to the side of the MM. There was a space between the front of the box and the tractor, and he went through it.

There are some things, he later reflected, that change every-thing else. Their breaking makes no sound yet fractures the world. Afterwards, nothing can be restored to its original order. It's Gone. But at the time, at the moment of domestic impression, Big Events don't appear to have any power at all, a single leaf falling. They don't seem as if they will be important. Their terrible reckoning is hidden from view.

He climbed onto the tractor and turned off the engine. The clat-tering died in a heavy denim flapping. He jumped down and stood over the mangled body. There was no question he was dead and no question he was July, doubled over like a fallen rag.

Jacob looked at the broken human form and felt, astonishingly, nothing. There was no mystery that required explanation. No laws had been broken. No dangers still lurked and no urgency spoke out of the vacant silence. Everything was done. July had been loading corn into his gravity box. His coat caught in the PTO. The shaft killed him. The look of resigned astonishment on the good side of his face was probably an accurate portrait of his last conscious moment; and even if it wasn't, it didn't matter. The thoughts passing through people's minds at the gate of death are always concealed from the living, and there was little point in speculation. July was dead. It was an accident. He had been working alone and should have been more careful. Maybe he was tired or preoccupied. No one could know. People died, sometimes accidentally. The death had been brutal, but that's the way with farming accidents. They were part of a hard life. The deflated, bluish look of the blood-drained body was normal. So were the open eyes. The look of death.

A pair of bright red male cardinals lit on the gravity box and hopped inside, disappearing from sight. A female joined them. The color of the dried blood, black and blue flies, and the scattered yellow kernels of corn lying among blades of green, green grass seemed almost beautiful.

When Winnie walked around the tractor, she pressed her hands against the sides of her face. Jacob unwound the denim coat from the PTO shaft and placed it over July. He put his arm around Winnie and turned her away, but she pushed him aside.

They walked to the house.

Jacob phoned for an ambulance. Winnie sat at the kitchen table with the crumbs from July's breakfast staring back at her. Beside the crumbs, she put her box of blackberries.

Jacob was still perplexed by how little he felt. It was just like a normal day, like yesterday and the day before. He noticed the fingers on Winnie's right hand rapidly tapping the top of the table.

"We'd better try to locate July's family," he said.

Winnie looked at him. "He doesn't have any close family," she said. "Maybe a cousin. At least that's what he told me once."

Winnie gripped her right hand with her left to stop it from tapping on the tabletop and then discovered that with her fingers in prison, other things were harder to contain. Without noticing how it happened, she had stood up. "Jacob, we've got to find someone to take care of the cows."

"Everyone's got some family, somewhere," said Jacob.

"We've got to find someone to take care of the cows," Winnie repeated.

Jacob walked through the living room and into the room July used for an office. Winnie heard him climbing the steps and walking around upstairs.

Then the house was quiet and Winnie cleared the dishes from the table. As she waited for the ambulance to arrive, she ran water in the sink and washed the frying pan.

She heard another sound, went upstairs, and found Jacob sitting on a wooden chair in a bedroom with a single bed. On his lap sat a shallow box of photographs and newspaper clippings. He was looking out the window, as though for the first time noticing that something had changed and that this day was nothing like the day before.

She walked across the room, stood next to him, and put her hand on his shoulder.

Jacob looked up at her. "I've known him more than five years, but he was private." He looked again into the box of photographs and newspaper clippings. "It says here that his wife was murdered many years ago, in Iowa. He never said anything about it. He never told me. Why wouldn't he tell me?"

"Are you sure it was his wife?"

"Not many people are named July."

Winnie noticed that several strands of tan thread in the seam of Jacob's shirt were unraveling in tiny loops. She felt awkward with her hand on his shoulder and took it off, held it in midair, then after a brief crisis of hesitation put it back on his shoulder. It felt better there. Through the bedroom window she watched an old convertible pull into the farmyard, and went downstairs.

Winnie opened the front door and Gail Shotwell walked into the kitchen.

"Hello," said Winnie. "I'm afraid we've never been officially introduced. I'm Winifred Smith."

"I know. I'm Gail. Is July around?"

"I'm afraid I have something to tell you," said Winnie.

Gail cast an impatient look around the room. Evangelists had trapped her before. "I don't have a lot of time, Preacher. I'm just here to pick up a pie pan that I left with July a couple days ago. I'm sure I can find it myself."

Winnie stood in the doorway of the living room, as though to block her from moving in that direction.

"Please, sit down."

"I don't want to sit down. What's going on? What are you doing here? Where's July?"

Noises could be heard upstairs.

"Is that July?" asked Gail.

"No," said Winnie. "That's Jacob Helm. We got here twenty minutes ago and found July by the corncrib. He was killed in an accident and we're waiting for the ambulance. He's dead."

"That's not true," said Gail, confidently.

"I wish it wasn't."

Their eyes met for the first time and the confidence immediately drained from Gail's face.

The house was quiet except for a faucet dripping into the dish-water. Gail sat down. "What's Jacob doing upstairs?" she asked, and as though in answer something above them smashed against a wall.

"Jacob's upset. They were good friends and he's having a hard time of it."

Upstairs, something else was thrown against a wall, accompanied by a curse.

"Men," said Gail. "They always think they can grieve with their fists and feet."

"We need to call someone to take care of the cows," said Winnie.

"I'll milk them," said Gail. "And I'll come back in the morning and milk them. Where did you say you found July?"

"He's in front of the corncrib."

"I'm going out there."

"That's not a good idea," said Winnie. "His coat was caught in the power takeoff."

"Oh," said Gail, sitting back down. "Drat, I don't think I want to see that."

Then she began to cry and Winnie sat next to her.

The ambulance arrived and left with July's body. The county sheriff's car came later. Standing in front of the corncrib, Winnie, Gail, and Jacob told the two men everything they knew about July—everything they could think to say.

After they left, Jacob did not talk again. He set the shovel inside the crib, went to his jeep, and drove away.

Winnie wasn't sure what she should do but decided to stay with Gail.

Gail found three bottles of beer in July's refrigerator and drank them.

SELLING LAND

GRAHM SHOTWELL PULLED A CULTIVATOR THROUGH A FIELD of soybeans. At first he only heard the name, the rest of the announcement obscured by the diesel's exhaust. He turned up the radio and waited for the next local news cycle. Afterwards, he climbed down from the tractor and stood in the middle of the field, rubbing his hands through his hair and looking at the recently sprouted soybeans. A hot, dry wind blew out of the south and the ground was hard.

Rain was forecast and it might be a week, perhaps two, before he would have another opportunity. The field had to be finished. He walked around the tractor several times, climbed back into the cab, and continued. He didn't know what else to do. It seemed he should respond in some way to the news but he couldn't imagine how. Even sudden, deadening grief had to be absorbed within a nonporous routine.

When he finished harrowing the field, Grahm left the tractor next to the road and drove his pickup to July's farm. Perhaps someone would know more about the accident than had been reported on the radio. There were several other cars there, but once he was in the farmyard he could not force himself to climb out of the truck and he drove back home.

That night he could not sleep and went outdoors before 4:00 a.m. Cora followed him a short time later and he told her to go back inside. He fed the calves, repaired a broken stanchion, ran feed into the bunkers, and milked his cows earlier than usual.

At ten o'clock he returned to July's farm. A light rain fell from the sky. His sister's car and Wade's pickup stood next to the barn. They were still milking, and he worked with them until they turned the cows into the pasture and drove back to Words.

Alone now, Grahm walked through July's other buildings.

Everywhere, things that couldn't move waited for July to touch them again. The Mason jar of arrowheads that July had picked from his fields sat on his tool bench, longing to be reseeded into the ground. Wrenches wanted to be picked up and fitted around a nut. It wouldn't be long, he knew, before they would be auctioned to someone else, along with the cows and everything else.

Someone, perhaps Wade, had driven the tractor into the machine shed, where it stood beside the gravity box. He climbed into the wagon and sat with his boots rooted in ears of corn. An owl inspected him from a darkened corner in the rafters, stepped off the beam, and flew out the open door with a single, silent pump of its wings.

He knocked on the front door of the house, found it unlocked, and went in. It was cooler inside and the air smelled stale. He thought about walking into the living room, but didn't.

He opened the refrigerator. The food, he suspected, would be thrown out—even the block of cheese sitting on a plate. No one would want to eat it.

Outside again, he stood on the front step. The bird feeder in the front yard was empty and he considered finding some grain and filling it. But he wasn't sure if July fed birds during the summer.

He went back to his truck and drove away.

At home, he walked through his own buildings, one after another, thinking about July and trying to imagine how someone might feel if he, Grahm, had died.

Standing beneath the tamaracks, he watched his children run across the yard, their short legs moving quickly, and he understood something: it was better to be wronged and do nothing about it than to do something wrong and regret it. A person could live with one but not the other. He remembered when he and Gail had run together, faster than the wind, between the trees.

In the kitchen, Cora was cooking. Grahm stood next to her and took off his cap. They sat together at the kitchen table.

"I'm going for a walk," said Grahm.

"Do you want some company?"

"No."

"The part for the skid-steer came in."

"How much is it?"

"Almost seven hundred."

"Do we have that much?"

"Not until milk check. You want something to eat?"

"No."

Grahm walked through the barn and into the pasture. He continued to the forty acres of old-growth forest that grew along the north boundary of his farm. Walking between the massive trunks felt like being inside a living cathedral. In the shade of the high canopy, he thought about his grandfather and grandmother, and then remembered the evening many years ago when July had stopped along the road where young Grahm was working and they had piled up dead sumac and set it on fire.

The memory, oddly enough, seemed uninformed about July's death. It presented its stored contents in the same manner it had presented them when July still lived. The portion of Grahm's mind that understood July's most recent circumstance did not communicate with the rest, and, strangely, his most recent circumstance seemed most in question, overwhelmed by the anecdotal preponderance of the more distant past.

We never really know another person, thought Grahm. We only have memories. If we really knew them, we couldn't bear it, so we only have memories.

The sparks from the burning woody stalks rose into the sky, and Grahm—not yet in his teens—wondered about July, a stranger who had walked into Thistlewaite County with nothing but a canvas sack. No one knew anything about him. He and July had piled up the wood and set it on fire. When the flames calmed down, Gail walked out from the house, wondering why Grahm had not come back for supper. She was not even five years old, and she looked at July as though he had arrived from a different world. The three of them had watched the fire burn into a level bed of coals, and then he and Gail had watched July drive away.

People never really know each other, Grahm concluded, but the memories they share hold them together enough to keep going.

Three hours later, he knocked on the front door of his sister's house. Gail let him in and they sat at the kitchen table.

"Are you milking at July's again tonight?" he asked.

"No, I'm supposed to be at work in an hour. Wade's going over after he leaves the cheese plant. They're auctioning the herd in the morning. You want something to drink?"

"Coffee?"

"I can reheat a cup."

"I sold the forty acres at the back of the farm," said Grahm. "I want you to have half of the money."

"Why?"

"Because that land belonged to you too, or should have. It wasn't fair of the folks to leave it to me."

"I got this house," she reminded him.

"Like I said, it wasn't fair."

"Who bought it?"

"Some guy named Leasthorse who works for the casino. He's been trying to buy it for several years. Wants to build a house, I guess."

"I didn't think you'd ever sell those woods, Grahm."

"I didn't either, but he's wanted it for a long time and he says there's an Indian mound in there somewhere. Anyway, we need the money. And I thought you'd want to go to music school or something."

Gail put a cup of coffee on the table and Grahm set a cashier's check next to it. She read it, and decided not to go to work.

"He must have wanted it pretty bad."

"He thinks he saw a cougar somewhere near there and I guess the hallucination gave him dreams of unspoiled nature."

"I never thought you'd sell it, Grahm."

"Things change. Forget the coffee. Let's go out somewhere and celebrate."

INSIDE THE CHURCH

W INNIE HAD NEVER BEEN IN CHARGE OF A FUNERAL BEFORE. Though the majority of her congregation was old, they had, so far, remained living. To make matters even more stressful, July had not been a member of a church and many attending the service most likely would come from that same persuasion. The language of Christian piety could not be relied upon to convey either empathy or solace, which she saw as her primary responsibility. Yet the trustees and other august members of the Words Friends of Jesus Church would expect her to seize the opportunity provided by the sudden death, assail unbelievers with the absolute certainty of life's uncertainty, and shepherd the unconverted into Christian membership with hard religious facts.

She had further reason to worry after meeting with the mortician in Grange. At the request of July's only known living relative, a cousin in Omaha—who apparently would not arrive in Words until the morning of the funeral—the body had been cremated.

"Because of pervasive structural damage," explained Bradley Worthington, looking up from his desk, "the reconstructive costs would have been very high."

Winnie tried to picture a funeral without a corpse and casket, without much success. Having the whole body present seemed mandatory. People needed to take leave of the chalky, habitual form. Seeing it in a box provided a fatal blow to the imagination's revolution against death's government. After the casket had been closed, rolled away, and buried, people could confidently conclude, "Well, that's over," and not have the lingering suspicion that it maybe wasn't. Traditions worked, praise heaven, and even if particular traditional practices were perhaps absurd and even ghoulish, they had comforting, human value. Through them people could face overwhelming

despair—could come together and, en masse, stare it down. Without
traditions there would be no expectations; without expectations
there would be no rules; without rules there would be anarchy. And
anarchy was no good.

Some older people in her congregation would have an especially
hard time with the urn, she knew. For many of them, cremation was
an atheist's last subterfuge in escaping Judgment, and there would be
no convincing them otherwise. They would look at the urn and their
faces would wrinkle like raisins. Many of them had probably never
even seen a cremation urn, unless they had seen one on television,
and its compact shape would be upsetting.

Death, Winnie knew, presented conceptual problems that many
people could solve only through extreme attitudes, ritualistically
enforced. The need for unity of belief was felt most keenly at these
times, yet no unity existed. Dead people were imagined going to
heaven, hell, and places in between. They were pictured writhing in
flames, dancing among the clouds, living with relatives who had died
earlier, dissolving in the belly of worms, vaporizing, and putting on
other life forms. Death was also thought to provide lessons in what
to do and what not to do, though the lessons varied as greatly as the
course offerings of a large university. For many Christians, the death
of unbelievers signaled divine condemnation, while the death of
believers revealed divine approval. Superstitions and firmly held es-
chatological fantasies surrounded every aspect of dying, and pastors
were somehow expected to find a way to accommodate all views—a
job for which little understanding and no sympathy existed.

"You may take the cremains now or leave them until Friday," said
the mortician.

Winnie placed the aluminum receptacle upright on the passenger's seat of her car and was more than a little upset when at the very
first corner it toppled over onto the floor.

You stupid woman.

It didn't matter if it fell over. It didn't matter. It was superstitious
to think it did. There was nothing inside but ashes! Everything important was gone and the urn had a screw top to assure against spill-
age. She hated herself for stopping the car and securing the container
in an upright position with the seat belt.

Winnie decided to keep the urn in the church rather than the parsonage, carried it inside, and temporarily set it in a pew. Orange-tinted late-afternoon sunlight fell through the tall west windows, the air unusually warm and soft. She sat beside the urn and took a Bible from the pew back, searching for passages that she could read during the funeral, but her attention was drawn again to the light on the other side of the room and the surrounding stillness. She set the book back in the pew and just looked at the colors, indulging in the sensuous solitude of the empty church.

I'll just lie down for minute, she thought.

When she woke up, the afternoon light had faded and though a silence remained, its character was no longer peaceful.

Am I going to be all right? she wondered, and thought about her father, whose death seemed the final confirmation of his disapproval of her. She sat in the pew and wondered when she should submit her resignation. Surely real people of faith never wavered in their beliefs, and never felt this inadequate.

When the back door to the church opened and slammed shut, Winnie jumped to her feet.

"I hoped I'd find someone here," said a voice. A body of flowers advanced toward her with two arms wrapped around it. She knew the voice and in the receding light recognized the thick hands, quickly pulled her hands through her hair, and backed away as Jacob Helm set the flowers on the end of the pew. An oily fragrance exploded in the air and she retreated further.

"Hope I'm not intruding. I thought I'd better come over. Wade and I went through July's house and I put together some pictures to display at the funeral. They're in the jeep. I have more flowers outside and was hoping there'd be vases here. Is that it?" he asked, pointing at the urn. "If you want, I'll get a casket and we can put it inside with the lid shut. It might be less upsetting for the old folks. They won't have to know he was cremated."

When their eyes met, Jacob rushed into the pew. "Winifred, what happened to your hair?"

"Violet helped me fix it," she said, backing up, her mind fastened on the sound of her name in his mouth.

"I hardly recognized you."

"I guess I can do what I want with my own hair."

He pursued her into the end aisle and followed her around the back. They moved in short, staggered steps, Jacob advancing and Winnie backing up, as though they were dancing to an ultraslow rhythm, and came to a full stop only when they arrived back at the place where the flowers rested on the pew.

"Of course, excuse me, it's just, well, it's just such a big change."

He came closer and she backed into the pew again.

"I'm sure there are some vases in the basement," she said, "and it's cooler down there. They'll keep better."

"I can't get over your hair. It's almost like you're a different person."

"You don't like it?"

"Are you crazy? It's perfect for you. It makes you look so, well, beautiful—in a more contemporary way than before. I know you don't like to think of yourself as beautiful, but, well, with that hair I'm afraid you'll have to get used to it."

Winnie conquered a quick smile that rebelled across her face by smothering it with her left hand.

"I'm sorry about the other day," said Jacob. "I abandoned you at the farm. I'm sorry."

"You couldn't help it, Jacob. I understood that. You needed to be alone."

As she spoke his name, she blushed, remembering the many times she had uttered the name in the room of her own thoughts, conjuring him up for a private meeting.

"I love you, Winnie," he said, and the intimacy of the sound of the words was surrounded by the strong smell of flowers and a faint odor of grease.

"Please, don't say anything else," said Winnie, with both of her hands on her face.

"True is true," he said. "What does it matter if it remains unspoken?"

"I'm not ready to hear it. I may never be ready."

"I know—we need so much time together, a lifetime. There's so much about you I'd like to know. Everything about you, from the first time I saw you—"

"Don't say any more, Jacob, please. I'm not ready for this. The funeral is overwhelming me. The only one I've ever attended was my mother's. I'm frightened."

"That's understandable," said Jacob. "Funerals are frightening. I'll bring in the rest of the flowers. I'm serious about the casket. The funeral home in Luster can have one here in an hour. I've talked several times with that Omaha cousin of July's, but he doesn't seem to know much—or want to know much. I'm not even sure he's coming. I've finished an obituary for the papers and I can read it at the service. Gail said her band would play if you want them."

"That would help," said Winnie. "They're quite good. Can they play acoustic?"

"I'm sure they can, but I'll ask them. Gail can rent a double bass from Barry Clark's Music in Grange. He has all kinds of instruments."

"Good," said Winnie. "Nothing wins over old people quicker than young people performing for them not too loudly."

"I can lead the congregational singing if you like. Believe it or not, I have some experience doing that."

"We have our own song leader," said Winnie.

"There won't be many people. He was kind of private."

"You sound as if you disapprove of that."

"I didn't understand how private he was. He hid things—things he shouldn't have hidden from me."

"You're angry with him."

"July accepted me for what I was and it wasn't fair of him not to give me the chance to accept him in the same way. He kept everyone at a distance."

"You're angry, Jacob. I can feel it."

"I'm angry with myself, but I can't explain it to you now. I was supposed to have been his friend. Friends are supposed to know things about each other. Do you think we can ever be forgiven for things we should have known but didn't?"

Without hesitation, Winnie said, "We can and are."

"Are you sure?"

"I am, but it would take too long to explain."

"That would be the shortest long time in the world for me," said Jacob.

Winnie laughed, and this time did not cover her face. "I told you not to say anything like that."

"I know," said Jacob. "I couldn't help it. I've never wanted anything more in my whole life as to know you better. I understood that last night. July and I had different expectations about the future. He had almost none, but ever since I met you my expectations have been running wild. I mean, I'm sorry if this seems like the wrong time to talk about this, and it probably is, but how do you feel about children? Have you ever thought that you'd like to have children, because for a long time I thought I could give up on the idea of children, but it seems that . . . forgive me, these things are hard to talk about because they mean so much. It just seems as though having a family and children might be a final solution to the ghost problem, perhaps the only way to take the purely interior and personal parts of ourselves and let them out into the world. It seems—"

Jacob stopped talking because Winnie looked like someone who has discovered the door to her most private room open and all her secret thoughts revealed.

"Stop!" she said and pushed her face into an armload of flowers, inhaling deeply.

THE FUNERAL

GOOD WEATHER, CONCLUDED WINNIE AS SHE STEPPED OUT OF the parsonage and into the churchyard: people wouldn't be getting wet at the cemetery. Overhead, huge roaming clouds, puffy, white, and popcorn-shaped were a welcome change from the leaden skies earlier in the week.

Three cars parked haphazardly near the back of the church and she hurried down into the basement to help with lunch preparations.

"Good morning, Pastor Winifred," sang Florence Fitch, ripping off an end of rolled white paper and taping it to a row of pushed-together tables. "Do you think scented candles would help with the mold smell?"

"I have some in the parsonage," said Winnie.

"I'll get them," said Violet. "You go upstairs. Those band people want to move the piano."

As Winnie climbed the steps she could hear single piano notes played in no particular rhythm or order, as if a bored child were trying them out on a rainy afternoon.

A head-high wall of flowers faced her from the front of the sanctuary and their thick fragrance boosted her spirits.

"We moved it," said one of the band members, standing near the new location of the piano, checking the tuning.

"Was that necessary?" asked Winnie, breaking for the first time her early-morning pledge to be less confrontational.

"It was pushed up against the wall, blocking the soundboard. How long has it been since this was tuned?"

He tapped another ivory-veneered key and frowned into a hand-held electronic meter with blinking lights. "We're talking major dissonance here."

The front doors banged open and two men in solid black suits rolled a copper-colored casket inside. They were from the funeral home in Luster.

Winnie walked back and greeted them. "Please clear some flowers out of the way and put it in front of the pulpit."

They guided the casket into the sanctuary.

"Excuse me," said the musician. "We still have drums to bring in. Could you set the casket on the other side of the room?"

Through the window, Winnie watched a maroon sedan come to a sedate stop in the parking lot. Louis and Edith Kotter, the oldest members of her congregation, were inside. She looked up at the clock on the wall—a full hour before the service.

The receptacle with the cremated remains of July Montgomery was still not inside the casket, and she hurried to the cabinet where she had put the urn several days ago.

When she opened the doors, the shelf was empty.

"Preacher, we've got to have more room here for the drums."

"Do you think drums are appropriate?" said the older and larger of the two men from the funeral home.

The cabinet was empty. Winnie's heart began beating in an uncontrollable manner.

"Pastor!" called Violet Brasso, climbing with difficulty up the back stairway. "I couldn't find those candles you talked about. We simply must have them, and the ham sandwiches are mostly frozen after sitting all night in the refrigerator. They're frosty, you might say, very cold on the teeth. The temperature from the freezer compartment must be leaking into the rest of the refrigerator. Land sakes, they moved the piano. Just look at that. Lyle and Esther donated the piano, you know. The last time it was moved there was real trouble. Well I declare, the casket is here. I wonder who picked out that color. Must have been a man."

"This piano has two stuck keys. Look, Buzz, now one of 'em doesn't even come back up."

The side door opened and the Kotter couple inched inside, dressed in their best dark clothes. They carefully selected the third pew on the left, sat down, and looked disapprovingly around the sanctuary like diners expecting to have been served an hour ago.

Then Gail Shotwell came in carrying an acoustic double bass that was taller and wider than she was. She positioned the wooden instrument next to the wall of bouquets, beside the guitar stand. Her first trial note loosened several flower petals, which dropped to the carpeted floor. The Kotter couple leaned together as though they were in a foxhole.

"Tune flat," said the dark-haired band member. "This piano is way off."

"You can't have all this music equipment here," said the man from Luster. "We need room for the casket."

"Who's this?" asked Gail.

"They brought the casket."

Another sedan, filled with more old people who did not want to miss anything, worry about finding a parking place, or be late, arrived in the parking lot. A silver dual-wheeled pickup parked on the street.

Winnie looked quickly through every place she could think of for the urn, checked the empty cabinet again, and remembered she had left the order-of-service handouts in the parsonage.

The side door opened and Rusty and Maxine Smith came inside. Rusty was smoking a cigarette and at Maxine's insistence flicked it out into the yard, but not before inhaling a final time. "Hello, niece."

"Good morning, Maxine," said Winnie.

"Scented candles," said Violet, noticing Winnie looking again in the cabinet. "They aren't in there. The cupboards were cleaned out several months ago, if you remember, Pastor. Those old hymnals used to be in there—the ones with the green covers and the drawing of Elijah's chariot. Maybe they were before your time. My lands, more flowers, more flowers."

Jacob Helm walked through the side door dressed in a new blue suit and carrying an armload of mums. Winnie went to him as fast as she could without running.

"I can't find the receptacle," she whispered.

Jacob deposited the mums in the back pew and returned to Winnie.

"I left it in the cabinet—you remember. It's gone, Jacob, it's gone."

"Pastor Winifred! We must have those candles. They need time to do their work. Just tell me where to look."

"Who's in charge here?" asked the man from Luster.

"You find the candles," said Jacob, ushering Winnie out the door, "I'll find the urn."

Winnie walked to the parsonage beside Violet, who earnestly recounted again how the parsonage used to be much smaller before it was added onto. And it had been added onto twice. The last time, the chief carpenter was one of the five children of Emil and Charlotte Poke, who had married a Short, one of the thick-haired twins—the fast-talking one, not the one who once fell off a roof.

Jacob paid the men from the funeral home for the casket and the use of their hearse and sent them back to Luster. Then he negotiated a compromise with Gail and the other band members about where to set up the drums.

While Jacob was installing his mums beside the other flower arrangements, he discovered the aluminum receptacle that two days earlier had contained July Montgomery's cremains. The ashes had been emptied out and it now contained water, ferns, and two dozen freshly cut long-stemmed lilies. The card in the middle of the display read, "In Remembrance, Violet and Olivia Brasso."

Jacob surrounded the aluminum container with other floral arrangements. When Winnie returned, he said he had found the urn and taken care of everything. Winnie touched his arm and looked relieved, placed the order-of-service notices on the entryway table, and carried her Bible and notes up front.

Four more old people from her congregation came inside and sat in the pews on the left side of the room.

Winnie became concerned that all her regulars were sitting on one side—farther away from the band—and Florence Fitch agreed to greet people as they entered and direct them to both sides. Since no family members were coming, only one pew, for the pallbearers, had been reserved.

The small parking lot soon filled up and later-arriving cars parked along the bean field, where the wind insulted the men's pant legs and the women's dresses and hair.

Even after being seated on the right side of the room, the regular members of the Words Friends of Jesus Church joined their friends on the other side, where they were joined by their neighbors and friends from other area churches. Soon, the community of church-goers was more or less segregated by the wide center aisle from the more casually dressed unchurched, who walked warily into the building and looked as though they expected to be asked by a member of the Federal Bureau of Investigation how much taxable income they had reported last year.

Seated on a small bench behind the pulpit, Winnie looked through her notes. The words swarmed together like black bees. A tightening in her chest and dizziness in her stomach slowly overtook her thoughts, and just before she was about to faint she discovered she was holding her breath. She breathed deliberately several times and the overhead lights stopped looking like clouds.

As more people continued to arrive, Jacob set up folding chairs in back.

Wade Armbuster carried in two pies and was directed down to the basement by Violet. When he came back upstairs, Violet sent him home for Olivia, who, she said, wasn't accustomed to keeping track of her own time, even though her new job selling cheese three days a week was forcing her to become more aware of it.

Grahm Shotwell and his children sat in the pew next to Winnie's uncle and aunt while Cora headed for the basement with a cake pan and a bowl.

The pew in front of Rusty Smith filled with a row of Amish in black hats and bonnets. Behind Maxine sat a man in a T-shirt reading SUPPORT YOUR LOCAL GUN DEALER.

Folding chairs were placed in the foyer.

Winnie couldn't remember ever having such a large crowd—more than two hundred, she estimated.

The band began to play quietly, the drummer using wire brushes and the piano player soft-pedaling the foot irons. The music drew the attention of the room to Gail. In her red coat, and surrounded by a sea of flowers, she looked like a cardinal in a spring apple tree.

Jacob joined Winnie on the bench behind the pulpit. "Are you all right?" he whispered. "You look perfect. That dress is ideal."

"I thought you said there wouldn't be many people."

"I was wrong. You want a glass of water or anything?"

"No. Please stop talking to me. I'm going over my notes."

"Sorry."

"Now go sit down. You can't be sitting here with me."

Downstairs, Cora arranged a platter of fresh vegetables: carrot sticks, pepper slices, celery stalks, broccoli heads, and clumps of cauliflower with a cream dip in the middle.

"Rice goes well with lamb," said Rachel Wood, sprinkling chives over the top of an enormous bowl of potato salad.

"That's what I told her," said Cora. "You'd think people who used to live on a farm would know something about food."

"Not necessarily," said Rachel. "They're both lawyers?"

"Our personal attorneys, actually. Leona clearly has the brains of the outfit, though. Tim's practically useless compared to her."

"Most men are."

"We're going to have more children," said Cora. "As soon as we get around to it."

"Really."

Upstairs, the band played "Power in the Blood" at about half speed, with a slightly altered cadence. The overall effect was ponderous, balladic and sad. Near the end, Gail played a solo on the double bass; but as so frequently happens with bass solos, about half the audience lost the thread of the tune, became distracted, and started talking to each other.

Wade came in the back of the church with Olivia on his arm, wearing a dress that glowed black, in heels and a top with bold white letters: SAY CHEESE. She looked twenty-five, if that, and sat next to Wade on the folding chairs in the foyer.

Winnie stood up, checked the fall of her dress, tossed her head in the manner to which she had become habituated during her many years with long hair, and stepped to the pulpit.

"Welcome," she said, trying not to look at Rusty, who was looking just like she remembered her father looking. "I'm Pastor Winifred Smith, and if you would please stand we will sing song number four hundred and forty-seven in your hymnbooks."

Leslie Weedle, the song leader, mounted the raised platform and stood behind a pole-mounted microphone. The band played the last measure of "Blessed Be the Name" and the congregation sang with enthusiasm, glad to have something to do.

Winnie asked a blessing on the service and the memory of July Montgomery, and invited everyone to sit back down.

Jacob read the obituary, recounting most of the conventional signposts in July's life—the place and date of his birth, the names of his parents, the school he attended, organizations he belonged to, places he'd lived and worked, and the name of his late wife. He ended with a brief description of July's accident.

The band performed "Precious Memories" and "What a Friend We Have in Jesus." Then they abandoned their instruments among the flowers and returned to the pew behind the pallbearers.

Winnie resumed the pulpit and read the Twenty-third Psalm. Then she explained that it was traditional to allow time for anyone who wished to share a memory.

She returned to the bench and sat perfectly erect. Jacob, sitting with the other pallbearers, spoke first and the right side of the room began recounting memories. As soon as one speaker sat down another stood up, recalling incidents that highlighted unique aspects of July Montgomery. Voices faltered, but there was also laughter— yes, that was him all right.

The people on the religious side of the room remained quiet. They had not known July as well and were cautious about talking at funerals. Older and more familiar with the precarious social dynamics of speaking inside a filled church, they knew better than to say something hastily. It was too easy to confuse a memory that presented the deceased in a favorable light with one in which an even brighter light was cast on the speaker. Vanity, they knew, was the most likely candidate to volunteer an encomium. That's what professional talkers were for. During life's most important times, a pastor was necessary to keep people from saying things they later regretted. Pastors were verbal stuntmen, protecting others from hurting themselves with their own talking.

But as the recounting of memories continued, it soon became clear to the speaking side of the room that the other side was not participating. An idea slowly began to congeal: perhaps the other half did not know July Montgomery at all, or even disapproved of him in some way.

Soon, memories in which July's suspicion of organized religion was the central issue, along with his fondness for cigars and European beer, were being shared. The fact that he didn't own a suit or tie but was tolerant, kind, and generous came up several times. It was mentioned that his only relative, a cousin in Omaha, was supposedly an extremely religious person but had not bothered to come to the funeral, which was typical of rank hypocrites, of which July Montgomery had not been one.

In the back of the church, Wade Armbuster rose to the tension in the room like a bass to surface bait. With his left hand on Olivia's shoulder, he declared July the most patriotic man he had ever known, and dared anyone to say otherwise. He said he owed the completion of his custom car and staying out of prison to July, who, he said, "stood like a mighty oak for justice, freedom, and decency." If the world were fair, he said, July would still be alive now and not stuffed inside a copper-colored coffin. "And if anybody doubts how unfair the present world is, they should just open the coffin and look inside."

Jacob went forward and he and Winnie picked up the short bench she was sitting on, carried it down the two steps, placed it in front of the casket, and reseated themselves on it. The movement imposed a temporary silence. Then several more people spoke and another brief silence followed.

Then Gail Shotwell came forward, alone, and moved the double bass near the microphone. Her voice shook as she explained that she wanted to sing a song she had recently written, and dedicated it to July. It was called "Along the Side of the Road". She played five or six deep, rising notes and began to sing.

It was a difficult song, with lyrical phrases that did not seem altogether connected to each other. The chorus was so different from the first verse that it seemed like an altogether separate melody. Finally, tears ran down her cheeks, her chin wrinkled, and her voice collapsed. She stopped playing and attempted to start over, failed again, wiped tears from her eyes, but wouldn't sit down.

Winnie looked anxiously at Jacob, and he stood up just as a woman with jet-black hair and green eyes rose in a pew near the middle, squirmed around the knees between her and the center aisle, and walked forward.

She smiled at Gail and, clearly accustomed to dealing with musical equipment, she moved the drummer's microphone next to Gail's, adjusted the strap on the acoustic guitar, and hung it around her shoulders.

"Start slower," she whispered, counted to four, and hit a diminished chord.

The two women sang. At the slower speed, the lyrics turned into poetry, assumed a meaning beyond the words themselves. Rural images bloomed inside themes of redemption and the sadness of unfulfilled longing. Tears flowed in every pew, and during the second verse Gail's voice broke free of her body and from a place somewhere above her held the room hostage to the sublime. Afterwards, everyone rose to their feet and applauded. A coal-black woman with a shaved head continued clapping after everyone else stopped, and then she stopped too. Then everyone sat back down.

After the singers sat down, Winnie stood up.

"First let me say how much I appreciate that you are all here. In preparing for today I wrote some things down, but I confess I don't know what the right things to say are."

She handed her notes to Jacob, glanced at her uncle, and continued, fear leading her to a higher castle.

"What I do know is that God loves us, completely, every one of us, all the time, and upon that single fact the hundred billion stars are hung. That love is both the source and the cause of all life."

Jacob watched as Winnie stepped further down the aisle, as though entering the room's center of gravity. She was beginning to gesture with her hands.

"We are here today to celebrate and mourn July Montgomery, and to do these things together.

"At moments like these it is hard not to wish for an end to suffering—a cancellation of it. But friends, a life without grief is hardly worth living, and someone who is not willing to give his or her life for something worth more than mere living is hardly alive.

"The things that wound us are the most important things we know, and the things that wound us deepest are things like July's dying in an accident.

"Why did it happen? What went wrong? What would be different if his life had not been interrupted? Instead of coming here today, we might have met him somewhere and he might have spoken to us. But that is no longer possible, and because it isn't, do things that are still possible have a different color?

"By all reports he was an honorable man, yet he died horribly. What does that mean? What obligation does it place us under? The grief hurts, but how will hurting change us? Will the suspicion that we might perhaps have done something to interrupt the flow of events that eventually ended his life haunt us into becoming different people?

"In our lives we make only a few important decisions—some of us only one or two—and the rest of our time is spent living them out. But what should we decide here today? How can we bear the responsibility of running our own lives when something like this happens to us?

"The remains of July Montgomery are behind me, inside the casket. We have them with us. That's the easy part, and we know quite well what to do with them. We'll take them to the cemetery and bury them. We can keep good track of material things. But what of July? Where will we look to find the part of him that convinced us to come today? Where will we locate the influence he continues to have on us? How will the stories he set into motion end?"

Winnie walked back to the bench and stood next to Jacob.

"Who was July Montgomery and where is he now?

"Friends, we are all connected in ways we cannot even begin to fathom. Our lives unfold through each other and within each other. What one suffers, we all feel. What one does changes others forever.

July was part of us and that part of us will never be gone. We can find him in each other. Everyone here has a part of him, and the part he was able to share with us we can share with each other.

"So we're united today not in belief but in grief—staring into the past, where July died alone. But though the world has cast him out, we never will. So long as we refuse to be separated from the love of God, which holds us all together, we will never lose July. We will never let him die. How we feel about him can never be taken from us. Nothing," she said, turning and looking straight at her uncle and smiling, "nothing can ever, against our will, separate us from the love of God, and we will do the best we can."

Pulling on the pew in front of him, Rusty stood up. He looked directly at Winnie and said "amen," in a manner that suggested he had never spoken the word before and was unlikely ever to speak it again, and sat down.

Winnie continued, "After these last songs I ask you to come with me to the cemetery."

Winnie sat beside Jacob and the Straight Flush took up their instruments and played "Bringing in the Sheaves."

Leslie Weedle came forward to lead the closing song. Afterwards, Winnie gave the benediction.

Six pallbearers rolled the casket to the front door and with surprising ease carried it down the steps and set it in the back of the hearse. A line of cars, pickups, vans, and buggies followed Jacob and Winnie and the casket to the cemetery, in the corner of a cornfield. Under two sugar maples an open grave waited.

Winnie said a prayer, and a dozen people placed flowers on top of the casket. Once it was in the ground, Gail Shotwell, Wade Armbuster, and Jacob Helm shoveled in a token amount of dirt, which landed on the flowers and plastic lid with a flat, hollow sound. Then everyone stood back and sang as much of "When the Roll Is Called Up Yonder" as they knew without songbooks and Leslie Weedle ended the song after the first verse.

Winnie said another prayer and the service was over. Some people stayed and talked, but most went back to the church for lunch, while eight men wearing work pants, T-shirts, and boots quickly shoveled the remaining loose dirt onto the coffin, filling the hole above ground level.

"Are you staying for the lunch?" Winnie asked Rusty.

"No, I should leave," said Rusty. "You did a good job with the service. I knew you would."

"Thank you."

"You're welcome."

"I've got to go back to the church now. This is Jacob Helm. Jacob, this is my uncle, Russell Smith."

"We've met," said Jacob and they shook hands.

In the church basement, Jacob asked for more potato salad. As Violet placed a heaping spoonful on his sagging paper plate, he inquired after the aluminum receptacle. "I just happened to notice," he said.

"Oh that," she said. "I found it in the cabinet."

"Nice vase," said Jacob.

"I know. Land sakes, just sitting there when I needed it, with a screw top if you can imagine, filled up with oak ashes."

"Oak ashes?"

"I'd recognize them anywhere. They're distinctive, different. We always used to burn oak. My father said it was the best wood for heat. Pound for pound, he said, oak was the best. Oh my, how that old stove used to puff and smoke. You couldn't come within ten feet of it when it was really cooking. I can remember as a little girl how the—"

"A vase filled with oak ashes?"

"That's what I wondered myself. It must have been some young person, as near as I can tell—thinking to have something to stand flowers up in. Bad idea really. Ashes are too caustic for growing things, takes the life straight out of 'em. Sand would be okay but not ashes. Who knows where young people get their ideas? Take Wade, for instance, he often doesn't seem to know anything about anything. Just the other day when he was helping me with the—"

"What did you do with the ashes in the vase?"

"I put them under the peony bushes in front of the church. Spread out, ashes are good, and they don't have to be oak. They neutralize the soil. That's what I try to do every couple years—get a good load of manure on the garden, not green manure, that's too ripe, and add some ash, you know, for lime. Helps work up better. Is that enough potato for you?"

"Yes. I wonder if I might buy that vase from you."

"What vase?"

"The vase you put the flowers in."

"Gracious no, it's not mine. It was just here. I guess it belongs to the church."

"How would I purchase it?"

"No one can buy it without a meeting of the trustees. In any case, you'd have to talk to the pastor."

"May I have some cake, please?" said Leslie Weedle, holding out a plate in an expectant manner.

"Which one?" asked Violet.

"Who made that one?"

"Leona Pikes."

"Give me the other."

"Nice funeral."

"I thought so. What did you think of the preaching?"

"Well, if you ask me it went on too long really. I don't know why things have to be so complicated—someone dies, they go to heaven, and we'll see them soon. That's all that's needed. I really liked the singing, though."

"That Shotwell girl does such a nice job."

"The black-haired woman has a band of her own, you know, and every person in it is a woman."

"Never mind about the cake, Violet. Are there any more frozen sandwiches?"

DRIFTLESS

A FTER THE CLEANUP IN THE CHURCH BASEMENT, WINNIE GAVE
Maxine a ride home.

"I'm sorry about this," said Maxine. "Russell doesn't like crowds so he left early."

"He wouldn't even stay to eat."

"Being around too many people is hard on his nervous system."

"He doesn't talk easily, it seems," said Winnie.

"It's true. We communicate well but don't talk much. Here, let me out by the road—I need to get the mail."

When Winnie returned to the church, it was empty inside. The evening air was floral scented, quiet and still.

She carried the few remaining folding chairs out of the sanctuary and into the basement, then picked up the discarded bulletins, gum wrappers, and other scraps of paper.

The band had not returned the piano to its proper place, and she made a mental note to find some people to move it back before Sunday morning. She also needed to distribute the flowers among the local nursing homes, keeping several of the arrangements brought in by her own people.

She closed the windows, slipped off her shoes, and settled into a middle bench, feeling her body relax. She attempted to pray, but as soon as her defenses were down she thought about July Montgomery and the look of death. What would it be like to know your coat had been caught and to understand you would perish? To die like that, alone, beaten to death by a machine, seemed terrible. Much of human life seemed ugly and brutal, and Winnie cried herself to sleep, lying on the pew.

It was well after dark when she woke up, the church as dark as the ocean floor. The smell of flowers was the first thing to greet her, joined by the coarse texture of the pew covering pressing against her cheek and the distant sound of a dog barking. These sensations coaxed her further into wakefulness and she climbed to her feet and turned on a light. Rubbing her face to remove the prickles, she began loading her car with flowers so they would be ready to take to the nursing home in the morning.

She recognized the aluminum vase as soon as she saw it and experienced a horror that reached all the way to the bottom of her.

But it did not last long. From the same psychic depths came a new feeling, and as it rose up it broke through all the gates, obstructions, and dams in its path.

She was angry, and her anger continued to mount until it burned white-hot.

Jacob Helm was up late. He sat in his living room staring into a small red fire, smoking his pipe and thinking about sitting next to Winnie on the short bench in the church—the smell of her soap. The little fire died to embers and he was putting on another log when the aluminum urn broke through the double-paned window and banged across the floor, spraying glass all over the room.

"You lied to me!" screamed Winnie from outside.

Jacob ran to the door. "Winifred!"

"You lied to me," she screamed again, standing in stocking feet in the wet, cool grass.

"I didn't."

"You did. How could you do that?"

"You're crying."

"I'm not crying, I'm mad. Can't you even tell the difference, you idiot?"

"Winifred, come inside. You're shaking all over."

"I can't trust you. I'll never trust you. You're a rotten liar."

"I was trying to protect you. And I didn't quite lie. I chose my words carefully. I love you."

"I told you not to say that," screamed Winnie. "I told you not to say that—you filthy liar."

"Why?"

"Because of how it sounds when I hear it. It mocks me. You don't know how lonely I am."

"I love you."

"I told you to stop!"

Jacob went to her and put his arm around her thin shoulders.

"Don't touch me," she said and pushed him away. "You let me go through that whole funeral believing something that wasn't true."

"What could I do? Violet Brasso had poured July's ashes on the peony beds in front of the church."

"You could have told me. At least I would have known."

"Come inside, you're shivering."

"No."

"Winifred, come inside."

"I won't ever."

"Then wait right here."

He ran inside and after much clattering and bumping returned with a stuffed armchair and a blanket. He wrapped the blanket around her and settled her into the chair, then sat in the grass in front of her.

"I'm sorry," he said. "I should have told you, you're right. I have no good excuse. Can you forgive me?"

"No."

"Come on, Winifred, be human."

"This is what being human *is*. You've been smoking."

"Yes, I was smoking."

"I didn't know you were a smoker as well as a liar."

"I rarely smoke. If it bothers you, I'll give it up."

"I loathe that smell."

"Then I will never smoke again."

Jacob's front door blew shut.

"My mother died from smoking cigarettes," said Winnie, and Jacob leaned back on his arms, watching her carefully.

"I'm sorry. Tell me about her. I want to know everything. Don't leave anything out. What was she like?"

Winnie was quiet for a long time.

"When I was little," she said, "I could look into her eyes and see heaven. She was the closest thing to a saint I ever hope to know. She could reach into her soul and find something for everyone. After she died, her memory was the only thing keeping me sane."

"She was religious then?"

"In every meaningful sense of the word, though she never attended church or read the Bible."

"Winifred, she would have been very proud of you."

"You say that but you don't even know me."

"That may be true, but how many times do I need to experience autumn or taste strawberry pie before I can say I know what autumn and strawberry pie are like? I know enough to think about you all day long. I go to sleep thinking about you and wake up thinking about you. I'd like to spend the rest of my life discovering you. There's something unquenchable about you. When I think of you I'm filled with something I can't describe. And being with you—nothing compares to it. Being with you makes everything else all right. Everything I learn about you, everything you say, everything about you brings me pleasure."

"I'm not a toy, Jacob, and certainly not a strawberry pie."

"Of course not—I should have said happiness instead of pleasure."

"Yes, you should have."

"Tell me more about your experience with Oneness—the one you told me about before."

"I can't talk about that now."

"I need to know everything. How did you feel at the time?"

"It was the most wonderful feeling. It was more than a feeling. It came from somewhere other than nerve endings."

"A passion," offered Jacob. "I'm sorry, I didn't mean to interrupt."

"Yes, a passion, but married to compassion! Breathing in joy and exhaling love, seeing it all around me. I lacked nothing and wanted nothing." She tossed her head and an arm popped out of the blanket, the fingers cupped in a gesture intended to shape the incorporeal object she was trying to describe. "It was a passion at peace with itself. It could not be divided or analyzed, and it was big enough to hold everything else inside it."

"Tell me more."

"That's the problem, telling more. I'm still trying to understand it myself. Until the day when Holiness is revealed to everyone and these experiences become commonplace—and I hope that they will be soon—there's no way to form consensus about how to refer to them. Our language only works when everyone is familiar with the things the words are talking about."

"Yes," said Jacob, looking at Winnie as though she were the thing she tried to describe. The moonlight reflected in her eyes in a small glimmer of flickering green.

"You shouldn't be sitting on the ground," she said. "It's cold. You'll catch sick."

"I'm fine."

"No, it's not good for you. Here, sit on this blanket."

"You need the blanket. I'm fine."

"No," said Winnie, standing up. "You sit here. I've got the blanket."

Jacob rose and sat in the chair. "Now you have no place to sit," he said.

"That doesn't matter."

"Let's go in the house," said Jacob.

"No!" said Winnie. "We're not going in there. Wait a minute." She unwound the blanket, seated herself on his lap, and pulled the blanket around them both. "There," she said.

"Tell me what you think of the stars," said Jacob, feeling unprepared for the sensations demanding his immediate attention. The veins in his neck pounded against her upper arm in a way that might be described as universal code. Her weight on his thighs had a strangely buoyant quality, a weightless weight. And the way she smelled was like the fragrance of spring after a long, bitter winter— a homecoming, lazy and deeply nourishing smell.

"I like the way ancient people used to think of the stars," said Winnie. "Pure spirits, that's what the Greeks thought—eternally luminous celestial bodies."

"Ah, the Greeks," said Jacob, breathing deeply.

"Though they were pagans of the worst sort, we owe much to them."

"Why?"

"They understood how full of wonder life is."

"What do you think the Greeks thought about the moon?"

"I can still smell that awful pipe, Jacob," said Winnie, realizing for the first time the alarming implications of her position on his lap.

She wondered how she had gotten here. That it had happened seemed irrefutable, but exactly *how* it had happened remained a mystery. She stretched out her legs and saw her feet inside her stockings. What had she been thinking? What foreign conspiracy had arranged this?

She simply had not been thinking at all—that was clearly the problem. She wondered how she could go backwards in time and end up three feet away, standing up.

The logistics of moving, however, even for such a relatively short distance, seemed fairly complicated. And perhaps he hadn't yet noticed where she was sitting, in which case moving would just draw attention to the fact. If she could sit perfectly still, avoid fidgeting or shifting her weight, leaning or blushing, everything might be all right.

Next she noticed that if she wasn't directly thinking about her seating arrangement in one particularly disturbing way, she was actually fairly comfortable and warm. Marshaling her thoughts along this narrow and strictly utilitarian path made everything seem fine.

She decided to ignore her present position and imagine, as clearly as she could, that someone else was sitting where she was. And in order to keep things running smoothly and not alert Jacob to the rude fact that someone had changed places with her, she decided to keep talking about tobacco, so she repeated, "I can still smell that awful pipe."

"I'm sorry."

"That's okay. It isn't so bad."

"I love the way you smell, Winifred, like a field of dandelions and hay."

"How awful."

"Earlier today I could smell your soap. This is better. This is you."

"Do you mean when we were sitting on the bench?"

"Yes."

Winnie wondered if perhaps now might be the time to inform

Jacob that she wasn't really herself anymore. The difficulties involved in explaining this, however, seemed insurmountable, so she gradually let herself again become the person taking up space inside her body—on a purely tentative basis.

"Does it matter to you that I've been married before, to someone I deeply loved?" asked Jacob.

The question had the effect of fully submerging Winnie in herself and she looked into his eyes. "You really don't know me if you could ask that. Nothing could be farther away from me than that thought. It makes no difference at all. If anything, your loving someone before me gives me reason to believe that—"

Jacob kissed her, and after a crisis of hesitation in which she evaluated both her astonishment at the sensation and the sensation itself, Winnie wrapped her arms around his neck and pulled their faces together at the two-way intersection of mouths. Then just as quickly she drew back.

"We can't do this," she said.

"Why not?"

"We must keep our pleasures separate; otherwise we might confuse one kind of happiness with the other. We can't let our bodies begin thinking for us. They're much cleverer than we give them credit for, with many rubbery joys to beguile us. Our thoughts must always remain two steps ahead of them. I'm not sure you always remember there is something higher, something better. That's why I worry I can't trust you. You would settle, I'm afraid, for this, for me."

"You're right," he said. "I would. I do."

"That's because you haven't experienced anything else."

"I don't need to. I love you."

"There you go again. You think that makes everything all right."

"It does."

"Not everything that seems right is. Some things should be stopped."

"And some things can't be stopped," said Jacob. "Your enormous spiritual ambitions and our love are inseparable. They belong together. We belong together. Your ideals make you who you are and I want all of you."

"There might be parts of me you don't want, once you get to know them."

"I doubt it."

A nightjar sang in the trees across the road, launching its voice into the dark surrounding foliage.

"Can we go inside now?" asked Jacob.

"Yes, very well. I guess it can't hurt anything. Here, move your hands, let me up."

From the doorway, Winnie saw the shattered window glass and the aluminum container on the floor.

"Jacob, we have to put those ashes where they belong."

"They're in a good place, fertilizing peonies. Come in."

Winnie stayed in the doorway. "We have to put them where people think they are, inside the casket."

"They're all spread out in the dirt. That's what Violet said. We'd never recover them all. They've drifted."

"Jacob, people believe July is buried in the cemetery. We can scoop up the dirt along with the ashes and put it all in the casket. It will make everything all right."

"That's a lot of work. What if someone sees us?"

"It's dark and we can be careful. No one will ever know."

"What difference does it really make, Winifred?"

"Things should be the way people think they are—when it's possible."

As a young man, **DAVID RHODES** worked in fields, hospitals, and factories across Iowa. After receiving an MFA degree from the University of Iowa Writers' Workshop in 1971, he published three novels in rapid succession: *The Last Fair Deal Going Down* (Atlantic/ Little, Brown, 1972), *The Easter House* (Harper & Row, 1974), and *Rock Island Line* (Harper & Row, 1975). In 1977 a motorcycle accident left him paralyzed from the chest down. He lives with his wife, Edna, in rural Wonewoc, Wisconsin.

READING GUIDE QUESTIONS

1. The prologue describes the geography of the region in which *Driftless* takes place, and the novel's title is taken from the name of the area. How does the Driftless Region, which Rhodes describes as "singularly unrefined . . . in its hilly, primitive form," influence the events of the book?

2. Words, Wisconsin, is a tiny town, not even located on maps of the region. How important is the rural setting of *Driftless*? How would the book be different if it were set in a city, or even in nearby Grange?

3. In many ways, *Driftless* seems to be a novel of oppositions— between the dairy corporation and the farmers, the Amish and the other residents, or a caregiver and a caretaker. What are some of the other oppositions in the book?

4. When July first arrives on the outskirts of Words, he observes that "the dead forever change the living." How does this assertion relate to July's experience? Is a statement like this more true in a small town like Words?

5. During Winnie's epiphany, she realizes that "boundaries did not exist. Where she left off and something else began could not be established." Is this notion and/or experience of unity displayed elsewhere in the book?

6. Early in the book, Winnie is told that "religion is irrelevant to the modern world." Do you agree? In this book, is religion a source for wisdom, naïveté, or a combination of the two?

7. Both Winnie and Gail are described as being "chosen"—Winnie through her epiphany; Gail because of the song she writes. What does the parallel between these two characters tell you about them? Are there other characters who are similarly paired?

8. *Driftless* is a collection of stories from many different characters. Do you think any one of the characters is particularly important or central? What is the effect of having many speakers narrate the story?

9. Grahm is forced to trust Cora's instincts when they lose their children in the snowstorm. In what way does that decision influence the rest of their story? Are there other characters who must trust in something beyond their control?

10. Words is described as a town "attached more firmly to the past than to the present." Some of the inhabitants of Words do seem firmly rooted in their history, but many of them also seem to be escaping their past. What role does the past play in *Driftless*?

11. Words, Wisconsin, is said to be named for Elias Words, the explorer who founded the town. Yet the name Words may also be metaphorical. What role does language play in the book? Which characters are good with words, and which are not? How does this affect their stories?

12. Rusty's attitudes toward the Amish seem out of line with his own neighbors' attitudes. Are his concerns justified? If Rusty's attitude has changed by the end of the novel, to what would you attribute that change?

13. In this book, corporations seem to be corrupt, and the government is little help. The most radical response to this problem is Moe Ridge's militia. His speech at the end of the book convinces some, but not all, of the characters to join his cause. What do you think of Moe?

14. The cougar July spots at the beginning of the book is an unfamiliar presence to the residents of Words. Are there other external forces facing Words? What do you think the future holds for the town?

15. After his death, revelations about July lead some of his friends to suspect that they didn't really know him, and yet a number of characters considered July a good friend. In retrospect, was July a good friend to the other characters in the novel?

Q & A WITH DAVID RHODES

1. How long have you been writing? Why did you start writing?

I've been writing since about the age of fourteen. Somewhere around that time I discovered that herding words into stories often gave rise to strangely satisfying states of mind—agitated, but satisfying. Maybe I was a little like a herding dog. That first glimpse of a pasture with bunched-together sheep had a different effect upon me than, say, a companion dog that looks at the same pasture and thinks, "Sheep, who cares?" As individuals we seek out activities we can lose ourselves in, and those activities, paradoxically, reveal things we couldn't otherwise know about ourselves.

2. This is your first book in thirty years. How did the accident affect your writing?

Driftless was my first *published* work in thirty years. I resumed writing within three or four years after the accident, but the results were dismal. I think serious physical injuries necessarily involve a hornet's nest of psychological problems and at least for me it was hard to begin again where I'd left off. All my equilibriums were disturbed. I didn't know myself any more, unconnected to the embroidered chain of memories and relationships that had earlier defined me. The activity of writing helped me work through this disjunction, though the end product of much of that work remained too dark and dimly focused for general consumption.

3. What draws you to rural life, both personally and in your work?

For me, rural life offers ample qualities of space. Wherever you look are unbounded areas of tumultuous nature, set against ever-expanding vistas of sky. In fiction, this vast roominess offers the psychological space needed for characters to explore their feelings, motivations, and sorrows, lending a depth that might not otherwise be available. As noted in the old fables of the country mouse and city mouse, the city has many wonderful and exciting things to offer, but for nurture, healing, and careful thought, the country is the place to be.

4. The character of July Montgomery is central to *Driftless,* and has appeared in some of your earlier novels *(Rock Island Line, The Easter House).* What is it about July that has you returning to him again and again?

Characters serve as receptacles for our own projected feelings and through characters we imaginatively encounter parts of ourselves. Characters teach us to loosen up, not take ourselves so seriously, see other points of view, and have fun. At their best, characters shine a light into otherwise dark areas—places we can't, or won't, go on our own. They help us explore our interior world. When I found July Montgomery, he immediately wanted to take me to places I was afraid of going. But his spirit was so courageous and resilient that I was willing to go along.

5. What inspired you to write *Driftless*?

The untimely death of a friend/neighbor provided the original impetus for the story. At his funeral I understood that I knew only a small part of him. The completed picture of my friend was held compositely among all those who knew him. This presented me with a new way of looking at personal identity, at who we are or think we are, and it was this more dynamic idea of collective interaction giving rise to the qualities of personal identity that I wanted to attempt to present in the book.

6. *Driftless* is a collage of stories, revolving around a large cast of characters whose lives intersect in various ways. How did you develop all of these characters and their stories?

> For me, there are three interconnected elements of a story. The first is a sense of place—in this case the Driftless Region of Wisconsin. The place limits the kinds of characters that can effectively be imagined living there, their ways of life, and to some extent their personalities. Once a group of characters have volunteered to live in a fictional setting, the plot or action of the story comes out of them. Certain characters will only do certain things. So place gives rise to character, which in turn gives rise to action. I waited for my characters to tell me what they would and would not do. After I had a general idea for what would happen, I began the long process of refining the individual voices and stories to lead in a certain direction, toward a particular feeling I wanted to develop. This took the longest time and is more difficult to talk about coherently.

7. What writers have influenced you over the years?

> I'm probably influenced by everyone I read, and I read incessantly. As a young writer I remember most wanting to learn how William Faulkner could speak for a whole family or community. His narrative voice was not an individual point of view, but rather a cultural force. Later, I came to appreciate Charles Dickens' unique abilities of characterization. All his social commentary and criticism took a second seat to his joy of human portraits, and he depicted the universal qualities of men and women through eccentric characterization. More recently I've been impressed with Louise Erdrich's ability to endow certain specific physical objects in her fiction, like a painted drum or violin, with such phantasmagoric histories that the objects themselves take on living, spiritual dimensions. I don't think I know of anyone else who takes such pains to do this.

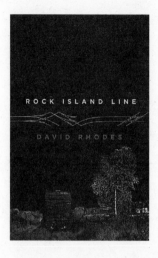

ROCK ISLAND LINE
David Rhodes

"A kind of dark but luminous *Candide, Rock Island Line* is beautiful and haunting in a way you have not encountered before. I read the book when it first came out over thirty years ago and it has lived in both my heart and head ever since."

—Jonathan Carroll,
author of *The Ghost in Love*

"Rhodes writes with both symphonic grandeur and down-to-earth humility in this galvanizing novel of 'the quick, naked bones of survival.' This is a descent into grief as resonant as James Agee's, an embrace of the heartland spirit as profound as Cather's and Marilynne Robinson's, a story that echoes Dreiser, Steinbeck, Gardner, and Bellow—and an authentically great American novel in its own right."

—*Booklist* (starred)

Born and raised in a small town not far from Iowa City, July Montgomery's early years are filled with four-leaf-clovers, dogs, and fishing. But this idyllic world comes to an end with the tragic death of his parents, after which July flees via the Rock Island Line, eventually landing in Philadelphia and fashioning a ghostly home beneath an underground train station.

When a young woman frees July from his malaise, they return together to the heartland. Restored to his ancestral home and yet perched on the precipice of a disaster that could herald his end, July must decide whether to continue running, or stand still and hope for the promised dawn of Paradise Regained.

THE EASTER HOUSE
David Rhodes

"*The Easter House* offers the tale of another tormented Midwestern clan, but in its pages no border exists between everyday life and the super-real. I wouldn't trade a word of *The Easter House* for anything."

—*New York Times Book Review*

"Rhodes proves that there is still vigorous life in the dark Gothic roots of great American novels."

—*Tennessean*

"This is [an almost impossible book to put down,] with its forceful narrative and striking characters. Rhodes is a brilliant writer and *The Easter House* a moving literary experience."

—*Cleveland Plain Dealer*

The largest residence in Ontarion, Iowa, looms over the town and three generations of the Easters. Ansel Easter—a minister favored by the townspeople until he rescued a Caliban-like creature from a carnival sideshow—paved a difficult path for his sons, C and Sam. After Ansel's violent death, no one in town was surprised when his children abandoned the house their father built in search of a new beginning.

Unable to shake Ansel's burdensome legacy from afar, the brothers return separately to the house. C and his wife start a junkyard in the expansive lawn of the Easter house and barter used appliances, cars, and random items for necessities. Eventually, C and Sam create a more lucrative business: the Associates, a group of men offering services for a fee. When a rash of deaths occur and the Ontarions suspect the Associates, the sins of the father appear to revisit the sons.

Shocking and suspenseful, *The Easter House* is an engrossing story of family redemption and survival. Originally published in 1974, David Rhodes' second novel captures the oppressive somnolence of a small community while intertwining elements of the American gothic tradition, illuminating the strangeness that lurks beneath the surface.

Available Fall 2009

Milkweed Editions

Founded in 1979, Milkweed Editions is one of the largest independent, nonprofit literary publishers in the United States. Milkweed publishes with the intention of making a humane impact on society, in the belief that good writing can transform the human heart and spirit.

Join Us

Milkweed depends on the generosity of foundations and individuals like you, in addition to the sales of its books. In an increasingly consolidated and bottom-line-driven publishing world, your support allows us to select and publish books on the basis of their literary quality and the depth of their message. Please visit our Web site (www.milkweed.org) or contact us at (800) 520-6455 to learn more about our donor program.

Milkweed Editions, a nonprofit publisher, gratefully acknowledges sustaining support from Anonymous; Emilie and Henry Buchwald; the Bush Foundation; the Patrick and Aimee Butler Family Foundation; the Dougherty Family Foundation; the Ecolab Foundation; the General Mills Foundation; the Claire Giannini Fund; John and Joanne Gordon; William and Jeanne Grandy; the Jerome Foundation; the Lerner Foundation; the McKnight Foundation; Mid-Continent Engineering; a grant from the Minnesota State Arts Board, through an appropriation by the Minnesota State Legislature, a grant from the National Endowment for the Arts, and private funders; Kelly Morrison and John Willoughby; an award from the National Endowment for the Arts, which believes that a great nation deserves great art; the Navarre Corporation; the Starbucks Foundation; Ellen and Sheldon Sturgis; the Target Foundation; the James R. Thorpe Foundation; the Toro Foundation; the Travelers Foundation; Moira and John Turner; United Parcel Service; U. S. Trust Company; Joanne and Phil Von Blon; Kathleen and Bill Wanner; Serene and Christopher Warren; and the W. M. Foundation.

THE MILKWEED EDITIONS EDITOR'S CIRCLE

We gratefully acknowledge the patrons of the Milkweed Editions Editor's Circle
for their support of the literary arts.

Kari and Mark Baumbach
John Beal and Barbara Brin
Valerie Guth Boyd and Geoff Boyd
Tracey and Jeff Breazeale
James Buchta
Emilie and Henry Buchwald
Bob and Gail Buuck
Timothy and Tara Clark
Ward Cleveland
Barbara Coffin and Daniel Engstrom
Margaret Fuller Corneille and Frantz
    Corneille
Dick and Suzie Crockett
Ella Crosby
Betsy and Edward Cussler
Mary Lee Dayton
Betsy David and Stephen Belsito
Kathy and Mike Dougherty
Julie and John DuBois
Camie and Jack Eugster
Kenneth and Grace Evenstad
Barbara Forster
Robert and Caroline Fullerton
Amy and Philip Goldman
John and Joanne Gordon
William B. and Jeanne Grandy
Hunt Greene and Jane Piccard
John Gulla and Andrea Godbout
Margherita Gale Harris
Libby and Ed Hlavka
Joe Hognander
Mary and Gary Holmes
John and Mary Jane Taber Houlihan
Cretia and Frank Jesse
Laura and Michael Keller
Constance and Daniel Kunin
Jim and Susan Lenfestey
Adam Lerner
Dorothy Kaplan Light and Ernest Light
Sally L. Macut
Chris and Ann Malecek
Charles Marvin

Sanders and Tasha Marvin
Susan Maxwell
Loretta McCarthy
Mary Merrill
Katherine Middlecamp
Sheila Morgan
Chris and Jack Morrison
Helen Morrison
John Morrison
Kelly Morrison and John Willoughby
Wendy Nelson
Ann and Doug Ness
Kate and Stuart Nielsen
Nancy and Richard Norman
Larry O'Shaughnessy
Steven and Linnea Pajor
Karen and Eric Paulson
Elizabeth Petrangelo and Michael Lundeby
Karin and Dean Phillips
Jörg A. and Angie Pierach
Margaret and Dan Preska
Deborah Reynolds
Cheryl Ryland
Cindy and Bill Schmoker
Daniel Slager and Alyssa Polack
Schele and Philip Smith
Cynthia and Stephen Snyder
Larry and Joy Steiner
Patrick Stevens and Susan Kenny Stevens
Barbara Gregg Stuart and Dr. David D. Stuart
Ellen and Sheldon Sturgis
Tom and Jeanne Sween
Moira and John Turner
Joanne and Phil Von Blon
Kathleen and Bill Wanner
Serene and Christopher Warren
Betsy and David Weyerhauser
Jamie Wilson and David Ericson
Eleanor and Fred Winston
Margaret and Angus Wurtele
Gary and Vicki Wyard
Kathy and Jim Zerwas

Interior design by Wendy Holdman

Typeset in Dante
by BookMobile Design and Publishing Services

Printed on acid-free Rolland Enviro
(100 percent post consumer waste) paper
by Friesens Corporation